He pulled ▮▮▮▮▮▮▮▮▮▮ **ran away from the burning storage unit into the field beyond, where they collapsed, arms still tightly wrapped around each other.**

His eyes met hers. "I thought I'd lost you," he whispered.

She took his face in both hands and pressed her lips to his, the kiss desperate in its intensity. Everything receded, burned away by passion.

He was the first to pull away, breaking the kiss. "You're the most amazing woman," he said.

"You're making a habit of saving my life," she said.

His expression hardened and he dropped his hand. "You don't owe me anything."

"This isn't about debts and payments," she said.

"Then what is it about?"

"It's about you making me feel more alive than I have in years. It's about...I don't know." She looked away. She had almost said *love*, but that was absurd.

"Maybe it doesn't matter why right now," he said. He pulled her close again.

COLORADO JUSTICE

CINDI MYERS

Previously published as *Saved by the Sheriff*
and *Deputy Defender*

 HARLEQUIN®

Recycling programs
for this product may
not exist in your area.

ISBN-13: 978-1-335-42730-4

Colorado Justice

Copyright © 2022 by Harlequin Enterprises ULC

Saved by the Sheriff
First published in 2018. This edition published in 2022.
Copyright © 2018 by Cynthia Myers

Deputy Defender
First published in 2018. This edition published in 2022.
Copyright © 2018 by Cynthia Myers

For questions and comments about the quality of this book,
please contact us at CustomerService@Harlequin.com.

Harlequin Enterprises ULC
22 Adelaide St. West, 41st Floor
Toronto, Ontario M5H 4E3, Canada
www.Harlequin.com

Printed in U.S.A.

CONTENTS

Cindi Myers is the author of more than fifty novels. When she's not plotting new romance story lines, she enjoys skiing, gardening, cooking, crafting and daydreaming. A lover of small-town life, she lives with her husband and two spoiled dogs in the Colorado mountains.

Books by Cindi Myers

Harlequin Intrigue

Eagle Mountain: Search for Suspects

Disappearance at Dakota Ridge

The Ranger Brigade: Rocky Mountain Manhunt

Investigation in Black Canyon
Mountain of Evidence
Mountain Investigation
Presumed Deadly

Eagle Mountain Murder Mystery: Winter Storm Wedding

Ice Cold Killer
Snowbound Suspicion
Cold Conspiracy
Snowblind Justice

Visit the Author Profile page
at Harlequin.com for more titles.

SAVED BY THE SHERIFF

For Lucy

Chapter One

Lacy Milligan flinched as the heavy steel door clanged shut behind her. After almost three years, that sound still sent a chill through her. She reminded herself she wouldn't ever have to hear that sound again after today. Today she was a free woman.

She followed the guard down the gleaming tiled hallway, the smell of disinfectant stinging her nose. At the door to a reception room at the front of the building she stopped and waited while a second guard unlocked and opened the door. Her lawyer, Anisha Cook, stood on the other side, beaming. She pulled Lacy to her in a hug and Lacy stiffened. That was something else she would have to get used to—being touched. Touching wasn't allowed in prison—even something as simple as a hug could lead to extra searches, even punishment. But those rules didn't apply to her anymore, she reminded herself, and awkwardly returned the other woman's embrace. Anisha, still smiling, released her, and Lacy noticed there were other people in the room— the warden, reporters, her parents.

"Lacy, what are your feelings, now that your conviction has been overturned?" A sandy-haired man shoved a microphone at her.

"I'm happy, of course," she said. "Ready to go home."

"Do you have anything to say to Rayford County Sheriff Travis Walker?" another reporter asked.

So Travis was the sheriff now. Putting a murderer behind bars had probably earned him points with the right people in town. Except he had arrested the wrong person. "I don't have anything to say to him," she said.

"Even though he's the one who came forward with the evidence that cleared your name?" the reporter asked.

Travis had done that? She shot a look at Anisha, who nodded. Lacy would have to get the whole story from her later. "That doesn't make up for the three years I spent behind bars for a crime I didn't commit," Lacy said. Three years of her life she would never get back.

"What are your plans now that you're free?" the sandy-haired reporter asked.

Plans? Plans were something a person with a future made—something Lacy hadn't had until yesterday, when word came down that she was to be released. She had been afraid to believe it was really going to happen until now. "I'm going to go home with my parents and consider my options," she said.

She caught her mother's eye across the room. Jeanette Milligan was openly weeping, tears running down her cheeks, while Lacy's dad held her tightly.

"We need to be going now," Anisha said. "We ask that you respect Lacy's privacy as she settles in." She put her arm around Lacy's shoulders and guided her toward the door.

Outside, her mother's green Subaru Outback waited—the same car she had had when Lacy had entered the Denver Women's Correctional Facility three years before. Lacy's dad embraced her and kissed her cheek, then it was her mother's turn. "I have your old room all ready for you," her mom said. "And we're having steak for dinner, and chocolate cake."

"Great, Mom." Lacy forced a smile. Moving back home had seemed the best choice right now, since she had almost no money and no job. It would only be temporary, until she figured out what she was going to do with the rest of her life and got back on her feet. But it still felt like going back in time while the rest of the world moved forward.

"We'll get together next week for coffee or something," Anisha said. "If you need anything before then, just call." She waved and headed for her own car, then Lacy slid into the back seat of her parents' car and they were off.

They tried to make small talk for a while, but soon fell silent. Lacy rested her head against the window and stared out at the summer-browned city landscape, which quickly gave way to the green foothills, and then the Rocky Mountains. Only five more hours until she was home in Eagle Mountain, the little resort town where her family had settled when Lacy was fourteen. Once upon a time, she had thought she would stay in Eagle Mountain forever, but now she wasn't so sure. Maybe there were too many bad memories there for her to ever be comfortable again.

Lacy slept, and woke only when her dad pulled the car into the driveway of the Victorian cottage just off Eagle Mountain's main street that had been their home for the past ten years. A lump rose in Lacy's throat as she studied the stone walkway that led up to the front porch that spanned the width of the house, with its white-painted posts and railings and lacelike gingerbread trim. The peonies under the railings were in full bloom, like big pink pom-poms filling the flower beds. A banner over the front steps declared Welcome Home Lacy!

She took her time getting out of the car, fighting the instinct to run up the steps and straight into her room. She was going to have to get used to facing people again, to dealing with their questions about what she had been through and what she planned to do next. She had never been good at that kind of thing, but she was going to have to find a way to cope.

She started up the walkway, but at the top of the steps, she noticed the uniformed man seated in the porch swing and froze. Travis Walker, all six feet of him, made even taller by the cowboy boots and Stetson he wore, stood and moved toward her. "What are you doing here?" Lacy asked, heart pounding madly. Had there been some mistake? Had he come to arrest her again?

Travis removed his hat, revealing thick brown hair that fell boyishly over his forehead. When Lacy had first met him in high school, she had thought he was the handsomest boy she had ever seen. Too much had passed between them for her to think that now. "I came to apologize," he said. "I know it doesn't make up for all I put you through, but I wanted to say I'm truly sorry. I've done what I can to make up for my mistakes."

"Your mistakes cost me three years of my life!" Lacy hated the way her voice broke on the words. "You humiliated me in front of everyone I knew. In front of people I've never even met. You accused me of the most horrible crime anyone could commit."

His face showed the strain he was feeling, his brown eyes pained. "I would give anything to take all of it back," he said. "But I can't. All I can do is say again that I'm sorry, and I hope you'll find it in your heart one day to forgive me."

"You don't deserve my forgiveness," she said, and rushed past him, tears stinging her eyes. She refused to break down in front of him.

She paused in the darkened living room, fighting for composure. Her father's quiet voice drifted to her through the opened screen door. "Give it a few days. This is hard for her—for all of us."

"I didn't mean to intrude on your first day back together," Travis said. "I just wanted her to know how I felt. It didn't seem right to wait any longer to apologize. It doesn't make up for anything, but it had to be said."

"And we appreciate it," her dad said. "We appreciate all you've done for her. It says a lot about a man when he's willing to admit he was wrong."

"I'll leave you alone now," Travis said. "You deserve your privacy and I have a lot of work to do."

"Thank goodness there's not a lot of crime in Rayford County, but I imagine the job has its challenges," her dad said.

"It does," Travis said. "But right now my priority is finding out who really killed Andy Stenson. I know now that Lacy didn't kill him, but I have to bring to justice the person who did."

TRAVIS WALKED AWAY from the Milligan home, down the street shaded by tall evergreens and cottonwoods, up a block to Main. He liked that the town of Eagle Mountain—the only incorporated town in Rayford

County—was small enough, and the sheriff's department centrally located enough, that he could walk almost anywhere. A big part of policing in a rural area like this was simply being a presence. Seeing uniforms on the street made people feel safer, and it made troublemakers think twice about acting up.

He passed under the large banner advertising Eagle Mountain Pioneer Days Festival, the biggest tourist attraction of the summer for the little town, with a parade and fireworks, outdoor concerts, crafts booths and anything else the town council could think of that would entertain people and induce them to stay a few days and spend money.

"Sheriff!"

He turned to see Mayor Larry Rowe striding toward him. Solidly built and energetic, Rowe was a relative newcomer to town who, after a year on the county planning committee, had spent a significant amount of money on his campaign for mayor two years ago—unusual in a town where most public officials ran unopposed. "Mayor." Travis stopped and waited for the older man to catch up.

"Sheriff, I wanted to talk to you about security for the festival," Rowe said.

"We'll have plenty of officers patrolling," Travis said. "I'm putting all of the reserves on duty, and as many of the full-time staff as possible."

Rowe nodded. "We don't want any trouble to detract from the festivities." He stared down the street, in the direction Travis had come. "I understand Lacy Milligan is back in town."

"Yes, I stopped by to see her."

"Oh?" The lines on either side of Rowe's mouth deepened. "How is she?"

"She's still processing everything that's happened, I think."

"I hope she doesn't have any plans to sue the city," Rowe said. "I'll have to consult our attorney, prepare for that possibility."

"I don't think she has any plans to sue," Travis said.

"Do whatever you can to see that she doesn't. I have to go now. You'll keep me posted if any problems arise with the Milligans."

"Yes, sir."

The mayor moved on, and Travis resumed the walk to his office. Though he didn't consider Rowe a friend, he appreciated that the mayor rarely involved himself in the operation of the sheriff's department. Travis was free to do his job as he saw fit.

A ten-minute stroll took Travis back to the office. His office manager, sixty-eight-year-old Adelaide Kinkaid, who refused to even consider retiring—and was sharper than most thirty-year-olds—looked up from her computer screen. "How did it go?" she asked.

"About like I expected." Travis hung his Stetson on the rack by the door. "She told me I'd ruined her life and tried not to let me see she was crying." He shrugged. "In her place, I'd probably feel the same way. I guess I'm lucky she didn't punch me."

"You're already beating yourself up enough," Adelaide said.

"Why are you beating yourself up?" Deputy Gage Walker, Travis's younger brother, emerged from his office. Taller than Travis by two inches and lighter than him by twenty pounds, Gage looked like the basketball forward he had been in high school, lean and quick.

"I went over to see Lacy Milligan," Travis said.

Gage's face sobered. "Ouch! That took guts."

"It was the least she deserved. Not that she thinks so."

"You did what you could," Gage said. "Now the ball is in her court."

"Not exactly."

"What do you mean?" Gage asked.

"I mean, I still have to find Andy Stenson's killer. And doing that will be easier with her help."

"Wait a minute—you proved she was innocent—but you think she knows something?" Gage asked.

"She can at least walk me through Andy's records, tell me about his clients. She was his only employee. She may have encountered his murderer, without knowing it."

"What about Andy's widow?" Adelaide asked.

"Brenda knows nothing about the business," Travis said. "She's told me everything she knows, but it's not enough. I need Lacy to help me."

"And I need a million dollars," Gage said. "But I'm not going to get it."

Travis moved into his office and dropped into his chair behind his desk, staring at the stack of papers in his inbox, thinking about Lacy. She was the first murderer he had ever arrested—the only one, actually. He was a deputy with only a few years on the force at the time, and murder was a rare crime in Rayford County. Sheriff's department calls ran more toward theft, vandalism, domestic violence and what he thought of as tourist calls—lost hikers, lost wallets, lost dogs and people who had locked themselves out of their cars.

The murder of young attorney Andy Stenson had been a shock to everyone, but the chief suspect had been pretty clear. Lacy Milligan's prints had been found on the murder weapon, she had been overheard arguing with Andy that afternoon and someone had seen a woman who matched Lacy's description—from her build to her dark hair—outside the office shortly before the time of Andy's death.

Travis hadn't wanted to believe Lacy was a killer. She had always been the pretty, quiet girl in high school. After she had graduated high school and had gone to work for Andy, Travis had occasionally seen her downtown and they would say hello. He had even thought about asking her out, but had never gotten around to it.

But then Andy had died and the only evidence Travis could find pointed to Lacy. She hadn't been able to produce anyone who could confirm her alibi—that she had been almost two hours away at her cousin's basketball game. The cousin hadn't seen her there, and no one else could remember her being there. And then the prosecutor had discovered funds missing from the law firm's account, and a deposit in almost the same amount in Lacy's account.

The jury had deliberated only a few hours before handing down a conviction. Travis had felt sick as he watched the bailiff lead Lacy from court, but he had been convinced he had done his job. He had found a murderer.

And then, only two months ago, he had been whiling away the time online and had come across a video someone had posted of a college basketball game—a

game in which a promising young player—now a major
NBA star—had made a series of free throws that hinted
at his future greatness. Watching the video, Travis had
recognized a familiar face on the sidelines. Lacy Milligan—a smiling, carefree Lacy—had stared out at him
from the screen. A time stamp on the video corrobo-
rated her story of being at her cousin's game. Further
research backed this up. Here was her alibi. When Andy
Stenson was stabbed in the heart, Lacy Milligan was
two hours away.

From there, the rest of the evidence began to fall
apart. Travis hired a former detective to review the case
and the detective—who had retired to Eagle Mountain after a storied career with the Los Angeles Police
Department—determined that what had looked like
missing funds was merely a bookkeeping error, and the
deposit in Lacy's account was, as she had said, the proceeds from the sale of some jewelry she had inherited.

Travis had felt sick over the error. He hadn't been
able to eat or sleep as he worked feverishly to see that
the decision in the case was vacated. He also did what
he could to publicize his efforts to clear the name of the
woman he had wronged. He wanted everyone to know
that Lacy was innocent.

Now she was home. He didn't blame her for hating
him, though it hurt to see the scorn in her eyes. All he
knew to do now was to work even harder to find the
real killer.

The phone rang and he heard Adelaide answer. A
moment later, his extension buzzed. "Sheriff, it's for
you," Adelaide said. "It's George Milligan."

Lacy's dad. Travis snatched up the receiver. "Mr.
Milligan, how can I help you?"

"I think you need to come over here, Sheriff." George Milligan's voice held the strain of someone who had taken almost more than he could bear. "We've had a, well, I'm not sure how to describe it. An incident."

Travis sat up straighter, his stomach knotting. "What's happened? Is someone hurt? Is Lacy hurt?"

"Someone threw a rock through our front window." George's voice broke. "It had a...a note tied to it. Just one word on the note—*murderer*."

"I'll be right over," Travis said. Hadn't these people suffered enough? Hadn't they all suffered enough?

Chapter Two

Lacy stared at the grapefruit-sized chunk of red granite that sat in the middle of the library table beneath the front window of her family home, shards of glass like fractured ice scattered about it. Strands of thin wire held the note in place, a single word scrawled crookedly in red marker, like an accusation made in blood.

Murderer! She had worn the label for three years, but she would never get used to it. Seeing it here, in the place she had thought of as a refuge, when she had believed her ordeal over, hurt more than she had imagined. Worse, the word hurt her parents, who had put their own lives on hold, and even mortgaged their home, to save her.

A black-and-white SUV pulled into the driveway and Lacy watched out the window as Travis Walker slid out of the vehicle and strode up the walkway to the door. Everything about him radiated competence and authority, from his muscular frame filling out the crisp lines of his brown sheriff's uniform to the determined expression on his handsome face. When he said something was right, it must be right. So when he had said she had murdered Andy Stenson, everyone had believed him. Men like Travis didn't make mistakes.

Except he had.

The doorbell rang and her father opened it and ushered Travis inside. Lacy steeled herself to face him. Travis hadn't thrown the rock through her parents' window, but as far as she was concerned, he was to blame.

"Hello, Lacy." Ever the gentleman, Travis touched the brim of his hat and nodded to her.

She nodded and took a step back, away from the rock—and away from him. He walked over and looked down at the projectile, his gaze taking in the broken window, the shattered glass and the note. He leaned closer to study the note. "Has anything like this happened before?" he asked.

It took her a moment to realize he had addressed the question to her. She shrugged. "Not really. There were a few letters to the editor in the paper during my trial, and a few times when I would walk into a place and everyone would stop talking and stare at me."

"But no direct threats or name calling?" he asked.

She shook her head. "No."

"I can't understand why anyone would do this now." Her father joined them. Her mother was upstairs, lying down with a headache. "Lacy has been cleared. Everyone knows that."

"Maybe not everyone." Travis straightened. "I'll get an evidence kit from my car. Maybe we'll get some fingerprints off the note."

Lacy doubted whoever threw that rock would be stupid enough to leave fingerprints, but she didn't bother arguing. Travis went outside and stopped on the sidewalk to survey the flower bed. Maybe he was looking for footprints? Or maybe he liked flowers.

He returned a few moments later, wearing latex

gloves and carrying a cardboard box. He lifted the rock and settled it in the box. "In order to hurl the rock through the window like this, whoever threw it would have to be close—either standing on the porch or in the flower beds," he said, as he taped up the box and labeled it. "I didn't see any footprints in the flower beds, or disturbed plants, so I'm guessing porch. Did you see or hear anyone?"

"We were all in the back of the house, preparing dinner in the kitchen," her father said.

"I'll talk to the neighbors, see if any of them saw anything," Travis said. "After the window shattered, did you hear anything—anyone running away, or a car driving away?"

"No," her father said.

Both men looked at Lacy. "No," she said. "I didn't hear anything."

"Who would do something like this?" her father asked. His face sagged with weariness, and he looked years older. Guilt made a knot in Lacy's stomach. Even though she hadn't thrown the rock, she was the target. She had brought this intrusion into her parents' peaceful life. Maybe moving back home had been a bad idea.

"I don't know," Travis said. "There are mean people in the world. Obviously, someone doesn't believe Lacy is innocent."

"The paper has run articles," her father said. "It's been on all the television stations—I don't know what else we can do."

"You can help me find the real murderer."

He was addressing Lacy, not her dad, his gaze pinning her. She remembered him looking at her that way the day he arrested her, the intensity of his stare making it clear she wasn't going to get away with not answering his questions.

"Why should I help you?" she asked.

"You worked closely with Andy," he said. "You knew his clients. You can walk me through his records. I'm convinced he knew his murderer."

"What if you try to pin this on the wrong person again?"

He didn't even flinch. "I won't make that mistake again."

"Honey, I think maybe Travis is right," her father said. "You probably know more about Andy's job than anyone."

"What about Brenda?" Lacy asked. "She was his wife. He would have told her if someone was threatening him before he told me."

"He never said anything like that to her," Travis said. "And she doesn't know anything about his law practice."

"I'm pretty sure all the files from the business are still in storage," she said. "You don't need my help going through them."

"I do if I'm going to figure out what any of it means. You can help me avoid wasting time on irrelevant files and focus on anything that might be important."

His intense gaze pinned her, making her feel trapped. She wanted to say no, to avoid having anything to do with him. But what if he was right and he needed her help to solve the case? What if, by doing nothing, she was letting the real killer get away with murder? "All right," she said. "I'll help you."

"Thank you. I'll call you tomorrow or the next day and set up a time to get together." He picked up the box with the rock, touched the brim of his hat again and left.

Lacy sank into a nearby arm chair. This wasn't how she had envisioned her homecoming. She had hoped to be able to put the past behind her once and for all. Now she was volunteering to dive right back into it.

TRAVIS CRUISED EAGLE MOUNTAIN'S main street, surveying the groups of tourists waiting for tables at Kate's Kitchen or Moe's Pub, the men filling the park benches outside the row of boutiques, chatting while they waited for their wives. He waved to Paige Riddell as he passed her bed-and-breakfast, drove past the library and post office, then turned past the Episcopal Church, the fire station and the elementary school before he turned toward his office. The rock someone had hurled through Lacy's front window sat in the box on the passenger seat, a very ordinary chunk of iron-ore-infused granite that could have come from almost any roadside or backyard in the area.

Who would hurl such a weapon—and its hateful message—through the window of a woman who had already endured too much because of mistakes made by Travis and others? Eagle Mountain wasn't a perfect place, but it wasn't known for violent dissension. Disagreements tended to play themselves out in the form of letters to the editor of the local paper or the occasional shouting match after a few too many beers at one of the local taverns.

When Travis had arrested Lacy for the murder of Andy Stenson, he had received more than one angry phone call, and a few people had refused to speak to him ever since. When he had issued a public statement declaring Lacy's innocence, most people had responded positively, if not jubilantly, to the news. He couldn't recall hearing even a whisper from anyone that a single person believed Lacy was still a murderer.

On impulse, he drove past the police station and two blocks north, to the former Eagle Mountain Hospital, now home to the county Historical Society and Museum. As he had hoped, Brenda Stenson was just locking up for the day when Travis parked and climbed out of his SUV. "Hello, Travis," she said as she tucked the key into her purse. A slender blonde with delicate features and a smattering of freckles across her upturned nose, Brenda seemed to be regaining some of the vivacity that had all but vanished when her husband of only three years had been murdered. "What's up?"

"Lacy came home today," he said. "I was just over at her folks' place."

"How is she? I saw her mom yesterday and told her to tell Lacy I would stop by tomorrow—I thought maybe the family would like a little time alone before the crowds of well-wishers descend."

"So you don't have any problem with her being out?" Travis asked, watching her carefully.

She pushed a fall of long blond hair out of her eyes. "Lacy didn't kill Andy," she said. "I should have spoken on her behalf at the trial, but I was so torn up about Andy—it was all I could do to get out of bed in the morning. Later on…" She shrugged. "I didn't know what to think. I'm glad she's out."

"Except that now we don't know who is responsible for Andy's death," Travis said.

"No, we don't. It makes it hard to move on, but sometimes these things never get solved, do they? I hate to think that, but I'm trying to be realistic."

"I want to find the real murderer," Travis said. "I feel like I owe it to you and Andy—and to Lacy."

"You didn't try and convict her all by yourself," Brenda said. "And you fought harder than anyone to free her once you figured out the truth."

"But I started the ball rolling," he said. "And this isn't really going to be over for any of us until we find out what really happened that day."

She sighed. "So what's the next move?"

"I know we've been over this before, but humor me. Do you know of anyone who was angry or upset with Andy—about anything? An angry husband whose wife Andy represented in a divorce? A drunk driving case he lost?"

"Andy hadn't been practicing law long enough to make enemies," Brenda said. "And Eagle Mountain is a small town—I know pretty much everyone who was ever a client of his. None of them seem like a murderer to me."

"I think the odds that the killer was a random stranger are pretty low," Travis said. "So one of those nice local people is likely the murderer."

Brenda rubbed her hands up and down her arms, as if trying to warm herself. "It makes me sick to think about it," she said.

"If I can convince Lacy to help me, would you mind if we go through Andy's case files?" Travis asked. "I figure she would have known his clients almost as well as he did."

"Of course I don't mind. Everything is in storage. I haven't had the heart to go through anything myself."

"I don't know if it will help, but it seems like a good place to start," he said.

"Stop by whenever you're ready and I'll give you the key to my storage unit," she said.

They said good-night and Travis returned to his SUV. He had just started the vehicle when his cell phone buzzed. "Hello?"

"Sheriff, Wade Tomlinson called to report a shoplifter at their store," Adelaide said. "He said he saw you drive past a few minutes ago and wondered if you could swing by."

"Tell him I'll be there in a couple of minutes." Travis ended the call and turned the SUV back toward Main, where Wade Tomlinson and Brock Ryan operated Eagle Mountain Outfitters, a hunting, fishing and climbing store that catered to locals and tourists alike. Technically, a call like this should have been routed through the countywide dispatch center. The dispatcher would then contact the appropriate department and the officer who was closest to the scene would respond. But locals were just as likely to call the sheriff department's direct line and ask for Travis or Gage or one of the other officers by name.

Wade Tomlinson met Travis on the sidewalk in front of their store. "Thanks for stopping by, Sheriff," he said. He crossed his arms over his beefy chest, the eagle tattoo on his biceps flexing. A vein pulsed in his shaved head. "Though I guess we wasted your time."

"Adelaide said you had a shoplifter?"

"Yeah, but he got away, right after I called." He led the way inside the shop, which smelled of canvas, leather and rope. Climbing rope in every color of the rainbow hung from hooks along the back wall, while everything from stainless-steel coffee mugs to ice axes and crampons filled the shelves.

Wade's business partner, Brock Ryan, looked up from rearranging a display of T-shirts. The one in his hand, Travis noted, bore the legend *Do It In the Outdoors*. "Hey, Travis," he said. "You didn't pass a skinny teenager in a red beanie on your way over here, did you?"

"No," Travis said. "Was that your shoplifter?"

"Yeah. I caught him red-handed shoving a hundred-dollar water filter down his pants. I sat him down up front by the register and told him we would wait until you got here before we decided whether or not to file charges."

Unlike Wade, who was short and stocky, Brock was tall and lean, with the squinting gaze of a man who had spent long hours in the sun and wind.

"What happened after that?" Travis asked.

"I turned my back to get a tray of fishing flies out of the case for a customer and the kid took off," Brock said, his face reddening.

"Did the kid give you a name?" Travis asked. "Did you recognize him?"

Both men shook their heads. "He wasn't from around here," Wade said. "He wouldn't say anything to us, so we figured we'd let you see if you could get anything out of him."

"Maybe you two scared him enough he won't come back," Travis said.

"Burns me up when somebody comes in here and tries to take what we've worked hard for," Brock said. He punched his hand in his fist. "If that kid ever shows his face here again, I'll make sure he never tries to steal from me again."

Travis put a hand on the tall man's shoulder. "Don't

let your temper get the best of you," he said. "If the kid comes back, call the office and one of us will take care of it."

Brock hesitated, then nodded. "Right."

A third man emerged from a door at the back of the shop—a lean, broad-shouldered guy in a black knit beanie. He looked as if he had been carved from iron—all sharp angles and hard muscle. He scanned Travis from head to toe, lingering a moment on the badge on his chest, and Travis wouldn't have called his expression friendly. "Do you have a new employee?" Travis asked, nodding toward the man.

Brock glanced over his shoulder. "That's Ian," he said. "A friend of mine."

Ian nodded, but didn't offer to shake hands. "I'll wait in back," he said to Brock, and exited the way he had come.

"Your friend got a problem with cops?" Travis asked.

"He's not comfortable with new people," Wade said. "He did four tours in Iraq and Afghanistan. He has trouble sometimes with PTSD."

Travis nodded. Maybe that explained the hostility he had felt from the guy. Or maybe Travis was more suspicious than most people. A hazard of the job, he supposed. "I doubt you'll have any more trouble from your shoplifter," he said to Wade and Brock. "You probably scared him off. But I'll keep my eyes open."

"Thanks."

Travis returned to his SUV and climbed in. He started the vehicle and was about to pull out of his parking spot when he glanced over at the passenger seat and slammed on the brakes. The box and the rock that had been thrown through Lacy's window were gone.

Chapter Three

"Why would someone steal the rock?" Lacy folded her arms over her chest and took a step back from Travis. He had shown up at her house this morning—supposedly to "check on" her and her family. But then he had come out with this crazy story about someone taking the rock that had been thrown through her window. "Do you think I took it or something?"

"No!" He put up his hands, as if he wanted to reach for her, then put them down. "I wanted you to know because you're the victim in this case, and you have a right to know what's going on."

She unfolded her arms, relaxing a little. She had insisted on talking with him on the front porch—mainly so her parents wouldn't overhear. Her mom and dad meant well, but they tended to hover now that she was back home. "So someone just opened the door of your sheriff's department vehicle and took the evidence box?" she asked. "How does that happen? Wasn't your door locked?"

"No one locks their car doors around here." He looked sheepish—an endearing expression, really—and she didn't want to feel anything like that for him. "Besides, it's a cop car. Who breaks into a cop car? And to steal a rock?"

"Maybe they didn't know what was in the box?" she said. "Or maybe somebody is pranking you—wants to give you a hard time."

"Maybe." He put one booted foot up on a metal foot-locker her mom used as a side table on the porch, and she tried not to notice the way the khaki fabric stretched over his muscular thigh. She didn't like being around Travis, but apparently her body couldn't ignore the fact that he was the sexiest guy she'd been near in three years. "Or maybe whoever threw the rock took it because they thought I could use it somehow to link them to the crime," he added.

She forced her mind away from ogling the sheriff's hot body to what was surely a more important matter. "Can you do that?" she asked. "Would a rock have fingerprints on it or something?"

"The surface was too rough to give good latent prints, and it looked like a common enough rock."

"What about DNA?" she asked.

He laughed. "No offense, but no one does DNA testing for an act of vandalism. It's expensive, and the results take a while to come back."

She lowered herself to the cushioned rattan love seat. Her mother had made the cushions out of flowered chintz, faded now by the summer sun, but all the more comfortable and homey for it. "If the person who threw the rock stole it out of your SUV, that means they knew you had it. They must have been watching and seen you come to the house to get it."

Travis sat beside her, the cushion dipping under his weight. She caught the scent of soap and starch and clean man, and fought to keep from leaning toward him. "Maybe," he said. "Or maybe they knew your family would call my office to report the threat, they saw my SUV and decided to take a look inside."

"Either way, I'm completely creeped out." She gripped the edge of the love seat. She had thought when she walked out of prison that she would feel free again, but she still felt trapped. Watched.

"I talked to Brenda Stenson yesterday," Travis said. "She's okay with us going through Andy's files."

Lacy nodded. "I'm not looking forward to that, you know."

"I understand. But I'm hoping coming at the files cold after a few years away, you'll spot something or remember something that didn't seem relevant before."

"What about the other evidence from the crime scene?" she asked. "Wasn't there anything that pointed to someone besides me as the murderer? Or did you conveniently overlook that?" She didn't even try to keep the sharp edge from her voice.

"I guess I deserved that," Travis said. "But no—there wasn't anything. Wade Tomlinson reported seeing a woman who looked like you near the office shortly before Andy would have died. Obviously, that wasn't you. It might help if we could find this woman, but we don't have much to go on—Wade admitted he only saw her from the back, and only for a few seconds, before she entered the office. I'll question him again, but I doubt he'll have anything useful to add."

"Right. Who remembers anything very clearly that happened three years ago?" Lacy sighed.

"I think Andy's files are the best place for us to start," Travis said.

"Andy hadn't been in practice very long," Lacy said. "Still, he had a couple of big cabinets full of files. Everything was backed up on the computer, too, but he had been trained by a man who liked to keep paper copies of everything, and Andy was the same way. It will take a while to go through everything."

"We can do a couple of boxes at a time. You could even bring them back here to look through."

"Do you trust me to look through them by myself?" she asked.

"It would look better in court if we went through them together," Travis said. "Otherwise, a good defense attorney would point out that you had a strong motive to make people believe someone else murdered Andy. They could suggest you planted evidence in the files."

She fought against her inclination to bristle at what sounded to her ears like an accusation. After all, she knew all too well how attorneys could twist the most mundane events to make someone look guilty to a jury. "I guess you're right," she admitted. She stretched her legs out in front of her. "So how do you want to do this?"

"I'll get together with Brenda this afternoon and go over to the storage unit with her. I'll select a couple of boxes to go through first, seal them in her presence, get her to sign off on them, then bring them here. We'll open them together and start going through the contents. Maybe I'll even video everything, just in case there's any question."

"You're very thorough."

"I'm determined not to make any mistakes this time."

And I'm determined not to let you, she thought.

ANDY STENSON'S STORAGE unit was located in a long metal shed at the end of Fireline Road on the edge of town. Weedy fields extended beyond the chain-link fence that surrounded the shed on all sides, the land sloping upward from there toward Dakota Ridge and the mountains beyond. With no traffic and no neighbors, the location was peaceful, even beautiful, with the first summer wildflowers blooming in the fields and a china blue sky arching overhead. But there wasn't anything beautiful about Travis's errand here today.

Brenda agreed to meet him, and when he pulled into the rutted drive, he found her waiting at the far end, key in hand. "You open it," she said, pushing the key at him. "I haven't been in here since before Andy died. I paid a cleaning company to move all his stuff out here."

"Are you okay being here now?" Travis asked, studying her face. Tension lines fanned out from her mouth, but she didn't look on the verge of a breakdown.

"I'm okay," she said. "I just want to get this over with."

He unfastened the padlock and rolled up the metal door of the unit. Sunlight illuminated jumbled stacks of file boxes. Furniture filled one corner of the unit—several filing cabinets and some chairs and Andy's desk, scarred and dusty. The chair he had been sitting in when he died, stained with his blood, was in a police storage unit, logged as evidence.

Brenda traced a finger across the dust on the desktop. Was she thinking about her young husband, who had been taken from her when they were still practically newlyweds? She squared her shoulders and turned to study the file boxes. "There's a lot of stuff here," she said. "Do you know what you want?"

"I want to look at his case files." Travis studied the labels on the boxes, then removed the lid from one with the notation Clients, A through C. "I know you said you didn't know much about his work, but who would you say was his biggest client at the time he died?"

"That one's easy enough. Hake Development." She pointed to a box on the bottom of the pile, with the single word *HAKE* scrawled on the end. "Andy couldn't believe his luck when Henry Hake hired him instead of one of the big-city firms. Mr. Hake said he wanted to support local business." She chuckled. "He did that, all right. Hake Development accounted for a big percentage of Andy's income that year." Her voice trailed away at these last words, as if she was remembering once more the reason the good fortune had ended.

"All right, I'll start with this one." Travis moved aside the stack of boxes to retrieve the Hake files, and found a second box, also marked Hake, behind it.

He set the boxes on the desk, then went to his car and retrieved the evidence tape and seals. "You're verifying that I haven't opened the boxes or tampered with them in any way," he said.

"I am." He ran a strip of wide tape horizontally and vertically across each box, sealing the tops in place, then asked Brenda to write her name across each piece of tape.

"I'll video opening the boxes," he said. "With Lacy's parents as witnesses. That ought to satisfy any court that we aren't up to anything underhanded."

Brenda watched him, arms folded across her chest. "I hope you find something useful in there," she said. "Though I can't imagine what."

"What was Andy doing for Hake, do you know?" Travis asked.

"Just the legal paperwork for the mining claims Henry Hake had bought and planned to develop as a vacation resort. It wouldn't have been a big deal, except that environmental group got an injunction against the development and Andy was fighting that."

"I remember a little about that," Travis said. "They had a Ute Indian chief speak at a council meeting or something like that?"

"He wasn't a chief, just a tribal representative—a friend of Paige Riddell's. She was president of the group, I believe."

"Maybe someone who didn't want the development thought taking out Hake's lawyer would stop the threat of the injunction being overturned," Travis said.

"If they thought that, they were wrong. Hake hired another firm to represent him—someone out of Denver this time. I don't know what happened after that, though I guess he hasn't done anything with the property yet."

"Wouldn't hurt to check it out," Travis said.

He picked up the first box as his phone beeped. Setting it down, he answered the call. "A car just crashed through the front window of the Cake Walk Café." Adelaide sounded out of breath with excitement. "Gage is headed there. Dwight and Roberta are in training today. I can call someone from another shift in if you want me to. The ambulance is en route from Junction."

"I'll handle it. I'm on my way." Travis hung up the phone and studied the boxes. He could take them with him, but after what happened yesterday, he didn't want to risk someone trying to get hold of them. He returned the keys to Brenda. "Lock up after I've left. I'll have to send someone to retrieve these later."

"Is everything okay?" she asked.

"Apparently, someone crashed into the café."

Brenda covered her mouth with her hand. "I hope no one was hurt."

"Me, too."

In the car, he called Lacy. "I picked out two boxes of files from Andy's storage and got them sealed, but now I have to go on a call. It will be a while before I can get back to them."

"I can pick them up," she said. "If they're already sealed, it shouldn't make any difference, should it?"

He debated as he guided his SUV down the rutted dirt road leading away from the storage facility. "Ride out here with Brenda and have her deliver you and the boxes back to your house." Before she could protest, he added, "It's not that I don't trust you, but I don't want to give any lawyers the opportunity to object."

"All right. I'd like to visit with Brenda, anyway."

"I'll get back with you to set a time for the two of us to get together," he said, and ended the call. As much as he wanted to find the person who had killed Andy Stenson, his job wouldn't allow him to focus all his attention on one case. Right now he had a mess to clean up at the café.

LACY ENDED THE call from Travis and looked out the front window. The glass company had been out this morning to replace the broken pane and she had a clear view of the street. The car she had noticed earlier was still there—a faded blue sedan that had been parked in front of a vacation cottage three doors down and across the street from her parents' house. The cottage had a For Sale sign in front, but Lacy was pretty sure no potential buyer had been inside the cottage all this time.

She retrieved her mother's bird-watching binoculars

from the bookcase by the door and returned to the window, training the glasses on the car. A man sat behind the wheel, head bent, attention on the phone in his hand. He was middle-aged, with light brown hair and narrow shoulders. He didn't look particularly threatening, but then again, looks could be deceiving. And it wasn't as if it would have taken that much brawn to throw that rock through the window yesterday afternoon.

She shifted the binoculars to the license plate on the car. BRH575. She'd remember the number and think about asking Travis to check it out. He owed her more than a few favors, didn't he? She had almost mentioned the car to him while they were talking just now, but she didn't want to give him the idea that she needed him for anything. She didn't like to think of herself as hardened, but three years in prison had taught her to look out for herself.

She brought the glasses up to the man in the car and gasped as it registered that he had raised his own pair of binoculars and was focused on her. She took two steps back, fairly certain that he couldn't see her inside the house, but unwilling to take chances. What was he doing out there, watching the house? Watching *her*? She replaced the binoculars on the shelf and headed toward the back of the house. As she passed her mother's home office, Jeanette looked up from her computer. A former teacher, she now worked as an online tutor. "Who was that on the phone?" she asked.

Lacy started to lie, but couldn't think of one that sounded convincing enough. "Travis canceled our meeting to go over Andy's files," she said. "He had to go on a call."

"I hope everything's all right." Jeanette swiveled her

chair around to face her daughter. "You're okay, working with Travis?" she asked. "I know you don't have the warmest feelings toward him, and I'll admit, I had my doubts, too. But when I saw how hard he worked to clear your name…" She compressed her lips, struggling for control. "I really don't think you'd be standing here right now if it wasn't for him."

"I wouldn't have been in prison in the first place if it wasn't for him, either," Lacy said.

Jeanette said nothing, merely gave Lacy a pleading look.

"I'm okay working with him," Lacy said. "I don't know how much good going through those old files will do, but I'm willing to help." She turned away again.

"Where are you going?" her mother asked.

"I thought I'd take a walk."

"That's nice."

Lacy didn't wait for more, but hurried toward the back door. All the houses on this street backed up to the river, and a public trail ran along the bank. She let herself out the back gate and followed this trail up past four houses, then slipped alongside the fourth house, crossed the street behind the blue sedan, and walked up to the passenger side of the vehicle. The driver had lowered the front windows a few inches, so Lacy leaned in and said, loudly, "What do you think you're doing, spying on me?"

The man juggled his phone, then dropped it. "You—you startled me!" he gasped.

"I saw you watching me," Lacy said. "I want to know why."

"I didn't want to intrude. I was merely trying to get a feel for the neighborhood, and see how you were doing."

"Who are you, and why do you care how I'm doing?" She was getting more annoyed with this guy by the second.

"I'm sorry. I should have introduced myself. Alvin Exeter. I'm a writer. I specialize in true-crime stories." He leaned across the seat and extended his hand toward her.

She ignored the outstretched hand. "I didn't commit a crime," she said. "Or don't you read the papers?"

"No, of course. And that's what I want to write about," he said. "I'm planning a book on your wrongful conviction and its aftermath."

"And you were planning to write about me without telling me?"

"No, no, of course not. I would love to interview you for the book, get your side of the story. I was merely looking for the right opportunity to approach you."

"Get lost, Mr. Exeter," she said. "And if you try to write about me, I'll sue."

"You could try," he said. "But you're a public figure now. I have every right to tell your story, based on court documents, news articles and interviews with anyone associated with you. Though, of course, the story will be more complete if you agree to cooperate with me."

"No one I know will talk to you," she said. Though how could she be sure of that, really?

"That's not true. Sheriff Travis Walker has already agreed to speak with me."

"Travis is going to talk to you about my case?"

"We have an appointment in a couple days." Alvin leaned back in his seat, relaxed. "What do you think the public will make of the man who sent you to prison speaking, while you remain silent?"

"I think you can both go to hell," she said, and turned and walked away. She could feel his eyes on her all the way back to the house, but she wouldn't give him the satisfaction of seeing her turn around. She marched onto the porch and yanked at the door—but of course it was locked, and she didn't have her key. She had to ring the doorbell and wait for her mother to answer.

"Lacy, where is your key?" Jeanette asked as she followed Lacy into the house.

"I forgot and left it in my room." Lacy stalked into the kitchen and filled a glass of water.

"What's wrong?" Jeanette asked. "You look all flushed. Did something happen to upset you?"

"I'll be fine, Mother." She would be fine as soon as she talked to Travis, and told him what he could do with Andy's client files. Travis Walker was the last person she would ever help with anything.

Chapter Four

Travis waited while Tammy Patterson snapped another photo of the red Camry with its nose buried in the pile of crumbling brick that had once been the front wall of the Cake Walk Café. She stepped back and gave him a grateful smile. "Thanks, Sheriff. This is going to look great on the front page of the next issue."

"I'll want a copy of those pictures for my insurance company." Iris Desmet, owner of the Cake Walk, joined Tammy and Travis on the sidewalk.

"Sure thing, Ms. Desmet," Tammy said. "And I'm really sorry about the café. I didn't mean to sound like this accident was good news or anything."

"I know you didn't, dear." Iris patted Tammy's shoulder. "I'm just relieved no one was hurt. It was our slow time of day and I didn't have anyone sitting up front."

Tammy pulled out her notebook and began scribbling away. Twenty-three but looking about fifteen, Tammy was working her very first job out of college for the tiny *Eagle Mountain Examiner.* What she lacked in experience, she made up for in enthusiasm. "The paramedic told me they think the driver of the car is going to be okay, too. They think he had some kind of episode with his blood sugar."

"Better confirm that with the hospital before you go printing it," Travis said.

"Oh, yes, sir. I sure will." She flashed another smile and hurried away, no doubt thrilled to have something more exciting to write about than the town council's budget meeting or the school board's decision to remove soda machines from the lunchroom.

Iris moved closer to Travis. "Do you think the guy will lose his license over this?" she asked, nodding toward the pile of rubble.

"I don't know," Travis said. "Maybe. Either way, he's probably going to have trouble finding someone to insure him."

"I hope he's got good insurance," Iris said.

"I guess you'll have to close the café for a while, to remodel," Travis said.

"I imagine so. Then again, I've been thinking how nice it would be to visit my sister for a few days. She and her husband live up on Lake Coeur d'Alene, in Idaho. Pretty country up there. Still, it'll be hard on my employees."

"I'll keep my ears open, let you know if I hear of anyone looking for short-term help, until you can get open again."

"Thanks, Sheriff." She looked him up and down. "And how are you doing?"

"I'm fine."

"I guess it's a load off your mind, with Lacy Milligan being home again, out of prison."

"I'm glad she's home," he said, cautious.

"But now you're back to the question you started with—who killed Andy Stenson?"

"I'm working on that," he said. "Do you have any ideas?"

"No. But I've been thinking, the way you do when you live alone and wake up in the middle of the night and can't sleep. I've always wondered about that woman."

"What woman?" Travis asked.

"The dark-haired one Wade testified he saw going into Andy's office shortly before Andy was killed," Iris said. "If it wasn't Lacy—and I guess it wasn't, since she was at that basketball game—but if it wasn't her, who was it?"

"Maybe it was Andy's killer," Travis said. "Or someone who saw the killer. But again—we don't know who it was. Do you have any ideas?"

"Maybe look for a client of Andy's who fits that description?" Iris shook her head. "I know I'm not helping, I just like to think about these things."

"Well, if you think of anything else, let me know," Travis said.

He walked back to his SUV and drove to the office. Adelaide rose to meet him. "Sheriff—"

"Not now, Adelaide," he said. "I'm not in the mood to talk."

"But, Sheriff—"

He walked past her, into his office, and collided with Lacy Milligan.

As collisions went, this one was more pleasurable than most, he thought, as he wrapped his arms around Lacy to steady them both. She squirmed against him, giving him plenty of opportunity to enjoy the sensation of her soft curves sliding against him. But he wasn't the kind to take advantage of the situation. As soon as he was certain neither of them was going to fall, he released his hold on her. "What can I do for you, Lacy?" he asked.

"Do for me? You've done enough for me," she said, voice rising along with the flush of pink to her cheeks. "I want you to stop. I want you to leave me alone."

Aware of Adelaide's sharp ears attuned to every word, Travis reached back and shut the door to his office. "Let's sit down and you can tell me what this is about. Is there something specific I've done that has you so upset?"

He lowered himself into the chair behind his desk, but she remained mobile, prowling the small office like a caged animal. "Alvin Exeter," she said. "How could you even think of talking to that man about me?"

Travis squinted, thinking. "Who is Alvin Exeter?"

"He's a horrible man who says he's writing a book about me—about what happened to me. He said he has an appointment to talk with you."

Travis picked up his phone and pressed the button to ring Adelaide. She picked up right away and he put her on speaker. "Do you want me to bring in coffee for you and your guest?" she asked.

"No. Do I have an appointment with someone named Alvin Exeter tomorrow?"

"Two days from now, 9:30 a.m."

"So you asked me if I wanted to talk to this Exeter guy and I said yes?"

He could picture her scowl as she assumed her chilliest schoolmarm tone. "I didn't have to ask you. You have a stated open-door policy for citizens who want to speak to you."

So he did. "What does he want to talk to me about?" Travis asked.

"He said he's writing a human interest story on rural law enforcement."

"Thanks." Travis hung up the phone and looked at Lacy. "Did you get all that?"

"You really didn't know you had an appointment with him?"

"No." Which perhaps made him look like a poor manager in her eyes, but better than looking like a traitor. "And, apparently, Adelaide didn't know the real reason behind the appointment. He lied about his purpose in wanting to see me."

"Are you still going to talk to him?"

"Only to tell him to leave you alone. That's really all I can do. I can't keep him from approaching other people and asking them questions. Though if he bothers you again, I can arrest him for harassment."

She dropped into a chair and glared at him. The memory of her warmth still clung to him, making him conscious of the short distance between them, of how beautiful and prickly and vulnerable she was—and how mixed up and charged his feelings for her were.

"You really are making this difficult, you know?" she said.

"Making what difficult?"

"For me to hate you. I spent the last three years building you up in my mind as this horrible monster and now that you're here, in front of me, you insist on being so… so decent!"

He told himself he wouldn't laugh. He wouldn't even smile. "If anyone bothers you—Exeter or anyone else— let me know," he said. "I've got your back."

"I don't need you to be my bodyguard," she said.

"My job is to protect the citizens of this county, and you're one of them."

"So that's what I am to you, then? Your job?"

"No." She was his biggest regret. His responsibility, even. He'd helped ruin her life and now he felt obligated to help her put it back together. If she had asked he would have found her a job or given her money, but she wouldn't ask for those things—she wouldn't take them if he offered. But he could do everything in his power to protect her—to shield her from the aftereffects of the damage he'd done to her. He couldn't tell her any of that, so instead, he tapped the badge on his chest. "You're someone I hurt and I want to make that up to you, but mostly, I want to make sure you aren't hurt again."

She looked away, cheeks still flushed, then shoved out of the chair. "I'd better go. I… I'll look at those files whenever you're ready."

"Iris Desmet over at the Cake Walk said something interesting to me this afternoon," Travis said. "She said we should look for any client of Andy's who matched the description Wade Tomlinson gave of the woman whom he saw at Andy's office about the time Andy would have been killed."

"I don't remember any clients who looked like me," she said.

"Think about it. Maybe a name will come to you."

"So that's your new theory about who killed Andy— this mysterious woman?"

"Not necessarily. But if she was around near the time when Andy was killed, maybe she saw something or remembers something." He frowned. "I should have followed up on that when Wade first mentioned her."

"But you didn't, because you thought he was talking about me," she said.

"That was a mistake. A big one on my part." One he wouldn't make again.

She turned to leave. "Let me know how it goes with Alvin Exeter," she said. "I'm curious to know what he has to say."

He walked her to the door. Even with her bad prison haircut and too-pale skin she was beautiful. The kind of woman a lot of men might underestimate, but not him. He would never underestimate Lacy Milligan again.

"IT'S SO GOOD to see you." Brenda greeted Lacy on the front porch of the Milligans' house the next morning with these words and a hug that surprised her with its fierceness. When Brenda pulled away, her eyes glinted with unshed tears. "I'm sorrier than you can know that I didn't contact you while you were in prison," she said. "I started to write more than once, but I just couldn't think what to say."

"I wouldn't have known what to say, either," Lacy said. After all, she had been convicted of murdering Brenda's husband. That went far beyond merely awkward. "I'm just really glad you don't have any hard feelings now."

"I'm thrilled you're home," Brenda said. "I could never accept that you had anything to do with Andy's death. When Travis told me he had found evidence that proved you were innocent, I was so relieved."

"Even though it means the real killer is still out there?" Lacy asked.

"I didn't think of that until later."

"So Travis told you he was going to try to free me?" Lacy asked.

"He told me before he told the press. He wanted to make sure I was prepared." Brenda touched Lacy's arm. "He told me you still have bad feelings toward him, and I don't blame you. But he really is a good man—one of the best men I know."

Lacy nodded. She might not be ready to forgive Travis Walker for stealing three years of her life, but she was woman enough to see the good in him, in spite of his mistakes. "I guess he told you why we're looking through Andy's files," she said.

"Yes. I don't think you'll find anything useful, but I guess we can hope." She pulled her keys from her purse. "Are you ready to go get the boxes? I would have swung by the storage unit and picked them up myself, but Travis said it was better to do things this way."

"After the mistakes he made at my trial, I guess he's being extra cautious," Lacy said.

"I can't help but hope that this time he finds the real murderer," Brenda said. "I think it would help all of us put this behind us." She climbed into the driver's seat of her car, while Lacy slid into the passenger seat.

"I do want to put this behind me," Lacy said. "I'm still adjusting to the idea that I'm really free."

"Do you think you'll stay in Eagle Mountain?" Brenda asked.

"I don't know," Lacy said. "This is my home, but even in three years, things have changed."

"Not that much, surely," Brenda said. She turned the car onto Main.

"There are new houses, new businesses, new people

I don't know. We even have a new mayor." Lacy gestured toward the banner that hung over the street. "And what's this Pioneer Days Festival?" she asked. "That wasn't around when I left."

"It's a whole weekend of events celebrating local history," Brenda said. "Jan came up with the idea when she was mayor and it's really been a boon for the town coffers." Jan Selkirk had been mayor when Lacy had left town, and, after leaving office, had taken over management of the history museum where Brenda worked.

"I guess I remember some talk about a local celebration to commemorate the town's founding," Lacy said. "I didn't think it would be such a big deal."

"I guess it morphed over time into a really big deal," Brenda said. "Tourists come and stay all weekend. All the local motels and inns are sold out, and we have all kinds of special events at the museum."

"Sounds like fun." Lacy swiveled in her seat as they passed a pile of wreckage. "What happened to the Cake Walk?" she asked.

"You didn't hear?" Brenda slowed as they passed the rubble, which was cordoned off with orange tape. "That was why Travis had to leave without picking up the file boxes. A guy ran his car right into it yesterday afternoon. Jan told me she heard the poor man had a stroke. They ended up taking him to the hospital. Fortunately, no one inside was hurt."

"I was at the sheriff's office yesterday afternoon and Travis never said a word about it," Lacy said.

"Oh? Why were you at the sheriff's office?" Brenda didn't try to hide her curiosity.

Lacy leaned back in the seat and sighed. "There's a man in town who says he's writing a book about me.

I complained to Travis about him." No point in going into her accusations that Travis was selling her out to this writer.

"Oh, dear. I suppose that was bound to happen," Brenda said.

"I'm surprised he hasn't gotten in touch with you yet."

"When he does, I'll tell him what he can do with his book project," Brenda said.

"He said he was going to write about me, whether I cooperate or not. I guess I'll have to get used to that kind of thing. He said I was a public figure now."

"Oh, Lacy." Brenda reached over and rubbed her arm. "I'm sorry."

Lacy straightened and forced a smile onto her lips. "It'll be okay. What's one lousy book in the scheme of things?"

For the next twenty minutes, the two friends discussed the Pioneer Days Festival, new businesses that had moved to town in Lacy's absence and a new television series they were both watching. By the time they reached the storage facility, they had relaxed into the easy banter of old friends.

"I remember this place," Lacy said as she climbed out of the car at the storage unit. "I used to give Andy a hard time about it being so far out here on the edge of town."

"I guess nobody really wants a place like this in their backyard," Brenda said. "Plus, the land is cheaper out here." She undid the lock and pulled up the door.

The first thing Lacy spotted was a Victorian lamp that had sat on her desk in the front office of Andy Stenson's law practice. Seeing it now, shade crooked and grayed with dust, gave her a jolt. Her gaze shifted to the big walnut desk where Andy had sat. It had usually been covered in papers, but she recognized the lovely dark finish. So odd to see these familiar things out of context.

"After Andy died, I was such a wreck," Brenda said, as if reading Lacy's mind. "I hired a couple of guys to clean out the office and put everything here. I hadn't even looked at any of it until I was out here with Travis yesterday."

"There was no reason you should have had to look at it," Lacy said. "I hope Travis is right, and we find something useful in all these papers."

"These are the two boxes he wants to start with." Brenda pointed to two white file boxes, their tops crisscrossed with red and white tape. "All the files for Hake Development."

"I was surprised when my mom told me Mr. Hake still hasn't done anything with that property," Lacy said. "I remember he had big plans for a bunch of luxury homes—even a golf course."

"An environmental group successfully got an injunction to delay construction," Brenda said. "I'm not sure what's going on with it now. Maybe Henry Hake changed his mind."

"Maybe." Lacy picked up one box, while Brenda carried the other to the car. Boxes safely in the back seat, Brenda locked up again and the two friends set out once more.

"They haven't done much to fix this road," Lacy said as they bumped over a series of ruts on the gravel track that led away from the storage units.

"I guess with no one living out this way, it's not a priority," Brenda said.

"Right." Lacy looked over her shoulder to make sure the file boxes hadn't slid off the seat, and was surprised to see a pickup truck following them. "If no one lives out here, I wonder who that is?" she asked.

Brenda glanced in the rearview mirror. "I don't recognize the truck," she said.

"Maybe it's a tourist," Lacy said. "He could be looking for somewhere to hike. Or maybe it's someone else with a storage unit."

"It looks like a ranch truck, with that brush guard on the front." The heavy pipe, gate-like structure attached to the front bumper would protect the headlights and grill from being damaged by brush when a rancher drove through the fields.

"I didn't see any other vehicles there," Lacy said. "And we didn't pass anyone on our way out here."

"Whoever he is, he's driving way too fast for this road," Brenda said.

Lacy glanced over her shoulder again. The truck was gaining on them, a great plume of dust rising up in its wake. "He's going to have to slow down," she said. "Or run us off the road."

Even as she spoke, the truck zoomed up, its front bumper almost touching the rear bumper of Brenda's car. The lone occupant wore a ball cap pulled low on his forehead, a black bandanna tied over his mouth and nose.

"What does he think he's doing?" Brenda's voice rose in alarm. The car lurched as she tapped the brakes and Lacy grabbed on to the door for support. The screech of metal on metal filled the vehicle, which jolted again as the bumpers connected.

Brenda cursed, and struggled to hold on to the wheel. Lacy wrenched around to stare at the driver once more, but she could make out nothing of his face. He backed off and she sagged back into her seat once more.

"He's crazy," Brenda said. The car sped up, bumping along the rough road. "As soon as I can, I'm going to pull over and let him pa—"

She never finished the sentence, as the truck slammed into them once again, sending them skidding off the road and rolling down the embankment.

Chapter Five

"All units report to Fireline Road for a vehicular accident with possible injuries." The dispatcher's voice sounded clear on the otherwise quiet radio. Travis, on his way to lunch, hit the button to respond. "Unit one headed to Fireline Road," he said. He switched on his siren and headed out, falling in behind Gage, an ambulance bringing up the rear of their little parade.

As he drove, he checked the GPS location the dispatcher had sent over. The accident looked to have occurred about two miles this side of the storage units, an area with a sharp curve and a steep drop-off. He slowed as the screen on his dash indicated they were nearing the site. Gage pulled to the side of the road and Travis parked behind him. He joined his brother on the rough shoulder, and stared down at a white Subaru Outback, resting on its side on the steep slope, wedged against a solitary lodgepole pine tree.

Gage raised binoculars to his eyes. "Looks like there's at least one person in there—maybe two," he said.

Two EMTs joined them—a freckle-faced young guy Travis didn't know, and Emmet Baxter, a rescue service veteran. "OnStar called it in," Baxter said, nodding to the wrecked Subaru. "They tried to contact the driver but no one responded. Since the airbags had deployed, it triggered an automatic call."

"I'll call in the plate," Gage said. "See if we can get a possible ID on the driver."

"Go ahead, but I know who it is," Travis said, the tightness in his chest making it difficult to take a full breath. "That's Brenda Stenson's car. And the passenger is probably Lacy Milligan. The two of them were supposed to drive out here to pick up some of Andy Stenson's files from storage." He pulled out his phone and punched in Brenda's number. It rang five times before going to voice mail. He got the same results with Lacy's number. He swore and stuffed the phone back in the case on his hip, then stepped down off the edge of the road.

Gage grabbed his arm and pulled him back. "Where do you think you're going?"

"I'm going down to them. They could be hurt."

"Yeah, and one wrong move could send the vehicle the rest of the way down the slope and you with it," Gage said.

Travis studied the car and realized Gage was right. "Get Search and Rescue out here. And a wrecker. We'll have to stabilize the car, then get the women out."

Gage made the call and then there was nothing to do but wait. Travis walked the roadside, studying the surface for clues to what had happened. Soon, Gage joined him. "You can see the skid marks where they went off here," Travis said, pointing to the long tracks in the gravel.

"Doesn't really look like an overcorrection, or like she was going too fast and missed the curve," Gage said.

Travis shook his head. "Brenda's not that kind of driver. Anyway, look at this." He pointed to another set of skid marks behind the first, these veering away from the edge of the road.

"Another vehicle?" Gage asked.

"Yeah." Travis walked a little farther and squatted down at a place where broken glass glittered amid the gravel in the road. "This is probably where it struck her car—broke the rear headlights." He glanced back as the first of the Search and Rescue team arrived.

"Accident or deliberate?" Gage asked.

"They left the scene. That's a crime, even if the collision itself was an accident. But this feels deliberate to me. The weather's good, light's good. No way a person traveling behind Brenda's car wouldn't have seen her."

"Maybe the other driver's brakes failed?"

Travis straightened. "How often does that really happen?"

He and Gage walked back to meet the SAR volunteers. Travis was relieved to see an orthopedic doctor who worked weekends at the emergency clinic in Gunnison, as well as a local mountain guide, Jacob Zander. "You remember Dr. Pete, right?" Jacob said.

The men shook hands, then turned their attention to the wrecked car. "We've got two women in the vehicle," Travis said. "We don't know how badly they're hurt, but they didn't respond to OnStar."

"We need to secure the vehicle before we can do anything," Dr. Pete said.

Another carload of SAR volunteers pulled onto the shoulder, followed by a flatbed wrecker with a driver and passenger. The wrecker driver climbed out and shambled over to join them.

"Got a challenge for you," Gage said, nodding to the wedged car.

The driver, whose jacket identified him as Bud, considered the scene below, then shrugged. "I've seen worse."

"Can you secure the vehicle so that the EMTs can get down to take care of the driver and passenger?" Travis asked.

"I'll take care of it." He returned to the wrecker and his passenger—who turned out to be a woman with curly brown hair—climbed out. They conferred for a moment, then both started climbing down the slope, draped in ropes and chains. Dr. Pete and Jacob followed.

"What should we do now?" Gage asked.

Travis leaned back against his SUV, arms crossed, eyes fixed on the scene below. "We wait," he said. And pray that his search for whoever had run Brenda and Lacy off the road didn't turn into a hunt for a killer.

LACY WOKE TO pain in her head, and the taste of blood in her mouth. She moaned and forced herself to open her eyes against the searing pain. "What's happening?" she asked.

The words came out garbled, and her mouth hurt.

"Don't try to talk, ma'am. You were in an accident."

"An accident?" She blinked, and the face of the man who was speaking came into focus. He was blond, with freckles and glasses.

"It looks like you hit your head," he said. "Can you tell me if it hurts anywhere else?"

"No... I don't know."

The man leaned in through the passenger-side window, which was broken. He shined a light into her eyes and she moaned again and turned her head away. When she opened her eyes, she stared at Brenda, who lay in the driver's seat, mouth slack, white powder covering her face and shoulders. "Brenda!" Lacy tried to lean toward her.

"We're taking care of your friend. We need you to stay calm." Her rescuer reached around behind her. "I'm going to put this brace on your neck," he said. "It's just a precaution. What's your name?"

"Lacy. Lacy Milligan." The brace felt stiff and awkward, and smelled of disinfectant. Her head felt clearer now—she was remembering what had happened. But with memory came fear. "Where is the truck that ran us off the road?" she asked.

"I don't know about any truck." She heard the ripping sound of a hook and loop tape being pulled apart and repositioned. "My name is Pete. I'm a doctor."

Then a second man was leaning in beside Pete. "Lacy, it's Travis. How are you doing?"

"My head hurts." She closed her eyes again.

"Stay with us, Lacy," Dr. Pete said. "Open your eyes for me."

"Tell me about the truck, Lacy," Travis said.

She struggled to do as they asked, fighting against a wave of nausea and extreme fatigue. "The truck was black," she said. "With one of those big things on the front—iron pipe welded to the front bumper."

"A brush guard?" Travis asked.

"Yes. One of those. And it came up behind us really fast. It just—shoved us and we went over." Her heart raced, and she fought to draw a deep breath as panic squeezed her chest. "Is Brenda going to be all right?"

"We're looking after Brenda," Dr. Pete said. "Try not to get upset."

"Do you remember anything else about this truck?" Travis asked. "Did you see the driver? Was there a passenger?"

"No. I mean, I don't know. The windows were so dark I couldn't see much of anything. I think he was wearing a ball cap. And a bandanna tied over his face— like a bank robber in a B movie. It all happened so fast." She tried to shake her head and pain exploded through her with a burst of light behind her eyes. She groaned.

"Do you remember anything about the license plate?" Travis's voice cut through the fog that was trying to overwhelm her. "Or what kind of truck it was?"

"I'm sorry, no."

"Okay, everybody get back, we're going to open this door." The voice came from beyond Lacy's field of vision. Travis and the doctor moved away. A deafening screech rent the air and the car rocked and slipped to the side. Lacy let out a cry and grabbed at nothing. Then the door was wrenched off the driver's side and two men rushed forward. One worked to cut away the steering wheel while two others slashed the seat belt and carefully moved Brenda onto a stretcher. Moments later, someone leaned in the passenger-side window and began sawing at Lacy's seat belt with a blade.

After that, things happened very quickly. A man helped Lacy move into the driver's seat, then she, too, was lifted onto a stretcher. As they strapped her in, Travis leaned over her, his eyes boring into hers. "I'm going to find who did this," he said.

Tears blurred her eyes. "My parents…"

"I'm going there now, to tell them in person and take them to the hospital," he said. "We'll meet you there."

And then he was gone, and all she could see was blue sky, as a group of people she didn't even know worked to carry her to help.

She told herself she was safe now. She was surrounded by people who would help her. But fear still made a cold fist in the middle of her stomach, and she couldn't shake the memory of the impact of that truck on Brenda's car, and the feeling of falling down the mountainside, knowing it was because someone wanted her dead.

TRAVIS PACED THE hallway outside Lacy's room, phone pressed tightly to his ear, shutting out the intercom summons for doctors to report to the emergency room and the rattle of carts as nurses traveled between rooms. "Tell me you've found something," he said when Gage answered the phone.

"I put out the APB like you asked," Gage said. "But we don't have much to go on. There are probably a hundred black trucks in this county alone, and a lot of them are beat-up old ranch trucks. You wouldn't be able to tell at a glance if any of the dents were new or had been there for ten years."

"There was only one black truck that was out on Fireline Road this afternoon," Travis said.

"Face it, Trav, that truck could be in New Mexico by now," Gage said. "Without more to go on, it's going to take a massive stroke of luck to find it."

"Yeah, and nothing about this whole investigation has been lucky. Did you at least get the files out of Brenda's car?" he asked.

"I picked them up myself," Gage said. "They'd been thrown around a bunch in the crash, but that tape you put on the lids actually held pretty well. One of them is kind of split on one side, but everything is in there. I put them on your desk."

"Lock the door to my office and leave it locked until I get there," Travis said.

"You think the guy who ran Brenda and Lacy off the road was after something in those files?" Gage asked.

"I don't know," Travis said. "But we can't afford to overlook anything."

"How are Brenda and Lacy?" Gage asked.

"Lacy has a concussion and a bunch of bruises," Travis said. "They're keeping her overnight for observation, but she should be able to go home with her parents tomorrow. Brenda regained consciousness briefly on the ambulance ride over, but has been drifting in and out ever since. Her head injury is worse, and she had three broken ribs and a punctured lung. They're keeping her in ICU."

"Are Lacy's folks there with her?" Gage asked.

"Yes." They had followed him to the hospital in their car. He had run lights and sirens the whole way, clearing the route, but when they arrived it was clear Jeanette Milligan had been crying, and George was as pale as paper. "They're understandably upset and afraid."

A woman in light blue scrubs came around the corner. "Are you Travis?" she asked.

Travis looked up. "Yes?"

"Ms. Milligan is asking for you."

"Got to go," Travis said, and ended the call.

Mr. and Mrs. Milligan stood on the far side of Lacy's hospital bed when Travis entered the room. Lacy wore a dark pink hospital gown, the black thread from a row of stitches just to the left of her right temple standing out against her pale skin. Both her eyes had begun to blacken, and her upper lip was swollen. Travis must not have done a good job of hiding his shock at her appearance, because she gave him a crooked smile. "They won't let me look in the mirror, but Dad says I look like I lost a boxing match," she said.

"Maybe if anyone asks, that's what you should tell them," Travis said. He moved closer and wrapped both hands around the bed rail, wishing instead that he could hold her hand. But she probably wouldn't welcome the gesture and it wouldn't be the most professional behavior for the county sheriff. Someone had placed a vase of flowers on the bedside table and the peppery-sweet scent of carnations cut through the antiseptic smell.

"Have you found out anything more about the person or people who did this?" Lacy's father asked.

"George." Jeanette gripped her husband's arm.

"It's all right, Mom," Lacy said. "I want to know, too."

All three looked at Travis. "We don't have anything yet," he said. "If you think of anything else that could help us, let me know."

"I'm sorry, no." She shook her head. "Brenda and I went to the storage units and picked up the two boxes you had marked. There wasn't anyone else around while we were there. I mean, there weren't any other vehicles, and it's not that big a place."

"Maybe they parked behind the storage sheds in the back. A truck could probably hide back there."

"Maybe," Lacy said. "It's not like we were looking around for anyone. But they would have had to have been there before we arrived. You can see the gate from the storage unit. That's the only way in, and you have to stop and enter a code to open it."

"It's bad luck no one else was out there who might have seen the guy who hit you," Travis said. "There aren't any houses out that direction, either. We're putting a plea out on the local radio station, and it will be in tomorrow's paper, asking anyone with any information to come forward. Maybe we'll get lucky and someone will know something useful."

"Why would someone do this?" Jeanette asked. "Why would anyone want to hurt Brenda or Lacy? Or was it just a madman, wanting to cause a wreck for kicks?"

"We don't know," Travis said.

"Do you think this is related to the rock that was thrown through our window?" George asked. "Maybe the same person? One of Andy's friends or relatives who still blames Lacy for his murder."

"I'll look into that angle," Travis said. "Though Brenda is the only relative of Andy's I've ever met. I don't remember any parents or siblings attending the trial."

"He was an only child," Lacy said. "His father was dead and his mother had remarried and lives in Hawaii. He didn't see her much. I don't think they were close."

"Still, I'll check and see what I can find," Travis said. "Maybe it was random, or maybe it was related to something else."

"The files!" Lacy put a hand to her mouth. "I just remembered. What happened to the files?"

"Gage got them out of Brenda's car and they're safe for now. Don't worry about them."

"Have you seen Brenda?" Lacy asked. "They told me she's in ICU?"

"I saw her for a few minutes," Travis said. "She's going to be okay, it's just going to take her a little longer. Her head injury was more severe, and she broke some ribs."

"I hope they're giving her good pain meds," Lacy said. "I feel as if, well, as if I was run over by a truck." She gave a small, hysterical laugh.

Her mother squeezed her arm. "You're getting tired," she said. "You need to rest."

"I'll go now," Travis said.

"Please let us know what you find out," Jeanette said. "We're anxious to put this all behind us."

"I will."

He was walking down the hall and was surprised to see Wade Tomlinson walking toward him. "I heard about the accident," Wade said. "I came to see if I could give blood or do anything else to help." He extended his arm to show the bandage wrapped around the crook of his elbow. "They said they didn't need it for Brenda or Lacy, but they could always use donations, and as long as I was here…" He shrugged.

"That was good of you," Travis said. "I was just in to see Lacy. She's pretty banged up, but she'll be okay. Her parents are with her now."

Wade nodded. "That's good. I hear Brenda is in ICU. Do you know what happened? I mean, the weather was good today, and Brenda doesn't strike me as the type to drive too fast on these mountain roads. Or maybe a deer ran out in front of her and she swerved or something."

Travis debated how much he should say about the accident. Then again, by the time the wrecker driver and the EMTs and the SAR volunteers got finished telling their stories, everyone in town would know what had happened. "Someone deliberately ran them off the road," he said.

Wade's eyes narrowed. "You're kidding me."

"I'm not. Do you know anybody who drives a black truck with a brush guard who might want to do something like that?"

"Half of our customers probably drive black trucks, and a lot of them have brush guards," he said. "Why would someone do something like that?"

"I don't know. But I'm going to find out."

The two men stopped at the elevators. "I'm glad I ran into you," Travis said. "I was going to stop by the store today or tomorrow to talk to you."

"What about?"

"The day Andy was killed—you said you saw a woman going into his office, about the time he would have died."

Wade nodded. "I thought it was Lacy—but I didn't really get a good look at her. I just saw her from the back. She had hair the color of Lacy's and she was the same height and build."

"Is there anything at all about her that you remember—anything that stood out?"

Wade shook his head. "That was more than three years ago," he said. "I couldn't tell you what I had for breakfast last week, so details about something that happened that long ago—they're just not there."

"I know it's a long shot, but if you think of anything, let me know."

"Sure thing. And I hope you find whoever did this to Brenda and Lacy." The elevator doors opened and they stepped in. "I guess the car is pretty wrecked, huh?" Wade asked.

"I imagine the insurance company will total it," Travis said.

"Brock said he saw Bud O'Brien's wrecker hauling it through town. He said looking at it you wouldn't guess anybody could walk away from the crash."

Lacy and Brenda hadn't exactly walked away, but Travis knew what he meant. "They were lucky," he said. "Whoever did this to them won't be when I find him."

"Bud can add the car to the collection at his yard," Wade said.

"We'll go over it for evidence first," Travis said. "I'm hoping the forensics team can get some paint samples from the vehicle that hit them."

"Yeah. I guess they can do all kinds of things like that these days." The door opened on the ground floor. "Good seeing you again, Sheriff."

Travis checked in with the office on his way to his SUV. "Gage put Eddie Carstairs on traffic patrol out on Fireline Road," Adelaide reported. "We had so many rubberneckers driving out there to see the crash site that he was afraid there would be another accident. And Eddie needs the training hours, anyway."

"Good idea," Travis said. "I'm leaving the hospital now. And before you ask, Lacy is banged up but awake and should be going home in the morning. Brenda is in ICU with a head injury and broken ribs, but she should recover fine."

"That poor woman." Adelaide clucked her tongue. "As if she hasn't been through enough already."

"I'm headed back out to the crash site," Travis said. "I know Gage and the crime scene techs already took pictures and measurements, but I want another look on my own. Call if anything urgent comes up."

"Will do, Sheriff."

As he was leaving the parking lot, Travis recognized Wade's truck in front of him. It was red, with the Eagle Mountain Outfitters logo on the tailgate. But Wade wasn't alone. A man sat in the passenger seat. As Wade turned right, Travis got a look at the passenger's profile and recognized Ian. Odd that Wade hadn't mentioned that Ian was with him. Then again, maybe they had been headed somewhere else when Wade decided to swing by the hospital. Wade had said that Ian was uncomfortable around new people, so maybe it wasn't surprising he had decided to wait in the truck.

Travis was halfway back to Eagle Mountain when his phone showed a call from Gage. "We may have found the truck," Gage said when Travis answered. "Though I don't know what good it's going to do us."

Chapter Six

"What do you mean, you don't know how much good the truck will do us?" Travis asked.

"Somebody set it on fire," Gage said. "A hiker saw the smoke and called it in. By the time the volunteer firefighters got there, it was toast. No license plates, and I'm betting when we examine the wreckage we'll find the VIN had been tampered with or removed."

"Where is it?" Travis asked.

Gage gave a location on the edge of a state wilderness area—but still in the sheriff department's jurisdiction. "I'll be there in about forty-five minutes," Travis said.

"I'm going off shift in fifteen minutes," Gage said. "Dwight is coming on to relieve me, but I can stick around if you need me to."

"Don't you have a class tonight?" Travis asked. His brother was studying for the sergeant's exam.

"I do, but I could miss it one time."

"No. Go to your class. Dwight can handle things."

Travis checked the clock on his dash—almost three, and he hadn't eaten since breakfast. He swung through a drive-through for a chicken burrito to go, then headed out to view this burned-out truck.

A fire truck and crew stood watching the smoldering remains of the blaze when Travis pulled up, along with Sheriff's Deputy Dwight Prentice. Dwight walked out to meet the sheriff. A rangy young officer who walked with the shambling, slightly bowlegged gait of a man who had spent most of his life on horseback, Dwight had surprised everyone when he had decided to seek a career in law enforcement after his return from active duty in Afghanistan, rather than take over the family ranch. "Good afternoon, Sheriff," he said when Travis climbed out of his SUV.

Travis nodded and looked toward the blackened remains of what had once been a pickup truck, the metal frame and parts of the seats and engine still visible amid the ashes. "That was about all that was left of it when I arrived," Dwight said.

The two men walked closer. Tendrils of smoke curled up from the wreckage and heat still radiated from it. "And why do we think this is the truck we've been looking for?" Travis asked.

"The hikers who called in the fire said it was a late-model black Chevy," Dwight said. "With a brush guard. You can still see the guard up front there."

The brush guard lay in the ashes near the front of the truck, blackened but intact. "Something like that would make it easy to ram another vehicle without tearing up your own ride," Dwight said.

"But we still don't know that this is the truck," Travis said.

"True," Dwight said. "But it looks like the fire was deliberate."

"Oh, it was deliberate, all right." Assistant Fire Chief Tom Reynolds joined them. "You can see they loaded up the bed with gas cans before they lit it." He pointed to the twisted remains of the cans in front of the rear axle. "The hikers said they heard a big explosion, and a couple of other people called it in, too."

"Adelaide said one woman called the station and wanted to know if they were blasting up at the Lazy Susan Mine again," Dwight said. "And it's been shut down for thirty years."

"I reckon whoever did this stood way back and set the fire by firing a flare gun into the gas cans," Tom said. "As soon as everything cools down enough to search, we'll get our arson investigator in here. He might be able to find the remains of the flare."

Travis nodded and looked around them. The country up here was pretty desolate—rocky and covered with knots of Gambel oak scrub, prickly pear cactus and stunted juniper trees. In the fall, hunters swarmed the area hoping to bag a mule deer or elk, but this time of year the only people who came to the area were more adventurous hikers, looking for a challenging route over Dakota Ridge, which rose on the horizon to the north. "If somebody drove the truck up here to dump it, then set it on fire, how did they leave? Did the hikers report seeing another vehicle?"

"Gage asked them that and they said no," Dwight said. "But it's possible they weren't in a position to see the road, so whoever did this could have had a second vehicle waiting to drive away. Or they could have walked out cross-county." He gestured past the burned-out vehicle. "There are a couple of trails you can access from here that will take you back to the highway. It would only be a hike of three or four miles."

"We'll ask around, but I'm not holding out a lot of

hope." He turned to Tom. "When is the arson investigator coming out?"

"Tomorrow morning. It would be a good idea if you posted someone here to guard the scene until we can give it a good look."

"I'll stay here until my shift ends at midnight," Dwight said. "Then Eddie will relieve me."

"I thought Eddie was on traffic duty on Fireline Road," Travis said.

"Gage sent him home, since the lookie-loos had apparently had enough. He told him to come back out here at midnight to relieve me."

"All right." Travis studied the still-smoldering wreckage. "What do you think a late-model Chevy is worth these days?"

"Depends on how old, but thirty or forty thousand at least."

"That's a lot of money to burn up," Travis said. "If this is the truck we were looking for, somebody was willing to get rid of it rather than risk getting caught."

"Some people will do anything to avoid going to jail," Dwight said.

"A good lawyer would try to plead down to reckless driving. Someone without a record might get off with probation and community service, maybe lose their license for a while."

"Or somebody who already had a criminal record might be looking at serious time," Dwight said.

"Or whoever did this is involved in something else they don't want us to find out about." Travis shook his head.

"Do you think this is connected to Andy Stenson's murder?" Dwight asked.

"Do you?" Travis asked.

Dwight nudged his Stetson farther back on his head. "Brenda is Andy's widow. Lacy was the woman everyone thought killed him. Targeting them seems like more than a coincidence. Maybe the real killer thinks they know something—or could learn something—that would point back to him or her."

"Maybe," Travis said. "Which makes me think the sooner I can see what's in Andy's files, the better."

"EVERY INCH OF me hurts, but I don't even care, I'm just so glad to be alive." Lacy sat on the wicker settee on her parents' front porch, a bowl of popcorn on one side of her, a glass of lemonade on the other, talking to her attorney, Anisha Cook, on the phone. The sweet scent of peonies drifted to her on the breeze and in spite of everything, she felt happier than she had since she had walked out of the door of the Denver Women's Correctional Facility. Although, who was to say some of that wasn't due to the painkillers the hospital had sent her home with?

"Do the police know who did this?" Anisha asked. "Are the drivers that bad over on your side of the Divide?"

Some of Lacy's euphoria evaporated. "Whoever did this deliberately hit us," she said. "I don't think the chances are very good that the police will find them, though Travis is apparently out questioning anyone and everyone."

"Travis? Do you mean Sheriff Travis Walker?"

"Yes. He seems to be taking this attack on me personally."

"Well, that is in-ter-est-ing." Anisha drew out the

last word, a hint of laughter in her voice. "Looks like he's appointed himself your personal knight in shining armor."

"Don't be ridiculous." The settee creaked as Lacy shifted position.

"It's no secret he feels guilty about what happened to you," Anisha said. "I had my doubts when he first came to me with the evidence he had found to clear you, but I think he might be the genuine article."

"What do you mean?" Lacy asked.

"A nice guy. And he's definitely easy on the eyes."

Lacy's cheeks felt hot, and she was glad Anisha wasn't here to see her. "You didn't call me to talk about Travis Walker," she said.

"No. I have some good news for you."

"What is it?"

"The state is cutting you a check for $210,000."

Lacy almost dropped the phone. "What?"

"It's the money they owe you for your wrongful incarceration—seventy thousand dollars a year for three years. All duly authorized by state law."

Lacy collapsed against the back of the settee. "I don't know what to say," she said. "I'm stunned."

"It's no less than you deserve," Anisha said. "It's money for you to use to start over. Maybe you want to use it for your education, to start a new career."

"I don't know what I want to do," Lacy said. "I haven't had time to think."

"There's always law," Anisha said. "I can recommend some good schools."

Lacy laughed. "I'm so grateful for everything you've done for me, but I'm not sure I'm cut out to be a lawyer. I'll have to think."

"You do that. And let me know if the check doesn't show up in a couple of days. They're supposed to be sending it directly to you."

Lacy ended the call and sat back, trying to let the news sink in. The money didn't feel real yet, but then, nothing about her situation did.

The door into the house opened and her mother stepped out onto the porch. "How are you doing out here?" she asked. "Do you need anything?"

"I'm doing well," Lacy said. "Great, even. I just heard from Anisha. The state is paying me a bunch of money. I guess there's a state law that says they have to."

Jeanette hugged her daughter. "That's wonderful. I'm so happy for you." She sat next to Lacy.

"I should use the money to pay you and Dad back for all you've done for me," Lacy said. "I know you took out a second mortgage on this house to pay my legal bills, and you used your savings…"

"Don't say another word." Jeanette put a hand over Lacy's. "We want you to use the money for your education, and for things you need—a car, maybe, or a place to live, though you are welcome to stay here as long as you like."

Lacy nodded. She would need all those things, wouldn't she? After so many months with no hope, she was going to have to get used to planning for the future again.

A familiar black-and-white SUV moved slowly down the street toward them. Lacy's heart sped up, though not, she had to admit, from fear. She no longer feared Travis Walker. And she had stopped hating him. But she wasn't indifferent to him, either. She couldn't decide where he fit in her categorization of people. He wasn't her enemy anymore, but was she ready to accept him as a friend?

Travis parked at the curb and strode up the walkway, confident and oh-so-masculine. He was one of those men who never looked rumpled or out of shape. "Good afternoon, ladies." He touched the brim of his Stetson. "I heard they let you out of the hospital, Lacy. How are you feeling?"

"Sore, but I'll live. Too bad it isn't Halloween, though. My face could be my costume."

He leaned closer to examine her face. "The bruises are turning Technicolor," he said. "Better start embellishing your story. Who did you say beat you in that boxing match?"

Lacy laughed in spite of herself. So much for keeping her emotions in check around this man. "What brings you here?" she asked. "Or did you just stop by to see how I'm doing?"

"I thought I should let you know the latest on the case, before the news got back to you through the Eagle Mountain grapevine."

"Eagle Mountain has a grapevine?" she asked.

"You know it. And half the time it starts in my office, with Adelaide Kinkaid."

"Sit down, Travis." Jeanette pulled up a chair. "Tell us what you've found out."

He sat. "We think we found the truck that ran you off the road," he said. "Someone drove it to an isolated area and set it on fire. We can't be 100 percent sure that it's the right one, but we think so. The Vehicle Identification Number was removed and there were no license plates. I don't know if we'll ever identify the owner."

"I wish you could find him," Jeanette said. "I hate thinking someone like that is out there, running free."

"We're doing the best we can," Travis said.

"I know that. And we appreciate it." She stood. "I have to get back to work. You stay and talk to Lacy."

They waited until her mother had shut the door behind her before either of them said anything. "I talked to—" she began.

"How are you—" he said.

"You first," he said, and motioned for her to continue.

"I talked to Brenda today," Lacy said. "She was pretty groggy, but awake. She thinks the doctors will let her go home tomorrow or the next day."

"That's great news."

"I got some more good news," she said. "The state is paying me a settlement. Apparently they have to, according to state law."

"I guess I had heard something about that," he said. "I'm glad. You can use the money to make a fresh start."

"I'm still trying to decide what to do with the money, but it does feel good to know it's there."

"I spoke to a friend of yours this morning," he said, a teasing glint in his eye.

"Oh? Who was that?"

"Alvin Exeter. We had an appointment, remember?"

"And what did he have to say?"

"I told him I knew he wasn't writing a piece on rural law enforcement and that I wouldn't talk to him about anything else. He said I must have spoken to you, but that refusing to do an interview with him wouldn't stop the book. He told me if I cooperated and spoke to him, he would be sure to present my side of the story. Otherwise I could come off looking like a stupid hick cop who took the easy way out on a case and got it wrong."

"He threatened you!" she said. "What a miserable worm. If I see him again—"

Travis's hand on her arm silenced her. "He isn't that wrong, you know," he said. "I did take the easy way out and I did get it wrong."

"You were inexperienced." She said the words without thinking. But she realized they were true. She had been twenty when she was sentenced for murder, but Travis had only been twenty-three. And he had never handled a murder case before.

"I should have done a better job," he said. "I will this time."

Lacy believed him, and she vowed to do what she could to help him. After all, she would only be helping herself. "I've been thinking about what happened," she said. "I have to wonder if whoever ran us off the road did so because he didn't want us to examine those files. It wouldn't be that difficult to figure out what we were doing out at Andy's storage unit. If he was watching us, he would have seen us put the files in Brenda's car."

Travis nodded. "I've thought of that, too."

"Where are the files now?" she asked.

"They're in my SUV." He nodded toward the vehicle parked at the curb. "I'm not trying to rush you, but when you're ready, I'd like to go through them."

"I'm ready now." She stood, fighting not to show how much it hurt.

"You just came home from the hospital," he protested.

"And I'm going nuts, sitting here doing nothing. Trust me, this is just what I need to distract me."

Chapter Seven

Lacy waited on the porch while Travis retrieved both boxes from the car and she held the door while he carried them inside. "Go through that archway on the right," she said. "We can use the dining table."

She flicked the light switch as she followed him into the room, illuminating the chandelier that cast a golden glow over the cherry dining set for eight that the family only used for holidays and formal occasions. Travis set the boxes on the table. "I'll be right back," he said, and went out again.

He returned moments later, carrying a video camera on a tripod. "This is probably overkill," he said as he positioned the camera. "But I didn't want to take any chances."

Camera in place and running, he broke the seal on the first box and removed the lid. The first file he opened on the table between them was the contract Henry Hake had signed, as president and CEO of Hake Development, with Andrew Stenson as his legal representative in the matter of Eagle Mountain Resort, a high-altitude luxury resort development.

"I remember the day Andy signed that contract," Lacy said. "He took me and Brenda to lunch and insisted on ordering champagne. We teased him that he was going to get a reputation as a lush, drinking at noon."

"It was a big contract for a fairly new lawyer," Travis said.

"The biggest. And totally out of the blue. We couldn't believe our luck when Mr. Hake contacted us. He said he wanted someone fresh, with new ideas, and that he believed in supporting local talent."

"Still, this development looks like a big deal," Travis said. "I'm surprised he didn't want someone who was more experienced in real estate law." He removed a folded paper from an envelope labeled Plat and spread it across the table. "Tell me about this," he said.

Lacy leaned over his shoulder, the soap and starch scent of him sending a tingle through her midsection. She forced herself to focus on the plat of the development, instead of on the way his shoulders stretched tight the crisp cotton of his uniform shirt, or the way his dark hair curled up at the collar, exposing a scant half inch of skin...

"These were all old mining claims, right?" Travis prompted.

"Right. Mining claims." She swallowed and shifted her gaze to the blue lines on the creamy paper. "Hake Development was able to buy up approximately fifty mining claims, all above nine thousand feet, an area that has traditionally been deemed unsuitable for development."

"Why is that?" Travis asked.

"Mostly because there's so much snow up there in the winter it makes it difficult to maintain roads," Lacy said. "Plus, there's a higher avalanche danger. Up at the higher elevations, above treeline, the ground is tundra, frozen year-round. That makes it unstable to build on. Hake had engineers who had devised plans for getting around those limitations—foundations anchored on rock deep in the ground, regular avalanche mitigation, roads on traditional mining trails, water piped up from far below in an elaborate network of aqueducts."

Travis whistled. "Sounds expensive."

"Oh, it was. But Hake swore he knew plenty of people who would pay a premium price to live with the kind of views and privacy you get at those elevations."

"Not everyone was thrilled about his plans, I'm sure."

"Oh, no. The Ute Indian tribe objected because some of that terrain overlaps areas they deem sacred. And the environmentalists were in an uproar over the potential damage to fragile tundra. They succeeded in getting an injunction to stop the development until environmental studies could be done."

"And were the studies done?" he asked.

"I don't know," she said. "But we could probably find out." The idea excited her. She had missed this—working on something constructive, researching and finding out things, instead of simply sitting back and letting each day stretch forward with no goal or purpose.

"You find out what you can about the injunction and any studies," Travis said. "Meanwhile, I'll talk to Henry Hake, and ask him to update us on the project."

"My mom said they haven't built anything up there," Lacy said. "Maybe he couldn't beat the injunction. Or he decided the project was too expensive to pursue. He supposedly had a lot of investors who wanted to put money into the resort, but maybe the injunction caused them to change their minds."

"I'll find out." He pulled another stack of files from the box and handed her half. "Let's see if anything stands out in these."

As Lacy read through the contents, it was as if she was sitting back in the little office on Fourth Street, twenty years old and ready to take on the world, excited to have found interesting work right here in Eagle Mountain, the place she loved best in the world. From the window by her desk she could look up and see Dakota Ridge, and the road leading out of town, Mount Rayford peeking up over the ridge, snowcapped year-round.

As she flipped through the files, she remembered typing memos and motions, and discussing the work with Andy over sandwiches at their desks. Sometimes Brenda would stop by to say hello and share a story about her work at the history museum. Though the world hadn't been perfect back then, it had sure seemed so at times.

"Find anything interesting?" Travis asked after they had been reading silently for almost an hour.

"Not really," she said. "Most of it is just routine stuff—surveyor's reports and court motions, tax paperwork—nothing out of the ordinary. How about you?"

"I found this." He pushed a piece of paper across to her. "Any idea what it means?"

The note was written on the blank side of a "While You Were Out" message slip. *Ask Hake about notes.*

Lacy made a face. "This is Andy's handwriting, but I don't know what notes he's referring to."

Travis set the paper aside and they searched through the rest of the first box. Lacy could tell when her pain medication wore off, as her head began to throb, her vision blurring from the pain. She put a hand to her temple, grimacing. "We should stop now," Travis said. "We can do the other box later."

"I guess you're right." Fatigue dragged at her—she could have put her head down and gone to sleep right there beside him.

"I appreciate your help," Travis said. "But don't overdo it."

She nodded. "What will you do now?" she asked.

Travis picked up the slip of paper he had set aside earlier. "I think I'll start by asking Hake about this."

GETTING AN INTERVIEW with Henry Hake proved to be more difficult than Travis had expected. When he had telephoned the number for Hake Development yesterday, a brisk-sounding woman informed him that Mr. Hake was out of town. "I can ask him to call you when he returns," she said. "But it may be some time before you hear from him."

"This is a police matter. I need to hear from him sooner, rather than later."

"Oh. Well, I'll certainly let him know."

"So you're sure you don't know when he'll be back in town."

The silence on the other end of the line went on so long Travis wondered if they had lost their connection. "Are you still there?" he asked.

"Mr. Hake may be back tomorrow—but you didn't hear that from me."

"What's the status of the Eagle Mountain Resort development?" Travis asked.

"I don't have any information on that to give you," she said.

"Is that because you don't know or because the official policy is to keep silent?" he asked.

"I'm sure I don't know what you mean," she said. "Is there anything else I can help you with?"

"No, thank you." He ended the call, then called Adelaide. "I need you to track down Henry Hake's personal number and address."

"Will do, Sheriff."

Travis turned to his computer and found a report from the county's arson investigator in his inbox. He settled back to read, finding no surprises. The truck was a standard model, probably from the last two or three years, judging by what little remained of the frame and engine. No VIN, no plates. The only nonstandard feature was the brush guard, which had been welded of heavy pipe and wasn't the sort of thing that could be ordered from a catalog. Travis called Adelaide again. "Who's on shift right now?" he asked.

"Dwight just came on. He's probably still in the parking lot, if you need him for something."

"See if you can grab him and tell him I want to talk to him for a minute."

A few minutes later, Dwight entered Travis's office. "What can I do for you, Sheriff?"

"I need you to check with any metal fabricators or welders around here, see if any of them made a brush guard like this for a guy with a black Chevy pickup." He slid a note across the desk with the description and dimensions of the brush guard.

"Sure." Dwight pocketed the note. "This have anything to do with the guy that ran Lacy Milligan and Brenda Stenson off Fireline Road?" he asked.

"Yes. I'm hoping we'll get lucky and turn up a lead, but it's a long shot."

Dwight hesitated in the doorway. "Is there something else?" Travis asked.

"I was just wondering how Mrs. Stenson is doing?" Dwight said. "I heard she was hurt pretty bad in the accident."

"She's doing much better," Travis said. "She should get to come home in a few days."

Dwight nodded, his expression solemn. "I'm glad to hear it. She and I were in school together. She was always a real sweet girl."

Dwight left and Travis sat back in his chair, staring at the computer, wondering what he should do next. He was tempted to call Lacy and brainstorm with her about the case—or better yet, go by and see her. He discarded the idea immediately. Though she had seemed to enjoy the time they had spent together, he wasn't going to delude himself into thinking she was helping him out of anything other than self-interest. Maybe once upon a time the two of them could have hit it off and been a couple. But too much had come between them now.

"Why are you sitting there with that moony look on your face?"

Travis looked up to find his brother standing in the doorway of his office. He sat up straight and assumed his best all-business expression. "I just sent Dwight out to try to track down the welder who made the brush guard on that burned-out truck," he said. "And I've got a call in to Henry Hake, trying to find out about a note we found in Andy Stenson's files."

"I thought Hake was out of town," Gage said.

"When I pressed his assistant, she admitted that he's supposed to return today."

"So you've been busy." Gage crossed to the visitor's chair across from the desk and sat. "When this is all over—when we've closed the case—are you going to ask her out?"

"Ask who out?" Travis stared at his computer screen, the words of the arson investigator's report blurring together.

"Lacy. And don't lie to me and say you aren't gone over her. You acted this same way about Didi Samuelson. I recognize the signs."

"Didi Samuelson was in eighth grade," Travis protested.

"Which only proves that love reduces all of us to immature shadows of ourselves," Gage said.

"And you know this because you've been in love so much."

Gage stretched his arms over his head. "I know this because I've studied how to successfully avoid falling victim to the dreaded love disease," he said. "And stop trying to change the subject. We're talking about you here, not me."

"I am not in love with Lacy Milligan." Travis kept his voice down, hoping Adelaide wasn't listening in, but doubting he would be so lucky. The woman had ears like a cat's. "I hardly know her."

"Right. So you only tied yourself in knots and practically killed yourself clearing her name because you wanted to do the right thing."

"Yes. Of course. I would have done that for anyone."

Gage laughed. "Pardon me if I have a hard time believing you would have gotten quite so worked up about some ugly guy with tattoos and a rap sheet as long as my arm."

"I made a mistake arresting her and I had to make up for it."

Gage leaned forward, his expression no longer mocking. "You did your job," he said. "You arrested her because the evidence pointed to her as the perpetrator of the crime."

"It was a sloppy investigation. The follow-up proved that. The money missing from the business account was a bookkeeping error. The money in Lacy's account really was from selling her grandmother's ring. She really wasn't in town at the time Andy was killed. If I had done my job and taken a closer look at the evidence, I would have found that out."

"You know what they say—hindsight is twenty-twenty. You could have looked at that evidence ten times back then and you might not have seen anything different."

"But I might have," Travis said. That knowledge would haunt him for the rest of his life. It had changed the way he looked at every case now.

"I know one thing," Gage said. "This whole situation has made you a better cop. And it's made all of us who work under you better cops."

"Yeah, it taught you not to make the mistakes I did," Travis said.

Gage sat back again. "And it taught us to man up and admit it when we do make a mistake, and to do what we can to right the wrong."

"Glad I could be such a shining example," Travis said sourly.

Gage stood and hitched up his utility belt. "Lacy is

still speaking to you, in spite of everything," he said. "That has to be a good sign."

"She's a good person."

"And so are you. Don't sell yourself short. I'm not saying you have to rush things, but don't give up before you start." He pointed a finger at Travis. "You taught me that, too."

He left the office. Travis stared after him, an unsettled feeling in his chest he wasn't sure he wanted to examine too closely. It could be his brother had stirred up something inside him—something like hope.

BRENDA CAME HOME from the hospital the next day, and the day after that Lacy delivered a box of fancy chocolates and a chicken casserole to her friend's door. "The casserole is from my mom, but the chocolates are from me," Lacy said as she carried her gifts into Brenda's house. It was the same house she and Andy had purchased shortly after moving to Eagle Mountain—a former forest ranger's residence originally built by the Civilian Conservation Corps in the 1930s, constructed of native stone and cedar, with hand-carved shutters and door lintels. They had updated the house with new windows and roof and a new heating system, part of the improvements paid for with money from Henry Hake's retainer.

"Thank you for both," Brenda said, gingerly lowering herself to the sofa.

"It still hurts, doesn't it?" Lacy asked, as Brenda sucked in her breath and winced.

"The doctor taped the ribs, but all I can do is wait for them to heal," Brenda said. "I still get dizzy from the head injury, and I can't read for long without getting a headache. The neurologist said those symptoms could take months to disappear, though she reassured me there's no permanent damage."

"That's going to make it tough at work, isn't it?" Lacy asked.

"Jan already called and told me not to worry. I know not everyone gets along with her, but ever since Andy died, she's been an absolute peach." She leaned forward to study Lacy's face. "You look pretty beat up yourself," she said. "How are you feeling?"

"Much better, actually," Lacy said. "The headaches are almost gone. I'm still a little stiff and sore, but that will go away eventually." She made a face. "I was hoping makeup would cover the worst of the bruising, but no such luck."

"You're still beautiful and it makes you look… I don't know—tough."

"That would have come in handy when I was in prison." At Brenda's stricken look, Lacy laughed. "It's okay, really," she said. "I don't mind talking about it. I figure better to get it out in the open and own it than to worry everyone's talking about it behind my back—which you know they are."

"I guess people are curious," Brenda said weakly.

"Of course they are. I would be, too. So don't be afraid to ask me questions. I'll answer if I can."

Brenda shook her head. "I don't want to know anything. All I care about is that you're here now. Though if I could ask a question of someone, I would want to know who tried to kill us the other day. And why?"

"Travis is following every lead, but he hasn't come up with much yet," Lacy said. "He and I started going through some of Andy's files, hoping we could find some clue—in case the guy who hit us was trying to stop us from looking through the files."

"Did you find anything?" Brenda asked.

"Only a note on the back of a 'While You Were Out' slip. It was in Andy's handwriting, and it said, 'Ask Hake about the notes.' Do you have any idea what that might mean?"

Brenda frowned. "I have no idea what it means. You know Andy—he was always making notes to himself about things he wanted to do or find out. For weeks after he died I would find little scraps of paper around the house."

"I'm sorry," Lacy said. "I didn't mean to upset you."

"No, it's okay." She straightened her shoulders. "It's actually been a lot better since you came home. I think I had that burden of guilt hanging over me, keeping me from moving on."

"I'd think it would be easier to move on if you knew who actually killed Andy," Lacy said.

"It would. But I'm getting used to the idea that that might never happen. I still have to live my life, so that's what I'm trying to do."

"You're still young. Maybe one day you'll meet another man you can love."

"Maybe. Though dating in a small town can be problematic."

"You mean, you can't really keep a relationship secret," Lacy said. "But at least we're luckier than some places. Single men still outnumber single women in these mountain towns, so we have a better selection to choose from."

"I don't care about a selection," Brenda said. "I just want to find the one right guy. But enough about me.

How many guys have asked you out since you came home?"

Lacy blinked. "None. Why would they?"

"Hello? Didn't we just say there are more single men than women around here? And here you are, a beautiful young woman who hasn't had a date in at least three years. I'm surprised they aren't lined up at your door."

Once again, Lacy cursed her tendency to blush so easily. "I was single before I went to prison, too," she said. "And I never dated that much." In fact, she had never had a serious relationship. She had always put it down to men seeing her more as a best friend than as a lover.

"There's a new guy in town who looks pretty interesting," Brenda said. "I saw him with Brock Ryan at the climbing wall in Ute Park when I cut through there to deliver an ad to the *Examiner* office. He was about halfway up the wall and, well, I'm not ashamed to admit I stopped and stared. And I wasn't the only one. The two of them had drawn quite an audience of female admirers. Adelaide Kinkaid was there, too."

"Adelaide is old enough to be Brock's grandmother," Lacy said.

"You'd have to be dead not to notice those two," Brenda said. "I mean, Brock is good-looking, but this new guy..." She fanned herself. "He was like a statue of some Greek god. Amazing."

"Then I hope I get a chance to check him out," Lacy said. "What's his name?"

"Tammy Patterson at the paper told me his name is Ian Barnes. He's a veteran and she thinks he's in town visiting Brock and staying at his place. She tried to get him to do an interview with her for the paper, but he wasn't interested."

"I don't guess I know Tammy," Lacy said.

"She moved here last year from Minnesota. Sweet kid, fresh out of college. She works weekends at Moe's Pub."

"That sounds like a good place to run into good-looking men," Lacy said.

"Except Tammy is apparently engaged to her high school sweetheart back in Duluth and staying true to him," Brenda said. "Which doesn't keep the men in town from pursuing her. I guess playing hard to get really is an effective strategy."

"You really do know all the gossip," Lacy said. "Is that because you've been studying, preparing to dive back into the dating game?"

"It's really because Jan keeps tabs on everything and everyone in town, and passes the information on to me," Brenda said. "She may not be mayor of Eagle Mountain anymore, but she still wants to know what's going on."

"I was surprised to find out she didn't run for reelection when her term ended," Lacy said. "She seemed to enjoy the job so much, and she was good at it."

"She said it was time to move on to something else. And Larry had already declared his intention to run, and he seemed really serious about wanting the job, so I guess she figured it was a good time to bow out."

"Maybe we should talk to her about Andy," Lacy said. "Maybe she knows something about the mysterious woman Brock saw near his office the day he died, or someone with a black truck who might have had it in for us."

"She holds court at a back table at Kate's Kitchen

every Thursday morning," Brenda said. "We could go there tomorrow if you like."

"I would like, if you're up to it."

"It's a date, then." Brenda picked up the box of chocolates. "Now, let's try out your gift. I get dibs on the caramels."

Chapter Eight

Henry Hake lived in a stone-and-cedar mansion near the base of Mount Rayford. A black iron gate blocked the winding paved drive, so Travis parked and called Hake's private number on his cell phone. "Hello?" The voice that answered was hesitant and higher-pitched than Travis had expected.

"This is Rayford County Sheriff Travis Walker. I need you to open the gate so I can come up and see you."

"What is this about?"

"We'll discuss that when I get there. Open the gate, please."

"I really don't have time for this. I'm on my way out."

"Then you shouldn't waste any more time discussing this. Open the gate and I'll be out of your way as quickly as possible." Silence stretched between them, but Travis could hear the other man breathing and knew he hadn't disconnected. He resisted the temptation to speak, letting the tension build. Finally, the gate groaned and began to swing open.

"I'll be up in a minute," Travis said, and ended the call.

He returned to his car and drove the quarter mile up to the house. Hake met him at the door. "Hurry. I don't have time to waste," he said, ushering Travis inside. A portly man in a light gray suit with worn cuffs, Henry Hake looked more like a schoolteacher than a millionaire businessman. Travis followed him down a mahogany-paneled hallway to a small, dark office, where Hake took a seat behind a cluttered desk. Dust coated the side tables and floated in the shaft of sunlight from the single window, where a leggy geranium sprawled across the sill. "What do you want?" Hake asked.

"I want to talk to you about Andy Stenson," he said.

Hake blinked. He clearly hadn't been expecting this topic of conversation. "What about him? He's dead."

"I'm trying to find out who killed him."

"Got that wrong the first time, didn't you?" Hake pawed through the papers on the desk until he unearthed a cell phone. He stared at the screen, then back up at Travis. "You've got five minutes."

"Why did you hire Andy Stenson to represent you and Eagle Mountain Resort?" Travis asked. "Why not a more experienced lawyer?"

"I wanted to give the kid a chance."

"Did you know him previously? How did you decide on him?"

"Never heard of the kid. A business associate suggested it."

"Who is this business associate?"

"That doesn't really matter. You're wasting your time."

The five-minute deadline was a bluff, Travis decided. As far as he could tell, Hake was alone in the house. It wasn't likely he could throw Travis out by himself. "What's the status of Eagle Mountain Resort?" he asked.

"We're restructuring."

"Who is we?"

"I have business partners—some of whom prefer to remain silent."

"You went to a lot of trouble to buy up the mining claims and develop plans for the resort. Why didn't you go through with them?"

"I really can't talk about that."

"Why not?"

Hake snatched the phone from his desk and shoved it into the inside pocket of his jacket. "It ought to be obvious to you, if you've done any investigating, that someone doesn't want that project to go forward."

"Who?" Travis asked. "The environmentalists?"

"Maybe. There was some sabotage that might have been their doing. What do they call it—monkey-wrenching? We had equipment destroyed, some property stolen."

Travis hadn't heard any of this. "Did you report this to the police?"

"We didn't want the bad publicity. We handled it ourselves by posting private security. After that we didn't have any more troubles."

"Who is we?"

Hake waved a hand as if shooing a fly. "The organization. Who doesn't really matter."

Travis took Andy's note from his pocket and passed it to Hake. "What can you tell me about this?"

Hake studied it. "What is this? It doesn't make sense."

"I found it in Andy Stenson's files."

Hake tossed the paper back toward Travis. "I have no idea what it's about."

Travis had given a lot of thought to what the note

might mean. He risked a guess. "Was someone writing you threatening letters? Is that what Andy wanted to know more about?"

Hake's face registered an internal struggle. "There were a couple of nasty notes," he said finally. "I never should have mentioned them to Andy, but I thought it would be a good idea if someone knew—for insurance."

"Do you think Andy decided to look into the threats on his own?" Travis said. "Is that what led to his death?"

Hake pushed out his lower lip. He had a cut on his chin, maybe from shaving. "I wondered at first, if maybe he had gotten too close to someone who didn't want to be found out."

"Why didn't you say something?" Travis tried to rein in his anger. "Your suspicions might have led us to look at other suspects in the murder."

"I thought if I opened my mouth whoever had killed Andy would come after me next."

"Who do you think killed him?" Travis leaned toward him. "If you have any ideas, tell me."

"I don't know who. And if I did, I'm smart enough to keep my mouth shut. I was so terrified at the time, I hired a bodyguard."

"Who did you hire?" Maybe the bodyguard knew more about these threats.

"A professional. He came highly recommended, but I don't remember his name. He didn't work for me for long."

"Why not?"

"After Andy died, the threats went away. The injunction stopped the development, so I guess our opponents got what they wanted."

"I'll need the names of your business partners so that

I can talk to them, too. Maybe they know more about the source of the threats."

"They don't know anything, I promise. Some of them aren't even alive anymore, and the others won't talk to you."

"Tell me their names, anyway."

"I'm sorry, I really can't help you. And I have another appointment." He rose.

Travis stood, also. "Did you keep any of the threatening notes you received?" he asked.

"No. I destroyed them a long time ago."

"And you have no idea who sent them?"

"None. As I said, it happened a long time ago." His eyes met Travis's. "I've put it behind me, and you should, too."

He walked Travis to the front door. As Travis drove away from the mansion, Hake's final words replayed in his head. Was the developer merely offering advice, or was he making a threat?

LACY AND BRENDA walked into Kate's Kitchen a few minutes after nine o'clock the next morning and found Jan Selkirk having coffee with Adelaide Kinkaid and two other women at a table near the back. The former mayor—a striking, fortysomething woman with big brown eyes and ash-blond hair in a tumble of curls around her shoulders—looked up and smiled at their approach. "Good morning, Brenda. I didn't expect to see you out and about so soon."

"I was going crazy, sitting around the house," Brenda said. She pulled out a chair and carefully lowered herself into it. "You know Lacy Milligan, don't you?"

Lacy leaned forward and offered her hand.

"I do. It's been a while," Jan said, with a firm hand-shake. "I hope you won't be offended, dear, but you look like you took a real beating. I'm so sorry. And the police have no idea who attacked you two?"

"If there's a clue to be found, Travis will find it," Adelaide said. "The poor man is working himself into the ground." She studied Lacy over her coffee cup. "I thought things would settle down once he got Lacy home, but I guess we're not going to be so lucky."

Lacy tried not to resent the implication that she was personally responsible for a new local crime wave. She took the chair next to Brenda and accepted the carafe of coffee one of the women passed her.

"We have a few questions since, as former mayor, you know pretty much everyone in town," Brenda said.

"What you mean is that she has the dirt on every-one," Adelaide said. She pushed out her chair and stood. "Come on, ladies. Let's leave these young women to it. I need to get to the station, anyway. If I don't, Gage will make the coffee and it will be so strong you could strip paint with it."

When Lacy and Brenda were alone with Jan, the older woman leaned back in her chair and studied them. "What do you want to know?" she asked.

"At my trial, Wade Tomlinson testified that he saw a woman outside Andy's office about the time Andy was killed—a woman who looked like me," Lacy said. "Obviously, that wasn't me, so do you know who it might have been?"

"I have no idea," Jan said. "I was too busy being mayor at the time to pay attention to anything that didn't pertain to the job."

"Yes, but can you think of anyone who was living

in the area at the time—or visiting—who looked like Lacy?" Brenda asked. "A slim young woman with dark hair?"

Jan put a hand to her own blond locks. "No one comes to mind," she said. "It could have been anyone."

"Maybe she was a client of Andy's," Lacy said. "I've tried to think if any of his clients had dark hair, but it was too long ago. I'm hoping when Travis and I look at the rest of Andy's files, it will jog my memory."

"You and Travis are going through Andy's files?" Jan looked amused. "I'll bet that's interesting. As I remember, there was no love lost between you and our young sheriff."

"We've decided to keep the past in the past," Lacy said, eyes downcast. No sense letting the town gossips think anything differently. Lacy's feelings about Travis were so all over the map she didn't need other people weighing in with their opinions.

"What about a newish black truck with a welded brush guard?" Brenda asked. "Do you know anyone with a truck like that?"

"Only half the ranchers in the county," Jan said. "I heard they found the one they think hit you burned out over on the edge of the public land out toward Dakota Ridge."

"Yes, but they don't know who was driving it," Lacy said.

"Whoever it is, let's hope he doesn't try again," Jan said. "Frankly, if I were you two I wouldn't want to be seen out in public together."

"Why do you say that?" Brenda asked.

"Well, since there's no way of putting it delicately, I'll just say it—you don't know who this maniac was really after, do you—you or Lacy. If you're not the one he wants, why take chances hanging out with the one he does?"

Lacy was still trying to digest this take on the situation when the door to the restaurant opened and a man entered. He wore a black watch cap, along with a black T-shirt that fit like a second skin, showing off every chiseled muscle of his shoulders and torso. Every female head in the room—including the two waitresses and the woman at the cash register—swiveled to track his progress to a table by the window. Jan leaned forward. "That's Ian Barnes," she said softly. "Now that is one beautiful man."

"I don't know," Lacy said, turning her back to him. "He's almost too beautiful. And does he ever smile? He looks almost…dangerous."

"Mmmm," Jan purred. "Some women like men like that. And you may not be interested in him, but he's definitely interested in you. He's looking right at you."

Lacy shifted in her chair. "I wish he wouldn't," she said. "Maybe someone should point out that it's rude to stare. He makes me nervous."

"He doesn't drive a black truck," Jan said. "I saw him yesterday in a beat-up Jeep." She sat back and sipped her coffee. "But I swear I've seen him somewhere before. That's not a body—or a face—a woman forgets. But I can't put my finger on where." She shrugged. "I'm sure it will come to me."

The door opened and a second man entered. Lacy let out a groan and turned back around. "Do you know him?" Jan asked.

"His name is Alvin Exeter," Lacy said. "He's a writer who says he's working on a book about me."

"I don't just say it, I'm writing it." Alvin stopped behind Lacy's chair, and the thought passed through her mind that this was what it must feel like for a mouse when a hawk hovered over it. Except she wasn't a mouse.

She turned to look up at the man. "Go away," she said.

"No." He pulled out the chair on her other side and sat.

"I don't have anything to say to you," Lacy said.

"I didn't come to talk to you. I came to talk to Ms. Selkirk."

"Oh?" Jan looked interested. "What about?"

"I understand you were mayor of Eagle Mountain when Andy Stenson was murdered," Alvin said. "I thought you would be the perfect person to give me a picture of what life was like here during that time."

Jan glanced at Lacy, then smiled at Alvin, coral-lip-sticked mouth stretched over big teeth. "I'm sorry, Mr. Exeter, but you'll have to write your book without my help. In fact, I think Lacy should write her own book. After all, it's her story to tell."

"Maybe I will," Lacy said, taking her cue, though she had no intention of reliving the last three years on paper.

Alvin's expression turned stormy. "If you don't help me, you have no say in how you're portrayed," he said.

"You're assuming we care," Jan said.

He shoved back his chair and left the café. Jan picked up the carafe and refilled their coffee cups. "What an unpleasant little man," she said.

"I caught him watching my house through binoculars," Lacy said.

"I don't suppose he owns a black truck," Jan said.

Lacy shook her head. "When I saw him, he was in a blue sedan."

"A pity. He's just the type I would like for the villain."

"I met plenty of very ordinary-looking people in prison who did horrible things," Lacy said. "For a while I celled with a white-haired grandmother who had poisoned three husbands."

The sudden silence that blanketed the café made her aware that everyone in the place was staring at her. Jan leaned forward and broke the tension. "Keep talking that way and they're all going to want to see your prison tattoos," she said.

"I don't have any prison tattoos," Lacy said, her cheeks burning.

"Everyone will be so disappointed," Jan said. "When people come through a horrible experience like that, we expect them to wear their scars on the outside." She leaned forward and grasped Lacy's hand. "Don't be afraid of shocking people. Sometimes that's exactly what we need to wake us up to the real world. It's very easy to get complacent, hidden away in this little town. We start to think we're special—protected from the bad things that plague other people. We don't like it when things—like murder—happen to remind us that's not true, but sometimes it's exactly what we need. You're exactly what we need."

Chapter Nine

Lacy was still trying to figure out what Jan Selkirk had meant at Kate's that morning when Travis called. "Do you have time today to get together with me?" he asked. "I have some more questions for you."

"I don't know," she said. "Let me check my calendar. After all, I'm so busy these days, what with being unemployed and losing that boxing match and all. Well, what do you know? I have an opening."

He chuckled. "Why don't I stop by around lunch time?"

"Are you offering to take me to lunch? Because I'm going crazy sitting around the house."

"All right."

When he pulled up in his SUV a little before noon, Lacy was waiting on the front porch and walked out to the street to meet him. "The bruises don't look so bad today," he said.

"You sure know how to lay on the compliments, Sheriff." She opened the passenger door and slid in. "Thanks for agreeing to go out. My mom has been through so much, I don't want to lose my temper with her, but her hovering is driving me nuts."

"She worries about you."

"Yes, but I need a little breathing space."

"Is it okay if lunch is a picnic?" he asked. "I picked up some sandwiches and stuff from Iris Desmet."

"The Cake Walk is open again?"

"No, but she's doing some catering and stuff out of her home. I guess being idle didn't suit her any more than it does you."

"A picnic is fine," Lacy said. "In fact, it would be nice to eat without everyone in the restaurant watching me. I'm beginning to feel a little bit like the local freak on display."

"People are curious, but it will pass," he said. "But it suits me if we skip the restaurant today. Your mother and my office manager aren't the only people in town who are interested in what we have to say to each other. And it's never a good idea to discuss a case in public. You never know who might overhear something they shouldn't."

"I don't think I was prepared for all the attention I'm attracting," she said. "I was in Kate's this morning and said something about being in prison and you would have thought I had confessed to kicking small children for fun."

"They'll get over it," he said.

"I guess that curiosity is what sells books like the one Alvin Exeter is writing," she said. "By the way, he came by Kate's this morning and tried to interview Jan Selkirk. She shut him down."

"Jan is quite a formidable woman. One of her last acts as mayor was to invite—or rather insist—that I present a report to the town council. She wanted to know what the youngest sheriff the county had ever had was planning for their community. It was like standing for inspection with an army drill sergeant. I thought she would send me away if I had a scuff on my boots or a spot on my tie."

"She told me I was what the town needed, to remind them they aren't as special and safe as people think they are here." She stared out the window, at the passing vista of mountains and wildflowers. "I was kind of hoping it *would* be special and safe here."

"I guess if that was really true, I wouldn't have a job," he said. "Though I would just as soon stick to helping lost tourists and chasing off the occasional shoplifter."

"You'd be bored silly if that was the case," she said. "Admit it—you like the adrenaline rush of going after the bad guys. You wouldn't be a cop if that wasn't true."

His hands tightened on the steering wheel. "All right. Maybe some of that is true."

"It's okay," she said. "I don't hold it against you." She could even say she admired that about him—his determination to right wrongs. Though that aspect of his character had helped put her in jail, it had also made him work tirelessly until she was free. Another man might not have been so willing to admit he had made a mistake.

He headed over the bridge out of town, to a picnic area on a small lake with a view of Mount Rayford. "I remember coming here for a cookout with the senior class of Eagle Mountain High," she said as she helped him carry their lunch to one of the concrete tables. They had the place to themselves and settled in the shade of the canopy over the table.

"A local tradition," he said. "The year of our picnic

it rained. You'd be surprised how many teenagers you can fit under one of these canopies."

"That all seems so long ago," she said. She had been a different person then, one who had thought the bad things of the world would never touch her.

"They still do those senior picnics," Travis said as he laid out their own meal. "One of the advantages of a smaller school—you're able to keep up traditions like that."

"It's nice to know some things haven't changed," she said. "I was only away three years and there's so many things I don't recognize—new people and businesses. And this Pioneer Days Festival—that's new."

"Some people thought Jan was crazy to suggest it," he said. "But it's been a big success. It's a real boost for local business. Though I'll admit, it keeps our department busy. Nothing big, but you bring a lot of people in from other places and crowd them all together, and you're bound to see an uptick in petty crime—shoplifting, public drunkenness, minor things like that."

"At least you're not up to your ears in serious crimes," she said. She bit into a ham sandwich.

"I went out to see Henry Hake this morning," he said, reminding her of the one very serious crime he was investigating. "He says he got some threatening letters from people who didn't want the resort project to go forward and Andy was looking into them."

Lacy set down the sandwich. A chill shuddered through her in spite of the warm day. "So whoever wrote the letters might have killed Andy to stop him?"

"Maybe. Did Andy mention anything like that to you?"

"No," she said. "What did the letters say?"

"I don't know. Hake said he destroyed them. But they frightened him enough that he hired a bodyguard for a while."

"The only people I know who were against the development were the Utes and Paige Riddell's environmental group. But they weren't subtle about their objections to the development—they went after Hake directly—in court. And they won."

"And Hake says after they won—well, after Andy died—the threats stopped. And the development never did go forward."

"That surprises me," Lacy said. "From what I remember, they had sunk a lot of money into the project."

"He says they're restructuring—'they' being him and some partners he insists want to remain silent." He took a bite of sandwich and chewed.

"I wonder if the partners know any more about the source of the threats?" Lacy asked.

"I'm going to see if the district attorney can subpoena him for the names," Travis said. "But that will take a while, and Hake says some of the original partners are dead."

"And that makes me wonder how they died." She plucked a grape from the bunch he had set in the middle of the table. "Then again, maybe I read too many murder mysteries. The prison library was full of them."

"I like that you don't mind talking about it," he said. "Especially around me."

"I can't pretend it never happened." She crunched down on the grape. "Later, I hope I don't think about it so much, but I'm still too close to it. I still wake up in the morning thinking I'm back there. I've missed head count and I'm going to lose my exercise privileges, or access to the commissary, or any one of a dozen punishments they can mete out for the slightest infraction."

He nodded, his mouth tight, the lines around his eyes deepening.

"I'm not telling you this to make you feel bad," she said.

"Why are you telling me, then?"

She considered the question, a warmth blossoming in her chest as the answer came to her. "Because I want you to know me," she said softly. "And that's part of me."

He slid his hand across the table and took hers, his fingers warm and slightly rough against hers. They sat that way for a long moment, holding on to something precious, neither wanting to break the spell.

A gray jay circled overhead, screeching at them in a bid for part of their lunch. Lacy pulled away and straightened, suddenly self-conscious. "I shouldn't keep you from your work," she said. "And my mother will be wondering where I've gotten to."

"I was hoping you'd have time to go through that second file box this afternoon," he said. "I want to see if we can find anything more about these threats of Hake's silent partners."

"As I said before, my afternoon just happens to be free."

TRAVIS FELT WARMED by more than the sun as he drove Lacy back to her house. There in the park, he had felt her truly softening toward him. When she talked about her time in prison, she didn't come across as someone who had been scarred by the experience. He would give her back those lost years, if there was any way possible, but at least he could let go of the feeling that he had ruined her life.

In the Milligans' dining room, they opened the second file box and each took half the papers. This box contained mostly legal documents—the deeds for the various mining claims that made up the proposed resort, copies of surveys, title searches, newspaper articles about the project and dense legal contracts relating to everything from water and mineral rights to public right of way on historic trails. After an hour, Travis tossed aside a sheaf of papers and rubbed his eyes. "I think I've found a cure for insomnia," he said.

Lacy laughed. "It does get a little dense at times," she said. "One reason I'd never want to be a lawyer."

"Have you found anything interesting?" he asked.

She shook her head. "Not a thing."

She stretched her arms over her head, a gesture that lifted her breasts and made his mouth go dry. He looked away and cleared his throat. "Maybe we'll find something in the other boxes."

"Let's go out there now," she said. "That is, if you have time."

"Let me check in with the office and see."

Adelaide reported that the office was "as dead as Methuselah's cat," and Travis wondered if she lay awake nights trying to come up with colorful expressions to add to her repertoire. "I'm going to make a run out to Andy Stenson's storage facility to look at some more files," he said. "Call me if anything pops up."

"Who else would I call?" Adelaide said breezily. "Say hello to Lacy for me."

"How did you know I'm with Lacy?"

"Your SUV is parked in front of her house. If you

really want to sneak around, you're going to have to learn to be more subtle."

"I am not sneaking a—" But Adelaide had already hung up.

Lacy said goodbye to her parents and she and Travis headed out the door. They were almost to his vehicle when Alvin Exeter stepped out from his car, which was parked across the street, and held a cell phone to his eye.

Lacy froze. "Did you just take our picture?" she asked.

Alvin grinned. "You two make a handsome couple—or you will when those bruises heal." He studied the screen of his camera. "This makes a more touching image, I think. The victim and the lawman."

"You're on thin ice, Exeter," Travis said, barely controlling his anger. "I've warned you about harassing Ms. Milligan."

"I'm standing in a public street and so are you. I know my rights as a writer."

Lacy took Travis's arm. "Come on, let's go," she said.

Travis held the passenger door for her, then went around the driver's side. Exeter watched, smirking and taking picture after picture with his camera. "I'd like to rip that phone out of his hand and stomp on it," Travis said.

"He gets a charge out of being confrontational," she said. "The best way to deal with someone like him is to ignore them."

Travis glanced at her. "You're pretty smart for someone so young."

"I keep telling myself the old children's rhyme still holds true," she said. "Sticks and stones may break my bones but words can never harm me."

He pulled into the street and headed for Main. "Words can do plenty of harm and we both know it," he said when they had left Exeter behind.

"Only if I let them," she said. "Being in prison was hard, but it taught me that I need to be my own best friend. I can't really rely on anyone else."

"You can rely on me," he said.

He could feel her eyes on him, though he kept his gaze on the road. "Yes, I'm beginning to believe that," she said.

They were both silent until he turned onto Fireline Road. A dusty brown Jeep blew past them and sped onto the highway.

"I think that was Ian Barnes," Lacy said, looking over her shoulder at the dust that hung in the wake of the Jeep's passing. "Jan said he drove an old Jeep. What was he doing out here?"

"There are some rock cliffs out this way that are popular with climbers," Travis said. "Maybe he was checking them out."

Lacy faced forward once more. "What do you know about him?" she asked.

"Not much. I met him at Eagle Mountain Outfitters. I think he's a friend of the owners. Wade Tomlinson told me he's an Iraq and Afghanistan veteran and suffers from PTSD. Why?"

She shrugged. "I don't know. There's just something about him I find…unsettling. Maybe it's the way he watches me."

"Maybe he's trying to work up the nerve to ask you out." His throat felt tight as he said the words.

"Hah! Trust me, the way the women around here are

always ogling him, he could get a date with any one of them. He doesn't need me."

"But maybe you're the one he's attracted to."

"Right." She brushed a lock of hair off her face. "Because I'm so attractive with two black eyes, a busted lip and a row of stitches across my head. Though maybe he's into zombie chic."

"So you don't go for the chiseled look?" he asked, keeping his voice light.

"Chiseled is right. He looked like someone carved him from granite."

"I wouldn't want to meet him in a dark alley. He looks like he could take me apart with his bare hands."

"You look like you could hold your own in a fight, Sheriff."

The air between them felt suddenly charged. "Are you saying you've been checking me out?" he asked.

"I've been locked up with nine hundred other women for three years," she said. "I check out every man I meet." But her smile seemed to say that she liked what she had seen when she looked at him. He had to fight the urge not to puff out his chest.

He stopped at the entrance to the storage facility and punched in the code Brenda had given him. The barrier rose and he drove to the first row of units on the right and parked. "I don't see anyone else out here," Lacy said as she and Travis climbed out of his SUV.

"I checked and only about half the units are rented," Travis said as he fitted the key into the padlock on the Stensons' unit. "Tom Reynolds owns the place and he told me most of the time people stash their stuff out here and don't look at it for years. The payment comes out of their bank account automatically every month and they probably never even think about the boxes of old clothes and papers or Grandma's furniture or whatever it is they're paying to store."

He shoved up the rolling metal door and it rose with a groan. Everything looked exactly as he had left it when he was here with Brenda, boxes and furniture piled haphazardly, everything smelling of dust and old paper. "Let me get the video recorder set up before you go in," Travis said. "We might as well do all this by the book."

Lacy waited while he set up the recorder on its tripod, then she moved into the unit ahead of him. "Where do we start?" she asked.

"The boxes are labeled alphabetically," Travis said. "Why don't you glance through a couple and see if anything catches your eye." He lifted a box from a stack and set it on top of Andy's desk. "And look for any *H*'s. The boxes we looked at already were labeled Hake, but maybe some papers related to the development ended up mixed in with the general files."

"All right." Lacy accepted the box he slid toward her and began flipping through the papers. Every few seconds she would pull up a file folder and examine it more closely. The sun beat down on the metal building and even with the door open, it grew stifling.

Lacy stopped to wipe sweat from her forehead. "Maybe we should just grab a couple and take them back to the house," she said.

"Good idea," Travis said. "Let me get my tape from the SUV and we'll seal up a couple to go through later."

He turned and had taken two steps toward the door when an explosion ripped through the air and knocked him to the ground.

Chapter Ten

The concussion from the blast slammed Lacy to the concrete floor of the storage unit and sent a tower of boxes tumbling over her. She lay stunned, head spinning, trying to make sense of the roaring in her ears and the pain in her knees and hands.

"Lacy!" Travis's voice rose above the roar.

She lifted her head. "I'm here!" she cried, the sound weak and barely audible even to her own ears. She took a deep breath, inhaling smoke, and coughed violently, then tried again. "Here!" she shouted, hoarse.

"Can you move?" Travis shouted. "Head toward my voice."

She rose up on her knees and shoved boxes and papers away from her. Then she felt the heat of the fire licking at her back. Terror sent her lunging forward, fighting against a wall of boxes and scattered furniture. "Help!" she shouted. "Help me!"

"I'm coming!" The wall of debris shifted, and a hand reached in, groping wildly for her.

Lacy took the hand and was yanked forward, half carried toward a blast of fresh air. Then she and Travis were rolling in the gravel, his hands beating at her back, and the flames that licked there. Then he pulled her to her feet and they ran, away from the burning storage unit, into the field beyond, where they collapsed, arms still tightly wrapped around each other. Even there, the tower of flame that reached toward the sky radiated heat over them.

Lacy's eyes filled with tears as she looked into his soot-streaked face. His eyes met hers, and he rested the back of his hand to her cheek. "I thought I'd lost you," he whispered.

She took his face in both hands and pressed her lips to his, the kiss desperate in its intensity. He wrapped both arms around her and rolled onto his back, carrying her with him, their lips still locked together, her body stretched atop his. Tears ran down her face and mixed with the soot. She tasted the salt of them as she opened her mouth to deepen the kiss. Everything—the roar of the fire, the ache in her knees, the stench of the smoke—receded, burned away by passion. Some part of her, banked and given up for dead all these years, roared to life, fueled by the feel of his hard, male body beneath her, by his searching lips and caressing hands. She wanted. She needed. She took.

He was the first to pull away, breaking the kiss and rolling her aside, then sitting up and taking both her hands in his. "I need to call this in," he said.

She nodded, unable to speak, adrenaline still pumping through her body. He released her hands, only to caress her cheek again. "You're the most amazing woman," he said.

"You're making a habit of saving my life," she said.

His expression hardened and he dropped his hand. "You don't owe me anything."

"This isn't about debts and payments," she said.

"Then what is it about?"

"It's about you making me feel more alive than I have in years. It's about… I don't know." She looked away. She had almost said "love," but that was absurd.

"Maybe it doesn't matter why right now," he said. He pulled her close again, so that her head rested on his shoulder. "I'm just glad you're okay. That we're both okay."

She turned her head to watch the fire. Other storage units had caught now, their contents feeding the blaze into even more of an inferno. "I heard an explosion," she said.

He nodded and, with one arm still wrapped around her, shifted to take out his phone. "This is Rayford County Sheriff Travis Walker. The storage units at the end of Fireline Road are burning. There was an explosion. We need the fire crew, an ambulance and a crime scene team out here." He listened a moment. "Just some burns. No fatalities. Get an officer out here to block the road," he said. "I don't want anyone back here but emergency personnel."

He ended the call and replaced his phone on his belt. "Why do we need an ambulance?" she asked.

"You've got blood on your hands, and you might have some burns." He took her wrist and turned her palm up to reveal the drying blood there.

"I scraped my hands and knees on the concrete when the blast threw me down," she said. "What about you? Are you hurt?"

He shook his head. "I was closer to the door, so the blast threw me forward." He squinted toward the blaze, black smoke billowing to the sky. "My SUV is probably on fire by now. And all of Andy's files."

"Do you think that's why this happened?" she asked. "So that we couldn't get to those files?"

"That would be my guess. I know one thing—I want to talk to Ian Barnes and find out what he was doing out here."

"Do you think he booby-trapped the storage unit or something?"

"Or something," Travis said. "Maybe he was just checking out places to climb, but he might have seen someone else out here."

Sirens sounded in the distance. Travis shoved to his feet, then offered her his hand and pulled her up beside him. "Sounds like the cavalry is on the way," he said. "Let's see if we can circle around to the road and meet them."

Lacy kept her hand in his as they hiked over the rough ground, around the still-raging blaze and out to the road. She had kissed him in an adrenaline rush of fear and elation, but she didn't regret the impetuous gesture. Danger hadn't changed her feelings for Travis, but it had made her see the foolishness of playing hide-and-seek with her emotions. Crazy as it seemed on the surface, the man who had been her worst enemy was fast becoming her best friend.

THE FRONT PAGE of the *Eagle Mountain Examiner* had a three-column color photo of the fire at the storage units, with a smaller inset picture of Travis and Lacy, scorched and ragged, standing surrounded by half a dozen emergency personnel. "You look like two extras in a low-budget horror film," Adelaide said as she laid the paper on Travis's desk.

Travis scowled at the photo. "I didn't even know this was taken."

"Tammy was at Kate's this morning, crowing about getting the story in just under deadline," Adelaide said. "You bumped a piece about the Eighth Grade Science Fair. She had to move the pictures of Olivia Dexter's first-place exhibit on DNA testing to page four."

"My apologies to Olivia," he said. "Have we heard anything from the arson examiner?"

"He says you're keeping him busy," Adelaide said. "He sent over his preliminary findings this morning—it was definitely a bomb, with some kind of trip mechanism, probably set to go off on a delay once someone triggered it."

"Adelaide, you aren't supposed to read official reports addressed to me."

"He sent it to the general office email and I'm in charge of the general office." She waited while he logged on to his computer and opened the email from the county's arson investigator. "You know, I think I read terrorists use those kind of bombs over in Iraq and Afghanistan," she said. "That way they can make sure all our soldiers are inside a building before they blow them all up."

"Go back to work, Adelaide," Travis said. "And close the door behind you."

He read the investigator's report, though everything was as Adelaide had said. The bomb wasn't sophisticated, but it was effective, and the kind of thing anyone with a rudimentary knowledge of explosives could use. He closed the file and left his office.

"Where are you going?" Adelaide asked as he passed her desk.

"Out."

He drove instead of walked, wanting the security of a vehicle around him. His SUV had been consumed in the blaze, so he was using the department's "spare" vehicle, an ancient 4Runner with a dented door, sagging seats and no air-conditioning. He would have to petition the county commissioners for funds for a new vehicle and probably wait for an insurance settlement to come through before he could get a new ride.

He parked in front of Eagle Mountain Outfitters and went inside. Wade looked up from the cash register, an outdoor magazine open on the counter in front of him. "Hey, Sheriff, what can we do for you?" he asked.

"I'm looking for your friend Ian," Travis said.

"He isn't here."

"Where is he?" Travis asked.

"Is something wrong, Sheriff?" Wade asked.

"I need to speak to Barnes. Where is he?"

"He's staying over at the Bear's Den," Wade said. "Paige Riddell's place. Why do you need to see Ian?"

"I just want to talk to him." Before Wade could question him further, Travis left the store, got back in his vehicle and drove three blocks to Paige Riddell's Bear's Den Inn. The faded brown Jeep he and Lacy had seen turning off Fireline Road yesterday sat in the driveway of the two-story Victorian home, next to Paige's red Prius. Paige answered when he rang the doorbell. She was a tall woman, with straight, shoulder-length, honey-blond hair and serious gray eyes. In addition to operating the bed-and-breakfast, she taught yoga at the local gym and headed up Eagle Mountain Conservationists, the environmental group that had succeeded in getting an injunction to stop Henry Hake's resort development. "Sheriff Walker," she said. "What can I do for you?"

"I need to talk to one of your guests—Ian Barnes."

Her eyes narrowed. "What about?"

"That's none of your business and you know it, Paige. Can I come in?"

She opened the door wider and let him walk past. "Ian is uncomfortable with strangers," she said. "He suffered horribly in the war."

Travis turned to study her. In her midthirties, and a little too serious for his tastes, but she might appeal to a man like Barnes. "You and he are friends?"

"No. But I respect his privacy."

"So do I. Which is why I won't tell you what this about. Is he here?"

"He's upstairs, in the sunroom off the back of the house." She nodded toward a set of carpeted stairs.

Travis took the stairs quickly, but Ian met him at the top. The muscular veteran in the black knit cap filled the doorway to the sunroom, his expression blank. "Sheriff," he said, no inflection to the word.

"Let's go into the sunroom where we can talk in private," Travis said.

Barnes backed into the room, keeping his gaze fixed on Travis. He sat in a square, heavy wood rocker in the back corner of the room. Travis pulled up a wrought-iron armchair. "I saw you out on Fireline Road yesterday afternoon," he said. "What were you doing out there?"

"I was looking for places to climb. I heard there were some good routes up Dakota Ridge back that way."

"Did you go by the storage units at the end of the

road? Maybe turn around there, or stop and take a look around?"

"No." His expression and his voice never changed, both as cold as a robot's. In Travis's experience, being interviewed by the police made most people a little nervous, even if they were innocent of any wrongdoing. The first time he had interviewed Lacy after Andy's murder, she had fidgeted constantly, and practically vibrated with tension. At the time, he had mistaken her unease for a sign of guilt.

Ian Barnes might have been talking to a store clerk or a complete stranger, for all the emotion he displayed. Was he that unfeeling—or simply more experienced at dealing with law enforcement? "You know about the bomb that went off out at the storage units yesterday afternoon," Travis said.

"I saw the paper."

"But you don't know anything about it."

"No."

"Someone suggested to me that this might have been the type of bomb used by terrorists in Iraq and Afghanistan, with a delayed timer. You must have run into that sort of device while you were serving over there."

"Yes."

"So you would know how to put one together. How to deploy it."

"I know a lot of things. Yesterday I was looking for places to climb. I don't know anything about your bomb." He stood, an imposing figure looming over Travis. It was hard not to read the gesture as an intentional threat.

Travis rose also, and found that he and Barnes were almost the same height. He looked the other man in the eye. "Why are you in Eagle Mountain, Mr. Barnes?" he asked.

"I'm visiting friends. Doing some climbing."

"Have you been to the area before?"

Something flickered in those impassive brown eyes, a shadow of something—guilt? Fear? "No."

Travis knew he was lying. All his words thus far might have been lies, but Travis was certain about this one. Ian could have said he had visited Wade and Brock before, or come here on vacation. Instead, he had lied. Why?

"If you had something to do with this, I'll find out," he said. He turned to leave, but at the door, Ian's words stopped him.

"If you want to know who has it in for you and your girlfriend, you should talk to that writer, Exeter," he said.

Travis turned to face Ian again. He could have protested that Lacy wasn't his girlfriend, but the memory of her in his arms after the fire cast doubt on the truth of that statement. "Why Exeter?" he asked instead.

"He was in Moe's Pub the other night, mouthing off about the power of the written word and making Lacy pay for being so rude to him."

"What did he say, exactly?" Travis asked.

Ian sat in the rocker again and picked up a book from the table beside it. "Ask him," he said, then opened the book, ignoring Travis.

Paige met Travis at the bottom of the stairs. "Did you upset him?" she asked.

"Do you really think anything upsets him?" Travis asked.

"Not everyone wears his feelings on his sleeve," she said. "Some are more stoic."

Travis headed for the door, then thought better of it and faced her again. "When that environmental group you head was opposing Henry Hake's resort development, did any of your members do more than protest?"

She wrinkled her forehead. "What do you mean? We filed an injunction against him in court and we won. We succeeded in stopping the development—which was a ridiculous idea, anyway. The environment at those elevations is far too delicate to support the kind of infrastructure Hake wanted to build—all so a few ultrarich people could enjoy looking down on the rest of us from their ridiculously oversize homes."

"Did you write threatening letters to him? Destroy equipment?"

Her eyes widened. "No! Our group doesn't just work for the environment—we're committed to peace. It's part of our core values and mission statement."

"But you don't control all your members," he said. "Maybe one of them stepped out of line."

"Not that I'm aware of."

Travis glanced up the stairs, wondering if Barnes was listening. "Someone threatened Henry Hake back then. Someone destroyed machinery on his property. Andy Stenson was looking into those threats. It may have been what got him killed."

Paige looked pained. "I don't know anything about that," she said. "It's horrible to even think about."

"Think about it," Travis said. "And maybe ask your guest upstairs how many men he's killed."

He left, shutting the door a little harder than necessary behind him. Maybe his last words had been a low blow. He hadn't meant to frighten Paige, only to warn her about the kind of man she might be harboring. Travis couldn't see how Ian Barnes had had anything to do with Andy Stenson, but his presence out on Fireline Road yesterday had to be more than coincidence. And when Travis looked into Barnes's eyes, he saw a man with no conscience. A man like that might do anything.

Chapter Eleven

Lacy stared at the check in her hand, at the machine-printed numbers—210,000 dollars. More money than she had ever seen in her life. "I'll have to open a bank account to deposit it," she said. She hadn't had a bank account since before she went to prison.

"Have you thought about what classes you'd like to take?" her father asked. "What career you'd like to pursue?"

She shook her head. "I don't know. I think I'd like to get a car first." Her eyes met his over the top of the check. "Nothing flashy. It doesn't even have to be new, but I'd like to be able to go places without borrowing Mom's car."

"Of course." Jeanette rubbed her daughter's shoulder. "And you have until August to decide about school. You might even be able to take some courses online at first, until you decide for sure on a major."

"Yeah. That's a good idea."

"Do you want me to take you to the bank now?" her father asked.

"Sure, Dad. That's a great idea. I'll just go upstairs and get my purse."

When she came back down, both her parents were

waiting by the front door. "I think this calls for a celebration," her mother said. "Maybe a special dinner."

"Sure." Lacy forced a smile. "But maybe here at home? We could order takeout so you don't have to cook."

"I don't mind cooking," Jeanette said. "We'll stop at the grocery store after the bank. We'll keep it simple—steaks and a salad. Is there anyone you'd like to invite?"

No. Yes. "Maybe... Travis?" Was she ready for that? Dinner with her family?

Jeanette's smile widened. "That's a wonderful idea."

Lacy wanted to tell her mother not to read too much into this. Travis was a friend. A friend she had been ready to jump right there on the ground next to the burning storage units, but she could blame at least part of that reaction on the sheer euphoria of surviving the explosion, right? "He might have to work," she said.

"Why don't you call right now and ask him?" Jeanette said. "We'll wait."

She realized both her parents were prepared to stand right there while she made the call, so she turned around and retraced her steps to her room, where she pulled out her cell phone—the one her parents had had waiting for her when she first arrived home, a first real symbol of her freedom.

Travis answered on the second ring. "Lacy. Is everything okay?"

"Why wouldn't it be okay?"

"You've never called me before."

"I wanted to invite you to dinner. At my house. With my parents. We're kind of celebrating. I got my check from the state." She said everything quickly, wanting to get it all out before she lost courage.

"Tonight?"

"Yes. I told them you might have to work, but I thought I would call and—"

"I'll be there. Unless some emergency comes up."

"Great. Be here about six."

She ended the call, feeling a little giddy, and almost floated down the stairs.

"He must have said yes," her mother said as Lacy joined her parents by the door.

"What makes you say that?" Lacy did her best to act nonchalant.

"You have that look in your eye," her mother said.

"What look?"

"A very pleased-with-yourself look." She reached out and touched the ends of Lacy's hair, where it skimmed her shoulder blades. One of the women on her prison block had cut it with a pair of contraband nail scissors in exchange for cookies Lacy purchased in the prison commissary. "We could stop by Lou's Salon on the way home and see if she could work you in," she said. "Maybe shape it up a little."

Lacy started to protest that she didn't want that—then realized she did. She wasn't an inmate who didn't care about her appearance anymore. "All right," she said. "That would be nice."

She was surprised at how nervous she felt about opening a bank account, but the clerk was professional and didn't even blink when Lacy handed over the check. "Would you like to deposit a portion of this in an investment account?" she asked. "I could make an appointment for you to speak to one of our financial counselors."

"Not today," Lacy said. "But next week would be good." One step at a time.

With a pad of temporary checks tucked in her purse, Lacy left the bank and headed across the parking lot with her parents. Her mother nudged her and leaned close to whisper in her ear. "Who is that good-looking young man who is staring at you?" she asked.

Lacy looked over her shoulder, starting when she recognized Ian Barnes.

Her father, who had just unlocked the driver's door, looked over the top of the car. "I think he's friends with the two guys who run Eagle Mountain Outfitters," he said. "I went in there looking for a bite valve to replace the one on my hydration pack that's been leaking and he was there. I think he's ex Special Forces or something."

"Well, he's certainly impressive," Jeanette said. She slid into the front passenger seat and cast a sideways glance at her husband, her cheeks rosy. "Well, he is. In an overly muscular kind of way."

"I wonder how he knows the mayor?" her father asked.

Only then did Lacy realize Ian was standing with Mayor Larry Rowe. She looked back and Larry clapped the younger man on the shoulder, then walked away.

"You know Larry," her mother said. "He makes it his business to know everyone in town. A good quality in a mayor, I guess. Lacy, have you met him before?"

"The mayor?" Lacy asked, deliberately misunderstanding her mother's question.

"No—that good-looking young man."

Lacy decided it was time to change the subject. "What's this Pioneer Days Festival like?" she asked. "Have you been?"

"It's quite the production," her father said. "There's a parade and a special display at the museum. Last year Brenda and Jan dressed in 1890s swimming costumes and sold lemonade and sugar cookies. There's a stage in the park with bands and crafts vendors, a baseball game and foot races and I forget what else."

"Fireworks," her mother said. "They shoot them off above town. They do a wonderful job."

"The whole thing was Jan Selkirk's idea," her father said. "She spent two years persuading the town fathers to adopt the idea, and then was able to gloat when it turned out to be such a big success. The new mayor, Larry Rowe, and his council have expanded on her original idea and attracted quite a bit of attention to our little town."

"They keep talking about creating a similar festival for winter, when business is slow," Jeanette said. "But the weather can be so iffy then."

"A big snow and avalanches could cut off Dakota Pass and everyone could be snowed in," George said. "The locals are used to it, but tourists might raise a fuss."

"I think it's enough having all those tourists in town for the summer," Jeanette said.

"Yes, but you're not a local businessperson," her husband countered.

Her parents continued the argument on the drive to the grocery store. Lacy sat in the back seat and let her mind drift to the place it always ended up these days—back with Travis and the kiss they had shared after the explosion. When she closed her eyes, she could still feel the scrape of the beard just beneath his skin as she pressed her cheek to his, the hard plane of his chest crushed against her breasts, the implements on his belt digging into her belly—the length of his desire confirming that he wanted her as much as she wanted him.

So what did she do? Instead of arranging to see him privately, where maybe they could see where that desire would take them, she had invited him to a family dinner, where she would be too uptight to even risk a kiss under her parents' watchful eyes. Not that her mother and father were prudes, but a new relationship—one she didn't even know how to define—required privacy.

Her father stopped and signaled for the turn into the parking lot of Eagle Grocery. A black-and-white sheriff's department vehicle, lights flashing and sirens blaring, sped by, followed closely by a second vehicle and an ambulance.

"My goodness, what's that all about?" her mother asked.

Lacy had already dug her phone from her purse and punched in the number for the sheriff's department. Adelaide answered immediately. "What's going on?" Lacy demanded.

"I'm not allowed to give out information about sheriff's department calls over the phone," Adelaide said. "You people ought to know that by now."

"This is Lacy Milligan. Just tell me—is Travis hurt?"

The silence that followed lasted so long Lacy thought Adelaide had hung up on her. "You can't tell anyone where you heard this," Adelaide said finally, her voice lowered.

"I won't. I promise."

"We had a report of an officer down, out at the storage units on Fireline Road. We don't know that it's Travis."

"Even I know the sheriff's department doesn't have that many officers," Lacy said. "We just saw two cars go by. If Travis wasn't in either one of those…"

"I have to go now, Lacy. I have a lot of other calls coming in. Try not to worry, but it wouldn't hurt to say a prayer."

Lacy ended the call to Adelaide and let the phone fall into her lap. "What is it, dear?" her mother asked.

Lacy swallowed, her mouth too dry to speak. *Keep it together*, she scolded herself. "There was an Officer in Distress call," she said.

"Travis?" her father asked.

"They don't know." The awfulness of those words settled over her like a smothering blanket, and it was all she could do to remain seated upright and breathing.

TRAVIS WAS AT the motel out on the highway, trying to track down Alvin Exeter, when the Officer in Distress call went out. As soon as he heard the address, he raced to his car, dialing his phone as he ran. He tried the office first, but the line was busy. No surprise there. Half the town had probably called in to see what was going on. The line was supposed to be for sheriff's department business only, but too many people knew about it and felt free to use it any time they wanted. He could have called Adelaide on the radio, but he didn't have time to waste.

He started the Toyota and hit the speed dial for Gage. "What's up?" he asked as he sped from the parking lot.

"Travis! Thank God!" Gage almost shouted the words. "We got the Officer in Distress call from Dispatch and they didn't know what unit. Since it was out at the storage units, I thought—"

"Where's Dwight?" Travis cut off his brother's relieved babbling.

"He's right behind me."

"No one else should be on duty," Travis said.

"They aren't."

"Then who put in the call?" He eased off the gas pedal, mind racing. "Is this some kind of trap?"

"Dispatch thought it was legit. Are we gonna risk not checking it out?"

"No, we aren't. But we need to be careful."

He was closer to Fireline Road than the other two units, but it wasn't long before they fell in behind him, a wailing, flashing parade of three sheriff's department vehicles, an ambulance and one state highway patrol car. Travis wouldn't have been surprised to see the fire department and Search and Rescue trailing them.

A red Jeep Wagoneer was parked in front of the gate at the entrance to the storage units. Travis swore when he recognized the vehicle. Gage's voice came on the radio. "Eddie," he said. "What's he doing out here?"

Eddie Carstairs was one of the reserve officers, called in when someone was out sick or on vacation, or when Travis needed extra manpower to work an accident or a festival. At twenty-two, Eddie looked about sixteen. His straight black hair flopped over a high forehead, and his face was long and droopy, which had led to the nickname Gage had saddled him with—"Hound Dog."

Travis pulled in beside Eddie's Jeep and shut off the Toyota, the engine sputtering twice in protest. From here he could make out a figure in jeans and a T-shirt, face down on the dirt a few yards from the blackened area that marked the reach of the fire. Travis pulled out his phone and called Eddie's number. "Officer Carstairs, this is Sheriff Walker. Can you hear me?"

The body on the ground didn't move.

Travis scanned the area around the body, then the hills beyond, searching for some clue as to what had happened. Gage and Dwight moved to his window, crouching down so that they were shielded between the Toyota and the Jeep. "What do you think?" Gage asked.

"What did Dispatch say about the call?" Travis asked.

"It came in on a private cell, not a police number," Gage said. "I called the dispatcher, Sally—you know her, the big blonde with the twins?" That was typical Gage. After five minutes with almost anyone, he would know their life history.

"What did she say about the call?" Travis prompted.

"She said the man on the other end sounded like he was having trouble breathing—or was in pain. All he said was 'Officer down'—and gave the address. Then he hung up or got disconnected."

Travis stared at the prone body, willing it to move. He took his binoculars from the field kit on the passenger-side floorboard and trained them on the figure.

"I think he's breathing," Dwight said.

"I think so, too," Travis said. Or was he imagining the faint rise and fall of the back? He laid aside the field glasses and looked at his two officers. "You two wearing your vests?"

They nodded in unison. "You think he was shot?" Dwight asked.

"That seems the most likely scenario."

"Could be a sniper," Gage said. "Up in the hills."

"If it is, I'm not risking him picking us off one by one," Travis said.

"If one of us could get behind one of the storage buildings, we could shoot up into the hills, maybe draw his fire," Dwight said.

"A smart shooter wouldn't fall for that," Travis said. "He'd wait until we were out in the open, where he could get a clear shot." He considered the situation again. "Gage, do you have the sniper rifle with you?"

"Yes. And two ARs and a shotgun, some smoke grenades and a case of ammo." At Travis's raised eyebrows, he shrugged. "When the call came in, I unlocked the arsenal and took everything I could grab. You never know what you're going to need."

"You take the sniper rifle and one of the ARs," Travis said. "Dwight, you get one of the ARs. I want one of you set up behind each of the intact buildings on either side of Eddie."

"Where are you going to be?" Gage asked.

"I'm going out to get Eddie. You're going to cover me."

Chapter Twelve

All thoughts of celebration vanished as Lacy and her parents drove home. Lacy started to suggest her dad drive out to Fireline Road to see what had happened, but quickly dismissed the idea. The officers didn't need civilians in the way. And it wasn't as if she could do anything to help. She would just have to sit at the house and wait.

She was surprised to find Jan and Brenda seated on the settee on the front porch when her dad pulled the car into the driveway. "We heard what happened," Jan said. "It's all anybody in town is talking about."

"But it might not be Travis," Brenda said, giving Lacy's arm a squeeze. "I called the dispatcher, Sally Graham, and she said the man who called didn't identify himself, but it wasn't Travis's phone number."

"Why don't we all go inside," Jeanette said. "I'll make coffee."

They all trooped inside and into the Milligans' living room, which overlooked the street. Jeanette and George left the three younger women sitting on the sofa and love seat and went to make the coffee. "Alvin Exeter came by the history museum this morning," Jan said. "He wanted to talk to me and to Brenda."

"We both refused to speak with him," Brenda said. "But he didn't want to take no for an answer. He was really nasty about it, too."

"He said he's thinking of taking the approach that you really got away with murder," Jan said. "Since no one is coming forward to contest that theory, he figures it will be an even better story than the one of your wrongful conviction—the kind of thing that's sure to attract a lot of attention and boost sales."

"I don't care what he says," Lacy said. "He can say I murdered ten people and it won't make any difference to me. He's just trying to bait people into talking to him."

Brenda glanced toward the kitchen, then leaned toward Lacy, her voice low. "You might not care, but your parents will," she said. "It would hurt them so much."

Lacy nodded. "There's nothing I can do to stop him."

Jan and Brenda exchanged glances. "You could talk to him."

"No," Lacy said. "Just…no."

"Or," Brenda said. "You could find out who really murdered Andy."

"That's what Travis has been trying to do," Lacy said. And because of that, he might even now be dead. She shoved the thought away. No. He would be okay. He had to be okay.

"There must be something in those files," Brenda said. "Something we forgot or overlooked."

"It doesn't matter now," Lacy said. "The files are gone. Destroyed by the bomb."

"It's horrible to think it, but all this violence must mean you're getting close to finding the real killer," Brenda said. "Otherwise, why go to so much trouble to stop you?"

"We thought it must have something to do with Hake Development, because that was Andy's biggest client," Lacy said. "But what if that's not it at all? After all, he had lots of clients. Maybe it's something small that we aren't thinking of at all."

"I still have Andy's computer," Brenda said. "I haven't turned it on since he died—I don't even know if it still works."

Jan and Lacy stared at her. "Why didn't you say something before?" Lacy asked.

"I didn't think of it," Brenda said. "Andy kept hard copies of everything. I figured anything important would be in his files."

"He probably had copies of a lot of stuff on his computer," Lacy said, excitement growing. "And if you haven't even turned it on in years, it should be just fine."

"I promise I'll take it to Travis first thing tomorrow," Brenda said.

"Better let him come to you," Jan said. "I wouldn't take a chance going anywhere with anything the killer might want."

"If Travis is okay," Lacy said.

Lacy's parents returned to the living room with a tray of cups and a coffeepot. "I turned on the radio to see if we could get a news report and find out what's going on," her father said. "But I couldn't find anything."

"Lacy, you have Travis's phone number, don't you?" her mother asked.

"Yes," she said. "I called him on it earlier."

"Have you tried calling him since all this has happened?"

"Mom, he'll be too busy to talk—" She fell silent, heart leaping in her chest. She laughed at her own foolishness and pulled out her phone. She didn't care if Travis yelled at her for interrupting him while he worked, as long as he answered.

She punched in his number and waited while the call connected and the ringer buzzed—once, twice, three times. "This is Sheriff Travis Walker. Leave a message at the beep."

She had heard the expression "crushed" before, but had never fully comprehended what it meant. She felt as if someone had dumped a truckload of bricks in the middle of her chest. She ended the call without leaving a message. "No answer," she said.

Brenda leaned over and squeezed her hand. "Don't give up hope," she said.

"I won't." Lacy took a deep breath and straightened. Three years in prison had taught her how to survive when things looked bleak—the only difference now was that so much more was at stake.

TRAVIS WAITED UNTIL Gage and Dwight were in position, then exited the Toyota. He wore a pack that contained blankets, a first-aid kit and water, and had unholstered his duty weapon and held it in his right hand. Eddie still hadn't moved, though a second check through the binoculars had revealed no pooling blood or obvious injuries. Still, he could be bleeding out from a chest wound or a gut shot and they might not be able to tell.

Gage signaled that they were ready and Travis began moving around to the west. His plan was to move far to the side, then rush in low, with Gage and Dwight laying down a screen of fire aimed at the hills within firing distance of Eddie. It wasn't the best plan in the world, but it was the only one he had right now. He could have waited for a helicopter or an armored vehicle from a neighboring department, but arranging that kind of backup could take hours, and Eddie might not have that kind of time.

He was halfway to the cover of the first storage unit, where Dwight waited, when his phone rang. He ignored it and silenced the phone. Everyone he needed to talk to was here right now and had better ways of communicating with him.

He stopped when he reached Dwight, who had been scanning the hills above the site with a pair of binoculars. "See anything?" Travis asked.

"Nothing." He lowered the glasses. "Could be our shooter is gone."

"Maybe." If he was, that meant they had lost their chance to pin him down, but it also meant it would be easier to get help for Eddie. He put his hand on Dwight's shoulder, the hard edge of the tactical vest beneath his palm. "You ready?"

"Ready."

Travis looked across at Gage, who nodded in acknowledgment, then took a deep breath. "Okay. I'm going out there."

He ran bent over, on a zigzagging path that was supposed to make it harder for a shooter to target him. Behind him, bullets ripped from the magazines of the two ARs fired by his deputies in a deafening blast. Travis couldn't tell if anyone returned fire or not, though no rounds hit the dirt around him—and more important, none hit him.

The shooting stopped as he knelt beside Eddie. He put a hand on the younger man's back and relief left him shaking as he felt the steady rise and fall of his breath. "Eddie." He shook the body. "Eddie, wake up."

Eddie groaned. Travis knelt in front of him and shoved him over. The younger man landed heavily on his back with a groan.

The first thing he noticed was that Eddie's nose looked broken. It was definitely crooked, with blood crusting around the nostrils, purpling bruises under both eyes. More blood seeped from a gash in the middle of his forehead. That might explain why the young man was unconscious. So what had happened? Had they gone to all this trouble because Eddie was clumsy and had tripped and knocked himself out?

Then Travis saw the wound—a dark, round hole in his shoulder, rimmed with blackish blood. He pressed on the wound and more blood seeped out, and Eddie groaned and stirred. His eyelids fluttered and he stared up at Travis. "Sheriff?" he asked hoarsely, and tried to sit up.

Travis pushed him back down. "Lie still," he said. "I'm going to call in the paramedics."

Thirty seconds later, a pair of paramedics swarmed around the wounded young man. Gage and Dwight, weapons in hand, emerged from the cover of the storage units and joined the growing crowd of law enforcement personnel who were milling around the area. "Get these people out of here," Travis said to Gage. "They could be compromising a crime scene."

"So he *was* shot," Dwight said.

"At least once, in the shoulder," Travis said. "Hit his head pretty good and broke his nose, too. That may be what knocked him out."

"What was he doing out here?" Dwight asked.

"Oh, he's going to explain all that, I promise," Travis said.

"My guess is he came out to look at the bomb site," Gage said. "He was hoping to be a hero and find something the arson investigator or the rest of us missed."

"So whoever set the bomb was *guarding* the place?" Dwight asked. "Why? There can't be anything in those ashes worth finding."

"I don't know," Travis said. "Maybe extra insurance? They're so paranoid they don't want to leave anything to chance?"

"Nobody is that paranoid," Gage said.

"You never worked for a big corporation, did you?" Dwight asked. "Or the government—especially the military. Some of those people are majorly paranoid."

"Ian Barnes was in the military," Travis said. "Maybe he's that paranoid. We'd better find out where he was and what he was doing when Eddie was shot."

A second team of paramedics wheeled a gurney over the rough ground to Eddie and lifted him onto it. One of the original first responders joined Travis, Gage and Dwight. "The bullet is still in him, but he's stable," he said. "We'll know more when they get some X-rays but my guess is he'll be okay."

"What about the head injury and his nose?" Travis asked.

The paramedic grinned. "He said he was trying to run for cover when he tripped and hit a big rock. Broke his nose and knocked himself clean out."

"It's a miracle the shooter didn't take the opportunity to finish him off," Gage said.

"Maybe he thought he had killed him and didn't want to stick around and find out," Dwight said.

"Or maybe killing him wasn't the point," Travis said. "Maybe he was just sending a warning."

"Yeah," Gage said. "After all, Eddie wasn't in uniform. He wasn't driving a police vehicle. The shooter probably didn't know he's a cop."

Travis watched as the paramedics strapped Eddie onto the gurney and fitted an oxygen mask over his face. He waited until they had rolled him away toward the ambulance before he moved over to examine the place where he had fallen. By now most of the other law enforcement personnel had moved on, but he had no doubt that within a couple of hours everyone in the county would have heard about the reserve officer who had knocked himself out fleeing from a shooter. Hound Dog might never live that story down.

"Here's where he hit his head," Gage said, nudging a cantaloupe-sized chunk of granite with the toe of his boot.

"There's some scuff marks here, like this was where he was standing when he was hit," Dwight said, indicating an area on the edge of the scorch marks where the Stensons' storage unit had once stood.

Travis moved to stand beside him, and stared up into the hills. He pointed to clump of pinion trees about halfway up the slope. "What do you think? In there somewhere?"

Gage squinted up toward the area Travis indicated, then nodded. "Yeah, I think so. Good cover, shade, a good view of this area, a good angle to shoot, with the sun behind you or directly overhead most of the day, after it came up over that ridge there."

"About two hundred yards," Dwight said. "You'd have to have a high-powered rifle and be a good shot."

"I could make it," Gage said. "So could you. So could a lot of people."

"All right. Let's go up there and see what we can find," Travis said, and led the way up the slope.

ADELAIDE KINKAID TELEPHONED Lacy at four thirty. "Travis is fine," she said. "Though when I see him, I'm going to read him the riot act for not letting me know himself. I had to find out from Pamela Sue Windsor, over at the hospital in Junction, when she called to get Eddie Carstairs's insurance information. That fool Eddie was up there, poking around at the bomb site where he had no business being, and got himself shot."

Lacy didn't know or care who Pamela Sue Windsor or Eddie Carstairs were. "Travis is okay?" she asked, collapsing back against the sofa. Around her, her parents and Jan and Brenda broke into relieved smiles.

"He's fine," Adelaide said. "He and Gage and Dwight are still out there, investigating the scene. Eddie is fine, too. They're operating to remove the bullet and they have to set his broken nose because the fool tripped on a rock and knocked himself out while he was trying to run away. I swear, that rock is probably smarter than he is. I'll tell Travis you called when he comes in. Or maybe I'll leave him a note, since it's almost time for me to go home."

"Oh, no, don't tell him," Lacy said. "Please don't." She was embarrassed to have him know how panicked she had been at the idea of him hurt or dead. Whatever was between them felt too new—too fragile for that.

"Have it your way, dear. I have to go now. I have a few more calls to make. I think I remember that Eddie has a girlfriend over in Delta—I'll need to get in touch with her and hold her hand a little. These men have no consideration."

Lacy slipped the phone back into her pocket and realized everyone in the room was looking at her. "He's fine," she said. "It was another officer who was hurt, but he's going to be okay."

"You have to know more than that," Jan said. "We want the whole scoop. What happened?"

"I don't know." Lacy held out her hand to stave off the chorus of protests. "I really don't. Adelaide said this other officer—Eddie—was out at the storage units and someone shot him. And I guess he tripped and fell and broke his nose and knocked himself out, but I guess he was able to call for help before that." She shook her head. "That's all I know, really." And Travis was okay. She knew that—and that was really the most important fact. The only one she cared about.

"I'm glad I decided to have a yard sale instead of renting a storage unit," Jan said. "Who knew they could be so hazardous."

"I think the sooner I get Andy's computer out of my house, the better I'll feel," Brenda said. "Whatever was in those files of his, someone wanted to protect the information badly enough to try to kill me and Lacy and Travis and now this Eddie fellow."

"Maybe they did kill Andy," Lacy said.

Jan stood. "Come on. We'll go get the computer now and take it to the sheriff's office," she said.

"Maybe you should wait and have Travis or one of his deputies go with you," George said.

"I'll go with you," Lacy said.

"Lacy—" Her mother managed to freight the one word with a wealth of worry.

"It's better than sitting around here," Lacy said. "It will be fine. I promise." And if they timed their arrival at the sheriff's department right, she might even run into Travis, and be able to see for herself that he was all right.

Chapter Thirteen

"I still can't believe you're only just now mentioning that you had Andy's computer," Jan said as she followed Brenda and Lacy into Brenda's house. "You knew the sheriff was looking for any information Andy might have had."

"I simply forgot it existed," Brenda said. "I was in the basement the other day, looking for that box of fossils I told you my father had given me—you remember we talked about using them in that ancient history display at the museum. I pulled a big plastic storage container out from under the stairs and when I opened it, I realized it was full of stuff from Andy's office. I thought everything was out at the storage unit, but apparently not. The computer was sitting right on top of everything else. I suppose whoever packed the stuff up for me thought I would want it here, but I'm not sure I ever knew I had it."

"If it's been safely packed away all this time, I'm sure it still works," Lacy said. "And computer files should be easier to search than paper ones."

"That doesn't mean there's going to be anything useful on it," Jan said.

"No," Lacy agreed. "But maybe it will help."

"I'll just go down in the basement and get it out of the storage box," Brenda said, crossing the kitchen to a set of stairs that led down. "You two can wait up here."

"I'll go," Jan said. "I know it's upsetting for you to see Andy's things."

"It was a shock, seeing them yesterday," Brenda said. "But I'm over that now. After all, it's been over three years. I'm not going to break down because I see an old law book that used to belong to him."

"Still, I'm sure I can go right to it, you've described the location so well." Jan moved past Brenda and Lacy to the top of the stairs. "Why don't you open a bottle of wine for us?" she said as she started down the stairs.

Lacy and Brenda's eyes met. "Is Jan always this bossy?" Lacy whispered.

"Jan is the type of person who likes to be in charge of any project," Brenda said. She opened a kitchen cabinet and pulled out three tall glasses. "Understanding that has helped me get along with her at work. I think instead of wine, we should have iced tea. I don't think we all want to show up at the sheriff's office with alcohol on our breaths."

While Brenda filled glasses with ice, Lacy descended the stairs to the basement. "Did you find it?" she called. She rounded the corner and spotted Jan bent over a large blue plastic bin.

Jan jerked her head up and saw Lacy, then straightened. The contents of the bin in front of her were all in a jumble—as if they had been hurriedly pawed through. "Brenda said the computer was right on top," Lacy said. "You shouldn't have to dig through the boxes."

Jan snapped the lid back onto the bin, then pulled a laptop computer off the shelf next to her. "I've been thinking," she said. "Maybe I should talk to that reporter—Alvin Exeter."

Just the mention of Alvin made Lacy's stomach churn. "Why would you want to do that?"

"Maybe if someone appeared to cooperate with him, he'd give up this crazy idea of portraying you as guilty." She led the way up the stairs. "I wouldn't tell him anything much about you, personally. I'd focus on the town, how much of a shock the crime was—and, of course, how we all knew all along that you couldn't possibly have murdered Andy."

Lacy couldn't help but wonder where "all" these people who knew she was innocent had been during her trial, but she could see little point in bringing that up now. "You're free to talk to whoever you like," she said, "but I doubt if you'll change his mind about anything. He strikes me as a generally nasty person."

Brenda met them at the top of the stairs. "I see you found the laptop." She reached out and Jan handed it over.

"There are actually several bins of things from Andy's office down there," Jan said. "I peeked in a couple of them and there are some books that might be worth some money if you want to sell them. And I saw a couple of photographs you might want to donate to the museum. I'll come over one day and we can go through them, if you like."

"Sure," Brenda said. "That would be great." She set the computer on the kitchen table and handed Lacy and Jan glasses of tea. "I decided we could wait on the wine until after we stop by the sheriff's department," she said.

"We don't have to all go see the sheriff," Jan said.

"When I leave here I'll take Lacy home, then drop this off on the way to my house." She opened the computer. "We ought to see if this turns on, don't you think?" Before Brenda could answer, she pressed the power button and the computer hummed to life.

"Looks like it's password protected," Lacy said, looking over Jan's shoulder at the screen that asked for the password. She and Jan looked at Brenda.

"I have no idea what the password is," she said. "We could guess, but I really don't care what's on there. I prefer to leave the snooping to the police."

"But snooping can be so fun," Jan teased. But she shut down the computer and closed the lid. "You'll feel better—and so will I—when you have this thing out of your house. Hopefully, whoever was out to destroy those files doesn't know yet that you have it."

Brenda froze, the glass of tea halfway to her lips. "How could they? I didn't even know myself until yesterday."

"One of the movers who helped clean out Andy's office might have remembered it," Jan said. She finished off her tea, then set down the glass and picked up the computer. "But probably not. Come on, Lacy. Let's take care of this. It's early enough, maybe you and Travis can have dinner together after all."

"How did you know about that?" Lacy asked.

"Your mother told me while you were in the bathroom," Jan said. She grinned. "I can't help it if I have a talent for finding out things about people. You'd be surprised how useful it can be."

She started toward the living room and the others followed. They were almost to the door when the bell rang. Brenda hurried forward to answer it.

Travis's uniform was streaked with soot and something dark that might have been blood. He had more soot smudged on one cheek and his nose, and he needed a shave, but Lacy had never seen a more welcome sight. She wanted to rush forward and throw her arms around him, but she held back, hovering behind Brenda as her friend ushered the sheriff inside.

He looked past the other two women and found Lacy, his eyes meeting hers. "Your mother told me I'd find you here," he said.

"I'm glad you're okay," she said.

"Sorry if I worried you," he said. "The dispatcher didn't know the name of the officer who called in, and people jumped to conclusions. By the time I got back to the station half the town thought I was the officer who had been wounded and the other half were ready to start planning my funeral."

"I'm sorry about the officer who was shot," Lacy said. "Is he going to be okay?"

"He will be."

"Do you know who shot him?" Jan asked.

"No." Travis was still watching Lacy. "I stopped by to see if you'd still like to have dinner with me."

"Um, sure." She was so aware of the other two women watching. She tried hard to appear casual and indifferent.

"Good." He looked down at the floor and for a long moment, no one said anything.

"Oh, really, go on, you two," Jan said. "It's at times like these that I'm reminded that the saying 'three's a crowd' is so true."

"But before you go." Brenda reached over and tugged

the computer from Jan's grasp. "We were going to bring this to your office, but you can take it with you."

"A laptop?" Travis examined the computer.

"It was Andy's," Brenda said. "I didn't even realize I had it until I was looking for something in the basement and found it in a box of books and other stuff from his office. It's password protected and I don't know the password, but I thought maybe the sheriff's department could get past that. So many things, like notes and letters and photographs, Andy kept in his files, but contracts and correspondence will probably be on there. Maybe you'll find something to help you."

"This is great," Travis said. "We'll find someone to get the information off it. Thank you, Brenda."

"I'm sorry I didn't think of it before," she said.

"Are you ready to go, Lacy?" he asked.

"I'm ready."

She followed him out the door and down the walkway, aware of the other two women watching them. "This is the oldest vehicle in our little fleet," he said as he opened the passenger door of the Toyota. "It's pretty rough."

"It doesn't matter," she said, sliding into the seat. She watched as he tucked the computer into a large plastic bag, filled out a label on the front of the bag, then sealed it. He laid the bag with the computer in it on the rear floorboard. "We'll put that in an evidence locker at the station." He looked up and his eye caught hers. "Later."

"Mom was thrilled you accepted her invitation to dinner," Lacy said, as he turned onto Main. "I was, too, of course. I thought maybe you would be too tired or too busy or…"

He put his hand over hers and she stopped talking. "It's okay," he said. "You don't have to be nervous."

"I'm not sure why I am," she said. She watched him through half-lowered lashes, not wanting him to look into her eyes and see the powerful desire and attraction that had her feeling a little out of control.

He laced his fingers with hers. "I told your mother I needed to take a rain check on the family dinner," he said. "I wanted some time for the two of us to be alone."

Lacy swallowed, her heart beating faster. "Oh."

"Is that okay with you?"

"Yes." She looked into his eyes. "More than okay."

He kissed the back of her hand, then turned it over and kissed her palm, and she suddenly felt hot and a little light-headed. "Where are we going for dinner?" she asked.

"How about my place?"

"Yes."

They held hands on the drive to the condo he rented in a development on the river. He retrieved the computer in its evidence bag from the Toyota and carried it inside, where he locked it inside a cabinet by the door. When he straightened, Lacy didn't hesitate, but moved into his arms.

The kiss was urgent, a little rough, his unshaven chin abrading her cheek, his lips crushing the still-healing cut on her mouth. But sheer pleasure overwhelmed the discomfort, and she angled her head to deepen the contact, reveling in the heat and strength of him. She wrapped her arms around him, pressing herself fully to him, and he slid his hands down to cup her bottom and draw her tight against him, leaving no doubt how much he wanted her.

When he finally lifted his head and looked into her eyes, she was shaky, her heart pounding. "Wow," she said.

"About dinner—" he began.

She wriggled against him. "I'm thinking maybe we should enjoy dessert first."

She whooped as he lifted her, his hands under her thighs, wrapping her legs around his waist. He kissed her again, bracing her back against the wall in the foyer. She squirmed, delighted at the way he groaned in response—then she was the one groaning as he brought one hand up to caress the side of her breast, and began tracing a series of warm, wet kisses along the line of her jaw.

She tugged at his shirt, frustrated by the equipment that jangled and poked from the belt at his waist. Even when she succeeded in undoing the top two buttons, she was blocked from further exploration by the hard black wall of his bulletproof vest. By this time he had her T-shirt pushed up under her arms and was trailing his tongue along the lace at the top of her bra.

"This isn't fair," she protested. "You're wearing too much stuff."

He raised his head and laughed, then wrapped his hands around her waist and gently lowered her to the floor. "Am I rushing things?" he asked, looking into her eyes.

"More like going too slow." She pulled his head down to kiss him again, then nipped his upper lip. "You're welcome to get naked right here and take me up against the wall, but don't you think a bed might be more comfortable?"

She whooped again as he picked her up once more,

this time scooping her up behind her knees and shoulders. He carried her down a short hallway to a large bedroom. She had a passing impression of dark furniture and a king-size bed before he dropped her onto the mattress.

She propped herself on her elbows and watched as he stripped off his utility belt and draped it on the arm of a chair next to the bed. He kicked off his boots, then finished unbuttoning the shirt and removed it. This was the kind of male body she could admire—masculine but not too hard, handsome but not too perfect.

There was nothing particularly sexy about the black protective vest he wore under the shirt—except that he was wearing it. He peeled it off, his skin damp in places beneath it. "I should take a shower," he said.

"Only if you take me with you," she said. His eyes met hers and she felt the force of the look deep inside, a tugging heat that settled between her legs. He finished undressing, then pulled her up from the bed. When she was standing beside him she pulled her T-shirt off over her head. Before she could remove her bra, he had unfastened it and was tracing his tongue around one nipple, and then the next, until she was swaying, her kneecaps having apparently melted in the onslaught.

Some time after that the rest of her clothes ended up somewhere on the bedroom floor, and the two of them tumbled into the shower, where warm water rushed over them, and she discovered how sensual the feel of soapsuds between two naked bodies could be.

She slid soapy fingers over the jut of his shoulders and the swell of his biceps, tracing the ridges of his ribs and smoothing across the flat plane of his stomach. When she wrapped her hand around his erection, he let out his breath and his eyes glazed.

He curled a hand around her wrist. "Better slow down," he said.

She smiled up at him. "I don't know," she said. "I kind of like having you at my mercy."

"Is that so?" His grin held a hint of wickedness that sent another thrill through her. The grin gave way to a slack-jawed sigh as he reached down and slid a finger into her, stroking gently. "Now...now who needs to go...slow," she stammered as he slid the finger in and out. "Remember...it's been a while for me."

With his free hand, he reached over and shut off the water, then kissed her again, their lips remaining locked together even as they moved out of the shower and wrapped themselves in towels.

They were still damp when they returned to the bed and tumbled onto the dark blue comforter. She scooted back onto the pillows and beckoned him to her. "I don't want to wait any longer," she said.

He leaned over and took a condom from the drawer of the bedside table. "Just so you don't get the wrong impression, these have been in there awhile," he said, holding up the foil packet. "But I think they're still good."

"Stop talking and put that baby on," she said.

"Yes, ma'am."

Watching him roll on that condom was enough to have her breathing hard again. When he finally moved over her she was more than ready for him, pulling her to him and sighing with happiness as he entered her.

She had expected a lot from this moment—physical satisfaction, a kind of completion, the thrill of being so close to him. But she hadn't counted on his gentleness, or how much he would *care* for her. He moved slowly at first, his eyes locked to hers, his focus entirely on her. He shifted slightly, and she felt the movement deep inside her. "Do you like that?" he asked.

"Yes."

"How about this?" He reached down to fondle her and her eyes lost focus. *Yeesss.* His hands and his hips worked a kind of magic over her, and she surrendered to it. "That's it," he whispered, his fingers caressing a sensitive place she hadn't even known existed. "Don't be afraid to let go."

So she let go, and rode the waves of pleasure each thrust of his body sent through her. She dug her fingers into his back and responded to his every movement, opening her eyes when she felt him still and tense, watching his release reflected on his face, then pulling him to her to hold him even closer, until they rolled to the side, still joined, to gaze into each other's eyes.

"To quote you—wow," he said, and he slid out of her. He disposed of the condom in the trash basket next to the bed, then lay back down beside her.

She laughed, feeling impossibly light, as if she might float off the bed. "Yeah—wow." She trailed one finger down his nose. "Now you're making me think I missed out in high school, not flirting with you."

"I like to think I've learned a few things since high school."

"Life has a way of doing that—teaching us things whether we want to learn them or not. You taught me that people can change—or at least, they can change their minds. You changed your mind about me. And I changed my mind about you."

He slid over to lay his head on her shoulder. "Let's

put that behind us," he said. "I want to focus on our future, not our past."

"Except we can't really put the past behind us," she said. "Not until we find Andy's killer—or whoever it is who keeps coming after us."

"You're right," he said. "We're going to stop them."

She eased him off her and sat up. "Why don't we start by taking a look at that laptop?" she said.

"What good will that do?" Travis asked. "Brenda said it's password protected."

"Yes, but I think I know the password. It's probably the same one Andy used for everything. That's what most people do, isn't it?"

The look he gave her held frank admiration. "I was right when I said you'd be the key to solving this case," he said.

"We haven't solved anything yet," she reminded him.

"No, but we will. And soon. I can feel it." He slid off the bed and took her hand. "Let's go check that laptop."

Chapter Fourteen

Travis couldn't stop looking at Lacy. He liked watching her when she was like this—completely relaxed and happy, her attention focused on the computer that was open on the coffee table between them. They sat on the sofa in his living room, thighs touching. She had put on one of his dress shirts, the cuffs folded back, the tails hanging down to midthigh. He had pulled on a pair of jeans. Just as well he didn't have the video camera here to film this, though he had made her sign off on the custody sheet, keeping to proper procedure.

"Andy's password for most things was brenda812," Lacy said as she typed. "They were married in August of 2012." She hit Enter and the screen shifted to reveal the desktop menu. "Eureka!" she cried, and clicked on a folder labeled Office.

A list of file names filled the screen. Travis leaned in closer. "Do you see anything?" he asked.

She highlighted the file named "Eagle_mtn_resort." The first thing that came up was a report from the county road commissioner. "It's about the roads in and around the resort," she said, scanning the page. "That doesn't look too pertinent."

She started to close the file, but Travis put out a hand

to stop her. "Wait a minute. Look at this." He dragged his finger across the touch pad to highlight a paragraph that began at the bottom of the page. "This mentions Fireline Road, see?"

She squinted at the screen. "It says they'll need to extend Fireline Road up over the ridge to provide a second access route to the resort." She looked at Travis. "Does that mean the resort is just over the ridge from the storage facility?"

He nodded. "Which would make it easy for anyone on the ridge to keep an eye on the storage facility, too. Maybe whoever shot Eddie was on Hake's land and saw Eddie from there."

"That still doesn't tell us why they would do something like that."

"No, but I think first thing tomorrow I'll drive to the resort property and see if it looks like anyone has been up there. Henry Hake said the group is restructuring, so I wouldn't think there would be any work going on."

"Don't go by yourself," she said.

"No. I'll take Gage or Dwight with me. And I'll be careful."

She turned back to the computer. "Let's see if there's anything else interesting on here." She scrolled through the list of file names and stopped when she came to a file named jan.

"Jan as in January?" Travis asked.

"Or Jan as in Jan Selkirk?" Lacy opened the file. The first page was a list of dates. 04/06/14, 07/29/14—seventeen different dates altogether.

"Those are all from the months prior to Andy's death," Travis said.

Lacy scrolled to the second page of the file. This

one was a photograph. She enlarged the photo on the screen. "That's Jan Selkirk," she said, staring at the wide-mouth brunette who was sitting on the lap of a burly blond man. "She's changed her hair color, but that has to be her. And is that—"

"Henry Hake," Travis said. "Keep scrolling."

The next four pages in the file were more pictures of Jan Selkirk and Henry Hake—the last two of them kissing passionately, his hand up her skirt.

Lacy scrolled until her cursor reached the end of the file. "That's all there is," she said.

"Jan Selkirk is married to Barry Selkirk," Travis said. "She has been for years."

"So Jan and Henry Hake were having an affair?" Lacy stared at the last picture, of the former mayor and the developer locked in a steamy kiss. "This explains why Jan was acting so strangely at Brenda's house this afternoon."

"Strange in what way?"

"She insisted on going into Brenda's basement to retrieve the computer herself, and when I went down to see what was taking her so long, I found her going through a box of things from Andy's office. Then she volunteered to take the computer to the sheriff's office herself. But then you showed up and foiled that plan."

"She must have suspected Andy had something on here that would damage her reputation," Travis said. "Not to mention her marriage."

Lacy looked ill. "Do you think Andy was blackmailing her?" she asked.

"If he was, that might have given her reason to want him dead." Travis tapped the screen. "Notice anything else about these pictures?"

"Her hair—it's dark brown, like mine."

"I don't remember when she changed it, but it may have been about the time Andy died," he said. "We might be able to find pictures in the newspaper archives."

"The woman Wade Tomlinson saw outside Andy's office the day he died—that could have been Jan."

"Maybe so." He tapped the keys to shut down the computer. "I need to take you home," he said. "I have to get this down to the station." He bent down and kissed her cheek. "Sorry we never got around to dinner."

"Oh, I don't know." Her smile sent heat curling through his stomach. "I thought dessert was pretty good."

"Only pretty good?"

"Awfully good." She kissed him on the mouth, then stood. "Let me know what happens with Jan," she said.

"I will. I'd like to put an end to this case as soon as possible."

"Yeah, I hate to think of Jan as a murderer."

"I'm going to make sure of her guilt before I ask the DA to file charges," Travis said. "I want to bring Andy's killer to justice, but I want to be sure we've got the right person this time."

"IF YOU WANT to discuss security for Pioneer Days, I don't see why we couldn't have done so at my office at the museum." Jan Selkirk swept into the Rayford County Sheriff's Department on a wave of expensive perfume, a bright blue Questions? Ask Me! button affixed to her blouse.

"What's with the button?" Gage asked as he escorted her into an interview room.

She glanced down at the four-inch button. "It's for Pioneer Days. I'm an information helper. We'll have them stationed throughout town. Anyone who sees this button knows they can approach that person and find out the schedule of activities, or where the restrooms are located or anything else they need to know."

Travis came into the interview room and closed the door behind him. Jan's smile faltered. "Why are we in here?" she asked. "Couldn't we go in your office?"

"I didn't ask you here to talk about the festival," Travis said.

Her color paled beneath her makeup. "What is going on, Sheriff?" she asked. "I don't have time to waste on trivial matters."

"Oh, I don't think this is a trivial matter. Sit down." He motioned to a seat at the conference table, then took the chair across the table for himself.

Jan hesitated, then sat. She glanced up at Gage, who remained standing by the door. "Am I under arrest?" she asked.

"Not at this time. We just want to ask you a few questions. You're free to go anytime."

She looked toward the door, as if debating leaving. Travis was gambling that she wouldn't. "I'm going to record the conversation," he said, and switched on the recorder that sat at one end of the table. "That's for your protection, as well as ours."

"You're making me very nervous," she said. "What is this about?"

Travis opened a folder and slid out a stack of photos—three of the pictures taken from Andy Stenson's computer enlarged to eight-by-ten-inch glossies. He arranged the photos in front of Jan. "Recognize these?"

She stared at the pictures, all the color bleached from her face. "Where did you get these?" she whispered.

"They were on Andy Stenson's laptop," Travis said. "You knew they might be there. They're why you tried so hard to get the laptop away from Brenda. I think you planned to destroy the machine, or maybe just erase the files."

"I don't know what you're talking about." But she continued to stare at the photographs, pain reflected in her eyes.

"You were having an affair with Henry Hake," Travis said. "An affair you didn't want your husband and the town council to know about. I looked up some council minutes from that time period and you were one of the strongest supporters for Hake's resort development, urging the council to pass resolutions that would make it easier for him to build his high-altitude luxury homes."

"I supported the development because it was a good idea. Not because I was sleeping with Henry Hake." Her voice was stronger, though the fear hadn't left her eyes.

Travis waited until her eyes met his before he spoke. "Was Andy blackmailing you?" he asked.

"No. Of course not!" She sat back, hands clutching the edge of the table. "You're thinking if he was I would have a good reason to kill him but I didn't kill him, I promise."

"We're going to subpoena your financial records," Travis said. "As well as Andy's bank accounts. They'll show if you were paying him to keep this quiet."

She shifted in her chair, hands clenching and unclenching. "All right—yes. He was blackmailing me. He said he wouldn't tell Barry or anyone else about the affair as long as I paid. He said he needed the money to finish the remodeling on his house. He let Brenda think all the money came from Henry Hake." She laughed, a hysterical sound. "I suppose in a way that was true, since I had to borrow money from Henry to pay Andy. But I didn't kill him. I wouldn't do something like that."

"A slim woman with dark brown hair was seen outside Andy's office about the time he died," Gage said. "We know now that woman wasn't Lacy—was it you?"

"I didn't kill him," she said. "I went there to talk to him—to tell him I couldn't keep paying him. I told him if he didn't stop harassing me I would make Henry Hake cancel his contract with Andy."

"I'm surprised you hadn't thought of that before," Travis said.

She made a face. "Henry didn't really have a say in who represented the development corporation," she said. "He was the public face of the company, but his business partners—the people behind the scenes—made all the decisions. Henry didn't think Andy was experienced enough to represent the group, but his objection was overruled."

"What happened when you went to talk to Andy that day?" Travis asked.

Her mouth tightened. "He laughed at me. He laughed. I didn't say half of what I wanted to say before he started laughing. He said he wasn't about to give up his very lucrative 'side job' and I'd better focus on finding a way to pay. He said Henry wouldn't fire him because he knew things about Henry that his business partners wouldn't want to know."

"What happened then?" Gage leaned over the table toward her. "Did you attack him in a fit of rage? Stab him in the heart with the letter opener he kept on his desk?"

"No! I ran out of there. I left by the back door so no one would see me. I was crying and I didn't want to have to make up some excuse if I ran into anyone."

"So you didn't see anyone when you were leaving?" Travis asked.

"No. The next day I heard Andy had been murdered and I was terrified. You can't imagine my relief when I heard Lacy had been arrested."

Travis tamped down his anger. "You really thought she killed Andy?" he asked.

"I just assumed he had been blackmailing her, too." Jan sniffed. "I wouldn't be surprised if Andy was getting money from other people in town. Everybody thought he was such a nice young man, but he had a sly streak."

"Who else do you think he was blackmailing?" Gage asked. "Besides you and possibly Henry Hake?"

"I don't know." She straightened, some steel back in her spine. "And I've said enough. Too much. I want a lawyer."

Travis slid back his chair and stood. "Call him. You can wait for him in here." He and Gage left the room, locking the door behind them.

Outside, at the end of the hallway, the brothers conferred. "What do you think?" Travis asked.

"She admits she was in Andy's office that day," Gage said. "It had to have been only minutes before he died. She's got a motive, since he was threatening to tell her husband about the affair."

"I don't think it's enough to hold her," Travis said.

"If we don't arrest her, she's liable to leave town and

try to disappear," Gage said. "She's got money and I bet she's got a passport."

"I wish we had more evidence against her."

"You're afraid of making the same mistake with her you made with Lacy," Gage said. "That isn't going to happen a second time."

"Let me call the DA, see what he says," Travis said.

The DA agreed with Travis that they probably didn't have enough evidence to arrest Jan at this time, but that she was a strong suspect. By this time both Barry Selkirk and the lawyer Jan had hired to represent her had arrived at the police station.

"My client—"

"My wife—"

Travis waved away the attorney and the husband's protests. "You're free to go, Jan," he said. "But I'll need you to stay close, in case I have more questions."

"I get it. Don't leave town." She stood, gathering her dignity. "Obviously, I've done some things I'm not proud of." She slanted a look at her husband. "But I did not kill Andy Stenson."

They watched her walk out of the door, flanked by her lawyer and her husband. "Do you believe her?" Gage asked.

"Yeah." Travis shoved his hands in his pockets, shoulders hunched. "Right now, anyway, I do."

"So what now?"

"I'm going to talk to Henry Hake and I'm going to check out the site of Eagle Mountain Resort. Why don't you search through Andy's computer and see if you can find anyone else he was blackmailing?"

"We might end up with a whole town full of suspects," Gage said.

"The only one I care about is the person who really killed him," Travis said. "Find him or her and we'll tie up a whole lot of loose ends."

"BLACKMAIL! AND JAN SELKIRK? I just can't believe it." Brenda sat between Lacy and Jeanette Milligan on the Milligans' sofa, a cup of coffee steadied on one knee.

"I was shocked, too," Lacy said. "I never would have believed Andy would do something like that. I knew he was doing better financially, but he told me you had inherited a little money from a favorite aunt, and that was enough for you to finish the remodeling on your house."

"I thought the money came from Henry Hake and the other new clients he had." Brenda sipped her coffee. Her eyes were red and puffy, and Lacy knew she must have been mourning this new revelation about her husband. "I thought I knew him so well," she said. "And to think all this time he was lying." Her voice caught on the last word and she bowed her head.

Jeanette pulled her close and handed her several tissues. "Andy was misguided, but he loved you," she said. "That's what you have to remember."

"Mom is right." Lacy patted Brenda's hand. "Andy did love you. I never knew him to even look twice at another woman."

Brenda nodded and raised her head. "To think I've worked with Jan all this time and I never knew she cheated on her husband. But I can't believe she killed Andy over it."

"I'm shocked, too," Lacy said. "Of course, I don't know her well, but the way Andy died—it never struck me as something a woman would do. It was just so…

brutal." She glanced at Brenda. "Sorry. I shouldn't have said that."

"No, it's okay," Brenda said. "It *was* brutal. The trial kind of numbed me to the whole thing, but I agree. It never set well with me when the prosecutor said Andy was killed by a woman. For one thing, he was a young, strong guy. You and Jan Selkirk just aren't big, physical women. I think Andy could have fought her off easily."

"I've been trying to think if there was anyone else Andy might have been trying to get money from," Lacy said. "Someone besides Jan who might have had a reason to kill him. There's Henry Hake, of course. He might not have wanted news of the affair getting out, and he certainly had a lot more money than Jan."

"I'm sure Travis has already thought of that," Jeanette said.

"Speaking of Travis." Brenda sat up straighter and dabbed at her eyes. "I don't think I was imagining the sparks flying between the two of you yesterday when he picked you up at my house."

"He canceled dinner with us in favor of a *private* dinner with Lacy," Jeanette said. "Though come to think of it, when she came in several hours later, she said she was starved because they had never gotten around to eating."

"Hmm. I wonder what two people could do for several hours that would make them forget all about food?" Brenda said.

Lacy's cheeks burned and she refused to look her mother or Brenda in the eye. "Travis and I have gotten close," she said.

Jeanette covered her ears. "I don't think I want to hear any more." She lowered her hands and smiled. "But your father and I think he's a very nice young man. And it's good to see you so happy."

"If anyone deserves it, you do," Brenda said.

"You deserve to be happy, too," Lacy said. "I'm so sorry about Andy. It feels as if he died all over again."

"There's something else about all this that's bothering me," Brenda said.

"What's that?" Lacy asked.

"Do the police think Jan is the person who ran us off the road in that truck, then burned the truck, and blew up the storage unit while you and Travis were inside?" Brenda asked. "And if she was, who shot Eddie Carstairs? Jan was with me when that happened—and then the two of us were with you."

Lacy stared at her. "I've been so focused on Jan as a suspect in Andy's murder that I didn't think of that," she said.

"If she could kill Andy, she might not hesitate to kill you or anyone else who threatened her," Jeanette said.

"Yes, but with a big truck?" Brenda asked. "Or a bomb? What does Jan know about trucks or bombs? And then she sets the truck on fire and hikes home cross-country?"

"I don't know her as well as you do, but I can't picture her doing any of that," Lacy said. She put a hand over her stomach, which felt as if she had eaten way too much pie. "I hope Travis isn't making another mistake."

"You should call and talk to him," Brenda said. "Not that you should tell him how to do his job, but maybe he'll put your mind at ease. He might have an explanation that we haven't thought of yet."

"Or maybe he thinks Jan had an accomplice or

something," Lacy said. She slipped her phone from her pocket and tapped in Travis's cell number. After two rings the call went to voice mail. "Call me when you get a chance," she said, hesitant to say more—especially with Brenda and her mother listening in.

Brenda set aside her half-empty coffee cup and stood. "Thanks for letting me vent," she said. "I have to get to work."

"The museum is open, even with Jan under suspicion?" Jeanette asked.

"Oh, yes. We're redoing all the displays and adding new ones for Pioneer Days." She picked up her purse and slung the strap over her shoulder. "It's coming up quickly, so I'd better get busy."

"I can help." Lacy stood, also. "I don't know the first thing about history, but I can put things where you tell me," she said. "Consider me your newest volunteer."

"That's the best offer I've had all day," Brenda said.

Jeanette rose and walked with them to the door. "If Travis stops by, I'll let him know you're at the museum," she said.

"Mom, you don't have to be my personal secretary."

"I know this is a little awkward," Jeanette said. "After all, you're not a teenager anymore. But just so we won't worry, if you're going to stay out overnight, text and let us know you're safe."

"Umm. Okay."

Lacy followed Brenda out to her car. "Did your mom just give you permission to spend the night with Travis?" Brenda asked.

"Yes. Talk about awkward!" Lacy rolled her eyes.

She could joke about it with Brenda, but she added "look for own apartment" to the top of her to-do list.

THE BIG IRON gate across Henry Hake's drive stood wide-open when Travis visited the house later that day. The sheriff parked in the paved circular drive and walked up to the massive oak entry doors. He rang the bell three times, but received no answer. No one answered when he called Henry Hake's private number, either.

Travis walked around the house, peering in windows, his boots crunching on the heavy layer of bark mulch in the immaculately tended landscape. Hake didn't strike Travis as the type to want to get his hands dirty, so he imagined an army of gardeners tending the lilacs and creeping juniper. The garage had no windows, so Travis couldn't tell if a car was parked inside, but the house itself had a deserted look, with no lights showing from within.

He returned to his vehicle and called the office of Hake Development. "This is Rayford County Sheriff Travis Walker," he told the woman who answered. "I'm out at Henry Hake's house and he doesn't appear to be home. It's important that I reach him."

"I'll put you through to Mr. Hake's administrative assistant," the woman on the other end of the line said.

Seconds later, the brisk woman Travis had spoken with before answered. Travis introduced himself once more. "It's very important that I speak with Mr. Hake," he said.

"You're from the police, you say?"

"The sheriff's office, in Rayford County, where Mr. Hake lives. I believe we spoke the other day. I'm at Mr. Hake's house now and he isn't home."

"Yes, I remember speaking with you. I was thinking I should call you later today, if I hadn't heard from Mr. Hake," she said.

"What about?" Travis asked.

"I'm afraid I can't tell you where Mr. Hake is right now, because I don't know. I haven't heard from him in a couple of days, and I'm starting to get worried."

"Does he often disappear without telling you where he's going?" Travis asked.

"Oh, no. He always stays in touch. That's why this is so unusual. And why I was going to call you."

"I'm not sure I understand," Travis said. "Do you think something has happened to Mr. Hake?"

"I couldn't say. All I know is that Mr. Hake is missing."

Chapter Fifteen

Volunteering at the history museum was not the most exciting work Lacy had ever done, but she enjoyed spending time with Brenda, and the work gave her something to do. Now that she had adjusted to life at home once more, she was growing restless. She needed a job, but a small town like Eagle Mountain didn't offer many employment opportunities, so for now at least, volunteering seemed the best solution.

The museum occupied the building that had once been Eagle Mountain's hospital, back at the turn of the nineteenth century, when the town had boasted five grocery stores, a dairy, a lumberyard, a train depot and a population five times what it was these days. The various rooms of the hospital housed themed displays, with space in the back for a classroom, archives and a workroom. Everyone from schoolchildren to tourists regularly filed through the building, which had developed a reputation as one of the finest small-town museums in the state.

Lacy finished tacking red, white and blue bunting around the large front windows and turned to find Brenda frowning at a computer screen behind the front desk. "What are you looking at that put that sour look on your face?" she asked.

Brenda turned away from the computer. "A customer came in yesterday, asking about a book we usually keep in stock, but were out of. I was trying to see if I could find out where Jan orders our books so I could get this lady a copy, but I'm having a hard time figuring out her system for organizing things."

"What will happen if Jan is arrested?" Lacy asked, joining her friend at the museum's front counter, which served as both check-in desk and retail checkout.

"Even if she didn't kill Andy—and I still can't believe she did—her affair will be a scandal," Brenda said. "The town owns this museum and I doubt if they'll keep her on."

"Will you apply to be the director, then?"

"I'd like to." She studied Lacy's face. "What about you? Want to be my assistant?"

"I would love to work for you, but I'm not in love with history the way you are." Lacy picked up an antique paperweight from the counter and turned it over in her hand. "I think I should use the money I got from the state to go to school."

"Do you know what kind of career you want to pursue?" Brenda asked.

"I was thinking maybe…education. My mom is a teacher and I like kids." She set the paperweight back on the counter. "I think I'd be good at the job."

"We certainly need good teachers. You should go for it."

"I already did some research," Lacy said. "I can enroll in the university in Junction and commute to classes from here."

"So you'd stay in Eagle Mountain?"

"This is home." Even with everything that had happened here—the tragedy of Andy's death and those awful months before and during her trial—Lacy still felt more comfortable here than she had anywhere else. "I don't want to leave."

"And a certain handsome sheriff is here…" Brenda's eyes sparkled.

Lacy laughed. "There is that. But I think I'd like to find my own place to live. My parents are happy to have me stay with them as long as I like, but it feels too much like I'm in high school, with them watching my every move."

"I know a place you can rent," Brenda said.

That got Lacy's attention. Rentals, like jobs, were scarce in small towns like Eagle Mountain. "Where?"

"Andy and I fixed up an apartment over our garage, thinking we would use it when relatives visited. It's been sitting empty all this time, but I'd love to rent it to you. You'd have your own entrance and could come and go as you please."

"That sounds perfect." Lacy leaned over the counter to hug her friend. "Just tell me when I can move in."

Brenda returned the hug. "You should look at the place first, make sure it's what you want," she said.

"Does it have room for a bed and my own bathroom?"

"And a tiny kitchen and living room," Brenda said.

"Then I love it already."

The bell on the front door rang, announcing someone had entered the museum. "I'll take care of this," Brenda said. "Would you go into the workroom and look in the closet and take out the box marked Pioneer Days Costumes? We need to go through those before the festival."

Lacy found the box in question and looked around for a pair of scissors to cut the tape. But voices from the front of the museum caught her attention and she froze, listening. "I didn't know you were interested in local history, Mr. Barnes," Brenda said.

Lacy tiptoed to the door of the workroom and peered out at the front reception area. Ian Barnes, his black Eagle Mountain Outfitters T-shirt stretched like a second skin over his powerful chest and shoulders, stood across from Brenda at the front counter. "Somebody told me you have a display of old climbing gear and some pictures," he said.

Brenda handed him some change and an admission token. "We do. It's in the Local Sports room—second door on the left." She indicated the hallway to her right.

Ian replaced his wallet in his back pocket. "Hello, Lacy," he said.

Lacy jumped. She hadn't realized she was standing where Ian could see her. Reluctantly, she stepped into the front room. "Hello," she said.

"Do you work here, too?" Ian asked.

"No. I'm, uh, volunteering."

He put his hand lightly at her back—a touch that sent a shiver up her spine. "Why don't you show me where this Local Sports room is?"

"Go ahead and go with him, Lacy," Brenda said.

"It's down this way." Lacy hurried forward, away from his touch, and led him to the room, which, in addition to historic photos of rock climbers and skiers, included a feature on a 1930s boxing champion who had hailed from the area and jerseys from local sports teams.

Ian stepped inside the room and Lacy turned to leave,

but he grabbed her by the wrist. "Stay a minute and tell me more about yourself," he said.

She pressed her back against the door frame, tamping down the urge to flee. Why did this man leave her feeling so unsettled? While every other woman in town seemed gone over the fact that he was so good-looking, what she felt in his presence wasn't attraction, but fear. "Why do you want to know about me?" she asked, keeping her voice light and focusing her gaze on the displays in the room.

"Oh, the usual reason." He smiled, and the effect was dazzling.

"What is the usual reason?"

"I'm a single guy, you're a pretty single woman." He leaned toward her, one hand on the doorjamb, over her head. "I'd like to get to know you better."

"I'm involved with someone, Mr. Barnes," she said, wincing inwardly at the primness of her words.

"The county sheriff. I've seen you two together. But you're not engaged or anything, right?"

"No."

He flashed the smile again. "Then you can't blame a guy for trying." To her great relief, he lowered his hand and turned to study the sepia-toned pictures of men in woolen knickers and heavy boots climbing up Dakota Ridge. "Somebody told me you used to work for that lawyer who was killed."

"Yes."

"I guess you knew all about all his clients then."

"Actually, no, I didn't." She edged toward the door. Why was he asking about Andy's clients?

"I think maybe you know more than you're saying,"

he said. "That's good. It's always good to know when to keep a secret."

The skin along Lacy's arms stood up in gooseflesh. Did Ian Barnes know about the blackmail? Had Andy blackmailed *him*? She backed out of the room. "I don't have anything to say to you or anyone else," she said.

"That's good." He turned and his eyes met hers, and the look in them froze her blood. His earlier flirtatiousness had been replaced by pure menace. "If I were you, I wouldn't tell my boyfriend, the sheriff, about our little conversation," he said. "After all, your parents have suffered enough, haven't they?"

Lacy all but ran back to the front room, past Brenda and into the workroom. Brenda hurried after her. "Lacy, what is it?" she asked. "You're white as a ghost. Did Ian do something to upset you? Should I call Travis?"

Lacy shook her head. "No. No, I'm fine. I just…" She put a hand to her head. "I just had a dizzy spell. I didn't eat breakfast this morning." She struggled to pull herself together, not to let her friend see how terrified she was. She felt confident enough to stand up to someone like Ian Barnes on her own. But when he threatened her family, he left her defenseless.

"Have some water." Brenda took a bottle from a small refrigerator under the counter and handed it to Lacy. "Are you sure this doesn't have something to do with Ian?"

Lacy drank some water and began to feel a little steadier. "He just makes me uncomfortable, that's all," she said.

"Yeah, he may be gorgeous, but have you noticed he never smiles?"

Lacy shuddered as she remembered the smile he had

fixed on her like a weapon. "I don't like him," she said, keeping her voice low.

"I'm sorry," Brenda said. "If he comes around again, I'll offer to give him a tour myself." She moved back up front and Lacy sagged against the counter and drank more water. Should she tell Travis about her encounter with Ian? Maybe he could find something on Andy's computer that would point to Ian as the victim of blackmail.

But what if word got back to Ian that she had told, and he made good on his threat to hurt her parents? Travis would offer to protect her family, but what if he couldn't?

"That's funny." Brenda came back into the workroom. "Ian left already."

"Did he say anything?" Lacy asked.

"No. When I walked back into the front room just now he was headed out. I called after him, but he must not have heard me. He got in that Jeep of his and drove away." She shrugged. "I guess all he wanted to see was the climbing gear and pictures. Some people are like that—they're only interested in items related to their hobby or history or family or whatever."

"Right." Lacy finished her water and tossed the bottle in the recycling bin. "I guess we'd better get back to work," she said. "What's next on the list?"

"Costumes." Brenda walked to the box Lacy had taken from the closet, opened it and pulled out a blue-and-white striped dress. Or, Lacy thought it was a dress—until she saw the attached bloomers.

"What is that?" she asked.

"It's an 1890s bathing costume." Brenda held the garment up to her body. "It's wool, and comes complete with a lace-trimmed cap and lace-up slippers. Jan and I wore them last year for Pioneer Days and they were a hit."

"You'll look adorable," Lacy said, trying hard not to laugh at the image she had of Brenda in the old-fashioned garment.

"Oh, I won't be alone." Brenda reached into the box and pulled out a second costume—this one red, with white ruffles at the neck and hem. "You and Jan are about the same size." She tossed the suit to Lacy. "And don't you dare say no. You promised to help, remember?"

"So I did." Lacy held the bathing costume at arm's length and made a face. It reminded her of a flannel nightgown. Not exactly the thing to turn the head of a certain sheriff.

"Please, Lacy," Brenda pleaded. "Don't make me look ridiculous all by myself. And I could really use the help."

"I'll wear it," Lacy said. "After all, you're going to be renting me my sweet new apartment." And at least volunteering at the festival would help take her mind off Ian Barnes. When she had a little more distance from her encounter with him, she would decide what to do.

TRAVIS SUMMONED HIS DEPUTIES, both regular and reserve, to the sheriff's department for a strategy session. "Eddie is out of the hospital but on medical leave," he said to begin the meeting. "Which may be permanent leave, when I've had more time to review his conduct that day. I don't need reserve officers who decide to interfere with investigations—on their days off or any other time." The pointed look he gave the two other reserve officers in attendance was enough to make them squirm.

"On to the next item of business," he continued. "Pioneer Days is this weekend. The sheriff's office has agreed to supply a couple of officers to help with crowd and traffic control, but four of us will be on duty throughout the weekend, and available to head off trouble if we see it developing."

"Check your schedules," Gage said to the reserves. "With Eddie out, I had to juggle things a bit."

"Moving on." Travis consulted his notes. "Henry Hake's administrative assistant, Marsha Caldwell, filed a missing person's report on him this morning. No one has seen or heard from him in the last forty-eight hours. There's no activity on his phone or credit cards, and his car is missing. But there's no sign of a struggle or violence at his home or office, so it's still possible he took a trip somewhere without telling anyone. He wouldn't be the first company executive to decide to take a break and shut off his phone for a long weekend."

"But you don't really think that's what happened," Gage said.

"No. Everything we've been dealing with lately— the reopening of the investigation into Andy Stenson's murder, the attack on Brenda and Lacy, the bombing of the storage unit, even Eddie's shooting—all have connections to Eagle Mountain Resort. We need to keep digging and see how they all link up."

"What's the next step?" Dwight asked.

"I want to check out the site Hake had planned for his resort. And I want you and Gage to go with me."

The meeting ended a few minutes later. The reserve officers left. Adelaide met Travis, Gage and Dwight in the front office. "It's a wonder your ears aren't burning, considering how the revelation that Andy Stenson was blackmailing Jan Selkirk, and Henry Hake's disappearance are all anybody can talk about."

"Anybody else confess to having been blackmailed by Andy Stenson?" Gage asked.

"Nah. Though Josh Lindberg at the hardware store is supposedly taking bets on whether Henry Hake left town because of the scandal with Jan, or whether Barry Selkirk ran him out of the county."

"That doesn't sound like Barry's style to me," Dwight said. "My guess is he'd be more likely to run Jan out of town."

"Word is he's sticking by her," Adelaide said. "Paid for a top lawyer from Denver and everything."

"I hope they work it out," Travis said. "We're headed up to the resort site to check things out. You know how to reach us if anything happens."

"I'd say we've had more than enough happen lately," Adelaide said. "I'm ready for the crime wave to be over. People are going to get the wrong idea about Eagle Mountain if this keeps up."

They set out, Gage and Dwight together in one SUV, Travis leading the way in the Toyota. The town was abuzz with preparations for the festival the following day. Wade Tomlinson and Brock Ryan were setting up a climbing wall for kids in front of Eagle Mountain Outfitters, and the Elks Club members were transforming the park into a mini-carnival, complete with a test-your-strength game, designed to look like a pioneer chopping wood, and a series of water troughs set up so that kids could pan for gold.

Travis had heard that Lacy was helping Brenda at

the museum, but he hadn't had a chance to talk to her, what with the craziness of Jan's confession that she was blackmailed and Henry Hake's disappearance. But they had made a date to meet up the day of the festival to watch the fireworks together. And maybe, he thought, go back to his place afterward and make a few fireworks of their own.

The proposed site for Eagle Mountain Resort was eight miles out of the town proper, near the top of Dakota Ridge, but Eagle Mountain had annexed the land three years previously, largely at the urging of then-mayor Jan Selkirk, on the theory that the luxury development would be a tax boon to the community. So far, that prediction hadn't come true. The sheriff's department vehicles drove through the twin stone pillars that marked the entrance to the resort, into a landscape of crumbling asphalt and abandoned building foundations. Grass and even small shrubs broke through the neglected streets, and the stakes marking lot lines had fallen over or were barely visible through the underbrush that had taken over. Staked trees and other landscaping that had died from neglect dotted the landscape.

They parked in front of a five-foot-by-four-foot sign that touted the amenities of the resort, with an artist's rendering of the development, the homes all soaring redwood beams and glass walls, luxury four-wheel-drive vehicles parked on cobblestone drives while elegantly dressed men and women smiled and laughed.

"Yeah, it sure doesn't look anything like that now," Gage observed.

"I never could understand how Hake thought he was going to sell a bunch of people on living way up here," Dwight said. "It's eight miles down the mountain to town, and in winter you could end up stuck up here for days. Not to mention the avalanche potential." He looked behind them, up the slope of Dakota Ridge.

"These aren't the kinds of homes people live in full-time," Gage said. He indicated the illustration on the sign. "People who build these kinds of places spend a few weeks in them at a time. When the weather gets bad they move to their villa in Tuscany or something."

"Let's take a look around," Travis said. He began walking, heading for a trio of curved metal air vents jutting up from a concrete pad.

"Looks like air vents," Dwight said. "Maybe venting an old mine, or an underground utility plant for the development."

"Maybe," Travis agreed. "They don't look that old, but maybe putting them in was one of the environmental requirements for building up here. Some of these old mines contain trapped gasses they might have had to vent."

"What exactly are we looking for?" Gage asked.

"Any signs of recent activity," Travis said. "I have a feeling whoever shot Eddie may have been coming from here."

"So you're thinking the shooting didn't have anything to do with the storage units?" Gage said.

"There wasn't any reason to shoot a man for digging through the ashes of a burned-out storage room," Travis said. "The fire destroyed everything, which even a casual observer could see. But if someone was coming over the ridge from this area—with something they didn't want anyone else to see—then they might be willing to kill for it."

The two brothers walked together along the development's main street, while Dwight explored among the foundations of buildings. "What does Eddie say about the shooter?" Gage asked.

"He doesn't remember anything," Travis said. "The knock on the head and the resultant concussion wiped out his short-term memory. He can't help us."

Mixed in among the modern foundations and survey markers were the signs of older occupation—weathered timbers with square iron nails and bent rusted spikes marked the path of tram lines that had carried raw ore from the mines. A new iron gate blocked the opening of a mine adit that had probably been constructed a hundred and fifty years before, and a rusting ore car positioned alongside the already-crumbling concrete foundation hinted at a future purpose as a flower planter.

"I may have something over here," Dwight called, about fifteen minutes into their search.

Gage and Travis joined him at the end of one of the streets, where the crumbling blacktop gave way to drying mud. Dwight pointed to a pair of impressions in the ground.

"Boots," Gage observed and squatted down for a closer look. "Some kind of work boots, or heavy-duty hiking boots."

"Army boots," Dwight said. "About a size thirteen from the looks of them. I've got the stuff in my unit to make casts of them if you want."

"Go ahead," Travis said. He walked from the mud in the direction of the storage units. Five feet farther on, he found a heel print that matched the boot print. Ten yards from there, he stood on a ledge that overlooked the storage facility and the end of Fireline Road.

"Sometimes you do know what you're doing," Gage said. He studied the ground at their feet. "I don't suppose we'd get lucky enough to find some shell casings."

"I think we're dealing with a pro," Travis said. "Someone who doesn't leave clues behind."

"The footprints were a mistake," Gage said.

"A mistake, or he knows they're not going to give us anything useful."

"It wasn't Jan Selkirk," Gage said.

"She was with Brenda when Eddie was shot," Travis said. "I'm not ruling her out for the murder, but not this. This was someone else."

"Come look at this." Dwight called them over.

On the back of a low rock wall that marked the boundary of the proposed resort, he had located tire imprints. "It's a good-sized truck," he said. "Not a tractor-trailer rig, but maybe a box truck. The tread pattern is still really sharp—they haven't had time to erode in the weather."

"So we know someone was up here," Travis said. He scanned the desolate surroundings. No trees grew taller than four feet, and the wind blew constantly. In summer, the sun burned through the thin air, fading paint, weathering wood and carrying an increased risk of skin cancer to anyone who stayed out in it very long. In winter, nighttime temperatures plunged to thirty below zero and snow piled up in drifts as tall as two-story buildings. Yes, the views were breathtaking, the air clear and the nighttime vista of stars unparalleled, but it seemed to Travis there were some places where it was better for people to visit and not try to dominate entirely.

They spent another half hour exploring the place, taking pictures and impressions of what they found. The few buildings that were intact were locked with heavy padlocks. "I'd love to see what's inside there," Travis said after he shook the door of a metal building half sunk in the side of a hill. "But I'd say our chances of getting a warrant to search this place are pretty much nil."

"Then why are we bothering with the impressions?" Gage asked.

"We had cause to come up here, tracking the shooter," Travis said. "If those impressions turn up anything, I'll make my case to a judge. But I'm not holding my breath we'll find anything."

They piled into their vehicles and headed back toward town. Halfway there, Travis got a call from Adelaide. "That writer, Alvin Exeter, is here in the office, demanding to speak with you," she said.

"Tell Mr. Exeter I have nothing to say to him."

"He says you'll want to talk to him," Adelaide said. "He says he has information about Eddie's shooting."

"Is he telling the truth, or only bluffing?" Travis asked.

"Well…" Adelaide paused, then said. "I don't know what kind of poker player he is, but I'm thinking you might want to talk to him."

Chapter Sixteen

Lacy had a restless night, replaying her interaction with Ian Barnes over and over again. By morning, she had decided she would tell Travis about Barnes and trust him to protect her and her family while dealing with Barnes's threats.

But when she came down to breakfast, she froze at the sight of a hunk of rusting metal resting in the middle of the kitchen table. She stared at it, a sinking feeling in her stomach that she had seen this artifact somewhere before—and recently. "What is that?" she asked.

"Your father thinks it's a piton," her mother said. "You know, the anchor things they drive into rock for climbers to attach safety lines to."

"Right." Lacy had a clear vision of a display of similar pitons on the wall in the Local Sports room at the history museum. "Where did you get it?" she asked.

Her father picked it up and turned it over in his hand. "The craziest thing—it was on the front porch this morning, right in front of the door. I can't imagine where it came from."

"Some climber probably dropped it in the street or it bounced out of a truck and the person who found it left it at the closest house," her mother said. "Though it looks old, antique, even."

"I thought if you were going to the museum again today you could take it down there," her father said. "Maybe they can use something like that—I sure can't."

Lacy had little doubt that she would find a missing space in the museum's display where, until yesterday afternoon, this exact piton had sat. Ian Barnes had brought it here and left it as a message to her. *I know where you live and I can practically come into your house without you ever knowing*, he was saying. *I can hurt you and the people you love and nothing you can do will stop me.*

"Lacy? Are you all right?" Jeanette put a hand on her daughter's shoulder. "You've gone all pale."

Lacy swallowed the bile that had risen in her throat. "I'm fine." She dropped into her chair at the table and forced a smile. "Nothing a cup of coffee won't fix."

"I'll wrap this up for you to take to the museum," her father said. "Tell Brenda hello from me."

Lacy had thought she would tell her parents that she had agreed to rent the apartment over Brenda's garage, but she needed to deal with Ian before she took that step. Living alone didn't seem like a good idea with him threatening her—and she needed to be near her parents to keep an eye on them.

"It's wonderful of you to help Brenda out at the museum." Lacy's mother placed a mug of coffee in front of her, then sat across from her. "That was so awful about Jan Selkirk. I couldn't believe it—her and Henry Hake. And Andy Stenson was blackmailing her?" She shook her head. "I couldn't say anything while Brenda was here yesterday, but it just goes to show you never can tell about people. I mean, I never would have thought Andy was a blackmailer, and I certainly wouldn't have picked Jan for a murderer."

"Mom, we don't know that Jan killed Andy," Lacy said. "We, of all people, should know better than to jump to conclusions about something so serious."

"Of course, dear." Jeanette stirred her coffee. "Still, someone killed Andy. I know it wasn't you, but knowing who really did it would finally put an end to all the speculation, and you wouldn't have any doubt hanging over your head. People think I haven't overheard their whispering. To some people you'll never be innocent until someone else is proven guilty."

"I don't care about those people," Lacy said. The only people she cared about were here in this room. And, well, Travis. She was beginning to care a great deal about him. Her gaze shifted once more to the rusted piton lying in the center of the table. She couldn't risk telling Travis about Ian. Not when there was so much at stake. She would never forgive herself if anything happened to her parents. And what if Ian hurt Travis?

She finished her breakfast, collected the piton her father had wrapped up for her and walked to the museum. She tried to slip through the door quietly, though the bell announced her arrival. The front room was empty, so she took the opportunity to tiptoe back to the Local Sports room and replace the piton in the display. By the time she made it back up front, Brenda had emerged from the workroom.

"I thought I heard you come in," Brenda said. "And just in time, too. The printer just delivered a bunch of brochures we have to fold and box up to hand out tomorrow. I'd forgotten Jan ordered them."

"I can definitely help with that," Lacy said, feigning cheerfulness. Though Brenda was as perfectly groomed and put together as ever, she had dark half-moons under her eyes, as if she, too, hadn't slept well last night. Between her hurt over the news about Andy and worry about her friend, Jan, she had a lot to deal with right now.

The two of them were well into the brochures when the bell over the door rang and Jan sashayed in. "Don't look so shocked to see me," she said. "There's lots of work to be done before tomorrow and until the town council relieves me of my duties, I'm still director of this museum."

She stashed her purse in the filing cabinet and locked the drawer, then turned to face them. "I'm only going to say this once, so pay attention. Brenda, I did not kill your husband. I was furious with him for extorting money from me and threatening to tell Barry about the affair, but really, I was furious with myself for getting into such a mess in the first place. I argued with Andy, but I never, never would have killed him. When I left his office that afternoon he was very much alive."

Brenda's eyes shone with tears. "I believe you," she said.

Jan turned to Lacy. "One of my biggest regrets is that I didn't speak out at your trial, when Wade Tomlinson told everyone he had seen you outside Andy's office that day. But I was too much of a coward. I told myself it didn't matter but I know I could have made a difference to you and I didn't. I don't blame you if you hate me for that."

Lacy told herself she should be angry with Jan, but the once-proud woman looked so pathetic. She seemed to have aged ten years overnight, her usually perfect manicured nails chipped and bitten, her lipstick crooked, her hair hanging limp. Jan would never be one of her favorite people, but she wasn't going to waste time hating her. "I'm through holding grudges," she said. Travis had taught her that lesson, hadn't he?

"What does Barry say?" Brenda asked.

Jan's expression grew more strained. "He's understandably upset, and he's moved into our guesthouse. But he's agreed we should see a counselor, so I'm hoping we can get past this."

"Did you know Henry Hake is missing?" Lacy asked. "I heard it on the news last night."

"I heard it, too," Jan said. "Travis contacted me to see if I knew anything about it. But I haven't seen the man in over a year, and we broke off our relationship before Andy died. That was one of the things I told Andy that day when I went to plead with him. I told Henry I couldn't take the stress and I wanted to try to make things better with Barry." She dropped into the chair behind the front counter. "Henry took the news much better than I expected. To tell you the truth, I was a little insulted that he took it so well. But I think I knew deep down inside that Henry was never really invested in a serious relationship. He's one of those perpetually distracted people—so many irons in the fire, so many deals and meetings. I was a bit of casual entertainment."

An awkward silence stretched between them, until Jan stood and picked up one of the brochures. "I'm not going to let my personal problems get in the way of making Pioneer Days as fabulous as possible. We have a lot of people counting on us."

"Right." Brenda picked up a stack of brochures. "Let's get to work, ladies."

ALVIN EXETER LOOKED as cocky as ever when Adelaide ushered him into Travis's office Friday afternoon, after Travis finally decided to talk to him. The writer offered a firm handshake, then dropped into the chair across from Travis's desk. "You're going to be glad you talked to me, Sheriff," he said. "All I ask in return is an interview for my book to get your side of the story. This is going to be great for both of us."

"I'm not interested in making any deals," Travis said. "If you know something that pertains to my case, you have an obligation to tell me."

"I don't know about that." Exeter pursed his lips. "After all, maybe I'm only speculating. And even if I did see something that might pertain to an investigation you're conducting, it's not a crime to keep it a secret, is it?"

"Then I have to ask myself—why would you say you know something about a shooting involving one of my officers unless you're an accessory to the crime?"

Exeter's mouth tightened. "There's no need to make threats."

Travis glared at the man. The guy really rubbed him the wrong way. "Either tell me what you know or quit wasting my time," he said.

Exeter sat back and crossed one leg over the other. "You suspect Jan Selkirk had something to do with the murder of Andrew Stenson," he said. "Don't deny it. The news is all over town. Her motive was that Stenson was blackmailing her over her affair with Henry Hake."

It was true what people said, Travis thought. You couldn't keep anything secret in a small town.

"So it stands to reason she's your chief suspect in the attack on Brenda Stenson and Lacy Milligan," Exeter continued. "As well as the explosion at the storage units."

"We haven't found any evidence linking her to those crimes," Travis said.

"But what if I could give you evidence?" Exeter uncrossed his legs and scooted to the edge of his chair. "That would be worth something to you, wouldn't it?"

"Get on with it, Exeter. I'm losing patience."

"What if I told you Jan Selkirk had an accomplice?" Exeter said. "A man who has the skills and the background to make him perfectly capable of running two women off the road or blowing up a building. And one who I don't think would hesitate to shoot a cop."

"Who are you talking about?" Travis asked.

Exeter grinned. "Ian Barnes."

Travis's heart beat a little faster at mention of the name. Barnes's military background certainly made him familiar with firearms, and explosives, too. And he had a certain menace about him. But looking tough didn't mean a man had broken the law. "What makes you think Jan and Barnes are working together?" he asked.

"Because I *saw* them. In the bar of the motel where I'm staying. Jan Selkirk was wearing sunglasses and a black wig, but I know it was her. She and Barnes had their heads together in a back booth, and then she handed over a stack of bills to him. He counted the money, slipped it into his wallet and told her she didn't have anything to worry about—he'd take care of things."

"What things?" Travis asked.

"He didn't elaborate, but I'm thinking it might be running those two women off the road, blowing up the storage unit—and maybe even shooting a cop."

Travis didn't know whether to be annoyed or intrigued by these revelations. "So you saw two people talking and one of them gave the other some money," he said. "That doesn't make either one of them guilty of a crime."

Exeter's expression hardened. "It does when one of them is a suspect in a murder case."

"Go back to your motel room and dream up a few more conspiracies, Exeter. Don't waste any more of my time."

The writer shoved to his feet. "You're not going to look into this?"

"I know how to do my job," Travis said. "You can leave now."

Exeter glared at Travis, then stormed out of the office. Adelaide swept in after him. "He didn't look too happy," she said.

"What's the local gossip about Ian Barnes?" Travis asked.

"Other than that it should be illegal for a man to look so good?" She grinned. "I heard he has PTSD, and that's what makes him so standoffish. He spends a lot of time in the mountains, climbing. I guess that's his big thing. He's friends with Wade and Brock, over at Eagle Mountain Outfitters. What else do you want to know?"

"Any links between him and Jan Selkirk?"

Adelaide hooted. "In her dreams. I think Jan's a little long in the tooth for Ian."

"Exeter said he saw them together and they were pretty cozy."

"If that's true, then she's more of a cougar than I ever expected," Adelaide said.

Travis rose and moved past Adelaide. "Where are you off to?" she asked.

"I'm going to have a chat with Mr. Barnes."

DWIGHT WAS ON DUTY, so Travis asked him to ride along to the Bear's Den B and B. Paige was clearly surprised to find two cops at her door. "Is there a problem?" she asked.

"We're looking for Ian Barnes," Travis said. "Is he around?"

"He checked out yesterday," she said.

"He wasn't going to stay around for the festival?" Dwight asked.

"He had a reservation through next week," Paige said. "But he said something had come up and he needed to leave." She shrugged. "I had a waiting list of people who wanted to stay here during the festival, so the early checkout didn't hurt me."

"Did he say why, exactly, he had to leave?" Travis asked.

"No, and I didn't ask. I believe in respecting people's privacy."

"So it didn't strike you as suspicious that he would leave so suddenly?" Travis asked.

"Work with the public long enough and nothing people do will surprise you," Paige said. "I thought maybe the idea of the crowds that are coming to town for the festival was stressing him out, so he decided to leave."

From the B and B, Travis and Dwight headed to Eagle Mountain Outfitters. Wade was manning the register and greeted the officers when they walked in. "No more sign of that shoplifter," he said.

"We're looking for Ian Barnes," Travis said.

"Haven't seen him for a couple of days," Wade said. "I think he was planning on doing some climbs out in Shakes Canyon. I'd have liked to go with him, but we've been too busy at the store."

"We were just over at the Bear's Den and Paige says he checked out yesterday afternoon," Travis said.

Wade frowned. "He didn't say anything to us. But then again, Ian's a different kind of guy."

"What do you mean by that?" Dwight asked.

"Oh, you know—standoffish. Not much for social niceties. He was probably just ready to leave and decided to go. It's a bummer, though, because he was supposed to help with the fireworks show tomorrow night."

"Why was Barnes helping with the fireworks?" Travis asked.

"Because he had experience with explosives in the military," Wade said. "We thought he'd be a natural to help set up the big fireworks display above town. The fire department and the Elks Club do most of the work, but they were happy to get an experienced volunteer."

"Where do they set up the display?" Dwight asked.

"Up the hills overlooking town. There's a big flat ledge there looking out over the town, with a backdrop of cliffs. The Elks cleared all the brush from the ledge years ago, so it makes the perfect spot to set up the explosives."

"Did Barnes say where he planned to head from here?" Travis asked.

"Nah. Ian doesn't like it when people ask too many questions. He's the kind of guy you have to accept at face value, on his own terms. He's an amazing climber, though. Being around him always ups my game."

They left the store. Out on the sidewalk, Travis studied the row of storefronts decorated for the festival. Tourists were swelling the population of the town and the festival promised to be bigger and better than ever. Not the time he wanted a possible shooter and arsonist on the loose. "Let's go talk to Jan," he said. "See what she knows."

"Where do we find her?" Dwight asked.

"Good question." Travis had assumed she would be at home, but what if her husband had kicked her out? He called the office. "Adelaide, where is Jan Selkirk staying right now?" he asked.

"She's still in her home. Barry moved into the guesthouse," Adelaide said. "But if you're looking for Jan, check the history museum. Amy Welch said she saw her over there this morning."

"Thanks."

They headed to the museum. Sure enough, Jan was there, along with Brenda and Lacy. "Hi, Travis," Lacy said, offering a wan smile. She was pale, with dark circles under her eyes, though the bruises from the accident had begun to fade. The stress of the whole situation with Jan must be getting to her.

He returned the smile, then turned to Jan. "We need to speak with you for a minute," he said.

He could tell she wanted to argue, but appeared to think better of doing so in front of Brenda and Lacy.

"Come back here," she said, motioning them to follow her into a room at the back of the building. She shut the door behind them. "I've answered all the questions I'm going to without my lawyer, Sheriff," she said.

"Just tell me where Ian Barnes is headed," Travis said. "He checked out of the B and B yesterday. I want to know where he went."

"How should I know where's he going?"

"Because the two of you are friends, aren't you?"

She looked away.

"I have a witness who saw you with him," Travis pressed. "You were at a motel bar, and you gave Barnes money."

Her face crumpled and she let out a strangled sob. The sudden breakdown of a woman who had always struck Travis as having ice water in her veins was shocking. "What do you have to tell us, Jan?" he asked.

"It wasn't supposed to turn out that way," she said through her tears. "That wasn't what I wanted at all."

"What wasn't what you wanted?" Travis asked. He led her to a chair and gently urged her down in it, then pulled up another chair opposite her, while Dwight stationed himself by the door. "Tell me about Ian Barnes."

She sniffed, and dabbed at her eyes with the tissue Travis handed her. "He was Henry Hake's bodyguard," she said. "I hadn't seen him for years and I didn't recognize him when he first came to town—when I knew him before, he had longer hair and a moustache. And he didn't call himself Ian Barnes then—he was Jim Badger. But he remembered me. He showed up at here at the museum late one evening, when I was working by myself. He said if I knew what was good for me, I wouldn't tell anyone I had known him before."

"Did he say why he was back in the area?"

She shook her head. "No, and I didn't ask."

"What about the money you gave him?"

"I think I'd better call my lawyer," she said.

"Call him," Travis said. "But I'm warning you now that when I find Barnes, I'm arresting him. If I find out you gave him money and he's involved in any of the other crimes I'm trying to solve—including the attack on Lacy and Brenda and the shooting of my deputy, I'll charge you as an accessory to attempted murder—and possibly murder." The threat was a bluff. While his suspicions were growing that Barnes was involved in the recent spate of local crimes—and maybe even Andy Stenson's murder—Travis didn't yet have enough proof to actually arrest him.

"I didn't have anything to do with any of those things," Jan said. She bit her lower lip so hard it bled.

Travis softened his voice. "If you need to tell me something, you should do it now," he said.

She glanced toward Dwight, then shifted her gaze back to Travis. "All right, I did give him money. I paid him to burn down the storage unit. I wanted to be sure Andy's files were destroyed, so that you wouldn't find out about my affair with Henry. He said he could set a fire and no one would ever figure out who did it. I didn't know he was going to put a bomb out there—or that you and Lacy would end up hurt." She grew more agitated. "I swear I didn't know."

Travis stood. "Call your lawyer," he said. "Then I want you both to report to the sheriff's department. Turn yourself in and we'll talk to the DA about the charges."

He left her sobbing, with Dwight standing guard.

Lacy met him outside the door. "What is going on?" she asked. "Is that Jan crying in there?"

"She's going to be all right," Travis said. "Are you okay?"

"A little stressed," she said, still watching the door to the workroom.

"It will all be over soon," Travis said. He touched her arm. "I can't say more, but trust me."

Her gaze met his and she nodded. More than anything just then, he wanted to kiss her, but the timing felt off. "I do trust you," she said.

"We're still on for the fireworks tomorrow night, right?" he said.

"Yes. I'm looking forward to it." Then she stood on tiptoe and gave him a quick kiss on the lips—a firm, warm pressure that sent a jolt of electricity through him. But before he could reach out and pull her closer, she had moved away. "I'd better let you get back to work," she said, and left the room.

But she had given him a good reminder of how much she was coming to mean to him. And of how much he wanted to clear this case, so that there would be nothing holding them back in the future.

Chapter Seventeen

Pioneer Days Festival in Eagle Mountain featured the kind of weather Coloradans love to brag about—balmy air, gentle breezes and a sky the color of blue china glaze, a few cottony clouds hanging around as if for the sole purpose of adding interest to photographs of the scenery. As it was, Lacy found herself part of that scenery. In her 1890s bathing costume, she handed out sugar cookies and lemonade and posed for photographs with families, children and a few grinning young men who flirted shamelessly but were otherwise harmless.

Crowds of people showed up to tour the museum, keeping Brenda and Lacy busy. Neither of them had seen or heard anything from Jan, who had left the museum the day before without saying a word. For once the town rumor mill wasn't churning with any information about the former mayor. Nobody had heard anything about her.

Mayor Larry Rowe made an appearance at the museum midafternoon to shake hands and congratulate everyone on helping to put together such a great festival. "Lacy, you're looking wonderful," he said, accepting a cup of lemonade. "I'm glad to see you're doing so well, making a fresh start."

What else was she supposed to do? she wondered, but she didn't voice the question out loud. She merely smiled and moved on to ladling more lemonade into cups.

Travis stopped by for a few minutes after the mayor left, but Lacy only managed to smile at him from behind the counter where she was pouring lemonade. He waved and moved on, but Lacy felt giddy from the brief encounter.

"You certainly look happy about something." Tammy, the reporter from the *Eagle Mountain Examiner*, focused her camera on Lacy. "Keep smiling like that." She clicked off half a dozen pictures, then studied the preview window of her camera. "Oh, those came out nice," she said. "You look great, and the museum and the crowds in the background might as well be an advertisement for Pioneer Days."

"I had no idea so many people would come to town for this," Lacy said.

"It's a draw," Tammy said. "Though we can thank the weather for the bigger-than-ever turnout, I think. And it's supposed to be perfect for the fireworks show tonight and, of course, the dance afterward." She snagged a sugar cookie from the tray to Lacy's left. "Only bad thing is that handsome Ian Barnes left town. I was hoping to wrangle at least one dance with that hunk. I probably wouldn't have worked up the nerve to ask him, but a girl can dream, right?" She took a bite of cookie.

"Ian left town?" Relief surged through Lacy.

"Yeah. Paige said he had reservations through the end of next week, but he came to her and said something had come up and he had to leave." She brushed cookie crumbs from the front of her shirt. "I'm thinking somebody told him about the crowds this festival attracts and he figured he didn't want to deal, you know?"

Lacy nodded absently. She leaned toward Tammy, her voice lowered. "Do you know what's up with Jan Selkirk?" she asked. "We haven't heard a word from her all day. It's like she's disappeared."

"Maybe she and her husband went away for a few days," Tammy said. "I heard they were trying to patch things up."

"Could she do that?" Lacy asked. "Would the sheriff let her leave town while the investigation is still ongoing?"

"I have no idea," Tammy said. "But I'll ask around. If I hear anything, I'll try to swing back by here and let you know."

"Thanks."

By six o'clock, when the museum closed, Lacy's feet ached and her head throbbed. But Travis had agreed to meet her at seven thirty. They planned to walk to the park and stake out a good spot from which to view the fireworks. They could do a little catching up while they waited for the show to begin, and maybe enjoy a glass of wine and a slice of pizza from one of the vendors in the park.

She walked back to the house without having to stop even once. The crowds had thinned and she guessed most of the tourists were eating supper or had headed to their hotels to change or put their feet up before the fireworks show and dance tonight. She let herself into the house and found a note on the hall table from her mom. "Having dinner with Dick and Patsy Shaw. Will probably get home after you leave. Love, Mom."

Lacy smiled. It was a rare occasion when she had the

house to herself. Too bad she didn't have time to enjoy it. She went upstairs and changed into capris and a knit tank with a matching cardigan for after dark, when the air would cool and she'd welcome another layer.

She still had half an hour before Travis would be here, so she poured a glass of iced tea and went out into the backyard. Here, where a wooden fence protected the space from hungry deer, her mother had created a sanctuary of flowers and fruit. Apple trees full of green apples gave way to paths lined with colorful hollyhocks. A copper birdbath and feeders attracted juncos, gold-finches, orioles and other birds, and wind chimes in the trees added their melody to the scene.

Lacy decided to pick a hollyhock for her hair, and headed toward a stand of dark pink blossoms near the back fence. As she leaned over to pluck the flower, something rustled in the bushes. Out of the corner of her eyes, she saw a flash of movement, then someone grabbed her from behind. She struggled as something was pulled over her head, blinding her, and she was thrown to the ground. "Make a sound and I swear I'll kill you now." The man's voice was low, his breath hot against her cheek. Something sharp pricked at the side of her breast and she sucked in a breath.

"That's right," the voice said. "Keep quiet or Mommy and Daddy will come home to find you butchered in their backyard."

AT SHORTLY AFTER SEVEN, Travis met Lacy's parents as they came up the walkway toward their house. "Are you coming to get Lacy?" Jeanette asked as George unlocked the front door.

"I stopped by the museum on my way over and

Brenda said she left about an hour ago to come home and change," he said, following them into the house.

"That old-fashioned swimsuit was so cute on her," Jeanette said. "Though she said the wool was a little itchy. Can you imagine wool for a swimsuit?" She stopped at the bottom of the stairs and called up. "Lacy! Travis is here!"

He waited, but heard no response. "Go on up," George said. "She's probably drying her hair or something and didn't hear you."

Travis climbed the stairs, though he heard no hair dryer or other noise as he neared the door to Lacy's room, which stood open. He paused in the doorway and knocked. "Lacy? Are you in here?" The antique swimsuit lay across the end of the neatly made bed. A laptop sat on her desk near the window, the top open but the machine shut off. Lacy's purse lay next to it, her phone tucked in a side pocket.

He checked the upstairs bathroom, and even peeked into a second bedroom he assumed belonged to her parents, but found no sign of Lacy.

"Did you find her?" Jeanette asked when he joined her and George in the kitchen.

"No. Her purse is on her desk in her room, but she's not upstairs."

George frowned. "That's odd. She's not down here." He looked at his wife.

"Maybe she decided to walk over to the park and meet you," Jeanette said.

"She would have taken her purse. Or at least her phone. It's upstairs in her purse." The bad feeling that had started when he had seen Lacy's empty bedroom was growing.

"Oh, this is just silly." Jeanette moved to the back

door. "She's probably sitting out here in the backyard and we're in here worrying."

But the Milligans' backyard was empty and silent, save for the faint sounds of celebration that drifted from the center of town and the gurgle of the creek just past their fence line. "Lacy!" Travis shouted.

But no answer came.

"What could have happened to her?" Jeanette clutched her husband's arm.

"She probably did walk downtown to meet me," Travis said, keeping his voice steady and his expression calm. "She's probably still not used to carrying a phone around with her and she forgot it. I'll go look for her."

"Let us know when you find her," George said.

"Of course."

He forced himself not to hurry out of the house, to assume the calm, easygoing saunter of a man who wasn't worried. But as soon as he was out of sight of the Milligans' home, he pulled out his phone and called Gage. "Lacy is missing," he said. "Spread the word to the others to keep an eye out for her."

"What do you mean, 'missing'?" Gage asked.

"She left the museum an hour ago and came home to change," Travis said. "Looks like she did that, but her purse and phone and keys are still here at her parents' house, only she's not."

"She probably just went downtown and forgot her phone," Gage said.

"I hope that's what happened," Travis said. "But I can't shake the feeling she's in trouble."

IAN BARNES HAD bundled Lacy into his Jeep and driven out of town, away from the crowds of people who might see her with him and act to help her. Once they had reached the vehicle, he had exchanged the knife for a gun and kept it pointed at her while he drove, one-handed, up a dirt road that led up Dakota Ridge.

"Where are you taking me?" she asked, hating the way her voice shook.

"I've been helping the Elks Club set up for the big fireworks show tonight," he said. "They were thrilled to get a guy with my experience with explosives to volunteer. They've cleared off a big ledge for the staging area for the show, but there's another ledge above that. Great view of the town, and when all the fireworks start going on, no one will be able to hear you when I kill you."

"Why are you going to kill me?" she asked, struggling to keep the tremor from her voice.

"Because you know too much."

"I don't know anything," she said. "Not anything to do with you."

"Some things you don't realize the significance of, but we can't risk you figuring them out later."

"Who is we?"

He gunned the Jeep up a steep slope, gravel pinging against the undercarriage, tires spinning until he gained traction. "That doesn't matter."

She stared at him, a cold, sick feeling washing over her. "You killed Andy, didn't you?" she asked.

Ian grinned. "I broke into the office while he was at lunch. I knew it was your day off and that he'd be alone. I hadn't counted on Jan coming by to see him, but it was easy enough to hide in the bathroom while she pleaded with him. She left out the back door and before he had time to even move, I stabbed him. He didn't suffer. I left by the back door and drove out of town."

"But why kill him?" she asked. "What did Andy ever do to you?"

"It was a job." He voice was matter-of-fact, as if he was talking about moving furniture or clearing brush. "He was poking his nose where it didn't belong. The people who hired me wanted him shut up."

"What was he poking his nose in?" She couldn't recall anything he had talked about, but that had been so long ago.

"I don't know and I don't care," Ian said.

"Did Henry Hake hire you?"

He laughed. "That loser? No. Hake had people above him who ran the show. They hired me."

"Why did you bother coming back to town? Why now?"

"I had a job to do."

"For the same people who hired you to kill Andy?"

"Maybe."

"Who are they?"

He glanced at her, his expression cold. "I don't see that that has anything to do with you."

"Were you the one who tried to run Brenda and me off the road that day?"

"Yes. I sacrificed a new truck to that one. It was hard, watching it go up in flames. But I had the old Jeep as backup."

"And the explosion?"

"Yeah, that was me. I miscalculated the delay on the timer, though. I should have set it for just a little longer."

"Did you shoot Travis's officer?"

"I can't tell you all my secrets, can I?" He parked the Jeep against a sheer rock face, shut off the engine, then leaned over and grabbed her by the arm. "Come on. The show starts in less than an hour. I want to be in place before everyone gets here."

TRAVIS PUSHED THROUGH the crowds of tourists and locals in the park, searching for Lacy. Once he thought he caught a glimpse of her dark hair in a group of women, but it turned out to be someone he had never seen before. As he circled the edge of the park, he came upon a group of firemen, climbing into the chief's truck. "Want to come help with the fireworks, Sheriff?" Assistant Fire Chief Tom Reynolds called.

"You don't need me in your way," Travis said.

"Come on," Tom urged. "We're a man short since Ian Barnes left town early."

"He left town?" a short, balding man next to Tom said. "That's funny, I could have sworn I saw his Jeep go by just a little while ago. I waved, but I guess he didn't see me."

"You saw Ian Barnes?" Travis asked.

"Yeah. I'm sure it was him. He had a woman with him."

Travis's heart pounded. "What did she look like?"

"I didn't see her face, but she had dark brown hair." He grinned. "Odds are, though, that she's a looker. A guy like that can have any woman he wants. My wife got this dazed look on her face every time she saw him."

"Which way was he headed?" Travis asked.

"The way we're going," the man said. "Hey, maybe he decided to stick around and help us and he went on ahead."

"Hey, Travis, where are you going?" Tom called as Travis took off across the park at a run.

Travis already had his phone out, calling Gage. "I

think Ian Barnes has Lacy," he said. "They're headed to that hill above town, where the Elks are getting ready to shoot off fireworks. Get Dwight and meet me up there. And alert Highway Patrol in case we need backup." He hung up as soon as his brother acknowledged the information. He had to get to Lacy. He only hoped he wasn't too late.

A LACEWORK PATTERN of glittering lights marked the town of Eagle Mountain, nestled in the valley below an uplift of mountains and cliffs. Lacy looked down at the town from the narrow ledge Ian had brought her to. Travis was down there somewhere, and her parents. They were probably wondering where she was, but she had no way of signaling to them, no way of letting them know what had happened to her.

Closer even than town, fifty feet below on a much larger ledge, a dozen men swarmed around the metal stands and boxes that contained the explosives set up for the fireworks display. If Lacy yelled, would they look up and see her here? Maybe—but if they did look up in response to her shout, likely all they would see was her death as Ian shot her. And then he would escape, driving away in his Jeep before anyone below had time to react.

"Come away from the edge," Ian said, and pulled her back against the cliff face. The gun dug hard into her side. "You don't want to fall, do you? A drop like that could kill you." He chuckled at his own joke, sending an icy tremor through her.

"Why are you doing this?" she asked again. "I haven't done anything to hurt you."

"It's nothing personal," he said. "It's a job. It pays well and it makes use of my talents." He leaned back against the cliff, his gaze still steady on her. "It's kind of a shame, though. I mean, you just got out of prison and you don't even get to enjoy a month of freedom before it's over. I'm sorry about that."

She looked away. How could she even comment on such an absurd statement?

"I was inside once," he said. "You did three years, right?"

"Yes."

"That's what I did, too. Course, I hear the women's prisons have it better than the men. But it wasn't too bad for me. I had friends inside and I knew how to work the system. You get respect, even inside, being a military veteran, and I never had to worry about anyone messing with me."

"I wouldn't know about that," she said.

"I remember you from before, you know," he said.

"From before what?"

"Before you went inside. When you worked for that lawyer."

"I don't remember you," she said. Surely she would remember if she had met him before.

"You never saw me. That's part of my job, too, not being seen. They won't see me when I kill you, and they won't see me when I leave."

She closed her eyes, not wanting him to read the fear there. Would those be the last words she ever heard?

THE BACK WHEELS of Travis's SUV skidded around a sharp curve as he trailed the fire department truck up the dirt road to the fireworks launch site. A number of men and vehicles were already at the site, their vehicles parked well away from the explosives, behind a protective wall of boulders. Travis drove right into the midst of the men working. "Something wrong, Sheriff?" one man asked, as Travis lowered his SUV's window.

"I'm looking for Ian Barnes," Travis said. "Have you seen him?"

"I haven't." The man looked around. "Anybody seen Ian Barnes?" he called.

"I thought he left town," someone said.

Tom walked up to Travis. "I don't see him or his Jeep," he said. "Maybe Walt was wrong about seeing him."

"I saw him." Walt walked up behind Tom. "But you're right that he's not here."

"Where else could he have gone?" Travis asked.

Both Tom and Walt registered confusion. "I don't know," Tom said. "There's nothing else up here."

Travis scanned the area. The road he had driven up continued past this ledge. "Where does that road go?" he asked.

"It just climbs up a little ways then peters out," Tom said. "There's an old mine site. I've been up there looking for artifacts, but it's pretty picked over. There's an adit, but the tunnel's full of water and the timbers are falling down, so it's not safe to go inside. There are warning signs posted, but no gate."

A flooded mine shaft. The perfect place to dispose of a body. Travis shut off the SUV and got out. "What are you doing?" Tom asked. "You can't just leave your vehicle here—not with the fireworks so close."

"Then you move it." Travis tossed him the keys. "I'm going up there to look around. When Gage and Dwight get here, tell them where I'm at."

"Okay, Sheriff," Tom said.

The noise and activity of the preparations for the fireworks show faded as Travis climbed. He kept to the shadows at the side of the road, moving stealthily, ears tuned to any sounds from above. The trail was steeper up here, and narrower, and Travis breathed hard on the climb. He doubted many people had the nerve to take a vehicle up something this steep, but Barnes apparently hadn't hesitated.

He crested the last rise and spotted Ian's Jeep first, the battered vehicle tucked in next to a cliff face. Freezing, he waited, listening. After a few seconds he heard the low murmur of voices—a man's, and then a woman's. A band tightened around his chest as he recognized Lacy's voice. He couldn't make out her words, but he felt the fear in her tone as a tightness in his own chest.

Travis drew his gun and began moving toward the voices, stealthily, placing one careful step at a time. By the time he reached the front bumper of the Jeep, he could make out the two shadowed figures against the cliff face and stopped.

He apparently hadn't been stealthy enough. "Step out where I can see you and toss your gun on the ground." Ian's voice was calm, the words chilling. "One wrong move and I'll blast her away right now."

Travis tossed the gun to the ground and raised his hands over his head. *Come on, Gage*, he thought. *Bring in the cavalry anytime now.*

"Come over here and stand next to your ladylove," Ian said. "When the fireworks start, I can shoot you both. And hurry up. They're almost ready."

At that moment, the first explosions from below shook the air. Lacy gave a cry of alarm and Ian turned to watch the first rockets soar overhead. "Now," he shouted, but before he could turn back to them and fire, Travis rushed him.

"Lacy, run!" Travis shouted.

LACY RAN, BUT not far. She made it only a few feet before she tripped and went sprawling. Gravel dug into her palms and her knees. Shaking with fear, she crawled to the cliff face and sat with her back against the rock wall, watching as Travis and Ian struggled on the ground. The two men rolled, grappling for the gun, while deafening explosions sounded overhead. Flashes of red and blue and gold illuminated the struggle, and bits of paper and ash rained down. Smoke and the smell of gunpowder stung her nose and eyes, but she blinked furiously and tried to keep track of what was happening.

Travis's discarded gun lay a few feet away. She crawled toward it and had almost reached it when a man stepped out of the shadows and scooped it up. "No offense, Lacy, but I'm probably a better shot with this than you are," Gage Walker said, joining her in the shadows.

"Are you alone?" she asked, looking over his shoulder.

"No. I've got Dwight and a couple of Highway Patrol deputies surrounding this place," he said. "But I'm not sure there's anything any of us can do right now but wait and hope one of us can get off a good shot."

Explosions continued to echo off the rocks. Lacy covered her ringing ears, but kept her eyes fixed on Travis and Ian, who continued to wrestle, gouging and kicking. In the flashes of light she thought Travis might be bleeding from a cut on his cheek, and Ian's shirt was torn. They rolled to the edge of the ledge, until Travis's feet hung over the edge. Lacy moaned. How could he win? He was in good shape, but Ian was phenomenal. She remembered Travis saying he wouldn't want to meet Ian in a dark alley. What about a dark mountain ledge?

The two men rolled away from the ledge, and Lacy let out her breath in a rush. Beside her, Gage did the same. She glanced over and saw that he was kneeling, steadying his gun with both hands, keeping it fixed on the two men as they moved. "All I need is one clear shot," he said in a lull between explosions.

The next round of volleys began, and then Travis was on top of Ian. He slammed the other man's head into the rocky ground, then lunged to his feet and staggered back.

"Freeze!" Gage yelled. "One move and I'll shoot."

"All right." Ian sat up, his hands over his head. "I give up." He struggled to his feet.

"I said freeze!" Gage shouted again, but already Ian had made his move, lunging toward Travis with a roar.

Gage fired, the explosion deafening, and Travis dodged to the side. With a scream that rose above the sound of fireworks and gunfire, Ian dove over the edge, the echo of his cry hanging in the air as he vanished.

Epilogue

"Goodbye, Jan. And good luck." Lacy faced the older woman, who had aged even more in the past few weeks. She had accepted a plea bargain in the charges against her involving her hiring of Ian Barnes to blow up the storage unit, and would serve a minimum of eighteen months in the Denver Women's Correctional Facility.

"It will be tough at first, but obey the rules and you'll get along fine," Lacy said. "Focus on doing your time and coming home."

"It helps a little, knowing you came out all right," Jan said. "I'm sorry again for all the trouble I caused you."

"I'm not worrying about the past anymore," Lacy said. "I'm focusing on the future, and so should you."

"You've got a lot to look forward to." Jan's gaze shifted to the man who stood behind Lacy.

Travis put a hand on Lacy's shoulder and nodded to Jan. "Good luck," he said. "I'll see you when you come home."

Jan turned away, and climbed into the sheriff's department van that would transport her to Denver. Lacy and Travis watched the van drive away. "I probably shouldn't, but I feel sorry for her," Lacy said.

"She brought it all on herself," Travis said. "And she got off lightly, considering."

She turned to face him and he pulled her close. She sighed—a sound of relief and contentment. "I'm just glad it's all over and you're all right."

"I'm all right. As for it being over—Henry Hake is still missing, you know."

In the whirl of activity in the days following the death of Ian Barnes, Lacy had forgotten all about the real estate developer. "No one has heard anything from him?" she asked.

"Not a word. According to the latest from Adelaide, public opinion is divided on whether he skipped town to avoid paying debts Eagle Mountain Resort had run up, or whether something has happened to him."

"Ian said people who were over Hake hired him to kill Andy," Lacy said. "Who was he talking about? I thought Henry Hake owned his own company."

"That's one thing I'm trying to find out," Travis said. "Ian may have been talking about investors—or maybe Hake had silent partners. And I'd like to know what Andy was looking into that got him killed. Knowing that might help me figure out who hired Barnes. Now that Exeter knows Barnes killed Andy, he has turned his focus to Barnes and Hake, as well."

"So there's still a lot of unanswered questions," Lacy said.

"I'm going to find the answers," Travis said. "It may take time, but I have plenty of that."

"Lacy! Travis!" Lacy looked up to see Brenda hurrying toward them. "Was that Jan leaving just now?" Brenda asked, a little out of breath as she joined them on the sidewalk in front of the sheriff's department.

"Yes," Travis said. "You just missed her."

"We said our goodbyes yesterday," Brenda said. "Though I meant to be here this morning. I got delayed at the museum." Brenda was the new director of the Eagle Mountain Historical Museum, a job that came with more responsibilities, but also a raise. Already, Lacy could see her friend blossoming in her new role.

"Have you seen Lacy's new apartment?" Brenda asked Travis. "She's fixed it up so cute."

"I have an invitation to dinner there tonight," Travis said.

Lacy hoped the blush that warmed her cheeks wasn't too evident. Now that she was settled into the apartment over Brenda's garage, she had invited Travis over for a little celebration, which she figured—hoped—would lead to him staying the night.

"I'd better get back to work," Travis said. "It was good seeing you, Brenda." He leaned over and kissed Lacy's cheek. "And I'll see you tonight."

"How are your parents taking the move?" Brenda asked, when Travis had disappeared inside the station.

"My mom cried, but then she cries at any change," Lacy said. "Truly, I think they're both happy for me." She and Brenda began walking back toward the museum.

"You may not need the apartment for long, if our county sheriff has a say in the matter," Brenda said.

"We've agreed to take it slowly," Lacy said. "I have a lot of adjustments to make. I start classes in just a few weeks. I'm pretty nervous about that."

"You'll do great." Brenda took her hand and squeezed it. "It's good to see you so happy. You deserve it."

"I'm happier than I ever thought I could be," Lacy

said. "While I was in prison, I told myself the key to surviving was to never give up. Now I know it can be just as important to have someone on the outside who will never give up on you."

"Travis was your someone," Brenda said.

"Yes." Travis Walker was her someone—her only one. The man who had saved her, and the one who had brought her back to herself. A man she thought she could love for a long time—for a lifetime.

* * * * *

DEPUTY DEFENDER

For Gaye

Chapter One

Yellow was such a cheerful color for a death threat. Brenda Stenson stared down at the note on the counter in front of her. Happy cartoon flowers danced across the bottom of the page, almost making the words written above in bold black ink into a joke.

Almost. But there was nothing funny about the message, written in all caps: BURN THAT BOOK OR YOU WILL DIE.

The cryptic message on the cheerful paper had been enclosed in a matching yellow envelope and taped to the front door of the Eagle Mountain History Museum. Brenda had spotted it when she arrived for work Monday morning, and had felt a surge of pleasure, thinking one of her friends had surprised her with an early birthday greeting. Her actual birthday was still another ten days away, but as her best friend, Lacy, had pointed out only two days ago, turning thirty was a milestone that deserved to be celebrated all month.

The message had been a surprise all right, but not a pleasant one. Reading it, Brenda felt confused at first, as if trying to make sense of something written in a foreign language or an old-fashioned, hard-to-read script. As the message began to sink in, nausea rose in her throat, and she held on to the edge of the counter, fighting dizziness. What kind of sick person would send something like this? And why? What had she ever done to hurt anybody, much less make them wish she were dead?

The string of sleigh bells attached to the museum's front door jangled as it opened and Lacy Milligan sauntered in. That was really the only way to describe the totally carefree, my-life-is-going-so-great attitude that imbued every movement of the pretty brunette. And why not? After three years of one bad break after another, Lacy had turned the corner. Now she was in school studying to be a teacher and engaged to a great guy—who also happened to be county sheriff. As her best friend, Brenda couldn't have been happier for her—and she wasn't about to do anything to upset Lacy's happiness. So she slid the threatening note off the counter and quickly folded it and inserted it back into the envelope, and dropped it into her purse.

"No classes today, so I thought I'd stop by and see what I could do to help," Lacy said. She hugged Brenda, then leaned back against the scarred wooden desk that was command central at the museum.

"I can always use the help," Brenda said. "But you're putting in so many hours here I'm starting to feel really guilty about not being able to pay you. If the fundraising drive is successful, maybe there will be enough left over to hire at least part-time help."

"You already rented me the sweetest apartment in town," Lacy said. "You don't have to give me a job, too."

"I'll never find anyone else who's half as fun for that garage apartment," Brenda said. "At least if I could give you a job, I'd still be guaranteed to see you on a regular basis after you're married."

"You'll still see plenty of me," Lacy said. "But hey—I hear Eddie Carstairs is looking for a job."

Brenda made a face. "I seriously doubt an ex–law enforcement officer is going to want a part-time job at a small-town museum," she said.

"You're probably right," Lacy said. "Eddie certainly thinks highly of himself. He's been going around town telling everyone Travis fired him because he was jealous that Eddie got so much press for being a hero, almost dying in the line of duty and all." Her scowl said exactly what she thought of her fiancé's former subordinate. "Obviously that bullet he took didn't knock any sense into him. And as Travis told him when he fired him, Eddie wasn't on duty that day and he wasn't supposed to be messing around at a crime scene. And he wasn't a full deputy anyway—he was a reserve officer. Eddie always fails to mention that when he tells his tales of woe down at Moe's Pub."

"Is Travis as upset about this as you are?" Brenda asked. She had a hard time picturing their taciturn sheriff letting Eddie's tall tales get to him.

"He says we should just ignore Eddie, but it burns me up when that little worm tries to make himself out to be a hero." Lacy hoisted her small frame up to sit on the edge of the desk. "Travis is the one who risked his life saving me from Ian Barnes."

"And anyone who counts knows that," Brenda said. Ian Barnes—the man who had killed Brenda's husband three years before—had kidnapped Lacy and tried to kill her during the town's Pioneer Days celebration two months ago. Travis had risked his life to save her, killing Ian in the struggle.

"You're right," Lacy said. "And I'm sorry to be unloading on you this way. You've got bigger things to worry about." She glanced around the museum's front room, comprising the reception desk and a small book-store and gift shop. Housed in a former miner's cottage, the museum featured eight rooms devoted to differ-ent aspects of local history. "How's the fund-raising going?"

"I've applied for some grants, and sent begging let-ters to pretty much every organization and influential person I can think of," Brenda said. "No response yet."

"What about the auction?" Lacy asked. "Are you getting any good donations for that?"

"I am. Come take a look." She led the way through a door to the workroom, where a row of folding tables was rapidly filling with donations people had contrib-uted for a silent auction, all proceeds to benefit the struggling museum. "We've gotten everything from old mining tools to a gorgeous handmade quilt, and a lovely wooden writing desk that I think should bring in a couple hundred dollars."

"Wow." Lacy ran her hand over the quilt, which fea-tured a repeating pattern of squares and triangles in shades of red and cream. "This ought to bring in a lot of bids. I might have to try for it myself."

"My goal is to make enough to keep the doors open and pay my salary until we can get a grant or two that will provide more substantial funds," Brenda said. "But what we really need is a major donor or two who will pledge to provide ongoing support. When Henry Hake disappeared, so did the quarterly donations he made to the museum. He was our biggest supporter."

"And here everybody thought old Henry was only interested in exploiting the town for his rich investors,"

Lacy said. "I wonder if we'll ever find out what happened to him. Travis won't say so, but I know since they found Henry's car in that ravine, they think he's probably dead."

Henry Hake was the public face of Hake Development and Eagle Mountain Resort, a mountaintop luxury development that had been stalled three and a half years ago when a local environmental group won an injunction to stop the project. Brenda's late husband, Andy, had been a new attorney, thrilled to win the lucrative job of representing Hake. But Hake's former bodyguard, Ian Barnes, had murdered Andy. Lacy, who had been Andy's administrative assistant, had been convicted of the murder. Only Travis's hard work had freed her and eventually cleared her name. But then Henry had disappeared. And only last month, a young couple had been murdered, presumably because they saw something they shouldn't have at the dormant development site. Travis's brother, Gage, a sheriff's deputy, had figured that one out and tracked down the couple's killers, but the murderers had died in a rockslide, after imprisoning Gage and schoolteacher Maya Renfro and her five-year-old niece in an underground bunker that contained a mysterious laboratory. A multitude of law enforcement agencies was still trying to untangle the goings-on at the resort—and no one seemed to know what had happened to Henry Hake or what the young couple might have seen that led to their murders.

"I guess I don't understand how these things work," Lacy said. "But it doesn't seem very smart to base a budget on the contributions of one person. What if Henry had suddenly decided to stop sending checks?"

"Henry's contributions were significant, but they

weren't all our budget," Brenda said. "When I started here four years ago, we had a comfortable financial cushion that generated enough income for most of our operating expenses, but that's gone now." Her stomach hurt just thinking about it.

"Where did it go?" Lacy asked. But the pained expression on Brenda's face must have told her the truth. "Jan!" She hopped off the desk. "She siphoned off the money to pay the blackmail!" She put her hand over her mouth, as if she wished she could take back the words. "I'm so sorry, Brenda."

Brenda had learned only recently that before his death, Andy had been blackmailing her former boss, Eagle Mountain mayor Jan Selkirk, over her affair with Henry Hake. "It's all right," she said. "I can't prove that's what happened, but probably. But if that is what happened, I don't know where the money went. I mean, yeah, Andy used some of it for the improvements on our house, and to buy some stuff, but not the tens of thousands of dollars we're talking about."

"Maybe Jan was giving the money to Henry, and his donations were his guilty conscience forcing him to pay you back," Lacy said.

"That would fit this whole sick soap opera, wouldn't it?" Brenda picked up a battered miner's lantern and pretended to examine it.

Lacy rubbed Brenda's shoulder. "None of this is your fault," she said. "And you're doing an amazing job keeping the museum going. These auction items should pull in a lot of money. Didn't you tell me that book you found is worth a lot?"

The book. A shudder went through Brenda at the thought of the slim blue volume she had found while going through Andy's things a few weeks ago. *The Secret History of Rayford County, Colorado.* What had at first appeared to be a run-of-the-mill self-published local history had turned out to be a rare account of a top-secret government program to produce biological weapons in the remote mountains of Colorado during World War II. Was that what had whoever left the threatening note so upset? Did they object to the government's dirty secrets being aired—even though the operation had ended seventy years ago?

In any case, Brenda's online research had revealed an avid group of collectors who were anxious to get their hands on the volume, and willing to pay for the privilege. Thus was born the idea of an auction to fund the museum—and her salary—for the immediate future.

"I still can't imagine what Andy was doing with a book like that," she said. "But I guess it's obvious I didn't know my husband as well as I thought."

"Whyever he had it, I'm glad it's going to help you now," Lacy said.

The local paper had run an article about the fundraiser, and listed the book among the many donations received. That must be where the letter writer had found out about it. Was it just some crank out to frighten her? Could she really take seriously a letter written on yellow stationery with cartoon flowers?

But could she really afford not to take it seriously? She needed to let someone else know about the threat—someone with the power to do something about it. "Can you do me a favor and watch the museum for a bit?" Brenda asked.

"Sure." Lacy looked surprised. "What's up?"

"I just have an errand I need to run." She retrieved

her purse from beneath the front counter and slung it over her shoulder. "It shouldn't take more than an hour." She'd have to ask the sheriff to keep the letter a secret from his fiancée, at least for now. In fact, Brenda didn't want anyone in town to know about it. She had been the focus of enough gossip since Andy's murder. But she wasn't stupid enough to try to deal with this by herself. She figured she could trust the Rayford County Sheriff's Department to keep her secret and, she hoped, to help her.

DEPUTY DWIGHT PRENTICE would rather face down an irate motorist or break up a bar fight than deal with the stack of forms and reports in his inbox. But duty—and the occasional nagging from office manager Adelaide Kincaid—forced him to tackle the paperwork. That didn't stop him from resenting the task that kept him behind his desk when Indian summer offered up one of the last shirtsleeve days of fall, the whole world outside bathed in a soft golden light that made the white LED glare of his office seem like a special kind of torture.

As he put the finishing touches on yet another report, he wished for an urgent call he would have to respond to—or at least some kind of distraction. So when the buzzer sounded that signaled the front door opening, he sat back in his chair and listened.

"I need to speak with Travis."

The woman's soft, familiar voice made Dwight slide back his chair, then glance at the window to his left to check that the persistent cowlick in his hair wasn't standing up in back.

"Sheriff Walker is away at training." Adelaide spoke

in what Dwight thought of as her schoolmarm voice—
very precise and a little chiding.

"Could I speak to one of the deputies, then?"

"What is this about?"

"I'd prefer to discuss that with the deputy."

Dwight rose and hurried to head off Adelaide's further attempts to determine the woman's business at the
sheriff's department. The older woman was a first-class
administrator, but also known as one of the biggest gossips in town.

"Hello, Brenda." Dwight stepped into the small reception area and nodded to the pretty blonde in front
of Adelaide's desk. "Can I help you with something?"

"Mrs. Stenson wants to speak to a deputy," Adelaide said.

"That would be me." Dwight indicated the hallway
he had just moved down. "Why don't you come into
my office?"

As he escorted her down the hall, Dwight checked
her out, without being too obvious. Brenda had been a
pretty girl when they knew each other in high school,
but she had matured into a beautiful woman. She had
cut a few inches off her hair recently and styled it in
soft layers. The look was more sophisticated and suited
her. He had noticed her smiling more lately, too. Maybe
she was finally getting past the grief for her murdered
husband.

She wasn't smiling now, however. In his office, she
took a seat in the chair Dwight indicated and he shut
the door, then slid behind his desk. "You look upset,"
he said. "What's happened?"

In answer, she opened her purse, took out a bright
yellow envelope, and slid it across the desk to him.

He looked down at the envelope. BRENDA was written across the front in bold black letters, all caps. "Before I open it, tell me your impression of what's in it," he said.

"I don't know if it's some kind of sick joke, or what," she said, staring at the envelope as if it were a coiled snake. "But I think it might be a threat." She knotted her hands on the edge of the desk. "My fingerprints are probably all over it. I wasn't thinking…"

"That's all right." Dwight opened the top desk drawer and took out a pair of nitrile gloves and put them on. Then he turned the envelope over, lifted the flap and slid out the single sheet of folded paper.

The capital letters of the message on the paper were drawn with the same bold black marker as the writing on the envelope. BURN THAT BOOK OR YOU WILL DIE.

"What book?" he asked.

"I can't be sure, but I think whoever wrote that note is referring to the rare book that's part of the auction to raise funds for the museum. It's an obscure, self-published volume purportedly giving an insider's experiences with a top-secret project to manufacture biological weapons for use in World War II. The project was apparently financed by the US government and took place in Rayford County. I found it in Andy's belongings, mixed in with some historical law books. I have no idea how he came to have it, but apparently it's an item that's really prized by some collectors—because it's rare, I guess. And maybe because of the nature of the subject matter."

Dwight grabbed a legal pad and began making notes. Later, he would review them. And he would need them for the inevitable report. "Who knew about this book?" he asked.

"Lots of people," she said. "There was an article in the *Examiner*."

"The issue that came out Thursday?"

She nodded. "Yes."

He riffled through a stack of documents on his desk until he found the copy of the newspaper. The article was on the front page. Rare Book to Head Up Auction Items to Benefit Museum—accompanied by a picture of Brenda holding a slim blue volume, the title, *The Secret History of Rayford County, Colorado*, in silver lettering on the front. "How much is the book worth?" he asked.

"A dealer I contacted estimated we could expect to receive thirty to fifty thousand dollars at a well-advertised auction," she said. "I thought that in addition to the money, the auction would generate a lot of publicity for the museum and maybe attract more donors."

"People will pay that much money for a book?" Dwight didn't try to hide his amazement.

"I was shocked, too. But apparently, it's very rare, and there's the whole top-secret government plot angle that collectors like."

"But this note wasn't written by a collector," he said. "A collector wouldn't want you to burn the book."

"I know." She leaned toward him. "That's why I'm wondering if the whole thing is some kind of twisted joke. I mean—that cheerful yellow paper..." Her voice trailed away as they both stared at the note.

"Maybe it's a joke," he said. "But we can't assume anything. Has anyone said anything to you about the book since this article ran?" He tapped the newspaper. "Anything that struck you as odd or 'off'?"

"No. The only thing anyone has said is they hope we get a lot of money for the museum. A couple of people said they couldn't imagine who would pay so much for a book, and one or two have said the subject matter sounded interesting. But no one has seemed upset or negative about it at all."

"Where is the book now?" he asked.

"It's at the museum."

The old-house-turned-museum wasn't the most secure property, from what Dwight could remember about it. "Do you have a security system there—alarms, cameras?"

She shook her head. "We've never had the budget for that kind of thing. And we've never needed it. We just have regular door locks with dead bolts, and we keep the most valuable items in our collection in locked cases. But we don't really have much that most people would find valuable. I mean, antiques and historical artifacts aren't the kind of thing a person could easily sell for quick cash."

"But this book is different," Dwight said. "It's worth a lot of money. I think you had better put it somewhere else for now. Somewhere more secure."

"I was thinking of moving it to a safe at my house."

"That sounds like a good idea." He stood. "Let's go do that now."

"Oh." She rose, clearly flustered. "You don't have to do that. I can—"

"I'd like to see this book, anyway." He gestured to the door, and she moved toward it.

"I'll meet you at the museum," he said when they reached the parking lot.

She nodded and fished her car keys out of her purse,

then looked at him again, fear in her hazel eyes, though he could tell she was trying hard to hide it. "Do you think I'm really in danger?" she asked.

He put a hand on her arm, a brief gesture of reassurance. "Maybe not. But there's no harm in being extra careful."

She nodded, then moved to her car. He waited until she was in the driver's seat before he got into his SUV, suppressing the urge to call her back, to insist that she ride with him and not move out of his sight until he had tracked down the person who threatened her. He slid behind the wheel and blew out his breath. This was going to be a tough one—not because they had so little to go on to track down the person who had made the threat, but because he was going to have to work hard to keep his emotions out of the case.

He started the vehicle and pulled out onto the street behind Brenda's Subaru. He could do this. He could investigate the case and protect Brenda Stenson without her finding out he'd been hopelessly in love with her since they were both seventeen.

Chapter Two

Brenda had come so close to asking Dwight if he would drive her to the history museum in the sheriff's department SUV. She felt too vulnerable in her own car, aware that the person who wrote that awful note might be watching her, maybe even waiting to make good on his threat. She shuddered and pushed the thought away. She was overreacting. Dwight hadn't seemed that upset about the note. And really, who could take it seriously, with the yellow paper and cartoon flowers?

She had always admired Dwight's steadiness. When they had been in high school, he was one of the stars on the basketball team. As a cheerleader, she had attended every game and watched him lope up and down the gym on his long legs. She had watched all the players, of course, but especially him. He had thick chestnut hair and eyes the color of the Colorado sky in a ruggedly handsome face. There was something so steady about him, even then. Like many of her classmates, he was the son of a local rancher. He wore jeans and boots and Western shirts and walked with the swaggering gait that came from spending so much time on horseback.

A town girl, she didn't have much in common with him, and was too shy to do more than smile at him in the hall. He always returned the greeting, but that was as far as it went. He'd never asked her out, and after graduation, they'd both left for college. She had returned to town five years later as a newlywed, her husband, Andy, anxious to set up his practice in the small town he had fallen in love with on visits to meet her family. Dwight returned a year later, fresh from military service in Afghanistan. Brenda would have predicted he would go to work on the family ranch—the choice of law enforcement surprised her. But the job suited him— the steadiness and thoughtfulness she had glimpsed as a teen made him a good cop. One she was depending on to help her through this latest crisis.

When they entered the history museum, Lacy was talking to a wiry young man with buzzed hair and tattoos covering both forearms. "Brenda!" Lacy greeted them, then her eyebrows rose as Dwight stepped in behind her. "And Dwight. Hello." She turned to the young man. "Brenda is the person you need to talk to."

"Hello, Parker," Dwight said.

"Deputy." The young man nodded, his expression guarded.

"This is Parker Riddell," Lacy said. "Paige Riddell's brother. Parker, this is Brenda Stenson, the museum's director."

Paige ran the local bed-and-breakfast and headed up the environmental group that had stopped Henry Hake's development. Brenda couldn't recall her ever mentioning a brother. "It's nice to meet you," she said, offering her hand. "How can I help you?"

Parker hesitated, then took it. "I was wanting to volunteer here," he said.

"Are you interested in history?" Brenda asked.

"Yeah. And my sister said you could use some help, so…" He shrugged.

"Well, yes. I can always use help. But now isn't really a good time. Could you come back tomorrow?"

"I guess so." Parker cut his eyes to Dwight. "Is something wrong?"

"No. Deputy Prentice is here to discuss security for our auction." Brenda forced a smile. That sounded like a reasonable explanation for Dwight's presence, didn't it? And not that far from the truth.

"Okay, I guess I'll come back tomorrow." Keeping his gaze on Dwight, he sidled past and left, the doorbells clanging behind him.

"What was that about?" Lacy asked Dwight. "He was looking at you like you were a snake he was afraid would strike—or a bug he wanted to stomp on."

"Let's just say Parker has a rocky history with law enforcement. I'd be careful about taking him on as a volunteer."

He sounded so serious. "Do you think he's dangerous?" Brenda asked.

Dwight shifted his weight. "I just think he's someone who should be watched closely."

"I'll keep that in mind." Brenda turned to Lacy. "Thanks for looking after things here while I was gone. You can go home now. I'm going to go over some things with Dwight, then close up for lunch."

Lacy gave her a speculative look, but said nothing. "We'll talk later," she said, then collected her purse and left.

Brenda crossed her arms and faced Dwight. "What's the story on Parker Riddell?" she asked.

He rubbed the back of his neck. "I probably shouldn't tell you."

"This is a very small town—you know I'll find out eventually. If anyone links the information back to you, you can tell them I was doing a background check prior to taking him on as a volunteer. That's not unreasonable."

"All right." He leaned back against the counter facing her. "He got into trouble with drugs, got popped for some petty theft, then a burglary charge. He did a little jail time, then went into rehab and had a chance at a deferred sentence."

"What does that mean?" she asked.

"It means if he keeps his nose clean, his record will be expunged. I take it he came to live with Paige after he got out of rehab to get away from old friends and, hopefully, bad habits. And I hope he does that. That doesn't mean I think it's the best idea in the world for you to spend time alone with him, or leave him alone with anything around here that's valuable."

"Do you think he might have sent the note?"

He frowned. "It doesn't fit any pattern of behavior he's shown before—at least that I know of. But I can look into it. I *will* look into it."

"I can't think of anyone who would do something like that," she said. "I mean, anonymous notes—it's so, well, sleazy. And over a stupid book."

"Show me the book."

"It's back here." She led the way into the workroom, to a file drawer in the back corner. She had placed *The Secret History of Rayford County, Colorado* inside an acid-free cardboard box. She opened the box and handed the book to Dwight.

He read the title on the front, then opened it and flipped through it, stopped and read a few lines. "It's a little dry," he said.

"Some parts are better than others," she said. "Collectors are mainly interested because of the subject matter and its rarity."

He returned the book to her. "Maybe someone is upset that this top-secret information has been leaked," he said.

"The whole thing happened seventy years ago," she said. "As far as I can determine, most of the details about the project are declassified, and all the people who took part are long dead."

"A relative who's especially touchy about the family name?" Dwight speculated. "Someone related to the author?" He examined the spine of the book. "S. Smith."

"The research I did indicated the name is probably a pseudonym," Brenda said. "In any case, since the author was supposedly part of the project, he would most likely be dead by now. Since his real identity has never been made public, what is there for the family to be upset about?"

"Someone else, then," Dwight said.

"Are there any new suspicious people hanging around town?" she asked.

He shook his head. "No one who stands out."

"Except Parker," she said.

"I'll check into his background a little more, see if I can find a connection," he said. He turned to survey the long table that took up much of the room. "Are these the items for the auction?"

"Everything I've collected so far," she said. "I still have a few more things people have promised."

He picked up a set of hand-braided reins and a silver-trimmed bridle. "You've got a lot of nice things. Should net you a good bit of money."

"I hope it's enough," she said. "I don't suppose you have any hope of finding Henry Hake alive and well and enjoying an island vacation, have you? He was our biggest donor."

Dwight shook his head. "I don't expect any of us will be seeing Henry Hake again," he said. "At least not alive."

"I figured as much. So all we need is another wealthy benefactor. I'm hoping that rare book will attract someone like that—someone with money to spare, who might enjoy getting credit for pulling us out of the red."

"What will happen if that benefactor doesn't materialize?" he asked.

She straightened her shoulders and put on her brave face—one she had had plenty of practice assuming since Andy's death. "I'll have to find another job. And this town will lose one of its real assets."

"I hope we won't lose you, too," he said.

The intensity of his gaze unsettled her. She looked away. "Sometimes I think leaving and starting over would be a good idea," she said. "But I love Eagle Mountain. This is my home, and I'm not too anxious to find another one."

"Then I hope you never have to."

The silence stretched between them. She could feel his eyes still on her. Time to change the subject. "Lacy was telling me Eddie Carstairs has been mouthing off to people about his getting fired, trying to stir up trouble."

"Eddie's sore about losing his job, but Travis did the right thing, firing him. Any other department would have done the same. The fact that he's making such a fuss about something that was his own fault shows he doesn't have the right temperament for the job. You can't be hotheaded and impulsive and last long in law enforcement."

Dwight had never been hotheaded or impulsive. He was the epitome of the cool, deliberate, hardworking cowboy. She replaced the book in the box and fit the lid on it. "I don't want to keep you any longer. I'll close a little early for lunch and you can follow me to the house—though that probably isn't necessary."

"No harm in taking precautions." He followed her into the front room, where she collected her purse, turned down the lights, then turned the sign on the front door to Closed. "After we secure the book in your safe, maybe I could take you to lunch," he said.

The invitation surprised her so much she almost dropped the book. Was Dwight asking her out on a *date*? *You're not in high school anymore*, she reminded herself. He was probably just being friendly. Her first instinct was to turn him down. She had too much to do. She wasn't ready to go out with another man.

Andy's been dead three and a half years. When are *you going to be ready?*

"Thanks," she said. "That would be nice."

He walked her to her car, and when his arm brushed hers briefly as he reached out to open the door for her, a tremor went through her. Why was she acting like this? She wasn't a schoolgirl anymore, swooning over a crush—but that's what being with Dwight made her feel like all of a sudden.

She murmured, "Thanks," as she slid past him into the driver's seat and drove, sedately, toward her home.

She laughed at herself, being so careful to keep under the speed limit. Did she really think Dwight would suddenly switch on his lights and siren and give her a ticket?

The house she and Andy had purchased when they moved back to Eagle Mountain had undergone extensive remodeling, expanding from a tiny clapboard-sided bungalow to a larger cottage trimmed in native rock and including a detached two-car garage with an apartment above. Only recently, Brenda had learned that those renovations had been financed not by Andy's law practice, as she had thought, but with money he received from people he blackmailed, including her former boss, Jan Selkirk. The knowledge had made her feel so ashamed, but people had been surprisingly kind. No one had suggested—at least to her face—that she had been guilty of anything except being naive about her husband's activities.

She pulled into the driveway that ran between the house and the garage and Dwight parked the sheriff's department SUV behind her. That would no doubt raise some eyebrows among any neighbors who might be watching. Then again, considering all that had happened in the past three and a half years, from Andy's murder to the revelations about his blackmail and Jan's attempts to steal back evidence of her involvement in the blackmail, everyone in town was probably used to seeing the cops at Brenda's place.

Dwight met her on the walkway that led from the drive to the front steps. "You haven't had any trouble around the house, have you?" he asked. "No mysterious phone calls or cars you don't recognize driving by? Any door-to-door salesmen who might have been casing the place?"

"If door-to-door salesmen still exist, they aren't in Eagle Mountain." She led the way up the walk, keys in hand.

He smiled at her, and her heart skipped a beat again. He really did have the nicest smile, and those blue, blue eyes—

The eyes hardened, and the smile vanished. She realized he wasn't focused on her anymore, but on her front door. She gasped when she saw the envelope taped there—a bright yellow envelope. Like a birthday card, but she was pretty sure it wasn't. Her name, printed in familiar bold black lettering, was written on the front.

Dwight put his hand on her shoulder. "Wait before you touch it. I want to get some photographs."

He took several pictures of the note taped to the door, from several different angles, then moved back to examine the steps and the porch floor for any impressions. He put away his phone and pulled on a pair of thin gloves, then carefully removed the note from the door, handling it by the edges and with all the delicacy one would use with a bomb.

Meanwhile, Brenda hugged her arms across her stomach and did her best not to be sick in the lilac bushes. Dwight laid the envelope on the small table beside the porch glider and teased open the flap.

The note inside was very like the first—yellow paper, dancing cartoon flowers. He coaxed out the sheet and unfolded it. Brenda covered her mouth with her hand. Taped to the top of the paper was a photograph—a crime scene photo taken of Andy at his desk, stabbed in the chest, head lolling forward. Brenda squeezed her eyes shut, but not before she had seen the words written below the photograph. THIS COULD BE YOU.

Chapter Three

Dwight could feel Brenda trembling and rushed to put his arm around her and guide her over to a cushioned lounge chair on the other side of the porch, away from the sick photo. He sat beside her, his arm around her, as she continued to shudder. "Take a deep breath," he said. "You're safe."

She nodded, and gradually the trembling subsided. Her eyes met his, wet with unshed tears. "Why?" she whispered.

"I don't know. I'm going to look at the note again. Will you be okay if I do that?"

"Yes." She straightened. "I'm fine now. It was just such a shock." She was still pale, but determination straightened her shoulders, and he didn't think she would faint or go into hysterics if he left her side.

He stood and returned to the note on the table. The image pasted onto the paper wasn't a photograph, but a photocopy of a photograph. Dwight couldn't be sure, but this didn't look like something that would have run in the newspaper. It looked like a crime scene photo, the kind that would have been taken before Andy Stenson's body was removed from his office and then become part of the case file.

"Have you ever seen this photograph before?" he asked Brenda.

"I think so," she said. "At Lacy's trial."

Dwight nodded. Lacy Milligan had been wrongfully convicted of murdering her boss. At the trial, the prosecution would have shown crime scene photos as evidence of the violence of the attack.

"Who would have had access to those photos?" Brenda asked. "Law enforcement, the lawyers—"

"Anyone who worked at the law offices or the courtroom," Dwight said. "Maybe even the press. This isn't one of the actual photos—it's a photocopy. The person who wrote the note included it to frighten you."

"Well, they succeeded." She stood and began pacing back and forth, keeping to the side of the porch away from the note and its chilling contents. "Dwight, what are we going to do?"

He liked that "we." She was counting on him to work with her—to help her. "You could burn the book," he said.

She stopped pacing and stared at him. "And give in to this creep's demands? What's to stop him from demanding something else? Maybe next time he'll suggest I burn down my house, or paint the museum pink. Maybe he gets off on making people do his bidding." Her voice rose, and her words grew more agitated— but it was better than seeing her so pale and defeated-looking.

"I'm not saying you should burn the book, only that it was one option."

"I'm not going to burn the book. We need to find out who this person is and stop him—or her."

She was interrupted by a red car pulling to the curb

in front of the house. Lacy got out and hurried up the walk, smiling widely. "Hey, Dwight," she said. "Still discussing security issues?" She laughed, then winked at Brenda.

Brenda's cheeks flushed a pretty pink. "You're certainly in a good mood," she said.

"I've been out at the ranch. The wedding planner needed me to take some measurements. It's such a gorgeous place for a wedding, and Travis's mom is as excited about it as I am." She sat in a chair near Brenda. "So what are you two really up to?" she asked.

"I've received a couple of disturbing letters," Brenda said. She glanced at Dwight. "Threatening ones."

"Oh no!" Lacy's smile vanished and her face paled. "I thought you were a little distracted this morning, but I assumed it was over the auction. I'm sorry for being so silly."

"It's all right," Brenda said. "The first note was taped to the door of the museum when I arrived this morning. We just found a second one here at the house."

"Threats?" Lacy shook her head. "Who would want to threaten you? And why?"

"The first note told me I should burn the rare book that's up for auction—or else," Brenda said.

"What did the second note say?" Lacy asked.

Brenda opened her mouth to speak, then pressed her lips together and shook her head. Lacy looked to Dwight. "You tell her," Brenda said.

"The second note contained a crime scene photo from Andy's murder, and said 'this could be you.'"

Lacy gasped, then leaned over and took Brenda's hand. "That's horrible. Who would do such a thing?"

"We're going to find that out," Dwight said.

"What are you going to do until then?" Lacy asked.

"Until this is resolved, I think you should move back in with your parents—or with Travis," Brenda said.

"You can't stay here by yourself," Lacy said.

Dwight was about to agree with her, but Brenda cut him off. "I'm not going to let this creep run me out of my own home," she declared. "I've been manipulated enough in my life—I'm not going to let it happen again."

Was she saying her husband had manipulated her? Dwight wondered. Certainly, Andy Stenson had kept her in the dark about his blackmailing activities and the real source of his income. "We'll put extra patrols on the house," Dwight said. If he had to, he'd park his own car on the curb and stay up all night watching over her.

"Thank you," Brenda said. "In the meantime, I'm going to contact the paper and let them know what's going on. I want whoever is doing this to see that I'm not afraid of him. Besides, if everybody knows what's going on, I'll feel safer. People complain about how nosy everyone is in small towns, but in a situation like this, that could work to my advantage."

"That's a good idea." He turned to look at the letter and envelope still lying on the table. "Let me take care of these, and I'm going to call in some crime scene folks to go over the scene and see if we missed anything. Come with me and we'll call the paper from there."

"All right," she said.

"I'll come with you, too," Lacy said. "Travis should be back from his class soon."

"Give me a minute," Dwight said. He walked out to his SUV to retrieve an evidence pouch. The women huddled on the porch together, talking softly. Brenda was calm now, but he could imagine how upsetting seeing that photograph had been for her. The person who had left that note wasn't only interested in persuading her to destroy the book. He could have done that with another death threat, or even a physical attack.

No, the person who had left that photo wanted to inflict psychological harm. The man—or woman—had a personal dislike for Brenda, or for women in general, or for something she represented. Or at least, that was Dwight's take, based on the psychology courses he'd taken as an undergraduate. He'd have to question her carefully to determine if there was anything in her background to inspire that kind of hate. With that photograph, the note-writer had gone from a possible annoying-but-harmless prankster to someone who could be a serious danger.

BRENDA RODE WITH Lacy to the sheriff's department, grateful for the distraction that talk about the upcoming wedding provided—anything to block out the horrible image of her dead husband on that note. The photo, more than the threat beneath it, had hit her like a hard punch to the stomach, the sickening pain of it still lingering. Dwight had been shocked, too, though, typical for him, he hadn't shown a lot of emotion. Somehow, his steadiness had helped her step back from the horror and try to think rationally.

Whoever had sent that note wanted to shock her—to terrify her and maybe, to make her reluctant to dig into the reason behind the threat. The letter writer mistook her for a weak woman who would do anything to make the pain go away.

She had been that person once. When Andy dismissed her questions about all the money he was spending on remodeling their home with an admonishment that she didn't need to worry about any of that, she had backed off and accepted his judgment. The idea made her cringe now, but she had been so young, and unwilling to do anything that might mar her happiness.

She wouldn't make that mistake again. Turning away from things that hurt or frightened her only made them more difficult to deal with later. Now she faced her problems head-on, and in doing so had discovered a strength she hadn't known she possessed.

Paige Riddell was waiting in the lobby of the sheriff's department, and confronted Dwight as soon as he walked in. "How dare you treat my brother the way you did this morning," she said before the door had even shut behind Dwight and the two women. "He was trying to help—to do something good—and you shut him down as if he were trying to rob the place. You wouldn't even give him a chance." Her voice shook on the last words—Paige, who to Brenda was the epitome of a tough woman. Paige, who had taken on Henry Hake's money and position and defeated his plans to build a luxury resort in an environmentally fragile location. Now she seemed on the verge of tears.

"Why don't we go into my office and talk about this?" Dwight gestured down the hallway.

"You didn't have any problem with confronting Parker in public, so we'll do this in public." Paige glanced at Lacy and Brenda. "I'm sure Dwight has already informed you that my brother has been arrested before. He's not trying to hide that. He made a mistake and he paid for it. He went through rehab and he's clean now, and trying to start over—if people like the deputy here will let him."

Dwight frowned, hands on his hips. "If Parker has a problem with something I said, he should come to me and we'll talk about it," he said.

"Parker doesn't want to talk to you. He didn't want to talk to me, but I saw how down he was when he came back from the history museum this morning, so I pried the story out of him. He said you looked at him like you suspected him of planning to blow up the building or something."

Dwight's face reddened. Brenda sympathized with him—but she also related to Paige's desire to protect her brother. Dwight clearly hadn't liked the young man, and his dislike had shown in the encounter this morning. "Paige, does Parker know you're here?" she asked.

Paige turned to her. "No. And when he finds out, he'll be furious. But he's been furious with me before. He'll get over it."

"Why was Parker at the history museum this morning?" Dwight asked.

"Because he's interested in history. It's one of the things he's studying in college. I told him the museum was looking for volunteers and he should apply."

"That's kind of unusual, isn't it?" Dwight said. "A guy his age being so interested in the past."

"Tell that to all the history majors at his school," Paige said. "Parker is a very bright young man. He has a lot of interests, and history is one of them."

"Any particular type of history?" Dwight asked. "Is he, for instance, interested in the history of World War II? Or local history?"

Brenda held her breath, realizing where Dwight was headed with this line of questioning.

Paige shook her head. "I don't know that it's any particular kind of history. American history, certainly. Colorado and local history, probably. Why do you ask?"

"Does your brother have any history of violence? Of making threats?"

"What? No! What are you talking about?"

"I can check his record," Dwight said.

"Check it. You won't find anything." She turned to Brenda and Lacy. "Parker was convicted for possession of methamphetamine and for stealing to support his drug habit. He was never violent, and he's been clean for three months now. He's going to stay clean. He moved here to get away from all his old influences. He's enrolled in college and he has a part-time job at Peggy's Pizza."

Brenda wet her lips, her mouth dry. "Do you have any yellow stationery at your place?" she asked. "With dancing cartoon flowers across the bottom?"

Paige's brow knit. She looked at Dwight again. "What is going on? If you're accusing Parker of something, tell me."

"Brenda received a threatening note at the museum this morning," Dwight said. "It was written on distinctive stationery." Brenda noticed that he didn't mention the note at her home.

"The only stationery I use is made of recycled paper," Paige said. "It's plain and cream-colored. And Parker didn't write that note. He wouldn't threaten anyone— much less Brenda. He doesn't even know her."

"I'm not accusing him of anything," Dwight said.

"Right." Paige didn't roll her eyes, but she looked as

if she wanted to. "I bet you're asking everyone in town about their stationery." She turned to Brenda again. "I know Parker would hate me if he knew I was asking this, but please give him a chance at the museum. He needs constructive things to fill his spare time, and he's a hard worker. And while he's not the biggest guy on the block, he knows how to take care of himself. He would be good protection in case the real person who's making these threats comes around."

Paige's concern for her brother touched Brenda. And she had always had a soft spot for people who needed a second chance. "Tell him to come around tomorrow and fill out a volunteer application. Most of my volunteers are older women—it will be nice to have a young man with a strong back."

"Thank you. You won't regret it, I promise." She squeezed Brenda's hand, then, with a last scornful look at Dwight, left.

Dwight crossed his arms over his chest. "I don't think it's a good idea for you to take on a new volunteer," he said. "Not until we know who's threatening you."

"I know you don't, but I trust Paige's judgment," Brenda said. "She's not a pushover."

"People often have blind spots for the people they love," he said.

She couldn't help but flinch at his words. She had certainly had a blind spot when it came to Andy. Her dismay must have showed, because Dwight hurried to apologize. "Brenda, I didn't mean…"

"I know what you meant," she said. "And I'll be careful, I promise."

The door opened again and Travis strolled in. The

sheriff looked as polished and pressed—and hand-some—as ever. If he was surprised to see them all standing in the reception area, he didn't show it on his face. "Hey, Brenda," he said. "What happened to the banner advertising the auction that was hung over Main Street at the entrance to town?"

"What do you mean?" she asked. "It was fine the last time I checked—just yesterday."

"It's not fine now," he said. "It's gone."

Chapter Four

"What do you mean, the banner is gone?" Lacy was the first to speak. "Did someone steal it?"

"I don't know," Travis said. "It was there when I left for my training this morning and it isn't there now."

"Maybe the wind blew it away," Lacy said.

"We haven't had any high winds," Brenda said. "And I watched the city crew hang that banner—it was tied down tight to the utility poles on either side of the street. It would take a hurricane to blow it away."

"Do you think this has anything to do with those nasty letters you received?" Lacy asked.

"What letters?" Travis was all business now.

"Let's take this into your office," Dwight said. "I'll fill you in."

They all filed down the hall to Travis's office. He hung his Stetson on the hat rack by the door and settled behind his desk. Lacy and Brenda took the two visitors' chairs in front of the desk, while Dwight leaned against the wall beside the door. "Tell me," Travis said.

So Brenda—with Dwight providing details—told the sheriff about the two threatening letters she had received: the cheerful yellow stationery, the black marker, the photocopy of the horrible crime scene photo and all about the book the letter writer wanted her to destroy. Travis listened, then leaned back, his chair creaking, as he considered the situation. "What's your take on this, Dwight?" he asked.

Dwight straightened. "I think this guy has a real mean streak, but he isn't too smart."

Brenda turned in her chair to look at him. "Why do you think he isn't smart?" she asked.

"Because if he really wanted to get rid of the book, why not try to steal it? Get rid of it himself?"

"Maybe he knew I'd keep something so valuable locked up," Brenda said.

"Maybe. I still would have expected him to try to get to it before resorting to these threats. There's a lot of risk in writing a note like that—the risk of being seen delivering the notes or of someone recognizing that stationery."

"He—or she—I'm not going to rule out a woman," Travis said, "must think there's a good chance he won't be noticed. Maybe he thinks people wouldn't be surprised to see him around the museum or your house, or he's good at making himself inconspicuous."

"So someone who looks harmless," Lacy said. "That could be almost anyone."

"Where is this book now?" Travis asked.

"It's in my purse." Brenda opened her handbag and took out the small cloth-bound volume and handed it across the desk. "After we found that second letter, we never made it inside to put it in my safe."

Travis opened the book and flipped through it. "I think you're right that this guy isn't very smart," he said. "By demanding you destroy this book, he's focused all our attention on it."

"Or maybe he's really smart and he's trying to divert our attention from what's really important," Dwight said.

Travis closed the book. "I think it would be a good idea to keep this here at the sheriff's department until the auction," he said.

"Fine," Brenda said. "I'll sleep better knowing it isn't in my house."

"You can't go back to your house," Dwight said.

He was giving an order, not making a request, and that didn't sit well with her. "I won't let some nut run me out of my home," she said.

"Someone who would threaten you with that crime scene photo might be serious about hurting you," Travis said. "We can run extra patrols, but we can't protect you twenty-four hours a day. We don't have the manpower. You need to go somewhere that will make it harder for this guy to get to you."

"And where is that?" she asked. "A hotel isn't going to be any safer than my home."

"We can try to find a safe house," Travis said.

"Sheriff, I have a job that I need to do. I can't just leave town and hide out—if I do, then this jerk wins. I won't let that happen."

The two men exchanged a look that Brenda read as *Why do women have to be so difficult?* She turned to face Dwight. "If someone were threatening you like this, would you run away?" she demanded.

He shook his head. "No." He rubbed the back of his neck. "But what about a compromise—somewhere near town where you would be safer, but still be able to work at the museum?"

"Do you know of a place?" Lacy asked.

"I do."

"Not with you," Brenda said. "No offense, but if you want to really start wild rumors, just let people find out I've moved in with you."

Something flashed in his eyes—was he amused? But he quickly masked the expression. "I don't want to start any rumors," he said. "And I'm not talking about moving in with me. But my parents have plenty of room at the ranch, and I know they'd love to have you stay with them. There are fences and a locked gate, plus plenty of people around day and night. It would be a lot more difficult for anyone to get to you there." He let a hint of a smile tug at the corners of his mouth. "And my cabin isn't that far from the main house, so I can keep an eye on you, too."

Brenda recalled Bud and Sharon Prentice as a genial couple who had cheered on their son at every basketball game and helped out with fund-raisers and other school functions. They were the kind of people who worked hard in the background and didn't demand the spotlight.

Lacy leaned over and squeezed Brenda's arm. "You don't really want to go back to your house alone, do you?" she asked.

"Where are you going to be?" Brenda asked.

Lacy flushed. "I think I'll be staying with Travis until this is settled. I'm no hero."

Brenda didn't want to be a hero, either—especially a foolhardy one. "All right," she said. "I'll take you up on your offer. But only for a few days."

"Let's hope that's all it takes to find this guy," Dwight said.

DWIGHT RODE WITH Brenda to his family's ranch west of town. He wasn't going to risk her wrath by coming right out and saying he didn't want her alone on the road, so he made an excuse about having to get his personal pickup truck and bring it into town for an oil change. He wasn't sure if she bought the explanation, but she didn't object when he left his SUV parked in front of her house and slid into the passenger seat of her Subaru. She had packed up her laptop and a small suitcase of clothes—enough for a few days at the ranch.

"Do you remember visiting the ranch when we were in high school?" he asked as she headed out of town and into the more open country at the foot of the mountains.

"I remember," she said. "Your parents threw a party for the senior class. I remember being in awe of the place—it seemed so big compared to my parents' little house in town."

"As ranches go, it's not that big," Dwight said. "To me, it's just home." The ranch had been the place for him and his brothers and sister to ride horses, swim in the pond, fish in the creek and work hard alongside their parents. For a kid who liked the outdoors and didn't enjoy sitting still for long, it was the perfect place to grow up. He had acres of territory to roam, and there was always something to do or see.

Brenda turned onto the gravel road that wound past his parents' property, the fields full of freshly mown hay drying in the sun. Other pastures were dotted with fat round bales, wrapped in plastic to protect them from the elements and looking like giant marshmallows scattered across the landscape. She turned in at the open gate, a wrought iron arch overhead identifying this as the Boot Heel Ranch.

"The house looks the same as I remember it," Brenda said. "I love that porch." The porch stretched all across the front of the two-story log home, honeysuckle vines twining up the posts, pots of red geraniums flanking the steps. Dwight's parents, Sharon and Bud, were waiting at the top of the steps to greet them. Smiling, his mother held out both hands to Brenda. "Dwight didn't give any details, just said you needed to stay with us a few days while he investigates someone who's been harassing you," Sharon said. "I'm sorry you're having to go through that, dear."

"Thank you for taking me in," Brenda said.

"I'm sure your mother would have done the same for Dwight, if the shoe had been on the other foot," Sharon said. "I remember her as the kind of woman who would go out of her way to help everyone."

Dwight remembered now that Brenda's mother had died of cancer while Brenda was in college. Her father had moved away—to Florida or Arizona or someplace like that.

"Thank you," Brenda said again. "Your place is so beautiful."

"I give Sharon all the credit for the house." Bud stepped forward and offered a hand. "I see to the cows and horses—though she has her say with them, too. Frankly, we'd probably all be lost without her."

Sharon beamed at this praise, though Dwight knew she had heard it before—not that it wasn't true. His mother was the epitome of the iron fist in the velvet glove—gently guiding them all, but not afraid to give them a kick in the rear if they needed it.

"Let me show you to your room," Sharon said.

"I can do that, Mom," Dwight said. He had retrieved Brenda's laptop bag and suitcase from the car and now led the way into the house and up the stairs to the guest suite on the north side of the house. The door to the room was open, and he saw that someone—probably his mother—had put fresh flowers in a cut-glass vase on the bureau opposite the bed. The bright pink and yellow and white blossoms reflected in the mirror over the bureau, and echoed the colors in the quilt on the cherry sleigh bed that had belonged to Dwight's great-grandmother.

"This is beautiful." Brenda did a full turn in the middle of the room, taking it all in.

"You should be comfortable up here." He set both her bags on the rug by the bed. "And you'll have plenty of privacy. My parents added a master suite downstairs after us kids moved out."

"Where do you live?" she asked.

"My cabin is on another part of the property. You can see it from the window over here." He motioned, and she went to the window. He moved in behind her and pointed to the modest cedar cabin he had taken as his bachelor quarters. "Years ago, we had a ranch foreman who lived there, but he moved to a bigger place on another part of the ranch, so I claimed it."

"Nice."

The subtle floral fragrance of her perfume tickled his nostrils. It was all he could do not to lean down and inhale the scent of her—a gesture that would no doubt make her think he was a freak.

"I hope you didn't take what I said wrong—about not wanting to move in with you," she said. "It's just—"

He touched her arm. "I know." She had been the center of so much town gossip over the years, first with her husband's murder, then with the revelations that he had been blackmailing prominent citizens, that she shied away from that sort of attention.

"I had the biggest crush on you when I was a kid," he said. "That party here at the ranch—I wanted to ask you to dance so badly, but I could never work up the nerve."

She searched his face. "Why were you afraid to ask?"

"You were so beautiful, and popular—you were a cheerleader—the prom queen."

"You were popular, too."

"I had friends, but not like you. Everyone liked you."

She turned to look out the window once more. "All that seems so long ago," she said.

He moved away. "I'll let you get settled. We usually eat dinner around six."

He was almost to the door when she called his name. "Dwight?"

"Yes?"

"You should have asked me to dance. I would have said yes."

SEEING THE ADULT Dwight with his parents at dinner that evening gave Brenda a new perspective on the solemn, thoughtful sheriff's deputy she thought she knew. With Bud and Sharon, Dwight was affectionate and teasing, laughing at the story Bud told about a ten-year-old Dwight getting cornered in a pasture by an ornery cow, offering a thoughtful opinion when Sharon asked if they should call in a new vet to look at a horse who was lame, and discussing plans to repair irrigation dikes before spring. Clearly, he still played an important role on the ranch despite his law enforcement duties.

Watching the interaction, Brenda missed her own parents—especially her mother. Her mother's cancer had been diagnosed the summer before Brenda's senior year of college. Her parents had insisted she continue her education, so Brenda saw the toll the disease took only on brief visits home.

She had met Andrew Stenson during that awful time, and he had been her strongest supporter and biggest help, a shoulder for her to cry on and someone for her to lean on in the aftermath of her mother's death. No matter his flaws, she knew Andy had loved her, though she could see now that he had assumed the role of caretaker in their relationship. By the time they married, she had grown used to depending on him and letting him make the decisions.

But she wasn't that grieving girl anymore. And she didn't want a man to take care of her. She wanted someone to stand beside her—a partner, not just a protector.

After dinner, she insisted on helping Sharon with the dishes. "That's my job, you know," Dwight said as he stacked plates while Brenda collected silverware.

"The two of you can see to cleanup," Sharon said. "I think I'll sit out on the porch with your father. It's such a nice evening."

"You don't have to work for your room and board," Dwight said as he led the way into the kitchen. "I could get this myself."

"I want to help," she said. "Besides, we need to talk. I never got around to notifying the paper this afternoon."

"You can do it in the morning," he said. "The deadline for the weekly issue is the day after tomorrow." He squirted dish soap into the sink and began filling it with hot water.

Brenda slid the silverware into the soapy water. "I've been racking my brain and I can't come up with anyone who would want to harm me or the museum."

"Maybe one of Andy's blackmail victims has decided

to take his anger out on you," Dwight said as he began to wash dishes. "We don't know who besides Jan he might have extorted money from, though the records we were able to obtain from his old bank accounts seemed to indicate multiple regular payments from several people."

"Why focus on the book?" She picked up a towel and began to dry. "Part of me still thinks this is just a sick prank—that we're getting all worked up for nothing."

"I hope that's all it is." He rinsed a plate, then handed it to her. "I want to dig into Parker Riddell's background a little more and see if I can trace his movements yesterday."

"Why would he care about me or a rare book?" Brenda asked. "He's a kid who made some mistakes, but I can't see how or why he'd be involved in this."

"I have to check him out," Dwight said.

"I know. I just wish there were more I could do. I hate waiting around like this." She hated being helpless.

"I know." He handed her another plate. They did the dishes in companionable silence for the next few minutes. The domestic chore, and the easy rhythm they established, soothed her frayed nerves.

Dwight's phone rang. He dried his hands and looked at the screen. "I'd better take this," he said. He moved into the other room. She continued to dry, catching snippets of the conversation.

"When did this happen?"

"Who called it in?"

"What's the extent of the damage?"

"I see. Yes. I'll tell her."

She set the plate she had been drying on the counter and turned to face him as he walked back into the room.

His face confirmed her fears. "What's happened?" she asked.

"There was a fire at your house. A neighbor called it in, but apparently there's a lot of damage."

She gripped the counter, trying to absorb the impact of his words. "How did it start?" she asked.

"They think it's probably arson." He put a hand on her shoulder. "We aren't dealing with a prankster here. Someone is out to hurt you, and I'm not going to let that happen."

Chapter Five

The smell of wet ashes stuck in the back of Dwight's throat, thick and acrid, as he stood with Travis and Assistant Fire Chief Tom Reynolds in front of what was left of Brenda Stenson's house the morning after the fire. The garage and apartment where Lacy lived were unscathed, but the main house only had two walls left upright, the siding streaked with black and the interior collapsed into a pile of blackened rubble. If Dwight let himself think about what might have happened if Brenda had been inside when the fire was lit, he broke out in a cold sweat.

So he pushed the thoughts away and focused on the job. "We found evidence of an accelerant—gasoline—at the back corner of the house," Tom said. "Probably splashed it all over the siding, maybe piled some papers or dry leaves around it and added a match—boom—these old houses tend to catch quickly."

"Do you think the arsonist chose that corner because it was out of view of the street and neighboring houses, or because he wanted to make sure the rooms in that part of the house were destroyed?" Dwight asked.

Tom shrugged. "Maybe both. The location was definitely out of view—someone in the garage apartment might have seen it, but he might have known Lacy wasn't in last night."

"Maybe they knew Brenda wasn't here last night, either," Travis said. He scanned the street in front of the house. "If they were watching the place."

"We'll canvass the neighbors," Dwight said. "See if they have any friends or relatives who have recently moved in, or if they've noticed anyone hanging around or anything unusual."

"What's located in this corner of the house?" Travis asked.

"I think it's where Andy's home office used to be," Dwight said. "I remember picking up some paperwork from him not too long after I started with the department." Brenda hadn't been home, which had disappointed Dwight at the time, though he had told himself it was just as well.

"That's probably where the safe was where Brenda wanted to stash that book," Travis said.

"Probably," Dwight said. "But safes are usually fireproof."

"Maybe whoever did this didn't know about the safe," Travis said.

"Or destroying the book wasn't even the point," Dwight said. "Frightening Brenda into getting rid of the book on her own would be enough for him."

"I guess I'd be frightened right now if I were her," Tom said.

"Brenda's not like that," Dwight said. "I'm not saying she's not afraid—but she's not going to destroy the book, either. This guy's threats are only making her dig her heels in more."

Travis checked his watch. "Thanks for meeting with us, Tom," he said. "I have to get back to the office."

"Yeah, I'd better get going, too," Tom said. "I'll get a copy of the report to you and to Brenda for her insurance company."

Dwight followed Travis to the curb, where both their SUVs were parked. "I'm supposed to meet with the DEA guy the Feds sent to deal with that underground lab we found out at Henry Hake's place," Travis said. "He's had an investigative team at the site and has a report for me."

"Mind if I sit in?" Dwight asked. "I've got a couple of questions for him."

"Sure. I asked Gage to be there, too."

Travis's brother, Deputy Gage Walker, met them at the sheriff's department. Two years younger and two inches taller than his brother, Gage's easygoing, aww-shucks manner concealed a sharp intellect and commitment to his job. "Adelaide told me you two were out at the Stenson place," Gage said as the three filed into the station's meeting room. "I drove by there on my way in this morning. The fire really did a number on the place."

"Tom says they're sure it was arson," Travis said.

"How's Brenda taking it?" Gage asked.

"She's stoic," Dwight said.

"She's been through a lot the past few years," Gage said.

Brenda had been through too much, Dwight thought. And most of it pretty much by herself. She had friends in town, but no one she could really lean on. He got the sense that Andy's betrayal had made her reluctant to depend on anyone. He wanted to tell her she didn't have to be so strong around him—but he didn't want her to take the sentiment wrong.

The bell on the front door sounded, and all conversation stopped as they listened to Adelaide greet a male visitor. Their voices grew louder as they approached the meeting room. "This is Special Agent Rob Allerton." Adelaide didn't exactly bat her eyes at the dark-haired agent, who bore a passing resemblance to Jake Gyllenhaal, but she came close. Gage grinned, no doubt intending to give the office manager a hard time about it later.

Allerton himself seemed oblivious to her adoration—or maybe he was used to it. He shook hands with the sheriff and each of the deputies as they introduced themselves. "Is this your first visit to our part of the state?" Travis asked as they settled in chairs around the conference table.

"My first, but not my last." Allerton settled his big frame into the metal chair. "You people are living in paradise. It's gorgeous out here."

"Don't spread the word," Gage said. "We don't want to be overrun."

"What can you tell us about your investigation of the underground lab?" Travis asked.

"Not much, I'm afraid," Allerton said. "So far our analysts haven't found any illegal drug residue, or really any signs that the lab has been used recently."

"What about World War II?" Dwight asked. "Could it have been used then?"

Allerton frowned. "Want to tell me how you came up with that time period?"

"The local history museum is having an auction to raise money," Travis said.

"Right, I saw the banner the first day I arrived in town," Allerton said.

The banner that had mysteriously disappeared—Dwight had almost forgotten about it in the flurry of activity since then. "One of the items up for auction—probably the most valuable item—is a book detailing a World War II project to produce chemical and biological weapons," Travis said. "Supposedly, the work was done in underground labs in this part of the country."

"No kidding?" Allerton shook his head. "Well, the equipment we found wasn't old enough for that. In fact, some of it appears to have been stolen from your local high school, judging by the high school name stenciled on the glass. There are some indications—marks on the floor and walls—that other equipment or furnishings might have been in that space previously. There's no way of knowing when they were moved. It would be an interesting historical artifact if that were true, but I can't see anything illegal in it."

"Somebody is upset about the book getting out there," Dwight said. "They made threats against the museum director, and last night someone burned down her house."

"That's bad, but I don't see any connection to this lab."

"Seen anybody up there at the site while you were there?" Travis asked. "Any signs of recent activity?"

Allerton shook his head. "Nothing. I see why this guy, Hake, wanted to build a development up there—it's beautiful. But the ghost town he ended up with is a little creepy."

"Where do we go from here?" Travis asked.

"Me, I go back home to Denver," Allerton said. "If

you have questions or need more help, give me a call. I'd love an excuse to get back out here."

He stood, and the four of them walked to the front again. Adelaide smiled up at them. Had she freshened her lipstick? Dwight forced himself not to react. "That didn't take long," she said.

"Short and sweet," Allerton said. "Though I know how to take my time when the job calls for it."

Adelaide blushed pink, and Dwight bit the inside of his cheek to keep from laughing. Allerton said goodbye and let himself out. When he was gone, Adelaide sat back in her chair, both hands over her heart. "Oh my! Did you see those eyes? He looked just like that movie star—what's his name? You know the one."

"Jake Gyllenhaal," Dwight said.

"That's him!" Adelaide crowed.

Travis and Gage stared at him. "You knew that?" Gage asked.

Dwight shrugged. "I like movies."

"He didn't find any signs of illegal activity in that underground lab on Henry Hake's property," Travis said. "That's all I care about."

"Mind if I go up there and take another look around?" Dwight asked. "I might take Brenda with me—she's a historian, or at least, that's her degree. I want to know if she sees anything that might link to the World War II labs that book talks about."

"Fine by me," Travis said. "Technically, it's still a crime scene, since that's where Gage and Maya and Casey were held after they were kidnapped, though I'm going to have to release it back to the owners soon."

"Who are the owners?" Gage asked. "Isn't Henry Hake's name still on the deed?"

"Apparently, the week before he went missing, he signed the whole thing over to a concern called CNG Development. I found out last week when I tried one of the numbers I had for Hake Development. I got a recording telling me the company had been absorbed by CNG, but when I tried to track down the number for them, I couldn't find anything. Then I checked with the courts and sure enough, the change was registered the day before Hake disappeared."

"Coincidence?" Gage asked.

"Maybe," Travis said. "But I'd sure like to talk to someone with CNG about it. The number listed on the court documents is answered by another recording, and the address is a mailbox service in Ogden, Utah."

"Be careful when you head up there," Gage said. "Allerton was right—that place is downright creepy."

TAMMY PATTERSON, the reporter for the *Eagle Mountain Examiner*, agreed to meet Brenda at the museum the morning after the fire. Dwight had tried to persuade Brenda to stay at the ranch and not go in to work that day, but she had refused. Dwight had gone with her the night before to see the house, when the firefighters were still putting out the blaze, but she had wanted to see it herself this morning, alone. She had driven in early and made herself stop at the house and stare at the ruins. Her first thought was that this couldn't really be her place—not the miner's cottage that she and Andy had worked so hard to remodel, the dream home she had lovingly decorated and planned to live in forever.

She had allowed herself to cry for five minutes or so, then dried her eyes, repaired her makeup and driven to the museum. She couldn't do anything about the fire right now, and crying certainly wouldn't bring her house back. Better to go to work and focus on something she could control.

"You don't know how glad I am you called," Tammy said when she burst into the museum, blond hair flying and a little out of breath. This was how Brenda always thought of her—a young woman who was always rushing. "Barry had me reading press releases, looking for story angles. Nobody else ever reads them, so we had this huge pile of them—most of them are about as exciting as last night's town council meeting minutes— which, by the way, I have to turn into a news story, too. So truly, you have saved me."

I'm hoping you can save me, Brenda thought, but she didn't say it—it sounded entirely too dramatic, and might have the wrong effect on Tammy's already-excitable personality. "Glad I could help," Brenda said.

Tammy plopped onto the wrought iron barstool in front of the museum's glass counter and pulled out a small notebook and a handheld recorder. "So what's this story you have for me?" she asked. "You said it was related to the auction, but not exactly? Something juicy, you said. Boy, could I use juicy. I mean, it's great that we live in such a peaceful town and all, but sometimes I worry our readers are going to die of boredom."

Brenda could recall plenty of non-boring news that had run in the paper—surrounding her husband's murder, the wrongful conviction of Lacy Milligan and her subsequent release from prison, revelations about Andy's blackmailing, Henry Hake's disappearance, etc., etc. But she supposed for a reporter like Tammy, that was all old news.

"So, did you find something scandalous in a donation someone made for the auction?" Tammy asked. "Or has some big donor come forward to shower money on you?"

"I wish!" Brenda pulled her own stool closer to the counter. "This has to do with that book we have up for auction—the rare one about the top-secret government plot to make biological and chemical weapons during World War II?"

"I remember." Tammy flipped back a few pages in her notebook. "*The Secret History of Rayford County, Colorado.* Do you have a bidding war? Or you found out the whole thing's a brilliant fake? Or has the government come after you to silence you and keep from letting the secret out of the bag?"

At Brenda's stunned look, Tammy flushed. "Sorry. I read a lot of dystopian fiction. Sometimes I get carried away."

"You're not too far off," Brenda said. "Apparently, someone is trying to silence me."

Tammy's mouth formed a large O. "Your house! I heard about that and I meant to say first thing how sorry I am. But I just thought it was old wiring or something."

"No, the fire department is sure the fire was deliberately set."

Tammy switched on the recorder, then started scribbling in her notebook. "How is that connected to the book?" she asked.

"I don't know. But before the fire, I received two different threatening notes—one here and one at my home, telling me if I didn't destroy that book, I could end up dead."

"Whoa! Do the cops know about this?"

"I told the sheriff, yes." Brenda leaned toward

Tammy. "I called you because I want you to make clear in your story that I'm not going to let some coward who writes anonymous notes and sets fire to my house bully me into destroying a valuable historical artifact. If he's so keen to destroy the book, then he can bid on it like everyone else."

"Ooh, good quote." Tammy made note of it. "Where is the book now? Or I guess you probably don't want to say."

"I don't have it," Brenda said. "It's in the safe at the sheriff's office, where no one can access it until the day of the auction." That wasn't exactly true, but she didn't picture Travis or his deputies taking the book out to show around to just anyone.

"You're right—this is definitely more exciting than the town council meeting," Tammy said. She paused and looked up from her notebook. "I hope that didn't sound wrong. I really am sorry about your house, and those threatening letters would have totally freaked me out."

"They were upsetting," Brenda admitted. "But now that I'm over the first shock, they just make me angry."

"Another good quote." Tammy made a note.

The doorbells clamored and both women turned toward the young man who entered. Parker Riddell froze in the doorway. "Um, you said I should come by about the volunteer work."

"Of course." Brenda pulled a clipboard with the volunteer application out from under the counter. "Tammy, do you know Parker? He's Paige Riddell's brother. Parker, this is Tammy Patterson. She's a reporter for the local paper."

"Uh, hi." Parker hesitated, then stuck out his hand.

"Nice to meet you." Tammy shook hands, then

turned back to Brenda. "I think I have enough here. I'll call you if I think of anything else."

"Thanks, Tammy."

When she was gone, Parker stood staring at the floor for a long moment, not saying anything. "I need you to fill out this application," Brenda said, offering the clipboard.

"Yeah, sure." He took the clipboard and looked around, then slid onto the stool Tammy had vacated. Brenda began straightening the shelves behind the counter, surreptitiously checking out the young man who labored over the forms.

Parker Riddell had the tall, too-thin look of a boy still growing into a man's body. His skin was so fair blue veins stood out on the back of his hands, while blue-lined tattoos of a skull, a scorpion and a crow—among those she could see—adorned his arms. He hunched over the clipboard, clutching the pen and bearing down on it as he wrote. He looked up and caught Brenda staring, his eyes such a dark brown the iris almost merged with the pupils. "Is something wrong?" he asked.

"You're the first person under the age of forty who's ever wanted to volunteer here," she said. "Well, except for Lacy, but she's my best friend. I'm curious as to why you did it. I'd think it would be boring for you."

He laid down the pen, still holding her gaze. "This whole town is boring for me," he said. "But I like history. I like old stuff." He shrugged. "It's weird, I know."

"It's not weird," Brenda said. "I always liked history, too." She moved to stand across from him. "Are you studying history in school?"

"Just one class this year—at the community college. But I'd like to take more." He signed the bottom of the form and turned the clipboard back to her. "You already know about my record, but it wasn't for a violent crime or anything. And you don't have to let me handle money or anything. I can file stuff or build stuff or, you know, whatever you need."

"Thanks." She smiled. Nothing about this young man seemed threatening. Of course, she had been fooled by people before, but she believed in second chances. "Why don't we start by having you help me pack up everything in our special exhibit room upstairs? I want to install a new exhibit on the war years in Eagle Mountain."

They worked the rest of the afternoon dismantling the installation on historic drugstores—including a mock-up of an old-time soda fountain. It took some time to take down and pack away, and Brenda was grateful for a young, strong and mostly silent helper.

"That was great," she said when she had taped and sealed the last box to go into storage in the basement. "When would you like to come again?"

"I have a class tomorrow, but maybe Thursday?"

"That would be great. Whatever you can manage."

He nodded. "Okay, I have to go to work now." He pulled out his car keys. "I deliver pizza for Peggy's."

"I'll remember that next time I need to place an order."

"Do you need me to carry these boxes down for you before I go?" He indicated the half dozen cartons piled around the exhibit space.

"No, that's okay. I need to decide where I'll put them first. They can stay in here until tomorrow or the next day." She followed him out of the room and pulled a velvet-covered rope across the doorway, then hung a sign that said New Display Coming Soon.

Downstairs, the bells on the door jangled. Brenda checked her watch. Ten minutes until five. She'd have to point out to whoever was down there that the museum would close soon and they would need to return tomorrow. But she took a step back when she recognized the man waiting in the reception area.

"Hello, Brenda." Eddie Carstairs smiled, showing the gap between his two front teeth. His straight black hair angled across his forehead and curled around his ears so that even when he had just had a haircut, he looked in need of another one. He wore a long-sleeved khaki shirt and pants—much like the sheriff's department uniform, sans any insignia. A utility belt equipped with flashlight, nightstick and holstered pistol added to his attempt to appear official. Or at least, that's how Brenda interpreted the look. Eddie had made no secret of his desire to be back in law enforcement since his discharge from the sheriff's department.

"What can I do for you, Eddie?" she asked.

Parker looked from Eddie to Brenda. "Do you want me to hang around a little bit?" he asked.

"No, she doesn't need you to hang around, punk," Eddie said before Brenda could answer. He rolled his shoulders back. "I'm here to protect her from people like you."

"It's all right, Parker, you can go," Brenda said. "And thank you again."

"Sure. See ya." He pushed out the door.

As it shut behind him, Brenda turned on Eddie. "What are you doing here?" she asked. "The museum is closed."

"Your boss, the mayor, decided after that fire at your

house, he didn't want to take any chances on the museum, so he hired me as a security guard."

"No one told me anything about this."

He shrugged. "It was just decided. You can call the mayor and ask him, if you like." He leaned one hip against the counter, as if prepared to wait all day.

"I certainly will." She grabbed the phone and retreated into the workroom, shutting the door behind her. She punched in the number for the mayor's office and waited impatiently as it rang and rang.

"Town of Eagle Mountain," a pleasant female voice answered.

"Gail, this is Brenda Stenson. I need to speak with Larry." Mayor Larry Rowe had been elected after Jan Selkirk had declined to run for reelection, running a well-funded campaign with promises of new jobs and opportunities for the town. He wasn't the friendliest person Brenda had ever met, but until now he had left her alone to do her job.

"I think he's still in, Brenda, let me check."

A few moments later Larry answered. "Brenda! What can I do for you?"

"Eddie Carstairs is over here at the museum saying you hired him as a security guard. Is that right?"

"Well, yes, but he wasn't supposed to start until tonight—after I had a chance to talk with you."

"I'm glad you thought it was a good idea to consult me on this."

Larry's voice hardened. "The city has a valuable investment in that museum, and since you seem to have attracted some unsavory attention, we find ourselves in the position of having to protect that investment."

"So this is all my fault?"

"The arson at your home seems to indicate the threats are targeted at you."

"There's no reason to think the museum is in any danger."

"There's no reason to think it isn't. Eddie came to us and offered his services, and we thought it prudent to take him up on the offer."

She hung up the phone and returned to the front room. "All good?" Eddie asked.

"Fine." She gathered up her purse. "You can follow me outside while I lock up."

"You can leave it unlocked and I'll hang out in here overnight," he said.

"You can follow me outside while I lock up and you can 'hang out' in your car overnight."

She could tell he wanted to argue, but thought better of it. He followed her onto the front porch and watched, frowning, as she locked the dead bolt. "You should be grateful to me for protecting your livelihood," he said.

"I may not have control over much in my life right now," she said, "but at least I get to decide for myself what and who I'm grateful for. Right now, you're not on my list."

The astonished expression on his face was almost worth the aggravation with the mayor. She stalked to her car, started it and had turned down the street toward her home when she remembered she didn't have a home to go to.

Part of her was tempted to keep driving—where, she had no idea. But she had never been one to run away from problems. So she turned around and headed out of town, to the ranch. Time to find out from Dwight how much longer she was going to be stuck in this limbo.

Chapter Six

Parker Riddell cruised slowly down Eagle Mountain's Main Street, careful to stay under the ridiculous twenty-five-mile-per-hour speed limit. He wasn't going to give the local cops any reason to hassle him—not to mention if Paige got a call from the sheriff's office about him, she would go ballistic. He didn't need another lecture about how she was doing him a favor and risking her own reputation and all she had worked for to look after him—yadda, yadda, yadda.

Nobody else was around after nine o'clock at night—talk about rolling up the sidewalks. This place was like a ghost town. The only cars were parked around Moe's Pub—it and Peggy's Pizza were the only businesses still open. There wasn't a movie theater or even a lousy bowling alley for a hundred miles. Paige always talked as if the lack of anything to do would help him stay out of trouble. Going to the movies and playing video games at the arcade weren't what had gotten him into trouble and she knew it.

But yeah, he was grateful for her—sort of—getting him away from his old hangouts. He'd worked hard in rehab and he didn't want to go back. But man, it wouldn't hurt to have a *little* excitement every once in a while, would it? He turned the corner and drove past the history museum. The pizza in the carrier on the passenger seat beside him was headed to one of Parker's regulars—a guy who worked second shift at the RV factory up in Junction. He ordered a couple times a week. Parker glanced over at the museum as he passed and was surprised to see two cars parked next to the old building. He slowed and craned his neck for a closer look. In the moonlight, he could make out that guy Eddie's pale face behind the wheel of a beat-up Jeep Wagoneer.

Eddie was talking to another man who had positioned his black SUV cop-style, so the drivers were door-to-door. What were they doing at the museum this time of night?

He made his delivery. His customer, Jason, tipped him a five, which was really decent of him. Parker slipped the five in his wallet and the rest of the money in the pouch for Peggy, then headed back toward the museum. He parked up the block and made his way in the darkness, sneaking up behind the two vehicles. He wasn't doing anything wrong, he reminded himself. Brenda clearly hadn't liked this Eddie fellow, and Parker owed it to her to make sure the guy wasn't ripping her off.

Parker hadn't thought much of the cop wannabe, either. It hadn't taken too many brains to figure out that Eddie was the guy Paige had talked about as the reserve deputy who had been fired and was trying to make trouble. And he'd looked at Parker like he was a dog he wanted to kick.

Parker heard Eddie and the other guy a long time before he got close enough to see them in the dark. Obviously, they weren't worried about being overheard. But Parker couldn't make out everything they said, just phrases that drifted on the night breeze.

"I'm taking care of it," Eddie said.

A mumble from the other guy.

"You don't have to worry. I know how to handle this. That's why you hired me, right?"

The other guy said something and they both laughed. Parker needed to get closer, to hear the whole conversation. He moved carefully, keeping to the shadows from a row of bushes alongside the alley where the cars were parked.

He didn't see the pile of debris set out for trash pickup until it was too late. He stumbled right into it, sending boxes and cans tumbling down, making a racket that could probably be heard a block away.

"Hey!" Eddie shouted.

The other man started up his SUV and sped away. Parker lurched to his feet and tried to run, but Eddie was on him, shoving him back onto the ground, the barrel of his pistol pressed to the side of Parker's face. "What are you doing sneaking around here?" Eddie demanded.

"I saw the cars. I wanted to make sure everything was all right."

Eddie shoved Parker's face further into the gravel. "Were you trying to steal something? I'll bet that's what you were doing. You 'volunteered' so you could check the place out and come back later and help yourself."

"No!" Parker squirmed, trying to free himself.

"Shut up." Eddie shoved the gun harder into Parker's cheek. "Maybe I ought to shoot you now and do everyone here a favor."

"Do you think you could get away from the museum one day and go with me up to the Eagle Mountain Resort site?" Dwight asked as he and Brenda did dishes that evening. Dinner had been grilled steaks on the back patio, and Brenda had done her best to smile and join in the conversation, but he could tell she was distracted. No surprise—she was probably worried about her house, and about whoever had targeted her.

"Why do you want me to go up there with you?" she asked.

"When we rescued Gage and Maya and her little niece, Casey, from those kidnappers last month, they were being held in an underground chamber on the resort land," he said.

"Yes, I heard about that." She added a dried plate to the stack on the kitchen table.

"What you probably didn't hear is that next to the chamber where they were held was another underground space that looked as if it had been used as a laboratory. The DEA has been investigating it, and hasn't found any sign of illegal activity. Now I'm wondering if it could be related to the labs the government established in the area to work on biological and chemical weapons—like that book talked about."

She stuck out her lower lip, considering. "The book does talk about some of the laboratories being underground—in old mines or caves. What does the DEA say?"

"They don't think any of the equipment is old enough, but they're not historians. I thought if you had a look, you might interpret things differently."

"But Wade and Brock kidnapped Maya and Gage and Casey," Brenda said. "And they're dead—right?" Finding out that the two men who ran the town's successful outdoor store were behind the kidnappings, and responsible for the murders of Maya's sister and brother-in-law, had shocked the town.

"They're dead, but we suspect they were working for someone else."

"The same person who's been threatening me?"

"Maybe," he said. "But maybe not."

She fell silent, mechanically drying plates and glasses and silverware, but Dwight couldn't shake the feeling that something was wrong. When the last dish had been put away, he turned to her. "Something's bothering you," he said. "Is it the threats or your house, or something else on top of all that?"

"I think that's enough to bother anyone," she said.

"It is. But if it would help to talk about it—if you need someone to listen to you, I'd like to be that person."

She straightened the dish towel she had just hung on the handle of the oven. "It will probably sound silly, especially considering everything else that has happened."

"I've never thought of you as particularly silly," he said. "What's happened?"

"The mayor—without consulting me—decided to hire Eddie Carstairs as a security guard for the museum. At a time when our budget is so squeezed we don't know if we'll be able to keep the doors open, he decided to spend money on this. And when I objected, he insinuated this was all my fault—that I had somehow put the museum property in danger."

Anguish colored the flood of words. He waited until she fell silent once more and said, "I can see why you're upset. The mayor isn't always the most diplomatic person." Larry Rowe had spent a lot of money and effort on his campaign for the office, but once elected, he had developed a reputation as a no-nonsense administrator who did whatever it took to get what he wanted.

"To make things worse, Eddie showed up while

Parker Riddell was still at the museum and treated him horribly. It was embarrassing."

"So Parker volunteered today?" Dwight kept his voice neutral, though he didn't like the idea of Brenda working closely with the troubled young man. Parker might be sincere in his desire to make a fresh start, but did Brenda have to be part of that?

"Yes, and he was wonderful. He's a very serious, quiet young man, and he's sincerely interested in history." Her shoulders sagged. "And I think he's lonely. There aren't a lot of people his age in this town for him to hang out with."

"It's great that you want to give him a chance," Dwight said. "Just…be careful."

"I will, I—"

His phone rang, interrupting her. "Sorry," he muttered, and took the call.

"Eddie Carstairs just hauled in Parker Riddell," Gage said when Dwight answered. "Eddie says he caught him trying to break into the history museum."

Dwight glanced at Brenda. "I heard that," she said.

"I'll be right down," Dwight said, and ended the call. He started toward the door, Brenda close behind him.

"I'm coming with you," she said.

"Brenda—"

"I'm in charge of the museum. And I agreed to take Parker on as a volunteer. If he was breaking in, then I need to address this, too."

He saw no point in trying to argue with her. "All right," he said. "Let's go see what this is all about."

BRENDA HAD NEVER been in this part of the sheriff's department—in the level below ground, and the single holding cell outside the booking area. Dwight had escorted her through a maze of locked doors without comment, until they stood outside the small cell where Parker sat, staring out from behind the bars. The young man looked angry, but behind the anger, she detected fear. Fear he was doing his best to hide, but she could see it.

"Brenda, I swear I didn't do the things he says," Parker said.

"Shut up, punk." Eddie, who had been talking with Gage at the far end of the booking area, turned to face them, frowning when he saw Brenda. "What are you doing here?" he demanded.

"I'm in charge of the museum," Brenda said.

"I'm going to check on a few things," Gage said to Dwight. "I'll leave you to look after things here."

Dwight nodded, then addressed Eddie. "What happened?"

"I caught him sneaking around in the alley, trying to pry open one of the windows," Eddie said.

"That's a lie!" Parker said.

"Quiet," Dwight ordered. "You'll have your turn in a minute."

"I did my job," Eddie said. "I cuffed him and brought him in."

"Why didn't you call nine-one-one?" Dwight asked.

"I didn't need backup to handle one punk."

Brenda balled her hands into fists. If Eddie used that word—*punk*—one more time, she might have to slap him.

"You aren't authorized to arrest anyone, much less bring them in and demand they be put in a cell," Dwight said.

Eddie folded his arms in front of his chest. "I made

a citizen's arrest," he said. "And apprehending a potential thief falls under my duties as security guard at the museum."

"He's lying," Parker said again, his voice less strident, more pleading.

"I'd like to hear Parker's side of the story," Brenda said.

Dwight turned to Parker. "All right, let's have it."

"I was driving home from delivering a pizza down the street from the museum. I saw this guy—" He pointed to Eddie. "He was sitting in a Jeep that was parked alongside the museum, in that alley. He was talking to another guy, in a black SUV."

Eddie leaned toward them, clearly about to object. Dwight held up a hand to stop him. "Let him continue."

"This afternoon, when I left the museum, I could tell Brenda was uncomfortable with this guy—Eddie—being there," Parker said. "I thought I should make sure he wasn't causing trouble."

Eddie laughed. "Oh, you'd know trouble, wouldn't you?"

Parker glared at him, then continued. "I wanted to hear what he and the guy in the SUV were talking about. I tried to get close enough to hear, but I tripped over some garbage and he heard me. The guy in the SUV took off and Eddie tackled me and held a gun to my head and demanded to know what I was doing there. He threatened to shoot me."

"Drama queen," Eddie said. "He's making that up. Wants you to feel sorry for him."

"Who was in the SUV?" Dwight asked Eddie.

"The mayor stopped by to see how things were going," Eddie said. "He knew Brenda was upset with me being there. We heard somebody rattling around in the alley and I ran back and caught Parker here trying to pry open a window. I figure he was going to steal some stuff to sell."

"No! I didn't try to break in," Parker said. "Go look for yourself. You won't find my fingerprints anywhere."

"You were probably wearing gloves," Eddie said.

"Then where are they now?" Parker asked.

Eddie shrugged. "You probably threw them away."

"Then they'd be in the alley, wouldn't they?"

"Eddie, did you threaten Parker with a gun?" Dwight asked.

"Of course not. I know better than that."

Brenda didn't believe him. Eddie wouldn't look Dwight in the eye—instead, his gaze kept darting to Parker.

"Look at my face." Parker pressed his cheek up against the bars. "You can see the bruises and cuts from where he pushed my face into the gravel." He turned to display the other cheek. "And there's a mark on this side where he held the gun barrel."

Brenda and Dwight leaned forward to view the faint round cut. "That could be from a pistol," Dwight said.

"The punk threatened me," Eddie protested. "I had a right to use force."

"You need to leave now, Eddie," Dwight said. "I'm going to take you upstairs and I'll deal with you later." He glanced at Brenda. "Will you be all right for a few minutes?"

"Of course."

Eddie opened his mouth, then closed it again. He followed Dwight to the first locked door, but before

Dwight could unlock it, it opened, and another deputy escorted Paige Riddell inside.

"What is going on?" Paige demanded. Then she saw Parker in the cell and rushed over to him.

"Rich, take Eddie upstairs and see him out," Dwight said.

"I didn't do anything," Parker said. "I was trying to help."

"I believe you," Brenda said.

"I'm going to send someone over to the museum to check," Dwight said. "If we don't find anything, we'll let you go."

"Eddie Carstairs is a liar and a weasel," Paige said. "He always has been. And he's never liked me, ever since I turned him down when he asked me out."

"I swear, I thought he and that guy in the SUV were up to something," Parker said. "That's the only reason I stopped."

"Next time you see something suspicious, call us," Dwight said. "Don't investigate on your own."

Parker looked at the floor, saying nothing. Brenda imagined for someone in his position, only recently out of jail and rehab, calling the cops wasn't the first line of action that came to mind.

The door opened again and Gage stepped in. "I checked the museum," he said. "I can't find any sign of tampering with any of the windows."

"Any gloves lying around anywhere?" Dwight asked.

"No. But I did find where it looks like Eddie and Parker scuffled—and two sets of tire tracks."

"Did you get a good look at the man in the other car?" Dwight asked Parker. "Was it the mayor?"

"I couldn't see him very well," Parker said. "And

I've never met the mayor, so I wouldn't know what he looks like."

"Clearly, Parker is telling the truth," Paige said. "You need to let him go."

"Brenda, do you want to press charges for trespassing?" Dwight asked.

"No." She shook her head.

"I think you should be charging Eddie with assault," Paige said.

"No, Paige," Parker said. "I just want to get out of here."

Dwight unlocked the cell, and Parker stepped out. He stopped in front of Brenda. "Thanks for believing me," he said.

"I do believe you." She lifted her chin. "I'm a good judge of character—not always, but most of the time. I think Eddie was the one lying, not you."

The four of them left together. "I'll take you home," Dwight said to Brenda.

She waited until they were in his SUV before she spoke again. "Why was Eddie lying?" she asked.

"I can't say for sure," Dwight said.

"But you have a theory. Tell me."

He sighed. "Eddie has always wanted to be the hero. I think, his first night on the job, he wanted to catch a burglar, prove it was a good idea for the town to hire him. But he always goes overboard. That's why Travis fired him."

"I think you're right," she said. "And I'm glad Travis fired him. He thinks wearing a gun makes him better than everyone else, and that's a dangerous attitude."

"Are you going to let Parker volunteer at the museum again?" Dwight asked.

"Yes. He did a great job for me today." She angled toward him, and studied the side of his face, illuminated by the dashboard lights. "Sometimes you have to go with your gut and trust people. And don't remind me I trusted Andy when he didn't deserve it."

"I wasn't going to say anything."

"I was younger then," she said. "And I was still grieving for my mother when we married. And later— later, I think I knew something wasn't right. It was why I kept questioning him about how we could afford all the work we had done on the house. But I was in love, and I wanted to believe him."

"I understand," Dwight said. "And I'm glad everything you've been through hasn't made you cynical."

"Not about everything," she said. "Though I don't trust as easily."

"That's all right. One thing being a cop teaches you is persistence."

She studied him, surprised by the word choice. "What is that supposed to mean?" she asked.

"It means I'm going to earn your trust. One of these days you're going to let down your guard with me and let yourself feel again."

She looked away. She didn't want to ask him what he thought she would feel. She could see it there, shining in his eyes. Dwight Prentice didn't think of her as just another crime victim who needed help. When he looked at her, he saw something more. He was letting her know that, but she wasn't sure what she was supposed to do about it. She wasn't ready to let down her guard with him or any other man. She wasn't ready to fall in love. The message Dwight had just sent her let her know he wasn't going to settle for less.

Chapter Seven

The next morning, Dwight met with Travis to review the previous night's events. "I spoke with the mayor," Dwight said. "Eddie's story about him stopping by last night checks out, though he says he doesn't know anything about Parker Riddell being there."

"What about the rest of Eddie's claim?" Travis asked. "Was Parker trying to break into the museum?"

"I don't think so," Dwight said. "I think the kid really was trying to sneak up on him and the mayor and Eddie overreacted—as usual."

"Gage didn't find any sign of an attempted break-in at the museum," Travis said.

"Brenda said she thought Eddie was lying, and I tend to agree with her," Dwight said. "He wouldn't look me in the eye."

"They could have chosen a better person for the job, but I don't think the town was wrong to hire a watchman for the museum," Travis said. "If the person who threatened Brenda thinks the book might be there, it's the next logical target."

"Brenda gave an interview to Tammy Patterson yesterday," Dwight said. "She said she told Tammy to make sure she stated in the article that the book was locked up at the sheriff's office."

"Good idea," Travis said. He leaned back in his chair, frowning. "Forensics didn't turn up anything on the notes. We did find the banner—ripped to pieces with a knife, probably a pocketknife—and stuffed into the Dumpster behind Moe's Pub. Nothing to go on there. The arson report on Brenda's house didn't turn up anything new, either."

"So we're back to wondering who wants that book destroyed and why," Dwight said.

"How's Brenda holding up?" Travis asked.

"Amazing. She's determined not to let this guy get to her. I thought later this morning I'd take her up to Eagle Mountain Resort and show her the lab—see if she spots any historical details the DEA missed."

"That's not going to prove a connection between what happened up there with Gage and Maya and what's going on with Brenda now," Travis said.

"No, but it might point us somewhere—to some collector and someone involved in the original project."

"When are you going?"

"She had some work to do at the museum this morning, then we're going to head up there," Dwight said. "Meanwhile, I want to take a look at that book."

"It's in the safe downstairs," Travis said. "Make sure you sign it back in when you're done."

"Yes, sir."

Dwight retrieved the combination to the safe, then got the book and sat down at his desk with it. After the first few pages, he struggled to keep going. The writer—S. Smith—had managed to take a potentially exciting subject and make it dry as sawdust. So he was relieved when the phone on his desk rang.

"There's a man here who wants to speak to you," Adelaide said. "A Professor Gibson."

Dwight closed the book and set it aside. "Send him in."

The professor was about eighty years old, thin and slightly stooped, with a full head of white hair and faded brown eyes peering from behind horn-rimmed spectacles. "The young woman at the newspaper suggested I talk to you," he said, peering into the office.

"Which young woman is that?" Dwight asked.

"Tammy? The reporter?" He stepped into the room and looked around.

"Why don't you sit down, Mr. Gibson." Dwight stood and closed the door behind the man.

"Val. Val Gibson." He lowered himself carefully into the chair across from Dwight's desk. "I'm a retired professor of history at Colorado State University."

Dwight returned to his seat. "Why did Tammy suggest you contact me?"

"She called me to get some information for a story she's working on—something to do with the government's activities in the state during World War II—Project Razor. She was researching the topic online and found an article I had written and realized I was a local. I retired to the area seven years ago."

"Project Razor?" This piqued Dwight's interest. "Do you mean the project to develop chemical weapons for use in the war?"

"Not just chemical weapons—biological ones, too."

"I'm not sure I'm clear on the difference," Dwight said.

"A chemical weapon uses a chemical agent to inflict

harm," Gibson explained. "So, for example, mustard gas in World War I or sarin gas. A biological weapon uses a pathogen, such as smallpox or anthrax."

"Aren't those against the Geneva Convention or something?" Dwight asked.

"The Geneva Convention of 1925 did ban the use of biological and chemical weapons," Gibson said. "But by World War II almost every major power, including the United States and Great Britain, had development programs in place. We don't believe the biological agents were ever used, but it wasn't until 1972 that a UN treaty was formed that forbade production of biological weapons—and even then, not every country is a signatory."

"How effective are biological weapons?" Dwight asked. "I mean, they sound terrible, but can't people be vaccinated or something?"

"Are you vaccinated against Q fever and tularemia?" Gibson asked.

"I've never even heard of them."

"Many of the agents used in biological warfare are obscure. As weapons, they can be devastating, but their effect isn't immediate, delivery methods are awkward, and you can't account for individuals who might have a natural immunity. So they're not seen as very practical for large-scale warfare. Still, there is some concern that terrorists could use them as another way to wreak havoc—release a vial of botulism spores in the air-conditioning system of a large office building and you could kill a lot of people and create a panic."

Dwight held up the book. "Are you familiar with this?"

"I'm very familiar with it," he said. "I have reason to believe that copy you're holding belongs to me."

Gibson spoke calmly, his expression pleasant. "Why do you think that?" Dwight asked.

"That young man—a lawyer—asked to borrow it years ago. Andrew Stenson. I was reluctant to lend it, but he was very persuasive. By the time I tried to get it back, he was dead." Gibson shrugged. "I tried to contact the widow, but the person who answered the phone said she was too upset to talk to anyone. They promised to look for the book and return it to me. I never heard anything back. I probably should have pressed the issue more, but it seemed petty, under the circumstances."

Was he telling the truth? Dwight couldn't tell. On one hand, maybe he was—Andy must have gotten this obscure title from somewhere. On the other, maybe this was a less-violent ploy to get hold of the book.

"Why did Andy Stenson want this book?" Dwight asked.

"He said he needed it for research he was doing on a case. He didn't elaborate, and I didn't pry. It's been my experience that lawyers as a group are fairly tight-lipped. Which I suppose is as it should be."

"Why didn't you say anything to Brenda Stenson when you saw that the book was up for auction?" Dwight asked.

"I didn't know it was up for auction until Tammy told me about it yesterday afternoon," Gibson said. "I don't take the local paper."

Again, maybe true—maybe not.

"I'll admit I haven't read the book," Dwight said. "It's a little...dry."

Gibson chuckled. "I suspect the author had written one too many government reports. It reads much like one. But as far as I've been able to determine, the information in the book is factual."

"Is there anything in there that might lead someone to want the book destroyed?" Dwight asked. "Something that incriminates an individual or casts a bad light on someone?"

"Destroyed?" Gibson looked puzzled.

"Someone sent Mrs. Stenson threatening notes, ordering her to destroy the book—or else. What kind of stationery do you use, Professor?"

"I have never threatened Mrs. Stenson, Deputy. And I'm not the sort of person who would ever destroy a book, or ask someone else to—especially not a valuable collector's item, like that one." He straightened. "And I don't use stationery. Who does in these days of emails and text messaging? I may look like a dinosaur to you, but I'm not."

Dwight remained skeptical. "You said Tammy contacted you because of an article you wrote about the project?"

"Yes. I've thought of writing a book about the history of biological and chemical warfare. The research has been a hobby of mine for some time now."

"Do you know where in Rayford County Project Razor took place?"

"I haven't been able to discover that, no." He nodded toward the book on Dwight's desk. "All that says is that abandoned mines were used for the laboratories, but considering how many of those are in the area, that isn't much of a clue."

"Do you know of anyone alive today who was involved in this research?" Dwight asked.

"No. From what I can gather, the scientists involved

were in their thirties and forties at the time. That would make even the youngest over a hundred years old."

"Then it's not one of them threatening Mrs. Stenson. Maybe a child or grandchild?"

Gibson shook his head. "There's nothing in the book to implicate anyone. As I recall the author, Mr. Smith— which I suspect is a nom de plume—didn't use any real names in his book. There's a disclaimer in the front that says so."

Dwight nodded. He had skipped over the book's front matter, but he had a vague recollection of an author's note. He'd go back and read it later. "Maybe this book isn't even the point," he said. "It could be a distraction to keep us from looking at the real reason for the threats."

"Why did Mrs. Stenson decide to auction the book?" Gibson asked.

"The museum she directs is in financial trouble. When she found the book in her late husband's belongings, she researched it online and saw how valuable it was, so she decided to sell it and use the money for the museum. She's been collecting donated items from others to auction, as well."

Gibson nodded. "I suppose I would rather see the book used for something like that than for personal gain."

"You could always bid on the book yourself."

He smiled. "My days of having that kind of money to spend on a hobby are gone. I lucked on to the book at a secondhand shop in Denver a good twenty years ago. I think I paid seven dollars for it at the time."

"Are you going to ask Mrs. Stenson to return the book to you?"

"I don't think so. I wasn't savvy enough to ask her

husband for a receipt or any other proof of the loan. That was my own foolishness." He stood. "Now that you've told me what Mrs. Stenson intends to do with the book, I'm happy to see it used for those purposes." He gave a wry smile. "As you observed, it's not exactly light reading material—and I never was one for owning things I wouldn't use or enjoy. Though I hope the threats toward Mrs. Stenson don't continue."

"We're watching the situation closely." Dwight walked with the professor toward the front of the station.

He was surprised to find Brenda waiting in the reception area. She stood as he approached. "I'm ready to leave when you are," she said.

"Brenda Stenson, this is Professor Val Gibson," Dwight said. "He—"

"I have some expertise in the history of biological and chemical weapons development in the US," Gibson said. "I wanted to offer my services to law enforcement in regard to the book that I understand has been the subject of threats to you."

"You know something about the threats?" Brenda asked.

"No, only about the book and its subject matter," Gibson said. "I'm afraid I wasn't much help." He nodded to her, then turned to Dwight. "Feel free to contact me if you have any questions."

As soon as the professor had left, Brenda moved closer to Dwight. "What was that about?" she asked.

"I'll tell you on the drive up to the resort. Come on." He led the way out the back of the building to his cruiser.

She waited until they were belted in and he had started the engine before she spoke again. "Why did the professor really come to see you?" she asked.

"You don't believe what he told you?" Dwight asked.

"You were about to say something about him when he interrupted." She sat back in the seat. "Don't ever play poker, Dwight. Your face is full of tells."

"You should have been the attorney in the family," he said. "You'd be good at interrogating witnesses. But before I answer your question, tell me if you've ever heard of Professor Val Gibson before."

"No. Who is he?"

"He's the man who owned that book before Andy. He said Andy wanted to borrow it to do some research for a case he was working on. The professor never saw the book again and had put it out of his mind until Tammy called him up yesterday to interview him for the article about the threats being made against you."

"Whoa, back up a little. Andy stole the book from the professor?" In addition to being a blackmailer, was her late husband a thief, also?

"I don't think he intended to steal it—I think he borrowed it and was murdered before he could return it. Then it just kind of fell through the cracks."

She nodded. "Does he want the book back? Is that why he came to you?"

"That may have been his intention originally, but after he learned about the auction to raise money for the museum, he seemed okay with that. And he admitted he didn't have any proof that it ever belonged to him."

"Maybe learning someone is threatening me because of the book made him think twice about wanting to own it," she said.

"That may have had something to do with it, too," Dwight said.

"I still don't understand how he ended up talking to you," she said. "Why not contact me directly?"

"Apparently, Tammy called him for some information for the article she's writing about the book and the threats to you," Dwight said. "She found him through an article he wrote about the top-secret government labs in Colorado during World War II and learned he was in the area. He told me he retired here seven years ago. When she learned he knew all about the book, she suggested he get in touch with me."

"But he wasn't able to help you?"

"He seemed to know a lot about what was in the book, and about the government's activities in general, but neither of us could think of any reason someone would want the book destroyed. He told me the author used pseudonyms for all the people who were involved in the project, and it's doubtful any of them are alive anymore, anyway."

"So he really wasn't much help."

"No. He doesn't know where the work was done, although he did say the weapons they developed were never used."

"I suppose that's comforting—sort of," she said.

"Everything okay at work this morning?" he asked.

"Eddie wasn't there and nothing was missing. No new threatening letters. So I'd call it good."

"Have you heard from Parker?"

"No, but I don't expect to. He said he had classes today." She shifted toward him. "I know you aren't crazy about Parker, but I really like him. I think at heart, he's a good kid."

"There's such a thing as being too trusting," he said.

"And there's such a thing as being too cynical," she shot back.

To her surprise, he grinned. "Guilty as charged. It's part of the job."

He looked so comfortable in his uniform, here in this cruiser, surrounded by the tools of his trade. "When we were growing up, I never would have pegged you as a future cop," she said.

"What did you think I would do?" he asked.

"I don't know—ranching, I guess. Or maybe business." He had always made decent grades, and been the serious, thoughtful type.

"I thought about both of those," he said. "But I have an uncle who is a small-town police officer in Wisconsin, and I always admired that. And I didn't want to sit behind a desk at a job where I'd be bored."

"I can't think law enforcement in Eagle Mountain is that exciting—at least most of the time."

"Some days are more of an adrenaline rush than others—for me, the pace is about right. And my ranching background comes in handy when we have to put cows or horses back in pastures."

She laughed. It was a local joke that the weekly sheriff's department activity reports printed in the local paper always contained a number of calls to put livestock back in pastures.

"It's good to hear you laugh, in spite of everything that's happened," he said.

"I'm still alive. I still have a job and friends, and I'm going to get through this." Saying the words made her feel stronger—and they were true. The threats were frightening, and she had lost things in the fire she would miss forever, but she still had so much.

"Yes, you are," he said. They fell silent as the cruiser headed out of town. Soon houses gave way to a solid wall of evergreens on either side of the road, and beyond that the red-and-gray cliffs of the mountains. "Have you ever been up here, to Eagle Mountain Resort?" Dwight asked.

"Once—they had some kind of ribbon-cutting or ground-breaking and I attended with Andy. That seems like a lifetime ago." It had been four years—she had definitely been a different person, then.

"What did you think?" he asked.

"That it was a shame to build fancy houses that would stay empty half the year in such a beautiful spot. I kept that opinion to myself. It didn't seem wise to criticize the man who was pretty much paying for the roof over my head and the food on my plate."

"You haven't been up here since?"

"No. Though I've heard it's a ghost town now. Paige and her group think it's an eyesore. Before Henry Hake went missing, they were lobbying him to restore the property to its natural state.

"I guess everything is in limbo until Hake is found."

"Hmm."

It was the kind of non-comment that made Brenda suspect Dwight knew more about Hake's disappearance—or about the future of the resort—than he was willing to say. That was probably part of being a cop, too—knowing things you couldn't talk about. But she didn't care. She had never been particularly fond of Henry Hake, and though she missed his regular donations to the museum, she couldn't pretend to grieve for him now that he was probably dead. As for his proposed resort, it would either be developed or not, and there were plenty of other people in town—like Paige Riddell and her environmental group—to worry about it. Brenda had other things to focus on—the upcoming auction, securing funding to keep the museum open, and finding a new place to live.

Dwight pulled the cruiser into a paved drive and parked in front of a pair of massive black iron gates. The gates stood partially open, remnants of yellow-and-black crime scene tape flapping from the crossbars. "Those gates aren't supposed to be open," Dwight said. He put the cruiser in Park and got out to examine the gates. A moment later, he was back. "Someone cut the lock," he said.

"Didn't you say the DEA had been up here, investigating?"

"I don't think they would have been so sloppy as to leave a broken lock hanging on the gate." He eased the vehicle through the opening and up the drive. Brenda studied the boarded-up buildings, crumbling foundations and dying landscaping that was all that remained of the proposed luxury development. Dwight steered around a waterfall of rock that spilled down an embankment and she knew without asking that this was where Wade Tomlinson and Brock Ryan had died, after they had left Gage and Maya and little Casey for dead.

Dwight stopped in front of a Quonset hut partially built into the hillside. "The lab is in here," he said.

She followed him out of the vehicle and walked to the entrance. The door—a massive metal rectangle with no window—leaned against the side of the hill. "Travis had that removed," Dwight said. "He didn't want anyone to end up locked inside—accidentally or on purpose."

Brenda repressed a shudder. "I'm glad he did. I'm not sure I'd want to go in if it was on there."

"Come on. I'll show you the lab." Dwight switched on his flashlight and led the way inside. The first room was a large, bare space, the dirt floor packed down and clean, save for a handful of dry leaves that skittered across the space, stirred by their entrance. A second door stood open at the far end of the room, and as they drew closer, Brenda realized it had been removed from its hinges also.

Dwight played the beam of the flashlight into the next room and swore under his breath. "What's wrong?" she asked, and moved up beside him to look inside.

"The place is cleared out," he said. "There was a workbench and tables and lab equipment in here before."

The space—with a floor of concrete, not dirt, and chains hanging from the ceiling that might have once held light fixtures—had been swept clean, not so much as a speck of dirt on the floors or walls, which were completely bare, except for a fly that crawled up one wall. "Maybe the DEA took everything away," she said.

"They didn't bother to mention it to us." He pulled out his phone and took several pictures.

Brenda's gaze shifted to the opening at the far end of the room. "Is that where Gage and Maya were held?" she asked.

"Yes." Dwight led the way across to it. Brenda hung back. "It's all right," he said. "There's nothing in here. It's pretty much like that first room—empty."

He was right, of course. It wasn't as if she were sight-seeing in a torture chamber. Still, she had to make herself cross the room to stand beside him. "Why are these rooms even here?" she asked.

"I don't know," he said. "Storage, maybe." He shone the light through the opening, and they both leaned in to examine the space. The beam of light illuminated a dirt floor, concrete walls—and something suspended from the ceiling—a suit of old clothes or a dummy or—

"Don't look." Dwight shoved Brenda back as the realization of what she was looking at hit her.

"Is that a body?" she asked.

He put his arm around her and hurried her toward the door. "We need to get down and call for help," he said. "I think we might have found Henry Hake."

Chapter Eight

Dwight stood beside his cruiser as the EMTs loaded the body into the back of the ambulance. Brenda sat inside, pale but silent, staring through the windshield toward the emergency vehicle's strobing lights. She hadn't said much of anything since they'd driven away from the resort to call for help, then headed back to wait for the sheriff and others to arrive. Dwight had tried to think of something to say to comfort her, but he hadn't been able to come up with anything. She was shaken but not hysterical, which pretty much described his own feelings.

When the EMTs had closed the doors behind them and driven away, Travis came over. "What made you think it was Henry Hake?" he asked.

"The suit," Dwight said. "Henry always wore those brown suits—I don't know. Something about it just struck me as him. I probably should have verified before I blurted it out like that."

"The coroner will verify, but it's probably Hake," Travis said. "There was a wallet in the back pocket, with Hake's driver's license. A money clip with the initials *HH*, but no money."

"Where's he been all this time?" Dwight asked. "It's been weeks."

"The body looked sort of—mummified," Travis said. "I didn't do a really thorough examination, but there wasn't any obvious sign of trauma. We'll have to wait for the medical examiner's report."

"When we got here, the lock on the gate had been cut and it was open," Dwight said. "And everything's been cleaned out of the lab."

"I saw that. I'll contact Allerton, but I don't think the DEA did that."

"Yeah. I'm guessing whoever left Hake's body cleaned out the lab, too. They must have known we'd find him."

"They've had plenty of time to cover their tracks," Travis said. "They could have left the area—even the country—by now." The ambulance drove past and he signaled the crime scene techs to move in. "There goes my theory that Wade and Brock killed Hake."

"You thought that?" Dwight asked.

"Why not? They killed Maya's sister and brother-in-law and would have killed Gage and Maya if they'd had the chance."

"But why?" Dwight asked. "What was in it for them?"

"I haven't come up with an answer to that yet." He glanced toward Dwight's SUV. "Why the threats to Brenda? Why burn down her house?"

"Do you think what's going on with her is connected in some way to Hake's disappearance and what happened with Maya and Gage?" Dwight asked.

Travis rubbed the back of his neck. "I don't know, but it feels that way. This is a small county—historically very low crime, and nothing very serious. And now we have a crime wave. Everything else has been related to this property, starting with Andy Stenson's murder three and a half years ago."

"Andy is the one who first got hold of that book the guy who's targeted Brenda wanted destroyed," Dwight said. "He told Professor Gibson he needed it to research a case. I'm wondering if the case had something to do with Hake—and if Andy was killed because he found out something he shouldn't have."

"Ian Barnes never said why he killed Andy," Travis said. "But he told Lacy he needed to kill her because she knew too much—something she didn't even realize the significance of. She has no idea what he was talking about."

"We've always assumed Maya's sister and brother-in-law were killed because they saw Wade and Brock with Henry Hake," Dwight said.

Travis nodded. "But what if they saw something else?" He glanced over his shoulder toward the Quonset hut. "Something to do with that lab, maybe."

"Every time we pull at one thread in this case, everything gets more knotted up," Dwight said.

"But we're going to keep pulling until we find the solution to the puzzle," Travis said. "I'll finish up here. You take care of Brenda."

Dwight returned to the SUV. "What now?" Brenda asked.

"If you feel up to it, you'll need to make a statement. We just need to get down your account of what happened for the case file."

She nodded. "I can do that."

"It's better to do it now, while it's fresh in your mind."

"Fine. I'll do it now."

"After that I can take you home. To my home, I mean."

"All right."

He started the cruiser and headed back toward town. Beside him, Brenda was still as a statue, not making a sound. She was too calm. Finding Henry Hake's body that way must have shaken her—it would have shaken anyone. It had shaken *him*. Yet she showed no emotion at all. Not reacting was probably a defense mechanism, especially considering how much tragedy she had faced recently. But walling off emotions never worked for long, and the fallout could be worse than giving in to tears now.

BRENDA DICTATED HER statement to Dwight, getting through the ordeal by pretending the events of that morning had happened to someone else. Every time she closed her eyes, she could see the shapeless figure in the baggy suit hanging there, twisting slowly in the breeze... Then she would snap open her eyes, take a deep breath, and focus on something else—the crooked diploma on the wall behind Dwight's desk, the chipped paint near the doorway of his office, the dust on the toes of her own shoes.

When she had signed the printed statement, he ushered her back to his car and drove out to his parents' ranch. She appreciated that he didn't try to talk to her. She didn't have anything to say. She felt empty—hollowed out and fragile, less woman than paper doll.

It wasn't until they passed the turnoff to his parents' house that she stirred. "Where are we going?" she asked.

"I'm taking you to my place," he said. "I thought you

might appreciate the peace and quiet there. My mom means well, but she tends to hover."

"Thanks." She had to speak around the lump in her throat. His thoughtfulness touched her. She cleared her throat. "I'm sure you have work to do," she said. "I shouldn't be keeping you from it."

"I don't have anything urgent right now." He glanced at her. "I want to make sure you're all right."

"I'm fine." She spoke the automatic lie she had been using for years now. The assurance kept people from prodding too deeply. She was keeping it together so they didn't have to worry.

Dwight said nothing, merely pulled up to his cabin and parked. The square cedar-sided cabin featured a porch across the front, and a gray tabby cat asleep in a rocking chair beside the door. The cat stood and stretched at their approach. "This is Otis," Dwight said, pausing to scratch behind the cat's ears before he opened the front door.

Otis purred like an engine humming along and followed them into the cabin, long tail twitching. "Oh, this is nice," Brenda said, stopping three steps into the front room. She wasn't sure what she had expected—something utilitarian and maybe a little worn, filled with hand-me-down furniture and the clutter of a bachelor life. Instead, the open, high-ceilinged room had the comfortable Western vibe upscale design magazines strived for, with a layer of authenticity that welcomed a visitor to sit down and kick off her shoes.

A Persian carpet in shades of red, black and blue covered the worn wooden floor, and a cast-iron-and-soapstone woodstove dominated one wall, flanked on either side by big windows that offered a view of golden hayfields and the mountains beyond, the peaks dusted with the autumn's first snow. A caramel-colored sofa and two matching armchairs were arranged around a table made from a slab of wood worn smooth by years of use. A flat-screen TV on an oak sideboard was the chief reminder that this was a modern home and not some backcountry retreat.

"Make yourself at home," Dwight said, motioning toward the sofa. "I'll fix us something to drink."

Not waiting for a reply, he headed toward the kitchen, which was separated from the living area by a massive island. Brenda moved to the sofa and sat, looking around at the shelves of books between the windows and the artwork on the walls—pen-and-ink drawings of elk, moose and other wildlife interspersed with paintings of rodeo cowboys. She leaned closer to peer at one of the paintings, of a young man in jeans and chaps carrying a saddle, a number pinned to the back of his leather vest. "Is that you?" she asked, when Dwight rejoined her in the living room.

"Me a long time ago," he said. "The artist is a family friend." He handed her a short, squat glass filled with ice and a dark liquor, and sat on the sofa beside her—close, but not touching.

She studied the drink. "What is this?"

"A brandy old-fashioned."

"Dwight, it's only one in the afternoon."

"Drink it. You need it after what you experienced this morning. I know I do." He took a long swallow of his own drink.

She took a tentative sip. It was sweet—and had a definite heat as it went down. She set the glass on the edge of the table and continued to look around the room.

"We should talk about what happened," Dwight said.

She turned to him. "I gave you my statement."

He frowned. "I don't mean the events that occurred—I mean, what's going through your head right now."

"Nothing's going through my head right now."

"And you don't think that's a problem?"

"I don't know what you mean."

He scooted forward to the edge of his seat and set his drink beside hers on the table. "Then I'll be frank. I'm worried about you. You've been through more awful things in the past few days—much less the past four years—than most people have to suffer through in a lifetime. Yet you go on as if nothing has happened. That's not normal."

She stiffened. "I'm not the hysterical type," she said. "And I did break down after Andy died." For months she had barely been able to function. She didn't want to go back to those helpless, out-of-control days.

He moved closer. "I'm not saying you have to get hysterical," he said. "But it's okay to let yourself feel. To acknowledge that some awful things have happened. And that it's not fair."

She nodded. She'd heard this advice before—read it in the books she turned to after Andy's death, told it to herself even. But taking the advice and letting go wasn't so easy. "Life isn't fair," she said. "I know that. And I don't see any point in dwelling on it."

Dwight took her hand. "I know you're tough. I admire that about you. But if you keep trying to bear the weight of all this by yourself, I'm afraid you're going to crumble."

His fingers twined with hers, so warm and strong. She held on in spite of herself, wanting to draw courage from him. "I don't know what you want from me," she whispered.

"I want you to trust me enough to believe that you don't have to put up walls between us," he said. "You've been hurt and it's okay to acknowledge that."

She stared down at her lap, her vision blurring. "I'm afraid," she said.

"Afraid of what?"

"Afraid if I let myself think about how awful things are right now, I'll start crying and never be able to stop."

"I'm no expert," he said. "But I think sometimes, if you let the hurt out, it makes room for good things to fill up that space."

"What good things?" The words came out harsh and full of bitterness she hadn't wanted to acknowledge. "I don't have a home. I may not have a job soon. Some maniac is threatening to kill me." Her voice broke. "I've never been so afraid or felt so alone."

He drew her to him, his arms a firm barrier to keep away harm. She buried her face against his shoulder, her tears flowing unchecked. She hated breaking down like this, yet it was such a wonderful release to do so. As the first wave of emotion subsided, she became aware of him stroking her back and gently kissing the top of her head. A different sort of emotion welled within her—a fierce awareness of Dwight as a man. New tears flowed, but these were tears of relief that after all she had been through, she could still feel the things a woman should feel—she was still alive and capable of desire and passion.

She tilted her face up to his and found his lips, pressing her body more firmly against his. He responded with an urgency that matched her own, pulling her onto his lap, one hand caressing her hip while the other cradled her cheek. She wrapped both arms around him, her breasts flattened against his chest, her mouth open, tongue eagerly exploring his mouth, reveling in thrilling, too-long-forgotten sensations shooting through her.

She rocked her hips and smiled as he let out a low groan, his erection hard and hot between them. He pressed his lips against her throat and spoke in a voice ragged with lust. "We'd better stop now unless you want it to go further," he said.

"Oh, I want it to go further." She trailed one hand along his cheek, the prickle of five-o'clock shadow along his jaw sending a fresh wave of heat through her. "I want you. I think I have for a while now, I just wasn't ready to admit it."

He grinned in answer and shoved to his feet, carrying her with him. She laughed, and he gripped her tightly and kissed her until she was dizzy and breathless. "Put me down," she pleaded, laughing.

"Oh, I'm not putting you down," he said. "Not until neither one of us is capable of standing."

He stalked toward the bedroom, her legs wrapped around his waist, his fingers digging into her buttocks. He didn't release her until they both collapsed onto the bed, and then only to begin stripping off her clothes as she tore at his shirt and pants.

Only when they were both naked, cuddling together side by side, did their fury give way to tenderness—still urgent, but more deliberate, each intent on savoring the moments. She trailed her fingers across the taut skin of his shoulders, tracing the contour of muscle and bone, memorizing the shape and sensation of him. He did the same, brushing kisses along her jaw and down the column of her throat, his tongue following the swell of her breasts and dipping into the valley between them, then sliding along to suck at first one breast and then the other, until she was quivering and all but whimpering with need.

She reached between them and grasped him, satin-smooth and hot, all but pulsing in her hand. "Do you have any protection?" she asked.

In answer, he gently pried her fingers from him and slid over to the side of the bed and took a condom from the drawer of the nightstand. He ripped open the package and rolled on the rubber, the movement leaving her dry-mouthed and ready to pounce on him.

Instead, he lay back and pulled her on top of him. "Ready to go for a ride?" he asked.

"Oh, yeah." She lowered herself over him, closing her eyes against the exquisite pleasure of him filling her. When she opened them again, she found him smiling up at her, his eyes full of such wanting and tenderness that it all but undid her. She began to rock, gently at first, then with more movement, drawing out their pleasure, holding back as the need built between them. He grasped her hips, encouraging her, and they began to move together, thrust and withdrawal, advance and retreat, until she shuddered, her climax overpowered her, filling and overflowing. "Dwight!"

His name still echoed around them as he found his own release. He pulled her close to him and kissed her hard, then rolled with her onto his side, where they lay, still connected, his eyes reflecting all the wonder she felt. "Feel better now?" he asked.

She laughed. "I do." She kissed the end of his nose. "Thank you."

"No thanks needed," he said. "I'm just glad you're here."

"Me, too." She hadn't felt all that glad to be anywhere in a long time, and though he wouldn't let her thank him for it, she was more than grateful that he had given her back this part of herself—this ability to feel so alive and whole.

Chapter Nine

Dwight never got around to taking Brenda up to the main house that night. His parents could see his cruiser parked at his cabin from their house, and he suspected they would draw their own conclusions about Brenda's whereabouts. He was happy to have her stay with him, and he wasn't about to put a damper on the new closeness they shared by suggesting she leave. Whatever barriers she had erected before had melted away somewhere between her flood of tears and the passion they had finally given in to.

She slept in his arms that night and woke early to make love again, a satisfying, leisurely coupling that left him so ridiculously happy he was afraid the grin he wore was permanently etched on his face.

He made breakfast while she showered, and when she joined him in the kitchen, smelling of his soap, damp tendrils of hair curling around her face, he had to focus to get his breathing under control. "Did you find everything you needed?" he asked, deliberately playing it cool.

"Oh, I think so." She moved to the coffeemaker and filled a cup.

Dwight turned back to the frying pan. "How do you like your eggs?" he asked.

"However you want to cook them. I'm not picky."

He scrambled eggs and made toast, aware of her eyes on him. Conversation, which had before now been easy with her, was apparently choked off by the lust that hovered like a cloud around him. How was it that at thirty, he could be reduced to the incoherence of adolescence?

She smiled when he set the plate down in front of her. "I could get used to this," she said.

"So could I."

She said nothing, but polished off the breakfast as if she were famished—which she probably was, considering they had never gotten around to eating last night. When she finally pushed her plate away, she sighed. "That was delicious."

"Thanks," he said. "I'm no gourmet, but I manage to feed myself."

She put her chin in her hand and studied him, her silent scrutiny making him nervous. "What is it?" he asked. "Why are you looking at me that way?"

"I'm just wondering why it is you're still single."

That definitely wasn't a question he had expected. "Last I heard, being single isn't a crime," he said.

"Of course it isn't. But you're an attractive man with a good personality, a nice home, a good job. There are plenty of unattached women in this county who would love to go out with you. But I can't remember you ever being in a relationship with any of them. Why?"

"You worried I'm gay?"

The pink flush that spread across her cheeks made her look even sexier. "Um, no."

"I've dated," he said. "I'm just discreet about it."

"Then you definitely have a talent for subterfuge. It's not easy keeping a secret like that in this town."

"I like to keep my private life private."

"So do I," she said. "But I haven't had much luck with that, so far. The *Examiner* might be broke by now if it weren't for me and those I'm close to supplying them with juicy headlines."

"You're not responsible for the things Andy did," he said gently.

"No, but I'm part of them. I can't get away from that. And as you might imagine, it hasn't made me eager to trust another man."

"You can trust me."

"Can I?" The expression in her eyes had hardened. "Haven't we already established that you're good at deception?"

"I don't deceive people I care about."

"I'm sorry. I didn't mean to suggest that." She looked away. "It's not you who's messed up, it's me."

"Don't say that." He leaned across the table toward her. "There's nothing wrong with you. You're perfect."

A choked laugh escaped her. "Oh, no I'm not."

"You're perfect for me. I've always thought that." He straightened. "Maybe you're the reason I'm not married. I was waiting for you."

"Dwight." She shoved out of her chair and stood, backing away from him. "Last night—what happened between us was amazing. But that doesn't mean I'm ready for more, I—"

"I know." He resisted the urge to move toward her, forcing himself to remain still, to rely on his words to reach her. "I'm not asking for anything. But you asked me an honest question—I figured I owed you an honest answer."

She considered this for a moment, then nodded. "All right. But what happens now?"

"Now I think I should take you to work." He stood, the movement slow and easy, as if she were an easily frightened animal. "Your car is still there, right?"

"Right. I'll get my things." She started to turn away, then stopped. "Thank you for being so understanding."

Oh yeah. He was understanding all right. Understanding that when it came to Brenda Stenson, he was pretty much at her mercy. Not a position he liked to be in.

BRENDA PRIDED HERSELF on keeping her emotions in check, but Dwight's declaration that he had been waiting for her had left her reeling. While last night had been an incredibly pleasurable and yes, healing, experience, she hadn't been prepared for what amounted to a declaration of love from a man she had always considered as taciturn and frankly, hard to read.

And now she had to sit here beside him in his cruiser and pretend that her emotions weren't all over the place. Wouldn't it be nice if she could have even a single day that wasn't full of drama? She'd almost forgotten what that was like.

Her morning didn't get any better when Dwight drove her to the museum and she spotted Eddie Carstairs seated on the bench beside the front door. "What is he doing here?" she asked as Dwight pulled his cruiser to the curb.

"Let's find out," Dwight said.

Her first instinct was to tell him that she could take

care of Eddie herself, but maybe it wasn't a bad idea to have a witness to back her up if things got heated. For whatever reason, Eddie seemed to have the mayor on his side, and since the town council was Brenda's employer, she ought to tread carefully.

"Hello, Eddie," she said as she climbed the steps to the front porch of the museum. "Did you need something?"

"Just keeping an eye on things," he said.

"I thought you were a night watchman," she said.

He ignored her, turning instead to Dwight. "I heard there was some excitement yesterday afternoon, up at Eagle Mountain Resort," he said.

"I imagine the news is all over town by now," Dwight said. But he didn't elaborate on what that news might be.

Eddie shifted from foot to foot. "Pretty funny to find Henry Hake up there after all this time, don't you think?" he said.

"I don't know of anyone who found it amusing," Dwight said.

Brenda opened her mouth to tell Eddie to get lost when he turned to her. "You were there, weren't you?" he asked.

"Yes." She crossed her arms over her chest. "But I don't have anything to say to you about it."

"I heard the body was practically mummified," Eddie said. "I figure his killer stashed him up there in one of those caves up on the cliffs. The Indians used to do that and the cool, dry air just desiccates the body. Sort of like beef jerky."

"I wouldn't know about that," Brenda said.

Eddie turned to Dwight again. "You must know how he died," he said.

"If I did, I wouldn't share it with you," Dwight said.

"You ought to think twice about that," Eddie said. "I know a lot of people in this town, see a lot of stuff. I might have information that could help you."

"If you have information, tell me what it is," Dwight said. "But the exchange doesn't work both ways."

The two men glared at each other like two roosters about to face off. Brenda was grateful when a new arrival interrupted.

"Hi, Brenda," Parker Riddell said as he headed up the walkway. "You said you might need help with that new display today."

"Yes, Parker." She offered him her warmest smile. "I'm glad to see you."

The two slightly older men studied the younger one as he mounted the steps to stand by Brenda. "Hello, Deputy, Eddie," Parker said.

Dwight greeted Parker, but Eddie only nodded, his lip curled in a sneer. Neither man gave any indication of budging. "Eddie, Dwight, you need to take this conversation elsewhere," Brenda said. "Parker and I have work to do."

Dwight's eyes met hers. She remained firm, but gave a slight nod, to show she wasn't holding anything against him. "Come on, Eddie," Dwight said. "Let's get out of Brenda's hair."

"This is public property," Eddie said. "I have a right to be here."

"Yeah, but if you waste the whole day standing around here, people are going to get the wrong idea," Dwight said.

"What do you mean?" Eddie asked.

"They're going to figure you don't have anything better to do. That you're too washed up to get a job."

"I have a job," Eddie said. "I'm establishing my own private security company."

"Right. Then go find some more clients. Don't stand around here harassing Brenda."

"I'm not harassing her. I—"

"Eddie!" Brenda snapped the word, more than tired of this conversation. "Get out of here or I'll call the mayor and tell him you're interfering with museum business."

She could tell he wanted to argue with her, but he set his jaw and stalked down the steps and across the yard to his Jeep.

"I'll be going, too," Dwight said, keys in hand.

"I'll see you later." Then, without another look back, she walked into the museum. For now, at least, this was her domain—the kingdom she ruled without a consort. Yes, it was lonely, but there was a kind of security in that loneliness, a way to keep her heart safe even if her head argued she was being stupid.

Parker followed Brenda inside, where she greeted Emma Waide, who had been volunteering at the museum since it first opened. "We're going to be working on the new exhibit if you need anything," she said.

"How is school going?" she asked Parker as they climbed the stairs to the second floor.

"It's okay. My history class is pretty interesting. Just basic American history, but still, the professor is good."

"The classes will get more interesting if you pursue the degree," she said. "You can home in on areas of particular interest."

"I like the World War II era. There was so much happening all over the world back then."

The exhibit in progress was just as she had left it the day before yesterday, with most of the material they would display still in boxes. Brenda consulted the plans she had drawn up. "I hope you're ready to work," she said. "I need you to move some shelves and tables around for me. Some of them are pretty heavy."

"No problem."

For the next two hours, they worked arranging the space. Parker proved both strong and fast, and able to work well without supervision—in other words, a dream volunteer. "I'd never get this done so quickly without your help," she said as she surveyed the newly arranged furnishings. "Now all we have to do is set out the items on display. Later today I'll work on printing out all the labels and signs."

"This is the fun part," Parker said as he opened a carton and lifted out a World War II-era uniform. "Like opening Christmas presents."

"It is sort of like that," Brenda agreed. "I've seen all this stuff before, but it's been packed away for a while. And some of it has never been on display. People give us things all the time that we have to save for the appropriate exhibit." She set a canteen and mess kit side by side on a shelf.

"What do we do with the clothes?" Parker asked, as he laid out a navy uniform next to the army gear.

"We have mannequins we'll need to dress," she said. "We'll save them for last."

After another hour, they had everything unpacked and arranged. Brenda might move some items later, after she had time to consider the flow of the exhibit.

The idea was to display things in a logical order that led visitors from one area of the room to the next. They retrieved the mannequins from her workroom and arranged them in the center of the room, the navy man clutching a pair of binoculars, his army counterpart holding a field radio.

"It looks pretty good," Parker said as he and Brenda stood in the doorway, surveying their work.

"It will look even better when the signs and labels are up. And I may add a few things in. Sometimes after a new exhibit goes up, someone will come in and donate something that fits the theme."

"What about that book you're auctioning?" he asked. "The one about the secret labs that were here in the county in World War II?"

She shook her head. "It's far too valuable—and apparently, controversial—to display."

"Do you think I could see it some time?" he asked.

"Why do you want to see it?" she asked.

He shrugged. "To try to figure out what all the fuss is about, I guess."

"The sheriff has the book and it's going to stay with him until the auction."

"Yeah, I guess that probably is best. Have you had any more threatening letters?"

"No. I hope the article in the paper will scare off whoever wrote the letters. I tried to make it clear that I was immune to threats."

"I hope you're right and you scare him off," Parker said. "And don't just make him angry and want to try harder."

His words sent a shiver through her. She watched him out of the corner of her eye as they moved empty boxes back into storage and swept up the room. Maybe he was only curious about the book and concerned about her—but what if he had other motives?

She said goodbye to him and the afternoon volunteer and prepared to lock up the building and leave herself. She hated feeling this way—untrusting and suspicious. Was Dwight's cynicism rubbing off on her? If that was the case, she wouldn't thank him for it.

Chapter Ten

"We have the coroner's report on Henry Hake." Travis distributed copies around the conference table, two days after Dwight and Brenda discovered the body. "There was a fair amount of deterioration, but he's ruled out physical violence as the cause of death. He found no sign of gunshots, knife wounds or asphyxiation."

Dwight skimmed the paperwork, flipping over to the end of the report. Next to "Cause of Death" was a single word: *Inconclusive*.

"Does that mean it's possible Hake wasn't murdered?" Gage asked.

"We can't rule out murder," Travis said. "Especially considering how the body was found. But the coroner did say the body was strung up after death—and that it hadn't been hanging where we found it long."

"We knew that already," Gage said. "The Feds only left the place three days ago."

"Maybe Hake was poisoned," Dwight said. "One of those poisons that leaves the body in a relatively short time."

"Did the coroner say how long Hake had been dead?" Gage asked.

"Approximately seven weeks—maybe a little more," Travis said.

"So he died not too long after he disappeared," Dwight said.

"The coroner did find evidence of heart disease," Travis said. "It's possible Hake was kidnapped and the stress brought on a heart attack. The kidnappers panicked, ditched the car and hid the body."

"Then why not keep the body hidden?" Dwight asked.

"Maybe because now we don't have a way of linking Hake to the killer?" Gage asked. "They think they're in the clear."

"Hake's car was found near the resort, and his body was found on the resort," Travis said. "The Hoods died because they saw something at the resort they shouldn't have. Wade and Brock kidnapped Gage and Maya and Casey and imprisoned them at the resort."

"So the resort is key to solving all of this," Dwight said. "What is going on up there that someone is willing to kill to protect?"

"We need to know that," Travis said. "And we need to know who." He consulted his notes. "Gage, you saw a black SUV at the resort when you were fired on. Casey reported seeing a similar SUV—and two men in dark suits—when she went for help. Wade and Brock were talking to those men before they were killed."

"So the suits were running the show." Gage nodded. "Two strangers in suits are going to stand out around here, where pretty much everybody wears casual clothing unless they're going to a wedding or a funeral. Even the bankers and lawyers seldom put on a jacket and tie."

"So why haven't we been able to find them?" Dwight

asked. "And why haven't we been able to find whoever is threatening Brenda?" Their canvass of the neighborhood had turned up not a single clue to help them find the arsonist who had burned down her house.

"The only link we can find between Brenda and the resort is the fact that her late husband was the lawyer who represented the development company," Travis said.

"And he was killed because of something he saw or said or did that didn't please his murderer's boss," Gage said.

"Ian Barnes was Henry Hake's bodyguard," Travis said. "But in talking with him before he died, I got the impression that there was someone above Hake who was calling the shots. My feeling is that that mysterious someone ordered Andy Stenson's murder."

"Why did Hake need a bodyguard?" Gage asked.

"Because he was afraid of the people over him?" Dwight asked. "He thought they were dangerous?"

"Or because those people had enemies who were dangerous," Travis said.

"Henry Hake had enemies of his own," Gage said. "Paige Riddell's environmental group didn't make any secret of their loathing for him and his development. And let's not forget his own lawyer, Andy Stenson, who was probably blackmailing him."

"So maybe Hake did order the hit on Andy," Dwight said. "But then who kidnapped Hake?"

"If he was kidnapped," Travis said, "we don't have any proof of that."

"When a guy disappears and his car ends up in a ravine—but his dead body is found hanging in an underground chamber a month later—that didn't all happen of his own free will," Gage said.

"And the coroner said no physical trauma," Dwight said. "So it's not as if Hake somehow managed to escape his car, only to die of his injuries later."

"And what—someone found the body and decided to hang it up as some kind of sick joke?" Gage asked.

Dwight shrugged. "Stranger things have happened."

"Right now all we have are a lot of questions and no answers," Travis said. "But maybe I'll get some answers this afternoon. I have a meeting with the new owners of the Eagle Mountain Resort property."

Dwight and Gage exchanged looks. "What was that company's name again?" Dwight asked.

"An investment group called CNG Development," Travis said. "I'm meeting with their representative on the property at two."

"Who is CNG Development?" Dwight asked.

"That's what I'm hoping to find out," Travis said. "As far as I can determine, at least some of the principals were silent partners in the original development. Before Hake disappeared, they signed an agreement with him to take over control of the property."

"How come nobody else knew about this?" Gage asked. "I mean, the way gossip spreads in this town, I would have thought someone would have said something."

"I think they kept it deliberately low-key," Travis said.

"Do they plan to go ahead with developing the property?" Dwight asked.

"That's one of the questions I'm going to ask them." Travis consulted his notes again. "What else do we have going on right now?"

"I'm working the high school basketball tournament this evening," Gage said. "Maya says the girls' team has a good chance of winning."

Gage's fiancée, Maya Renfro, had snagged a position teaching English at the high school when another teacher's husband was transferred. A former avowed city girl, she had thrown herself into small-town life and signed on as assistant coach of the girls' basketball team.

"Dwight, what are you working on?" Travis asked.

"I'm going to take another look at that book of Brenda's, see if I can figure out what Andy might have been looking for when he borrowed it from the professor. And I'm going to touch base with Brenda and see who has made a bid on the book so far."

"I thought the auction wasn't until next Saturday," Travis said.

"It isn't, but she said bidders had the option of mailing in a bid ahead of time. I want to know if anything has come in that might raise a red flag."

"There's a reception next Friday night where people can view all of the items up for auction, including the book," Travis said. "I want as many of us as possible there, keeping our eyes open for anyone suspicious."

Everyone was beginning to look suspicious to Dwight—not a feeling he especially liked.

"We still have our regular patrols," Travis said. He read off their assignments for the day and they dispersed.

Dwight resisted the urge to drive by the museum first thing. Brenda had been polite but decidedly cool toward him since he'd made the mistake of revealing his true feelings to her yesterday morning. So much for the honesty women said they wanted.

But maybe that wasn't a fair judgment, either, he admitted. Brenda had made it clear she wasn't ready for a relationship, and he could see how his comment might make her think he was trying to rush things.

Instead of saying he had remained single because he was waiting for her, he should have shared another bit of truth: staying single was a lot easier than navigating the land mines inherent in any relationship.

WITH THE AUCTION fast approaching, Brenda spent the next few days working long hours at the museum, proofing the final copy of the auction catalog and updating listings on the website she had established as new items continued to come in. The work needed to be done, but when she was being honest with herself, she admitted that staying late at the office gave her an excuse to avoid Dwight. She couldn't think clearly when she was with him, what with her body demanding to be back in his bed and her mind focused on the benefits of sticking close to a man with a gun and a desire to protect her. She could shut up her mind with a reminder that she had received no more threatening letters. Her body, awakened from long dormancy, wasn't so easily reasoned with. Better to avoid the object of her lust until she had gained a little perspective.

Work was one thing that allowed her to focus. The interest and support from the people of Eagle Mountain and the surrounding county touched her. Surveying the growing collection of items in her workroom, it seemed as if half the residents of the area had raided basements and attics for great-granddaddy's miner's lamp or great-grandmother's Victrola to contribute to the museum's fund-raising efforts.

But their generosity wasn't going to be enough. The money the auction would bring would keep things going for a few more months, at most, but an ongoing donor was needed to insure continued operation—and Brenda's continued employment. In addition to getting ready for the auction, she continued to send letters to potential sponsors, both corporate and private.

She was composing such a letter, long after the museum had closed, on the Tuesday before the auction when a pounding on the door broke her concentration. A glance out the window showed a distinguished-looking man in a dark suit standing on the porch. Annoyed but curious, she opened the door. "The museum is closed," she said. "You're welcome to come back tomorrow morning after nine." She tried to see past him, into the parking lot. Wasn't Eddie supposed to be around somewhere, doing his security guard duties? She hadn't seen any sign of him all evening.

"I'm here to see Mrs. Brenda Stenson." He offered a smile that transformed his expression from businesslike to breathtaking. Of average height and build and in his forties, he had the thick dark hair and piercing gray eyes of a matinee idol. "Would that be you?"

"Yes." She maintained her composure under the force of his movie-star smile. "What can I do for you, Mr...?"

"Brownley. Robert Brownley. Could we go inside to talk? It's awkward, standing here on the doorstep."

If she admitted she was alone in the building, would that make her more vulnerable? She had certainly been alone in the museum with strangers many times, given that she operated with a skeleton staff. But always before, that was during regular business hours, when another person could have walked in any time. She should tell Mr. Brownley to come back tomorrow.

"I have a financial proposal to make," he said. "I would have come earlier, but my business demands my attention during working hours. I saw your car out front and decided to take a chance that you were here."

He certainly looked like a man who had money to give away—his deftly tailored suit, gleaming leather shoes and even his haircut advertised wealth—and the black SUV parked beside her Subaru was a brand she was sure retailed for close to $100,000. That didn't mean he wasn't a serial killer, but could she really afford to pass up the chance that he was going to offer up a much-needed donation to the museum? She stepped back, holding the door open wider. "Come in."

He strode past her, the spicy fragrance of his cologne trailing in his wake. He admired the photographs on the walls and the books displayed on the shelves. Brenda perched on the high stool next to the cash register, keeping the glass display case that served as the front counter between them. "What can I do for you, Mr. Brownley?" she asked.

"I'm interested in one of the items you have listed for auction," he said.

"Oh." She tried not to show her disappointment. "You're welcome to make an early bid online, or attend the live auction Saturday night," she said.

"I'm prepared to make a preemptive bid now," he said. "I'll beat any subsequent bid you might obtain."

"What's the item you want to bid on?"

"It's a book. *The Secret History of Rayford County, Colorado.* An esoteric item, I admit, but I'm a collector, and you know how collectors are obsessive about completing our collections."

The hair on the back of her neck stood at attention at the mention of the book, but she remained cool. "We've had quite a bit of interest in that item," she said. "As I'm sure you're aware, it's quite rare."

"Yes." Did she imagine that his smile held less warmth? He looked around the room, scanning the titles on the shelves, as if he expected to find the book there. "And as I explained, I am prepared to meet or beat any other bid you receive, provided the volume meets with my expectations. I'd like to see it and assess its condition."

"The book is in a secure location. Off-site," she added. "All the auction items will be on display at the reception Friday evening, which you're welcome to attend. And of course, you can see everything the morning of the auction."

No smile now. Without it, his expression was forbidding. "I'm prepared to offer a substantial sum to acquire this volume," he said. "I don't think it's too much to ask for a private showing ahead of time."

"That isn't possible," she said. "The book isn't here. It isn't anywhere I can get to it."

"That's a very poor way to do business," he said.

"That may be your opinion, but it's how we've chosen to handle it." She pulled her cell phone from her pocket. "I think you'd better go."

He scowled at the phone, then turned and stalked out. When the door had slammed behind him, she laid the phone aside and slumped on the stool. She hated confrontation. But even worse, she hated people who tried to push her around.

Five minutes later, the jangle of the doorbells had her grabbing up the phone again, heart pounding. Dwight stepped into the room, and the sight of his lanky figure in the familiar khaki uniform left her weak with relief. "Everything okay here?" he asked.

She laid down the phone and smoothed her damp palms on her skirt. "Fine. I'm just working late on auction stuff."

"Who was that in the black Land Rover that just went tearing out of here?" he asked.

"A man who wanted to place an auction bid. I explained he could go to the website or attend the live auction Saturday."

Dwight's alert posture didn't relax, and his gaze remained fixed on her. "What did he want to bid on?"

She opened her mouth to tell him, but what came out was, "Oh, it doesn't matter." She began shutting down her laptop. "I'm about ready to call it a night."

He quickly crossed the room and placed his hand over hers. "I thought you were going to trust me."

Yes. She wanted to trust him. But the encounter with Robert Brownley had shaken her, reminding her of how vulnerable trusting made her.

But this was Dwight, not an angry stranger. Dwight, who had loved her so fiercely and held her so tenderly and stayed by her side even when she pushed him away. "He said he wanted to bid on the book. He said he was a collector and he was anxious to complete his collection. He promised to outbid anyone else."

"Did he give you a name?" Dwight asked.

"Robert Brownley."

"I'll try to verify that. So you told him he'd have to bid online or at the auction Saturday?"

"Yes. But he asked to see the book. I told him it was being kept at a secure location—not here. He didn't like that."

"Did he threaten you?" The words were almost a growl.

"No." She smiled weakly, recalling Brownley's re-action. "He said that was no way to run a business, or something to that effect—as if that would make me give in to his demands. It was ridiculous, really."

"And then he left?" Dwight asked.

"Then I picked up my phone and told him to leave. I would have dialed nine-one-one if he hadn't headed for the door. I'm sure he knew that."

"He lit out of here fast enough," Dwight said. "I would have stopped him for speeding if I hadn't been concerned about you."

"You didn't have to worry about me." Though she had been relieved to see him when he walked in. "I think he was just a rich businessman who's used to always get-ting his way. When I dared tell him no, he stormed off in a fit of temper. If he wants the book as badly as he said he did, I'm sure he'll come back Saturday."

"If you see him before then, let me know," Dwight said. "In the meantime, I'll see what I can find out about him."

"I invited him to the auction reception Friday eve-ning," she said. "I hope he shows up. If he's as wealthy as he appeared to be, and a collector, maybe he'll see a few more items he can't live without."

She closed her laptop and slipped it into her bag. "I'm leaving now. What about you?"

"I'm headed home, too. I'll follow you out to the ranch."

"I really need to find somewhere else to stay," she

said as she walked with him out of the museum. "I can't keep imposing on your parents, and it's going to be months before my house can be lived in again."

"My parents are happy to have you." Dwight waited while she locked the door.

"I need my own place."

"Fair enough. But where? Eagle Mountain doesn't have much in the way of affordable rentals. That's why Lacy ended up in your garage apartment, and one reason Maya and Casey are living with Gage."

Brenda thought he would suggest she move in with him and was grateful when he didn't. "It may take me a while to find something," she said. "So I should start looking now."

"Then let me help," he said. "I'll put the word out and let you know if anything comes up. We can put Adelaide to work on it, too. She knows everyone and everything—at least to hear her tell it."

"All right. I'd appreciate that."

Dwight walked her to her car. "Where's your security guard tonight?" he asked.

"I don't know." She looked around, half expecting to see Eddie lurking in the shadows. "I don't know what kind of schedule he and the mayor worked out. They haven't bothered to inform me."

Dwight switched on his flashlight and played the beam over the darkened lot. He stopped with the light shining down the alley. "Isn't that Eddie's Jeep?" he asked. He shifted the light and Brenda gasped at the sight of a figure slumped over the steering wheel.

"Call an ambulance," Dwight said, and took off running for the Jeep.

Chapter Eleven

Dread filled Dwight as he raced toward the Jeep, but when he reached the open driver's-side window he realized Eddie wasn't dead. The figure slumped over the steering wheel snored softly and mumbled when Dwight shook his shoulder. Dwight leaned in closer and spotted a half-eaten pizza on the passenger seat. He sniffed, but didn't smell alcohol—only sausage and pepperoni. He shook the security guard again. "Come on, Eddie, wake up."

But Eddie only leaned sideways, mouth open, snoring away.

"The ambulance is on its way." Brenda joined him and stared in at Eddie. "Is he drunk?" she asked.

"I don't think so," Dwight said. "I think he's drugged."

"Drugged? By who?"

"I don't know. But he was eating a pizza."

Brenda frowned at the pizza, in its cardboard box with Peggy's Pizza on the front. "Do you think someone put something in his pizza?"

"I think we'd better have it tested, just in case."

"Has anyone else been to the museum—or in the parking lot—in the last half hour or so?" he asked.

"No one's been inside except Mr. Brownley," she

said. "When I answered his knock, his was the only vehicle I saw. But why half an hour? Couldn't someone have done this earlier?"

"I'm just guessing, but the pizza is still warm." He frowned at Eddie's slumped figure. "I'll find out from the mayor what time Eddie was supposed to start his shift."

A wailing siren announced the arrival of the ambulance. The paramedics parked and jogged up to the Jeep. "What have we got?" Merrily Rayford, one of the squad's senior paramedics, asked.

Dwight nodded to Eddie. "I think he's been drugged. No idea with what."

She and her partner donned gloves and opened the door of the Jeep. While they examined Eddie, Dwight retrieved an evidence bag from his cruiser and bagged the pizza, box and all. Brenda moved in beside him. "You don't think Parker had anything to do with this, do you?" she asked.

"I don't know what to think," Dwight said. They watched as the paramedics shifted Eddie onto a stretcher.

"His vitals are good," Merrily said. "I don't think he's in any danger, but we'll take him in for a closer look."

"I'll want to question him about what happened," Dwight said.

"From the looks of him, it might be a while," Merrily said. "Maybe in the morning."

"I'll check with the hospital later." He held up the evidence bag. "Meanwhile, I'll get this to the lab."

Brenda waited by her car, arms hugging her stomach, as the ambulance left the lot. "I need to take this in and file a report," Dwight said. "I probably won't be in until late."

She nodded. "Eddie isn't my favorite person, but I hope he's all right."

"I'll let you know." He wanted to kiss her, but settled for squeezing her shoulder. "Go home and try to get some rest. Try not to worry about this."

"It's been so long since I didn't have anything to worry about, I've forgotten what that's like," she said.

THE NEXT MORNING, Dwight and Gage faced a sullen Parker Riddell in the sheriff's department interview room. Gage had picked up the young man at his sister's house, where he and Paige were eating breakfast. Paige had argued against him going to the sheriff's department and had wanted to call a lawyer, but Gage had persuaded her that wasn't necessary. All they wanted was for Parker to answer a few questions. The young man had agreed, as much, Dwight suspected, to get his sister off his back as to placate the cops. He sat now, clothes rumpled and the dark shadow of a beard across his jaw, tattooed forearms crossed over a faded black T-shirt advertising a metal band that had been old when Dwight was a teen.

"I didn't deliver a pizza to Eddie," Parker said in answer to Dwight's first question.

"You were working last night," Dwight said. He had verified this with Peggy at her home earlier this morning.

"Yeah. But I didn't deliver a pizza to that jerk. If he says I did, he's lying."

Eddie wasn't saying anything yet—he was still out of it at the hospital in Montrose. When Dwight had called to check on him, the nurse on duty had reported that he was sleeping well and not in danger, but they didn't expect him to wake before midmorning.

"He had a pizza from Peggy's on the seat beside him when we found him last night," Dwight said. "He was unconscious."

Parker only looked more sullen. "I don't know anything about that. He must have picked up the pizza at the store."

"Peggy says Eddie didn't pick up a pizza, and he didn't order one delivered, either."

"Then I don't know what to tell you," Parker said.

"Maybe you made up this pizza special and delivered it between your regular orders," Gage said.

"Why would I do that?" Parker's voice rose. "The guy hates me. I wouldn't want to give him a free pizza."

"Maybe you told him it was a peace offering," Dwight suggested. "You were trying to get him to see you aren't a bad guy."

"I don't have any reason to want to impress him."

"What do you know about zolpidem?" Dwight asked.

"It's a sleeping pill, right?"

"So you have heard of it."

He shrugged. "I've heard of lots of things. I mean, I read books, and I watch movies."

"Do you have any zolpidem?" Gage asked. The lab report had come in that morning, showing that the pizza was loaded with the stuff—probably in the form of ground pills sprinkled on top. "Know where to get any?"

"No!" Parker uncrossed his arms and sat up straighter. "I don't have anything to do with drugs anymore. Even when I did, I didn't use downers."

"But they might be a good way to get back at some-body," Gage said. "Load a pizza up with them, put them out of commission for a while."

"Is that what happened to Eddie? I didn't do it. Why would I?"

"Revenge?" Dwight asked. "Or maybe you wanted to break into the museum and didn't want him around."

"I don't want to rob the museum. And it would have been stupid to pull that kind of thing last night—Brenda was working late at the museum."

"How do you know that?" Dwight leaned over him. Was this kid stalking Brenda?

Parker shifted in his chair. "I drove by there on the way to one of my deliveries and saw her car."

Dwight sat back. "I'll bet that disappointed you," he said. "Here you'd gone to all the trouble to make that special pizza for Eddie, and Brenda was foiling your plans."

"No! I told you, I didn't have anything to do with that pizza. Ask Peggy. She would know if I made a pizza."

"She said she left the kitchen to use the bathroom for a few minutes," Dwight said. "You could have slipped in and thrown one together then."

"And she would have noticed if the ingredients were missing. Not to mention it takes more than a few min-utes to put together a pizza."

Dwight tried another tack. "When you drove by the museum and saw Brenda's car, did you see Eddie or his truck?"

"No."

"Anyone else?" Gage asked.

"No one else was there—just Brenda's Subaru."

"What time was this?" Dwight asked.

Parker paused, as if considering the question. "I was delivering a Mountain Man special to Mr. Wilbur over on Sixth Street. So that was about seven. A little after."

When Dwight and Brenda found Eddie, it was after nine.

Parker held Dwight's gaze, defiant. "Are you going to charge me with something, or can I go? I have class this morning."

"You're not being charged with anything." Dwight stood. "We appreciate you coming in for questioning."

Parker said nothing, but left in a hurry. Dwight and Gage returned to Gage's office. "Peggy was pretty insistent that Parker didn't make an extra pizza," Dwight said.

"Her place is pretty small," Gage said. "Even from the bathroom, I think she'd have heard someone messing around in her kitchen."

"She's also positive Eddie didn't order or pick up a pizza," Dwight said.

"Maybe someone else ordered it, added the sleeping pills and took it to Eddie," Gage said. "It's not hard to imagine he's made other enemies."

Dwight grunted in assent. He reviewed their conversation with Parker, searching for any inconsistencies and finding none. "What's a Mountain Man special?" he asked.

"Pork carnitas, green chili and onions," Gage said. "A personal favorite."

Dwight let this pass. "Parker is the most obvious suspect," he said. "But maybe that's just what someone wants us to think."

"Yeah," Gage agreed. "The kid strikes me as smarter than that."

"Drugs can make even smart people do dumb things," Dwight said. "But I think you're right. So, who else had it in for Eddie?"

"Or for Parker," Gage said. "Whoever did this wasn't trying to kill Eddie—just put him out of commission for a while and make it look as if Parker did it."

"So—somebody who wanted to get into the museum?" Dwight shook his head. "Brenda was there until the two of us found Eddie."

"Nobody else was there with her?"

Dwight sat up straight. He'd almost forgotten about Robert Brownley. "A man stopped by to ask about bidding on that book she has up for auction," he said. "He was just leaving when I showed up—in a black Land Rover. Said his name was Robert Brownley. He wasn't too happy when she told him he couldn't see the book."

"So—before he goes in to see Brenda, he delivers a doctored pizza to Eddie?" Gage shook his head. "Why?"

"To get him out of the way? Maybe he planned to try to take the book if Brenda wouldn't sell it to him."

"I'm definitely going to do a little more checking into Brownley."

"We should be able to interview Eddie in a few hours," Gage said. "Maybe he can solve this whole puzzle."

"Or he'll just throw in another piece that doesn't fit," Dwight said. Every new development only made this case more frustrating.

BRENDA HAD INTENDED to work through lunch the day after her encounter with Robert Brownley and all the excitement with Eddie, but Lacy showed up and insisted she take a break. "You have to eat," Lacy said. Fresh from the hair salon, she looked young and happy—looking at her, Brenda felt old and exhausted.

"I have so much to do," Brenda said, indicating her full desk. "I don't think I can spare the time."

"The work will be here when you get back," Lacy said. "Besides, we need to catch up. We don't see each other as much, now that I'm not living next door."

Brenda did miss her friend. "All right," she said. "You've convinced me."

They walked to Kate's Kitchen on the town's main street. A brisk breeze made a jacket necessary, but the sun shone brightly, and the aspens in people's yards and on the mountainsides above town glowed gold.

"How do you like living at the ranch?" Lacy asked when they were settled into a booth at the café.

"It's very comfortable, but…" Brenda didn't finish the sentence, pretending to study the menu.

"But it's not your place," Lacy said. "You're a guest."

Brenda should have known her friend would understand. "I need to find a place of my own," she said.

"What's the word on your house? Are you going to rebuild?"

"I don't know," she said. "I have a meeting with someone from my insurance company this afternoon. I hope that will give me an idea of how much money I have to work with. I'll probably rebuild, though something different." Something that would be just hers—not the grand house Andy had convinced her she wanted. "Whatever I do, I'll need someplace to live for the foreseeable future. But you know how scarce housing is around here."

"I wasn't thrilled about moving back in with Mom and Dad, but it's only until the wedding," Lacy said.

"I wondered if you would move in with Travis."

"I considered it, but I guess I'm a little old-fashioned. I want to wait until we're married to live together."

The waitress arrived to take their orders. Brenda opted for the chicken salad, while Lacy chose a burger. As soon as they were alone again, Lacy resumed the conversation.

"Another reason I'm waiting to move in with Travis is that once we're husband and wife, I'll have free rein to redecorate his bachelor pad," she said. She made a face. "It definitely needs some changes."

Brenda thought of Dwight's cabin. There wasn't much about it she would change.

"Dwight has a cabin out at the ranch, doesn't he?" Lacy asked as though reading Brenda's mind. "Have you seen it? What's it like?"

Brenda cursed the blush that heated her face, but she tried to play it cool. "It's really nice," she said. "Comfortable. He has better taste than I expected."

"I'd say he has excellent taste."

Brenda ignored the knowing look in her friend's eyes, and was saved from having to answer by the arrival of their iced teas.

"I'm dying to know the scoop on what happened with Eddie Carstairs," Lacy said. "Travis mentioned he was in the hospital after someone tried to poison him or something. He said you and Dwight found him."

"We found him as we were leaving the museum last night." Brenda added a packet of sweetener to her tea and stirred. "He was slumped over the steering wheel of his Jeep. I thought he was dead."

"That must have given you a turn," Lacy said. "Especially after what happened with Henry Hake."

Brenda shuddered. "Yes. Thankfully, Eddie was just drugged."

"What, did someone shoot a poison dart into him or something?" Lacy asked.

The waitress arrived with their food, her expression not giving any indication that she had heard this alarming question. Brenda crunched a potato chip, then said, "There was a half-eaten pizza on the seat beside him. Dwight sent it to the lab to see if the drugs were in there."

"Ooh, that makes it interesting." She bit into her burger and chewed.

Both women ate silently for a few minutes, then Brenda said, "I think Dwight suspects Parker Riddell." Saying the words out loud made her realize how upset she was by the possibility that Parker—a young man she had grown to like—might be responsible for something so horrible.

"He works at the pizza place, right?" Lacy asked. "Did he and Eddie have some kind of run-in?"

"You know Eddie," Brenda said. "He likes to throw his weight around."

"And I guess Parker had some trouble with the law before." At Brenda's startled look, Lacy held up her hands. "I'm not gossiping—Paige told me."

"Yes, but he's trying to put that behind him," Brenda said. "He's going to school and working at Peggy's Pizza and volunteering at the museum. I think he's a good guy—and I don't think he hurt Eddie, even though Eddie gave him a really hard time. Parker is trying to make a fresh start." Something she also wanted desperately to do. Not that any of the trouble she had been through was her fault, but she longed to take her life in a different, calmer direction.

"Okay, so why don't you think Parker did it?" Lacy asked.

"He's too smart to do something so obvious," Brenda said. "I mean, putting the drugs in a pizza points the finger right at him."

"So you think someone set it up to look like Parker was the guilty party," Lacy said. "But who? And why?"

"I don't know," Brenda said. She stabbed at her salad. "I'm just hoping that for once, it doesn't have anything to do with me or the museum."

"Or maybe whoever doctored the pizza *is* the same person who's been threatening you," Lacy said. "Dwight can arrest him and then you wouldn't have to worry about him anymore."

"Right." She could go back to worrying about her job and where she was going to live. Those were the kinds of problems most people had to solve at one time or another. It had been a while since she had had anything that resembled a "normal" life. She thought she'd welcome the change.

"What you need is a real break," Lacy said. "Why don't we call Paige and Maya and the four of us go out tomorrow night? Dress up, dinner, drinks—just fun. No men, no worries allowed."

"I don't know," Brenda said. "I've got so much to do with the auction and the reception Friday night."

"If I know you, you've already got everything done. If you sit at home tomorrow you'll just fret over all the details you've already gone over a dozen times."

Brenda had to smile at this. "You do know me, don't you?"

"Come on—how about it? We can call it my pre-bachelorette party. Or, I know—we'll say it's an early party for your birthday."

"I don't know," Brenda said. "I'm not much on big celebrations."

"It'll just be four of us. And you need to do something to mark your thirtieth."

Brenda nodded. "All right." She had had her nose pretty firmly to the grindstone the last few weeks. Maybe a night out was exactly what she needed.

NO GROWN MAN could avoid looking ridiculous in a hospital gown, Dwight decided, as he and Gage entered Eddie Carstairs's hospital room. Eddie, paler than usual, with dark circles under his eyes, pulled the sheet up farther on his chest when he recognized them. "I hope you two have come to get me out of here," he said.

"You'll have to talk to your doctor about that," Gage said. "We're just here to interview you about what happened at the museum last night."

"The doctor was supposed to stop by here an hour ago to sign my discharge papers," Eddie said. "But he's disappeared."

"Then you've got time to talk to us." Dwight stopped beside the bed, while Gage took up position on the opposite side.

Eddie looked from one to the other of them. "The nurse told me someone tried to kill me with poisoned pizza."

Of course Eddie would go for the most dramatic story first, Dwight thought. "Someone added ground-up sleeping pills to the pizza," he said. "But there wasn't enough there to kill you. It looks like whoever did it wanted to put you out of commission for a while. Who would want to do that, Eddie?"

Eddie looked away. "How should I know?"

"Where did you get the pizza?" Gage asked.

"It was the Tuesday special from Peggy's," he said. "Pepperoni and sausage."

"Peggy says you didn't order a pizza from her last night," Dwight said.

Eddie said nothing.

"Did someone deliver the pizza to you?" Gage asked. "A friend who knew you were working last night?"

Eddie pressed his lips together, as if holding back words. Then he burst out, "That punk Parker Riddell probably put drugs in the pizza to get back at me," he said.

"Did Parker deliver the pizza to you?" Dwight asked.

Again, Eddie didn't answer right away.

"Do you want us to find who did this or not, Eddie?" Gage asked. "Because we have other things we could be spending our time on than finding out who wanted you to take a long nap."

"Parker didn't deliver the pizza," Eddie said. "But he works at Peggy's. He probably knew it was for me and messed with it."

"Who delivered the pizza?" Dwight asked again, struggling to keep his temper. Gage was right—they had plenty to do without wasting time like this.

"A friend," Eddie said. "But he wouldn't do something like that."

"What is the friend's name?" Dwight asked.

"I don't have to tell you that."

Dwight stared at the man in the bed. "If you know he's innocent, why not give us his name?"

"Because I don't want to."

Dressed in that faded hospital gown, his hair uncombed, mouth set in a stubborn line, Eddie reminded Dwight of an obstinate little kid. He stepped away from the bed. "Call us if you change your mind," he said.

"I'd be careful accepting any more gifts from your friend," Gage said. "Next time, he might decide instead of putting you to sleep, he'll finish you off."

It was possible Eddie went a shade paler beneath the day's growth of beard, but he said nothing as Dwight and Gage left him. They were in Dwight's cruiser before Gage spoke. "Do we know who Eddie's friends are?"

"No. But I'll be asking around." He put the cruiser in gear. "Let's start with the mayor."

"The mayor?"

"He stopped by to talk to Eddie the night Eddie arrested Parker," Dwight said. "Maybe he was there last night, too."

"With a pizza?" Gage asked.

"That's what we're going to find out."

Chapter Twelve

Mayor Larry Rowe's office was so small it scarcely had room for his desk, a filing cabinet and a credenza so covered with piles of paper its surface wasn't visible. When Gage and Dwight entered, he looked up from the screen of a laptop computer, scowling. "What's wrong now?" he barked.

"We just have a few questions for you." Dwight pulled out a chair and sat, while Gage remained standing by the door.

"I don't have time for questions," Larry said, turning his attention back to the computer.

"When was the last time you saw Eddie Carstairs?" Dwight asked.

"I don't know. A few days ago."

"You didn't see him last night?" Dwight asked.

"I went to dinner in Junction with my brother."

"Who's your brother?" Gage asked. "Does he live here?"

"He lives outside of Boston. He's an actor—Garrett Rowe."

Dwight and Gage exchanged glances—neither one of them had ever heard of the mayor's brother. "What time was your dinner?" Dwight asked.

"We left here at five, drove to Junction, had cocktails, then dinner, and lingered, catching up. I don't get to see him that often. I probably got back to my place about midnight."

He swiveled his chair toward them. "Why are you asking these questions?"

"Eddie Carstairs is in the hospital," Dwight said. "Someone fed him pizza laced with sleeping pills."

Larry made a snorting sound that might have been a laugh. "Eddie never did turn down a meal."

"Do you have any idea who might have given him the pizza?" Gage asked.

"None. Eddie Carstairs is a city employee, not a personal friend."

"Is your brother still in town?" Dwight asked. "We'd like to confirm your story with him."

Larry stiffened. "Are you saying you don't believe me?"

"It's just standard procedure."

"I can give you his number. He's gone back to Boston."

Dwight took the number, and he and Gage left. "What do you think?" Gage asked.

"We'll check with the brother. Not that I think the mayor is really involved, but I don't like to leave loose ends."

AS BRENDA PULLED into the drive at her house, her phone pinged with a text from the insurance appraiser, telling her he was running a few minutes late. She sat for a moment, phone still in hand, studying the charred ruins of what had once been her dream home. The stones that had trimmed the foundation stuck up like blackened teeth arranged around a jumble of fallen timbers and empty window frames. She had avoided looking at any of this since the fire, but she was going to have to deal with it sooner rather than later. If nothing else, her neighbors were probably already tired of looking at this eyesore.

She stuffed the phone in her pocket and got out of the car and walked up the stone path to what had been the front door. Everything in the house was a total loss. She still had her laptop and the few clothes she had packed to take to Dwight's parents' home. It didn't matter, she tried to reassure herself. It was all just stuff.

But it was all stuff that she had, for the most part, personally chosen over the years—things it pleased her to look at and to use—the transferware teapot decorated with kittens, the dishes with a pattern of morning glories, the ginger jar bedside lamp with the pale green silk shade. She would miss these little items more than she would grieve the loss of the bedroom furniture and wedding china.

She spotted something glinting in the sunlight and stepped over the threshold and bent down to fish a silver teaspoon from the rubble, blackened, but intact. She found two more nearby, along with the silver top to a teapot and a silver salt cellar—though the walnut buffet that had held them all was a heap of charred wood nearby.

She picked her way across the rooms to the back corner that had been Andy's home office. The fire had started here, and everything in the room had been destroyed, all the little things she kept of her husband's reduced to ash—his desk and chair, a few law books, his university and law school diplomas, his law license. It didn't feel as awful as she would have imagined to lose those things. She supposed she would have eventually put those items away somewhere. They didn't have any children to save them for.

Brakes squealed as a car slowed, and she turned to watch a silver Toyota pull into the driveway and a tall, thin man in khakis and a blue polo unfold himself from the front seat, a folder tucked under one arm. She walked out to meet him. "Alan Treat." He introduced himself and handed her a card, then turned to survey the house. "I understand it was arson," he said.

"That's what the fire department investigator determined, yes."

Treat fixed her with a watery blue eye. "Have they determined who set the fire?" he asked.

"No. Someone has been making anonymous threats. They assume the arsonist was the same person."

His eyebrows were so bushy they looked fake, pasted on like a stage costume. One rose in question and she had a hard time not staring, to see if she could spot the glue. "What has a woman like you done to receive threats?" he asked.

She resented the implication that she had done anything to bring this on herself. "I don't see what any of that has to do with you," she said. "I only want to know what the settlement will be on the house, so that I can make plans."

"We don't pay claims where homeowners burn down their own homes," he said.

"I didn't burn down my own house!" She had raised her voice and glared at him. "I sent a copy of the fire investigator's report to your office. Did you even read it?"

"Most home arson fires are set by the homeowner," he said, his expression bland.

"Well, mine wasn't. And if that's all you came to say to me today you can leave, and I will be contacting my attorney."

"Now, now, there's no reason to fly off the handle."

As far as she was concerned, she had every reason to be upset with him, including but not limited to the fact that she absolutely hated being placated with phrases such as "now, now."

"Mr. Treat," she said through clenched teeth, "are you going to discuss the insurance settlement I am entitled to, or not?"

He sighed and opened the folder. He handed her a single sheet of paper. She scanned it until she came to the number at the bottom. She blinked and read it again. "The house was worth far more than this," she said.

"Your settlement is not based on the market value of your home," he said. "It is based on the amount you chose to insure the home for, less your deductible, less the cost of things that weren't destroyed in the fire."

"Everything was destroyed in the fire," she said.

"Not your foundation and the portion of the house below ground level."

She stared at the paper again, trying to make the numbers add up in her head. "I was expecting more," she said.

"Your policy had not been updated in several years," he said. "We do recommend an annual policy review and increased coverage to reflect current market conditions. You are, of course, welcome to appeal, but these things seldom come out in the homeowner's favor."

She looked at the ruins of the home again. "I understand there wasn't a mortgage on the home," Treat continued. "So you will receive a check made out to you, to do with as you wish, though you will, of course, have to pay for cleanup of this lot. I'm sure there is a city ordinance to that effect."

Yes, she would have to pay for cleanup. And then what? She had already considered building a less elaborate home, but would the amount the insurance company was offering be enough?

"If I could have your signature here, we can get the check in the mail to you in a few days." Treat pointed to a blank line at the bottom of the page.

"I don't want to sign anything right now," she said.

Treat closed the folder. "Call us when you're ready." Then he turned, got back in his car and drove away.

When Brenda was sure he was out of sight, she swore and kicked at the front stoop. But that only made her swear more, her toe throbbing. She felt like screaming and throwing things, but had no inclination to provide a free show for neighbors or passing motorists.

A familiar SUV pulled to the curb and Dwight got out. "Are you following me?" she demanded as he walked toward her, his slightly bowlegged gait so distinctive.

He stopped. "No," he said. "I saw you were here and stopped to talk. Do you want me to leave?"

"No. I'm sorry." She held up the paper, as if in explanation. "The insurance appraiser was here. Mr. Treat. And he wasn't."

"He wasn't a treat?" Dwight started forward again and came to stand beside her.

"No. He was a jerk. He accused me of burning down my own home. And then he offered me this paltry settlement and as much as said it was all my fault for not updating my policy."

Dwight glanced at the paper in her hand, but didn't ask to see it. "Is it enough money to rebuild?" he asked.

"I don't know. I don't think so." She shoved the paper at him. "And he's right—I didn't update the policy. Andy always did those things and I assumed he had purchased replacement coverage. The premium certainly went up every year. I'm mad at Andy all over again for not taking out enough insurance, and angry at myself for not thinking to review the policy once the house was in my name alone. And I'm furious with whoever put me in this position." She glared at the burned-out house. If the arsonist had come along and confessed at that moment, she thought she could have strangled him with her bare hands.

"You've had a rough morning," Dwight said.

"Yes, and you came along at just the wrong time."

"I can take it."

"I don't suppose you're any closer to knowing who did this?" She gestured toward the house.

"I'm sorry, no."

She started back toward her car, and he walked with her. "What are you up to this afternoon?" she asked, making an effort to be more cordial than she felt.

"I'm meeting Gage in a few minutes to head up to Eagle Mountain Resort. We're supposed to meet a representative of the new owners."

"New owners—already? I mean, Hake's body was only just found." A small shudder went through her at the memory.

"Apparently, these people officially took over only a few days before he disappeared."

"Who are they?"

"Another real estate development company, out of Utah, I think."

"I wonder what they plan to do with the property."

"That's one of the things we're hoping to find out." He held open the car door and returned the settlement statement to her. "What are you doing this afternoon?"

"I'm putting the finishing touches on preparations for the reception tomorrow night and the auction Saturday. Everything is almost in place. Then, tonight, I'm going out with Lacy and Paige and Maya."

"That's a good idea. You've been working hard—it will be good for you to relax a little." His eyes met hers, so serious and at the same time, tender. "I'm on duty. But call me if you need anything."

"What would I need?" She tried for a flirtatious tone, but wasn't sure she succeeded. "Are you expecting trouble?"

"I didn't mean it that way," he said. "Just that I'm here for you. Whenever."

She waited for the automatic resistance she expected at such a statement, but it didn't come. Instead she felt warmed—comforted by his words. "That's nice to know," she said. "So if I drunk-dial you at two a.m. you won't hang up on me?"

He laughed. "I promise I won't. Though I can't imagine you doing something like that."

"You never know," she said. "I'm beginning to think it's time to try a lot of new things in my life." Maybe even trusting this kind, patient man who was coming to mean so much to her.

DWIGHT TRIED TO put Brenda's troubles out of his mind and focus on work as he and Gage headed out of town toward the Eagle Mountain Resort property. "I talked to the mayor's brother, Garrett, this morning," Dwight said.

"Oh?"

"Yeah. I looked him up online. He actually has quite a few acting credits—dinner theaters, some commercials, some walk-ons in movies. So Larry was telling the truth about that."

"What about their dinner?" Gage asked.

"He confirmed that he met Larry in Junction about six and they were together until after eleven. So the mayor is off the hook."

"Yeah, well, he wasn't at the top of our list anyway," Gage said. "My money is on the guy who was with Brenda—Brownley."

"I haven't been able to find out much about him," Dwight said. "But I'm still looking."

"I ran some more background on these folks we're meeting," Gage said. "Came up with nothing. The company itself—CNG Development—is a subsidiary of a subsidiary of a holding company, and part of a consortium of capital improvement corporations, etc. etc. etc." He waved his hand. "One of these big corporate tangles even the IRS can't figure out, which I guess is the whole point."

"What about the men we're meeting today?" Dwight asked.

"Pierpoint and Reed," Gage said. "Sounds like a law firm. Nothing on them, either. Low-level corporate drones."

Dwight nodded. That was all he'd been able to come up with, as well. "I don't expect to get much out of them," he said. "They'll tell us about as much as a press release, but at least we'll be able to size them up."

"Size them up, and let them know we'll be keeping an eye on them," Gage said.

Marcus Pierpoint and Bryce Reed met the two deputies at the entrance to the property. Dressed in gray business suits and white shirts with no ties, they were cut from the same mold—middle-aged and serious, with firm handshakes and big smiles. Pierpoint was the taller of the two and did most of the talking. Reed tended to echo whatever his colleague said.

"Thanks for meeting with us this afternoon, officers," Pierpoint said after the introductions, as if the meeting had been his idea and not the sheriff's. "We're always interested in establishing good relations with local law enforcement."

"Always good to have the police on our side," Reed agreed.

"What do you know about the activities that have gone on here the past few months?" Dwight asked.

The two businessmen exchanged looks. "You're referring to illegal activities?"

Dwight and Gage said nothing.

"We're aware that wholly unauthorized persons have used the property for illegal activities," Pierpoint said.

"Wholly unauthorized," Reed echoed.

"Did you know any of these persons?" Dwight asked. "Wade Tomlinson or Brock Ryan?"

"No," Pierpoint said, while Reed shook his head.

"What about Henry Hake?" Gage asked.

"What about him?" Pierpoint asked.

"When was the last time you saw him?" Gage asked.

"We never met Mr. Hake," Pierpoint said.

"Do you know anything about his disappearance and subsequent death?" Dwight asked.

"No." Pierpoint shook his head emphatically. "We had nothing to do with any of that." He looked around the property, at the bare limbs of the aspen trees, and the piles of golden leaves among the concrete foundations of buildings that had never been completed. "We were, of course, horrified to learn of the goings-on up here. I assure you both that we intend to put a stop to anything like that."

"Oh?" Dwight waited for Pierpoint to fill in the silence that followed. He struck Dwight as a man who liked to talk.

"We will be installing new gates and locks to keep out trespassers," Pierpoint said. "And we're going to be hiring a security service to patrol the area. We want to make sure everyone knows that this is private property and trespassing will not be tolerated."

"What about the public trail?" Gage asked.

Again the look between the two. "What public trail?" Pierpoint asked.

"The one on the west side of the property," Gage said. "A court case last year established that it is a public right of way and can't be blocked."

"We contest that assertion and will be appealing," Pierpoint said.

Did the man always talk like he was presenting a case in court? Dwight wondered. "Until the court order is overturned, any gates or locks you install blocking the trail will be removed," Dwight said.

Pierpoint's expression made it clear he didn't like this, but wisely didn't argue.

"What are your plans for the property?" Gage asked.

"We will be building a private research facility on-site," Pierpoint said.

"What kind of research?" Dwight asked.

"We're not at liberty to say, but the remote location and high altitude could prove beneficial," Pierpoint said.

"Was the laboratory we found here on the property, in the underground bunker, yours?" Dwight asked.

"No," Pierpoint said. "That has nothing to do with us. We'll be building a completely modern, state-of-the-art facility."

"You'll be applying for all the proper permits from the county," Gage said.

"Of course." Reed apparently decided it was time for him to get another word in.

"Is there anything else we can do for you?" Pierpoint asked. He pulled a set of car keys from his pocket. "We have another meeting we need to get to."

"That's all for now," Dwight said.

He and Gage returned to Dwight's SUV. Pierpoint and Reed followed and Reed shut and locked the gate behind them. Dwight waited until he was on the road again before he spoke. "What do you think?" he asked Gage.

"Hard to say if they were telling the truth or not," Gage said. "I can't think of any good reason they would be linked to Henry Hake's disappearance and death—the transfer of the property was completed before he died. And it doesn't make sense they would have a connection to Wade and Brock." He shrugged. "But stranger things have happened."

"Interesting that they're going to use the place for a research facility," Dwight said.

"I don't know," Gage said. "I think high-altitude research is kind of a thing these days. There are a couple of facilities around Denver—and one in Crested Butte—studying climate and who knows what else."

Dwight nodded. "I guess so. Just seems like a remote place to do research."

"Maybe the remote location is an advantage," Gage said. He shifted in his seat. "The environmental folks might like that idea better than a big resort."

"Maybe. And the place is an eyesore in the condition it's in now."

"Do you really think they had no idea what was going on up there?" Gage asked. "I mean, that underground lab, what happened with me and Maya—and don't forget someone shot at me and at Travis on different occasions. It was like they were using that place as a headquarters for something."

"These guys are based in Utah," Dwight said. "I can see how they might not know if someone was up to something on the place. And I can see how it would attract the wrong element—all those empty buildings and the remote location. I'm glad they're going to be looking after the place now."

"That public trail is going to be a sticking point. If they try to close it, Paige and her group will fight them on it."

"Let's hope we don't have to get involved," Dwight said. "I'd be happy if I never had to go up to Eagle Mountain Resort again."

Chapter Thirteen

It didn't take long for the four women to agree that a proper night out on the town meant a town other than Eagle Mountain. "There's only one bar there, there's no place to dance, the only fancy places to eat are full of tourists, and everyone we know will see us and gossip about every move we make." Paige ticked off all the reasons the quartet had to leave town if they were really going to cut loose.

"Just how wild do you plan on this evening being?" Maya asked. A recent transplant from Denver, the high school teacher with dip-dyed blue hair probably had more party girl experience than any of them.

"I don't know," Lacy said. "Do you think we can get enough drinks in Brenda that she'll dance on a table?"

"It will never happen," Brenda said. "You know I don't drink that much. And someone has to stay sober enough to drive."

"I've already taken care of that," Lacy said. "No worries about any of us getting behind the wheel with too much to drink."

"What do you mean?" Paige asked, clearly skeptical.

"We have a driver." She gestured to the window and the street outside her parents' house. A young man dressed in jeans, a navy blazer, and a chauffeur's cap saw them all peering at him and tipped his hat.

"Parker!" Paige exclaimed.

"He had the night off, he doesn't drink as a condition of his parole, and he's a good driver," Lacy said. "I figure it would be the perfect solution."

"I'm not sure how I feel about going out with my kid brother," Paige said as the women gathered their purses and wraps and headed for the door.

"He's not going to go into the restaurant or club with us," Lacy said. "And I've already told him that if he tries to take any photographs of any of us in compromising positions, I'll take his phone and step on it." She extended one foot to display a wicked-looking stiletto heel. "I think he believed me."

Parker drove them to Junction, a college town about an hour away, in the dark blue Toyota sedan he usually used for pizza delivery. Paige had made the dinner reservations, selecting a Japanese grill where they sat on cushions around a low table while a chef made their meals to order—and flirted outrageously. They took turns daring one another to eat unfamiliar foods—they all tried the octopus, but Paige was the only one who would brave eating eel.

By her second glass of wine, Brenda realized she had laughed more in the last hour than she probably had in the last year. While a waitress cleared away their dinner plates, she excused herself to use the ladies' room.

"I'll go, too," Lacy said, and hurried after her.

"Thank you for pulling this together," Brenda said when the two friends found themselves alone in the ladies' room. "You were right—this is exactly what I needed."

"It's what I needed, too," Lacy said. "I've been working so hard at school and on plans for the wedding—it feels great to relax with friends. As much as I love Travis, being with him isn't the same as being with female friends, you know?"

Brenda nodded, too choked up to speak. In the months following Andy's death, she had too often cut herself off from others. Only recently had friends like Lacy reminded her how important other people were in her life.

A few moments later, they emerged from the restroom into the hallway that divided the restaurant into two halves—their table was in a large space full of low tables, colorful cushions, shoji screens and traditional Japanese décor. The other side of the restaurant had a more Western vibe, with dark booths and small tables.

Brenda glanced into this space and stopped short.

"What is it?" Lacy asked.

Brenda took a step back, behind a large potted firm. "That booth on the far side of the room—the second one from the left." She kept her voice low, just above a whisper. "Is that Eddie Carstairs?"

Lacy peered around the firm. "It is him! But who is he with?"

The two women stared between the fronds of the fern at Eddie, who was dressed in a dark suit a little too big for his slight frame, and at the man across from him. This man also wore a dark suit, though better tailored and obviously more expensive than Eddie's. His upper face was in shadow, only his chin visible. "I can't tell who that is," Brenda said.

"Eddie looks upset about something," Lacy said. At that moment, Eddie leaned forward, jaw set, and stabbed his finger at the man opposite. The man didn't even flinch, merely waited for Eddie to finish whatever he was saying.

Brenda tugged on Lacy's arm. "It doesn't matter. Let's get out of here before he sees us." Having to deal with Eddie would definitely put a damper on the night.

"What do you think Eddie is doing here?" Lacy asked.

Brenda shook her head. "I don't know. Maybe his brother is in town. Or a friend from college or a cousin. Or maybe it's a business meeting." The more she thought about the scene at the table, the more it struck her that way—very businesslike. Or maybe it was just that the other man seemed like a businessman to her—the tailored suit, the stoic demeanor.

"I told them to go ahead and bring our checks," Paige said when Brenda and Lacy returned to the table.

"What's next on the agenda?" Brenda asked as she fished her wallet out of her purse.

"We're going to a great club a friend told me about," Maya said. "They have a fantastic DJ and a big dance floor. Plenty of room for the four of us to get out there and show our stuff." She laughed at what must have been the expression on Brenda's face. "It's okay to dance without men, you know," she said. "Women do it all the time at places like this."

"Sure," Brenda said. "It sounds like fun." Though she couldn't help feeling a little pang of nostalgia for the times she and Andy had danced arm in arm. For all his faults, he had been a great dancer.

They paid their bills, then gathered their belongings and filed out of the dining room. Brenda and Lacy waited while Maya and Paige went to the ladies' room.

They were standing in the foyer when two men emerged from the other side of the restaurant and almost collided with them. "What are you doing here?" Eddie demanded. He glared at Brenda, face flushed.

"We're having dinner," Brenda said. "The same as you." She glanced behind him, toward his companion, but the other man was already gone. She'd been so focused on Eddie, she had never gotten a good look at him.

"You must be feeling better," Lacy said. "Have they caught whoever it was who tried to poison you?"

"It wasn't poison," Eddie said. He glared at the two women. "I have to go." Then he turned and hurried out the door.

"Was that Eddie Carstairs?" Paige joined them, Maya close behind.

"Yes," Lacy said. "He apparently decided to have dinner here, too."

"I guess he won't want pizza for a long time." Maya covered her mouth and giggled. "I'm sorry, that was probably mean."

"He wasn't happy to see us, that's for sure," Brenda said. The women trooped out to the parking lot, where Parker met them at the car. He had opted to go across the street to a popular burger place for dinner.

"How was your dinner?" Brenda asked as he unlocked the car for them.

"Good. I met a couple of cute girls." He grinned. "One of them gave me her number."

"Since when are you such a flirt?" Paige asked.

"You should try it sometime, sis," he said. "It's fun."

"Oh no!"

At the cry from the rear of the car, the others turned

to find Maya staring down at the rear wheel. She looked up at them, dismayed. "We've got a flat."

"Let me see." Parker moved to her side and knelt to check the tire, which was, indeed, deflated.

"You have a spare, right?" Paige asked.

Parker stood and walked around the rear of the car to the other side. "I have one spare," he said. "But both rear tires are flat."

"Did we run over nails or something?" Lacy looked around, as if expecting to find the cause of the tire damage nearby.

"Or something." Parker turned to Paige. "Maybe you'd better call the cops."

"Why?" she asked, even as she pulled out her phone.

"We didn't run over anything," Parker said. "Both tires have been slashed."

"EDDIE'S THE OBVIOUS suspect for slashing the tires, but he denies everything," Dwight said when he saw Brenda the next night before the museum reception. Whereas when she had called last night to tell him about the incident in the restaurant parking lot she had been clearly upset, tonight she was the picture of calm, in an ankle-length midnight-blue dress that bared her shoulders and clung to her curves, subtle silver threads shimmering with every movement. She wore her blond hair piled on top of her head, delicate tendrils framing her face. The overall effect was elegant and incredibly sexy.

He had traded in his uniform for a dark gray Western-cut suit and polished python boots, though he was technically on the job, his service weapon in a holster beneath the jacket. Travis and Gage were in attendance as well, to beef up the security provided by Eddie. They would keep an eye on the valuable auction items, but Dwight's main focus was on protecting Brenda.

"I don't think Eddie did it," she said. "I don't see how he would have had time. We were talking to him in the lobby of the restaurant right up until we walked out to the car."

"What about his friend?" Dwight asked. "The man he was having dinner with. You said he left the restaurant ahead of Eddie."

"Maybe." She frowned. "But why? Neither Lacy nor I recognized him. We really didn't get a good look at him. His face was in shadow in the restaurant."

"I wish you had seen him. I'd love to know who he is."

"Do you think he's the same person who brought Eddie the doctored pizza?" she asked.

"Maybe." Dwight had already considered this—whoever had dosed that pizza with sleeping pills had been someone Eddie either wanted to protect, or didn't want to admit to knowing. "But then, why would Eddie go out to dinner with him a few nights later?"

"Maybe Eddie set up the meeting to confront the guy about the pizza. He wanted to do it away from Eagle Mountain, where someone might see them together. That would explain why he was so upset to run into us."

"Maybe." He looked around the crowd. At least eighty people were in attendance, drifting through the rooms of the museum, sipping cocktails and nibbling canapés, admiring the items on display and checking out the auction items arrayed on tables in the front rooms. Attire ranged from business suits and cocktail dresses to jeans and T-shirts. He didn't recognize a dozen or more of the guests, though he spotted the mayor across the room, in conversation with the woman who headed up the local beautification committee. "Is Robert Brownley here?" he asked.

"I haven't seen him. Why?"

"I tried to find out some background information on him, but I couldn't come up with anything."

"I did an online search, too," she admitted. "But nothing I came up with sounded like him. But if he's as wealthy as he seemed, maybe he purposely keeps a low profile."

"Maybe." There were too many maybes involved in this case.

"Oh look, there's Professor Gibson." She touched Dwight's arm. "Excuse me, I want to speak to him."

"Of course." Dwight watched her cross the room and greet the professor. She smiled at the older man, and Dwight felt a now-familiar catch in his chest. He would never get tired of looking at that smile, of watching the play of emotions on her face. He could imagine himself looking at her this way when they were both twenty or forty or sixty years older. The problem was—how could he persuade her to see that kind of future? She had been hurt so much in the past, he had the sense that she was afraid to look too far ahead.

Patience, he told himself. That was the key to dealing with Brenda—and the key to investigating any case. He went to join Travis by the auction display. The sheriff wore a black Western jacket, black jeans and a black Stetson, with a white shirt and string tie. Lacy, in a sleeveless red cocktail dress trimmed with fringe, stood beside him. They made a striking couple.

"Hello, Lacy." Dwight touched the brim of his hat and nodded to her.

"Don't you look handsome." She turned to Travis. "All of you clean up so well."

Travis's answer was a grunt. Lacy laughed. "You'd rather be in uniform, wouldn't you?" She kissed his cheek. "Dwight has a look in his eye like he wants to talk shop, so I'm going to visit with Paige." She smiled at Dwight and left them.

"Anyone particularly interested in the book?" Dwight asked.

"Nope." Travis glanced toward where the book sat on a raised platform in the very center of the table to their left. "A couple of people have looked at it, but no one has lingered." He shifted toward his deputy. "How's Brenda doing?"

"She seems calm. I think the whole episode with the tire annoyed her more than it frightened her."

Travis nodded. "She doesn't frighten easily."

"She said Robert Brownley hasn't shown up."

"Anybody else here who shouldn't be?"

"Brenda didn't mention anyone." Laughter rose from a knot of people near the door to the hallway and he turned to look toward them. "There are quite a few people from out of town."

"Let's hope they bid high and the museum makes some money," Travis said. He looked toward the auction items again. "Lacy has her heart set on that quilt. I put in a bid on it—thought it might make a good wedding present."

"I imagine it would." This brought to mind the question of what *he* should give the happy couple as a gift—something that hadn't occurred to him until this moment.

Fortunately, he didn't have to wrestle with this question for long. The arrival of Eddie Carstairs interrupted him. Unlike the dressed-up sheriff and deputies, he wore khaki pants and shirt that looked very much like the Rayford County Sheriff's Department uniforms, though in place of the sheriff's department patch, his shirt had a dark blue star with the word *Security* embroidered in gold lettering across it. "What are you two doing hovering around the auction items?" Eddie asked.

"Just keeping an eye on them," Travis said.

"That's my job." Eddie rested his hand at his hip, very near the holster for a pistol. He had a permit for the weapon, and his sheriff's department training would have ensured he knew how to use it safely, but the sight of it still made Dwight uncomfortable. Maybe that was behind Dwight's decision to make Eddie uncomfortable in turn.

"Who were you having dinner with last night?" Dwight asked.

Eddie's cheeks flushed. "We already went over all that," he said. "It's none of your business."

"It's my business if he slashed the tires on the car Brenda and her friends were in." Dwight could feel Travis's steady gaze on him. Was the sheriff going to reprimand him for interrogating a witness in a public place like this? Or was Travis merely waiting to see what Eddie would say?

"Maybe Parker slashed the tires himself to make me look bad," Eddie said. "Did you ever think of that?"

Dwight looked over Eddie's shoulder to where Parker Riddell, in black pants and a white long-sleeved shirt that hid his many tattoos, offered a group of silver-haired women a tray of bacon-wrapped shrimp. He had considered the idea that Parker had slashed the tires, ei-

ther to frighten the women or to call attention to himself
for some reason. But everything he had learned from the
people who knew and worked with him confirmed that
Parker was staying on the straight and narrow. Brenda
certainly thought so, and her opinion carried more and
more weight with Dwight.

"What is he doing here, anyway?" Eddie asked. "He
doesn't have any business being around all these valuable items. If anything disappears, he's my number one
suspect."

Travis and Dwight both ignored the comment.
Dwight could almost hear Eddie's teeth grinding in
frustration at his failure to elicit a response.

"Who is that man Brenda is talking to?" Eddie asked.

Dwight followed Eddie's gaze to where Brenda
stood with Professor Gibson, their heads inclined toward each other, deep in conversation. He was tempted
to tell Eddie the man's identity was none of his business, but Travis answered, "That's Professor Gibson.
He owned that book—*The Secret History of Rayford
County*—before Andy Stenson got hold of it."

Eddie studied the couple. "He and Brenda certainly
look cozy," he said. He turned to Dwight. "You might
have some competition, Prentice."

Dwight glared at him. He could either deny anything
was going on between him and Brenda—which would
be a lie—or remain silent and confirm Eddie's suspicions. The man was a worse gossip than Adelaide, and
in Eddie's case, Dwight always had the sense Eddie
was searching for any scrap of information he could
use to his own advantage. He decided to play it cool.
"I wasn't aware we were running a race. Excuse me. I
see someone I'd like to speak with." The mayor had just

entered the room, and as long as he was here, Dwight wanted to find out where Brenda's boss—and Eddie's, for that matter—had been when Brenda's tires were being slashed.

"PROFESSOR, I'D LIKE you to meet Parker Riddell. He's one of my best volunteers—and he's studying history at the community college." Brenda had waylaid the young man as he hurried past with yet another tray or hors d'oeuvres.

"Always good to meet a young person who's interested in history." Professor Gibson offered his hand. "Is there a particular period you'd like to focus on?"

Parker shifted the serving tray and shook the professor's hand. "I'm not sure, sir. American history. The West. And I'm really interested in World War II."

Gibson nodded and asked a few more questions about the classes Parker was currently enrolled in, and made some recommendations of books he should read. "History isn't the most lucrative field these days," he said. "But it can be a very rewarding one."

"I hope so, sir." Parker shifted the tray again. "I'd better go pass these out before they get cold. It was nice to meet you."

"Nice to meet you, too, young man."

When Parker had left them, the professor turned back to Brenda. "You've done a wonderful job with this place," he said. "It's a real gem."

"We think so," Brenda said. Now seemed as good a time as any to bring up what was, after all, an awkward subject. "I want to thank you for being so understanding about *The Secret History of Rayford County, Colo-*

rado. I truly had no idea my late husband had borrowed it from you when I listed it for auction."

"If I thought you had, I might not have been so understanding," Gibson said. "As it is, proving my claim would have been difficult, and I'm pleased to have the sale go to support a worthy cause. I'm curious, though—did you read the book?"

"I did. More than once. And I made quite a few notes."

He nodded. "At one time I tried very hard to determine where the secret lab might have been located. My theory is the government destroyed it once the project ended. Otherwise someone would have found it by now."

"The sheriff's department found what looked like a laboratory up at Eagle Mountain Resort, but it apparently wasn't nearly old enough to have been used during the war."

"Government documents are being declassified all the time," Gibson said. "I imagine before too many more years, someone will find out the location. In the meantime, that book attracts attention from everyone from conspiracy theorists to serious collectors. I hope it brings a high price to help support the museum."

She looked around, past the well-dressed guests to the photos and displays on the walls. To many people, the items in these rooms were just old junk, relics of a time long past. But to Brenda and other history lovers, they were links to the past—a look at how the people who had settled this part of the country had once lived. She believed those people still had lessons to teach. "I love this place," she said. "And I'm determined to do everything I can to keep it going."

"I have some ideas about that I'd love to talk to you about," the professor said. "I know—"

But a terrified scream cut off his words and silenced the conversations of those around them. A man Brenda didn't know, face blanched paper-white, staggered into the room. "Upstairs...a body...hanging," he gasped.

Chapter Fourteen

Dwight pushed through the crowd toward the stairs, Travis close behind him. "Police! Let us through!" he shouted, over the panicked voices of those rushing down the narrow staircase. Men and women turned sideways to let him pass, their frightened faces a blur as he mounted the steps two at a time. At the top, he paused and looked around.

"In there!" A man motioned toward a room to the left. Travis moved up beside Dwight, his gun drawn. "You take right. I'll go in on the left."

Dwight nodded. They had no reason to believe anyone dangerous was inside the room, but best to be prepared. Heart hammering, he moved to the right side of the door. Travis positioned himself across from him. At his nod, they went in, guns drawn.

Dwight's breath caught as he came face-to-face with a man in white—then he felt foolish, and a little shaky, as he realized the figure was actually a mannequin in a World War II sailor's uniform. He scanned the rest of the room, which was filled with old military paraphernalia, from helmets and maps to a Vietnam-era field radio and navy semaphore flags.

The body hung from the ceiling in the corner, positioned so that someone had to enter the room to see it. In the dimmer light in that part of the room, it did indeed look human—but closer inspection revealed that this, too, was a mannequin, dressed in the olive drab of a World War II-era sergeant.

Travis holstered his weapon. "Someone's idea of a sick joke," he said.

"What is it? Someone said there was a body?"

Eddie, red-faced and out of breath, appeared behind them, his gun drawn.

"Put that weapon away," Travis barked. "And go back downstairs."

Eddie holstered the gun, but made no move to leave. "I'm the security guard for the museum," he said. "I need to know what's going on."

"Nothing's going on," Dwight said. He gestured to the hanging mannequin. "Some joker decided to play a prank."

Eddie started to approach the mannequin, but Travis waved him back. "Stay out of the crime scene," he ordered.

Eddie laughed. "Crime scene? It's a mannequin."

"Someone wanted to frighten the people here tonight," Travis said. "I want to know who."

Brenda appeared behind Eddie in the doorway to the room, looking pale but determined. "What is going on?" she asked.

"Someone hung one of your mannequins from a ceiling beam," Travis said. "Then someone looked in, thought it was a body in the dim light and panicked."

Brenda moved into the room and looked toward the mannequin in the corner. She shuddered. "It certainly does look like a body from here. Who would do such a thing?"

"Where have you been, Eddie?" Dwight asked.

"Are you accusing me of doing something like this? I've been working, protecting the visitors to the museum and the museum's valuable property."

Dwight didn't let his disdain show on his face. Eddie acted as if he had personally been guarding every exhibit.

"The auction items!" Brenda's eyes widened and she started to turn away.

"Gage is guarding them," Travis said.

Dwight nodded. "You thought this might be a distraction—get us all up here and the thief could help himself to whatever he liked downstairs."

"It was a possibility." Travis looked up at the dangling mannequin. "Let's close off this room until we can get a crime scene team in to take a look. And we'll need to talk to whoever was up here when it was discovered."

"Some people have already left," Brenda said. "I think we can safely say this has put a damper on the evening." She turned around to look toward the hallway. "There have been dozens of people in and out of these rooms all night. How could someone do this without being seen?"

Dwight studied the layout of the room. "You can't see this corner from the hallway," he said. "If our prankster had the rope handy, he could wait until he was alone in here and loop it around the mannequin's neck. Throw the rope over the beam, hoist up the mannequin, secure the rope and stroll out. It might take less than a minute."

"You can ask if anyone saw anything," Brenda said. "Maybe you'll get lucky."

"Maybe." Travis didn't sound convinced.

"Do you have a guest list or anything with the names of everyone who attended tonight?" Dwight asked.

"There's a guest book—but whether or not people signed it was up to them."

"Let's go get it."

He descended the stairs right behind her, and a crowd of people surrounded them, firing questions—most versions of "What happened?"

"False alarm," he said, one hand at Brenda's back. He leaned closer to whisper in her ear, the floral scent of her perfume momentarily distracting him, but he forced his attention back to the task at hand. "You'd better make an announcement and send them home."

She nodded and climbed back up a few steps until she was above the crowd. Everyone fell silent. "Thank you all so much for coming tonight," she said. "I hope we see all of you at the auction tomorrow morning. You'll be able to get another look at all the items available tomorrow starting at nine a.m. See you then."

Eddie had appeared on the stairs behind Brenda as she spoke. As he came down after her, Dwight snagged his arm. "Help herd everyone out the door," he said.

Eddie opened his mouth as if to argue, but apparently thought better of it. He nodded and moved on, murmuring, "Good night," and, "Thank you for coming," as he urged people toward the open front doors.

"I want to check with Gage that the auction items are all right," Brenda said to Dwight.

"Good idea." They fought their way against the flow of the crowd to the next room, where Gage stood between the tables of auction items. "Any problems?" Dwight asked.

"Everything is still here, and I didn't notice anyone paying particular attention to me or the merchandise," Gage said. "What happened up there?"

"Someone hung a mannequin from a ceiling beam," Dwight said, keeping his voice low, though only a few people remained, waiting for their turn to exit.

"Sick joke," Gage said.

"Maybe," Dwight said.

"Eddie is supposed to be on duty all night," Brenda said. "But I'd feel better if one of you would take the book back to the station and lock it in the safe until morning." She picked up *The Secret History of Rayford County, Colorado*. "It's by far our most valuable item."

"I'll make sure it's safe." Dwight took the book from her. Gone was the sparkling, happy woman of earlier in the evening. She looked exhausted, weighed down by worry. "We don't know that the hung mannequin had anything to do with the book," he said.

"No, but too many unsettling things have been happening." She looked around the room. "I need to get you that guest book."

He followed her back to the entry hall, where they found Lacy with Travis. "Do you need me to stay and help with anything?" Lacy asked.

"No, thank you," Brenda said. "I'm going to go in a few minutes myself."

"We'll be here a little while longer," Travis said. "We'll lock up when we leave, and we'll be back in the morning for the auction."

"So will I." Lacy squeezed Brenda's shoulder. "Are you okay?"

Brenda nodded. "I'm fine."

Lacy frowned, but didn't say anything else. "I'll walk

you to your car," Travis said, and they headed out the door.

"The guest book is over here," Brenda said, walking to a small desk to the right of the door. The guest book, bound in blue leather, lay open on the top, a brass can filled with pens next to it. Signatures half filled the open page. Brenda picked up the book and flipped through it. "I don't see Robert Brownley's name here," she said. "And I didn't see him among the guests. Maybe he changed his mind about bidding for the book."

"Or maybe, since he plans to outbid everyone else, he'll be here tomorrow." Dwight slid the book from her hand, closed it and tucked it under his arm. He stroked her cheek. "Are you okay?"

She sighed. "I'm ready for all this to be over." She shook her head. "I don't know why that stupid mannequin upset me so much. It's just a sick joke, like Gage said. But it took me back to when we found Henry Hake…"

Her voice trailed away. Dwight set the book on the desk once more and pulled her to him. She rested her head on his shoulder, and he held her tightly for a long moment, saying nothing. He closed his eyes and let himself revel in the sweet scent and soft feel of her. When all this was over, he'd ask her to go away with him somewhere—a beach where they could lie side by side on the sand and sip fruity drinks. He smiled, picturing Brenda in a bikini.

"What are you smiling about?" She pushed away from him.

"How did you know I was smiling?" he asked, his expression solemn once more.

"I felt it." She rested a hand on his chest.

"I'll tell you later," he said. "Now, go home and get some rest. I'll take care of everything here."

She looked past him, at the crime scene techs filing up the stairs. "I feel like I should stay."

"There's nothing you can do. Go home and rest."

"All right. Let me get my purse." He waited while she retrieved her purse from her office, then walked with her to her car.

"We'll talk in the morning," he said. "Try not to worry."

She nodded. "I'm not going to let a stupid prank get the best of me." She rose on tiptoe to kiss his cheek. "I was thinking…instead of going to the ranch house, I might wait for you at your cabin."

The words sent a current of heat through him. "I'd like that." He fished his key from his pocket and pressed it into her palm. "You'll need this."

"Try not to be too late."

No, he'd be wrapping up his business here as quickly as possible. One lifeless mannequin couldn't compete with the very live woman he would have waiting for him.

AT LEAST HER bold suggestion to Dwight had provided a welcome distraction from the terrible way the evening had ended, Brenda thought as she drove through town. When he had pulled her to him and held her—just held her, without offering empty words or advice—she had felt so comforted and *supported*. He wasn't hovering or trying to control her or dismiss her or any of the things she had experienced at the hands of other men. Dwight was simply there for her, letting her find her own strength by lending her some of his. His calm, practical nature was exactly what she needed.

But Dwight was more than a calming presence or a strong friend. He was a man she wanted to be with more and more. Time to stop denying that and admit what was happening. In spite of all her efforts to resist— all the *logical* reasons this shouldn't be happening— Brenda had fallen in love with Dwight. The realization made her a little light-headed.

Maybe, when things had calmed down—after the auction at least—she would find a way to tell him.

That is, if she could get through the auction with no more disasters. At least it hadn't been a real body hanging in the display room, but who would do something like that? Was someone trying to frighten her?

Everyone in Eagle Mountain—and anyone who read the local newspaper—would have known that she and Dwight had found Henry Hake hanging in that underground laboratory at Eagle Mountain Resort. Was that mannequin supposed to be a sick reminder of that event—or some kind of warning?

She rubbed her temple, trying to ward off the headache that was building there. It didn't make sense, but then, nothing that had happened really did. She went over all the events in her mind—the two threatening notes on cheery yellow stationery, the crime scene photo from Andy's murder, the stolen banner announcing the auction, the fire that had destroyed her house, the slashed tires on the car that had been transporting her and her friends—and now this hanging mannequin. It was such a crazy combination of shocking violence and almost juvenile pranks. Everything seemed to have been aimed at either her or the museum, but why?

She turned onto the county road that led from town up to the Prentices' ranch. She couldn't keep from going over the events in her mind. It was like trying to find a missing piece in a jigsaw puzzle—find that piece, that link, and everything would make sense. She would have a clear picture where there had been only chaos before.

Glaring lights filled the car, reflecting off the rear-view mirror and into her eyes as a vehicle with its brights on came up behind her. Brenda put up a hand to shield her eyes from the glare and stepped on the brakes. She pulled the Subaru toward the shoulder, hoping the rude person behind her would pass. The car—or probably a truck, judging by the height of the headlights—was approaching very fast, obviously in a hurry to get somewhere. She would have pulled off the road altogether, but there wasn't room. The Eagle River followed the road here, the waters spilling over rocks some ten feet below.

She shifted her gaze to her side mirror and realized the other driver wasn't slowing down. He was traveling much too fast for this narrow, winding road. She took her foot off the brake and sped up, thinking she should drive until there was a safe place to pull over. But she had no time to gain much speed before the other vehicle was on her. Horrified, she realized the other driver wasn't going to stop. He hit her full-on, throwing her forward, her airbag exploding with painful violence, the car skidding off the pavement, rocketing down the bank of the river and into the icy water.

Chapter Fifteen

Pain throbbed in Brenda's head, and her chest hurt. She moaned and tried to shift into a more comfortable position, held upright by her seat belt. Confused, she opened her eyes and stared through the spiderwebbed windshield into a tangle of broken tree limbs and underbrush illuminated by one headlight. The lights on the dash bathed the interior of the car in a faint blue glow. The airbags had deflated, though their powdery residue lay like a dusting of sugar over everything. As her still-painful head began to clear, Brenda realized the car was still running. She felt around on the steering column and found the key, and turned it to cut the motor.

She had expected silence, but instead heard a car door slam and someone approaching, clumsy footsteps slipping and sliding on the steep embankment down from the road. The memory of the bright headlights rushing toward her sent panic through her, and she grappled to unfasten the seat belt. If her attacker was coming after her, she would have to run, to hide—

She was still fumbling with the seat belt when her door was wrenched open. A tall, dark figure, face covered by a black ski mask, grabbed her arm and shook her. "Give it to me!" he demanded, in a gruff, unfamiliar voice.

"G-give you what?" Brenda stared up at him, fighting for calm. She had to think, but her head hurt so much—the pain made her nauseous.

"Give me the book!"

The book. She wished she had never laid eyes on that cursed book. "I don't have it," she said.

"It's not at the museum. Where is it?"

"The sheriff has it."

Her attacker let loose a stream of invective that had her shrinking back. But even as she did so, she put her right hand down by her side, on the button to release the seat belt. As soon as she saw her chance, she would leap from the car and run. Better to risk the dangers of the mountainside than this madman.

"You're lying!" He punctuated this statement by thrusting a pistol in her face. Brenda had seen plenty of firearms in her life. Her father had collected guns. The museum owned several antique pistols and rifles. But she had never been eye to eye with a weapon that was pointed directly at her. She was both terrified and icily calm.

"I'm not lying," she said, shocked by how even her voice sounded. It was almost as if some other person— a cooler, more courageous person—had taken over her body. "The sheriff has the book."

"Give me your purse." He thrust the gun toward her.

"It's in the passenger seat," she said. "You're welcome to it."

He reached past her and grabbed the purse, as well as the tote bag that contained auction paperwork she had planned to look over before she returned to work in the morning. He riffled through these items, then tossed them onto the ground at his feet. She bit her tongue to keep from pointing out that she had already told him she didn't have the book. Why wouldn't he believe her?

"Where were you going tonight?" he asked, the end of the barrel of the gun only a few inches from her forehead.

"I was going home," she said.

"You don't live out this way," he said.

I didn't until you burned down my house, she thought. But then, maybe this man hadn't burned her house. She had no way of knowing. "I'm staying with friends," she said.

"Friends? Or one particular friend?" He reached over and unsnapped the seat belt, then dragged her from the car. "You're staying with that cop, aren't you? The tall, dark-haired one."

Brenda said nothing.

"He lives on a ranch, doesn't he?" the man asked. When she didn't answer, he yanked on her arm—hard.

She cried out and tried to pull away, but he only held on tighter and dragged her after him. "Come on," he said.

"Where are you taking me?" she asked.

"To wait for your boyfriend."

WRAPPING THINGS UP at the museum took longer than Dwight had wanted. Usually, he appreciated how methodical and thorough Travis could be, but tonight the routine had chafed. Brenda was waiting, and Dwight didn't want to lose the chance to be with her—not just to make love, though he certainly hoped they would do that, but to talk to her about something besides the case. About their future.

Finally, he had gotten away, with a reminder from Travis that he would need a report on his desk in the morning. Dwight had suppressed a groan and nodded, then hurried away, leaving Travis and Gage to lock up the museum. He pushed the SUV on the drive to the ranch, though the narrow, curvy road limited how fast he could safely travel. He watched the sides of the road for deer or elk that might decide to leap out in front of him. He had attended more than one wreck caused by wildlife. Most of the people involved escaped with only minor damage, but he still remembered one young woman who had been killed when her truck rolled down the embankment, crushing her, after she swerved to avoid a deer.

His headlights glanced off a vehicle parked ahead, half on the shoulder, half in his lane, and he braked. The car appeared empty, not running. Had someone abandoned it like this? He prepared to pull in behind it. He might have to call a tow truck to retrieve the big SUV—another delay, but necessary. Parked as it was, the vehicle was a real hazard.

But as he pulled in behind the SUV, two figures emerged ahead of the vehicle, climbing up from the stream bank. The larger figure—a man—appeared to be dragging the smaller one—a woman—behind him. Dwight hit his brights and recognized Brenda's battered face even as his windshield was shattered and the sound of a gunshot echoed around them.

Dwight threw himself to the floorboard, drawing his pistol as he wedged himself beneath the steering column. "You can come out now, Deputy," a man's voice shouted. "Come out with your hands up and I promise I won't shoot you. But try anything and I'll kill your girlfriend here."

Dwight didn't answer. He glanced at the radio, wondering if he could reach it and call for help. But a woman's scream, sharp and filled with pain, froze him. "Come out now!" the voice demanded. "Unless you want me to kill her now."

"I'm coming out!" Dwight answered, and raised his hands, though the rest of him remained shielded by the cruiser's door.

"Throw out your weapon."

Dwight tossed the gun onto the ground.

"Now come out with your hands up."

Everything within him resisted the idea of stepping out and exposing himself to the shooter, but the idea that Brenda could die if he hesitated propelled him to open the door and step into the open. A stocky man with a black knit ski mask pulled over his face held Brenda by one arm, a long-barreled pistol pressed to the side of her head. Brenda locked her eyes to Dwight's, determination shining through the fear. She trusted him to get them out of this, and that knowledge made him stronger.

"What do you want?" Dwight asked.

"I want the book," the man said.

"The Secret History of Rayford County?" Dwight wished he had urged Brenda to burn the book when she received the first threatening note.

"Yes. I want it."

"I don't have it."

The man drove the barrel of the gun into Brenda's cheek so that she cried out. "Don't lie to me!"

"The book is at the sheriff's department," Dwight said. "In the safe."

"Then we're going to go get it," the man said. He adjusted his grip on Brenda's arm. "But we don't need her to get it."

Instinct overwhelmed reason as Dwight realized what the man intended to do. With a roar, he launched himself at the other man, even as the pistol flashed in the darkness and the explosion of gunfire rang in the night stillness. Brenda's scream merged with his own cry of rage as he and the shooter grappled on the ground. Dwight clawed and kicked at the other man, who was shorter but heavier than him. And he knew how to fight.

He slammed his fist into the side of Dwight's head as Dwight grabbed hold of the pistol and tried to wrench it away. Dwight drove his elbow into the man's stomach, then thrust up his head, striking his assailant's chin and forcing his head back. The man roared in either pain or anger, and punched Dwight in the nose. Pain exploded behind his eyes and his vision went black, but he kept hold of the gun and struggled onto his knees, battling for equilibrium.

When the other man tried to kick him, Dwight scrambled out of the way, keeping hold of the gun and forcing the man's hand back at an awkward angle. The man cried out in pain, and Dwight shoved harder, putting all his weight behind the move. The man's fingers loosened, and Dwight seized the gun and trained it on the man.

But the other man shoved up to his feet and ran, the black of his clothing blending into the darkness. Dwight fired, but the shot went wide. Seconds later, the man was in the big SUV. Dwight steadied the gun with both hands and fired again, but only succeeded in taking out one taillight as the vehicle sped away.

Dazed and vaguely aware of blood streaming down his face, Dwight clutched the gun and tried to steady his breathing and think past the pain. A low moan cleared some of the fog engulfing him. "Brenda!" He looked around and heard the moan again, to his right. He unhooked his MagLite from his belt and played the beam along the shoulder of the road until he saw her. She lay back in the gravel and leaf litter, blood bathing her torso, her face ghostly white, her eyes closed.

"Brenda!" He shouted her name, but she didn't stir. He shoved to his feet and ran to her, dropping to his knees beside her. "Brenda!" He took her hand, staring at the blood covering the front of her shirt.

She moaned again, and her eyes fluttered open. "Dwight." She struggled, as if trying to sit.

"Don't move." He put one hand on her shoulder to keep her from rising. "Where are you hurt?"

"My shoulder."

He trained the light on her left shoulder and surveyed the round hole that was seeping blood. The blood loss was a concern, but at least she hadn't been shot in the chest or stomach or head. "Lie still," he said. "I'm going to call for help and get the first aid kit from my cruiser."

"All right."

He ran to the cruiser, ignoring the pain from his nose, which was probably broken. Once there, he grabbed the radio, identified himself, asked for an ambulance for a gunshot victim and gave his location. "The shooter is a man about five ten, a hundred and eighty pounds, driving a black Land Rover, license Alfa, Foxtrot, Sierra, two, two, eight."

He retrieved the first aid kit and returned to Brenda. "I'm going to put some gauze on this wound and apply pressure to try to stop the bleeding," he said. "It might hurt, and I'm sorry about that."

"It's okay." She blinked at him, clearly dazed. "What happened to your face?"

He reached up and touched his nose, and winced as a fresh jolt of pain made him catch his breath. "I think the guy who shot you broke it."

"He ran me off the road," she said. "My car is down by the creek somewhere. My head hurts." She closed her eyes.

Did she have a concussion, too? Other injuries he didn't know about? "Talk to me," he said. "Try to stay awake. Do you know the guy? Did you recognize him from anywhere?"

"No. He wore a mask. Why did he shoot me?"

"I don't know." He made a thick pad from the gauze and pressed down hard on the wound. Brenda cried out and tried to roll away, but he held her firm. "We need to stop the bleeding," he said. "The ambulance will be here soon." Or he hoped it would be. If the ambulance crew were out on another call, it could take a while before they reached them. Meanwhile, he would do everything he could to help. "Do you think the man was Robert Brownley?" he asked.

She furrowed her brown. "Robert Browning? The poet?"

"Robert Brownley. The man who came to see you at the museum and wanted to bid on the book."

"I… I don't know." She looked at him, eyes full of questions behind the pain. "Why do you think that?"

"I recognized the SUV he was driving." In which case, Robert Brownley probably wasn't the man's real name, but Dwight had alerted his fellow law enforcement officers about the license plate of the Land Rover and the fact that it only had one taillight. He hoped someone would stop Brownley before he had time to ditch the vehicle and switch to another.

"I don't know," Brenda said. "I can't think very clearly right now."

"Don't worry about it now. Do you hurt anywhere else—besides your head and your shoulder?"

Before she could answer the question, headlight beams illuminated them, and tires crunched on gravel as a red Jeep Wagoneer pulled in in front of Dwight's cruiser. Still pressing down on the gauze pad, Dwight squinted over his shoulder at the vehicle and the man who climbed out of the driver's seat.

"What happened?" Eddie Carstairs asked, hurrying toward them.

"Brenda's been shot," Dwight said. "An ambulance is on its way. Maybe you can walk down the road a little ways and watch for it and flag it down."

"Sure." Eddie took a few steps closer. "Is she okay?"

"I'm going to be fine," Brenda said before Dwight could answer. The strength in her voice encouraged him. He reached out to stroke the side of her face.

"Yes, you're going to be fine," he said. "I think the bleeding has almost stopped."

"What happened?" Eddie asked again.

"Some guy ran her off the road and shot her," Dwight said. "He wanted that book—the one about the World

War II laboratories. I got his plate number and every cop in the state will be looking for him soon."

"Looks like he almost got the better of you," Eddie said, leaning down to peer at Dwight's face.

"Eddie, what are you doing here?" Brenda asked. "You're supposed to be at the museum."

"I came to find you. You and Dwight." He reached behind him and drew his gun. "I need you to take me to the book."

Chapter Sixteen

Dwight reached for his weapon, but Eddie lashed out, kicking him viciously. Brenda's scream echoed around them as Dwight fell back. When he sat up, Eddie had the gun trained on Brenda. "You need to cooperate with me or I'll shoot her." His voice shook a little, but his hand remained steady. "Don't think I won't do it."

"Eddie, why?" Brenda asked.

"Nothing personal against you," Eddie said. "But I'm sworn to do my duty." He motioned to Dwight. "Stand up. We need to get going."

Dwight stood, and Brenda struggled to prop herself up on one elbow. "What do you mean, your duty?" she asked.

"I don't have time to explain now." He took Dwight's elbow. "We have to go."

Where is that ambulance? Dwight thought. "I'm not leaving Brenda," he said.

"Of course not," Eddie said. "Do you think I'm stupid enough to leave her to tell the paramedics where we are and what we're doing? She's coming with us."

"She's injured," Dwight protested. "She needs medical care."

"Then I'll just have to finish her off." Eddie shifted the gun toward her.

"No!" Brenda struggled to sit, one hand keeping the gauze pad in place over her wound. "I'll go with you. You just have to help me up." This last she directed at Dwight. He wanted to argue that she should lie still, but he didn't trust Eddie not to carry out his threat to kill her. The security guard looked desperate and a little unhinged.

"It's going to be all right," Dwight whispered in Brenda's ear as he helped her to stand. "Just hang in there." Eddie thought they were at his mercy, but at the first opportunity, Dwight would prove he was wrong.

BRENDA FOUGHT WAVES of nausea and dizziness as Dwight half carried her to Eddie's Jeep. Her shoulder throbbed with pain, and she took shallow breaths, trying to avoid moving it. But that didn't help much, as every step over the rough ground jarred the wound. Dwight pressed the gauze tightly against her, adding to the agony, though she knew it was necessary to keep her from bleeding to death. She fought back panic. She wasn't going to die. Not over some stupid book.

Not when she had finally found Dwight.

Eddie stood beside them while Dwight helped her climb into the Jeep. She loathed the idea of sitting next to Eddie, but he wasn't giving her any choice. When Dwight had buckled her seat belt, Eddie prodded him with the gun. "Now let's take care of your cruiser."

"What about my cruiser?" Dwight asked.

"You don't think I'm stupid enough to let you leave it here, where anyone coming along might see it and call in a report about an abandoned cop vehicle?" He jabbed Dwight in the shoulder with the gun. "Come on."

Dwight looked at Brenda. Maybe if she'd been in better shape, she could have used this opportunity to run for help, but it was taking every ounce of strength she could muster to remain upright in the truck. "I'll be right back," Dwight said.

She nodded.

As soon as he had left her, she closed her eyes, but opened them again as that seemed to make the dizziness worse. She studied the contents of Eddie's Jeep—fast-food wrappers and discarded cups stained with coffee littered the floormats, while gas receipts, maps and other papers almost obscured the dashboard. She saw nothing in the debris that gave her a clue as to why he was doing this. Were he and the man who had shot her working together—or were they rivals, both wanting *The Secret History of Rayford County, Colorado* for some reason?

Maybe all this had something to do with money, she thought. Eddie struck her as a man who was very motivated by money. He was always talking about how hard up he was since he had been let go from the sheriff's department—even though as a reserve officer, he had worked only part time and made very little. But it was probably easier to blame Travis for his woes than admit that his own actions had led to his downfall.

An engine raced, startling her. She raised her eyes to the rearview mirror and gasped as Dwight's SUV rolled toward the drop-off on the opposite side of the road. The front wheels left the pavement and the vehicle lurched forward, then tumbled over the edge, the sound of it hitting and bouncing off the rocks echoing in the still night air.

The two men returned to the Jeep. Dwight's hands were cuffed behind his back—Brenda assumed with his own handcuffs. Eddie waited until he had slid into the passenger seat beside Brenda, then he shut the door and walked around to the driver's side. "What are we going to do?" Brenda whispered.

"Wait for an opportunity," Dwight said.

Eddie slammed the door behind him and put the Jeep into gear. He held the gun in his right hand, his left on the steering wheel. "Just remember, Dwight. If you try anything, I'll shoot Brenda. I know you don't want that."

Dwight said nothing, though Brenda felt his tension, the muscles of his forearm taut beside her. "Where are we going?" she asked as Eddie turned the truck back toward town.

"We're going to get that book out of the safe."

"Why do you want the book?" she asked.

But he didn't answer as the flashing lights of an ambulance approached, the siren wailing. Eddie slowed and edged to the shoulder, turning his face away as the ambulance passed, bathing the interior of the Jeep in red light. When it was past, Eddie pulled onto the highway again.

Maybe someone will be at the sheriff's department when we arrive, Brenda thought. But as soon as they pulled into the dark, empty lot, she knew that was a false hope. The force was so small they often had only one or two officers on duty overnight, and they spent most of their time in the field, patrolling. No one else was out at this late hour, either, the streets empty of cars or pedestrians. A quarter moon rose over Dakota Ridge, stars like sequins on a cocktail dress shining around it. Under other circumstances, she would have admired the view. A new pain shot through her as she wondered if this would be the last night she ever saw these stars.

Eddie drove around the back of the sheriff's department and parked in the shadow of the building. Security lights bathed the area around the back door in a silvery-white glow, but inside Eddie's truck was pitch-black. "Where are your keys?" he asked Dwight.

"My front pocket."

Eddie nudged Brenda with the gun. "Get them," he ordered.

She looked to Dwight. He nodded and lifted his hip to make it easier for her to reach into his pocket and retrieve the keys. She handed them to Eddie. "All right," he said. "We're going to all go in, and you're going to get the book out of the safe. And remember—you try anything and Brenda is dead."

The words sent a chill through her, but she fought back the fear. She had to stay calm and alert for any chance to help get them out of this. They climbed out of the Jeep. She had to hold on to Dwight's shoulder to stand, she felt so shaky and weak. "Come on," Eddie said, one leg bouncing with agitation. "We don't have all night."

They made their way toward the door. Before they reached it, Eddie shot out the security camera focused over it. Brenda stifled a scream as the report of the gun rang in her ears. A second shot took out the light. Maybe someone would hear the shots and come to investigate, she thought. If only they would come in time.

The security keypad beside the door glowed with a red light. "What's your code?" Eddie asked.

Dwight said nothing.

"Give me the code." Eddie grabbed Brenda's arm—the wounded one—and jerked her toward him. Pain blinded her and she screamed, her knees giving way.

"One six three four," Dwight said. He bent over Brenda. "Are you all right?"

It was a moment before she could speak. She struggled to control her breathing and managed to nod, then, realizing he might not be able to see her in the dark, said, "Yes."

"Get up," Eddie said, then he turned and punched in the code.

Hands bound behind his back, Dwight couldn't help her, but he braced himself so that she could pull herself up against him. She leaned on him for a moment, still breathing hard, while Eddie opened the door. Then he motioned them inside.

He led the way down a flight of stairs to a small room at the back of the building, and used a second key to unlock it. When he flipped on the light, Brenda saw shelves full of guns and ammunition. Eddie moved aside a cardboard box labeled "SWAT" to reveal a small safe. "What's the combination?" he asked.

"It's in the sheriff's office," Dwight said.

Eddie looked at Brenda.

"I'm telling the truth!" Dwight said. "Why would I have the combination to the safe?"

"You put the book in the safe after you took it from the museum tonight, didn't you?" Eddie asked.

"It was open. The book was the only thing in the safe, so when we removed the book, we left it open. All I did when I put it back in there was close the door."

"Then come on." They trooped back down the hall

and up the stairs to Travis's office. The door was closed, but not locked. "Where does he keep the combination?" Eddie asked.

"There's a shelf that pulls out on the right-hand side," Dwight said.

Eddie found the shelf and pulled it out. A piece of paper was taped to it. From her position by the door, Brenda could see what looked like a list of phone numbers, but apparently, the combination to the safe was there, too.

"I really need to sit down," she said, and sank into the chair across from Travis's desk.

Eddie scowled at her. "Get up."

"I can't," she said, her voice so weak she could hardly hear it. She closed her eyes. She didn't really care what happened to her now. She was beginning to think she was going to die, anyway.

"Leave her alone," Dwight said. "You've got your combination. Go get the book."

Eddie glared at them, as if about to argue, then jerked his head up. "Is that a siren?" he asked.

Brenda heard nothing, but Dwight said, "Someone must have heard those shots you fired."

Eddie sprinted out of the office and down the hall. Dwight bent over Brenda. "Hang on just a little longer," he said.

She opened her eyes and focused on his hands, the wrists bound with the silver cuffs. "Do you think someone is really coming?" she asked.

"I didn't hear anything," he said. "I think Eddie might be cracking up, but we'll take advantage of that. Can you get the key out of my pocket and unlock these cuffs?" He turned so that his other side faced her.

Energized by the prospect of freeing him, she found the key. He turned his back and held out his hands to her. She fumbled with the lock at first, but after a moment, he was free.

He rubbed his wrists, then put his hand on her uninjured shoulder. "Come with me to my office and hide there," he said.

He helped her up and together they made their way as quietly as possible across the hall to the office Dwight shared with Gage. She sat in his chair while he slid open the bottom drawer of the desk and took out a pistol. He checked to make sure it was loaded, then bent and kissed her cheek. "Wait here," he said, then slipped quietly out of the room.

Brenda clutched her wounded shoulder and rested her head on the desk. She prayed this nightmare would be over soon—and that Dwight would come out the winner. Eddie definitely seemed unbalanced, but that just made him more dangerous.

DWIGHT MOVED AS quickly and as soundlessly as possible toward the door of the armory. Eddie probably had the safe open by now. What would he do when he had the book? Would he simply leave? The supposed siren had seemingly spurred him to grab the book and make his escape, but maybe he would come back to finish off the witnesses to his crime.

Dwight stopped outside the door to the room. Eddie had turned on the overhead light and he stood beside the safe, the book in his hand. He was tearing pages from the book, a few at a time, and dropping them into a metal trash can. As Dwight stared, he took a cigarette lighter from his pocket and touched the flame to the edge of one of the pages. The paper flared, and Eddie dropped it into the trash can with the rest.

Dwight braced himself and aimed the gun. "Eddie Carstairs, you're under arrest," he said.

Eddie turned, openmouthed, and started to raise his gun. Dwight fired, and Eddie lurched away, so that the bullet caught him in the shoulder—almost exactly the spot where Brenda had been shot.

Eddie dropped the gun and sank to his knees beside the trash can, the contents of which were burning brightly, filling the small room with smoke. Dwight scowled at the blaze, then kicked Eddie's gun out of the way. He grabbed him by the arm and hauled him up. "Get up!" he ordered. "Or do you want to give me an excuse to shoot you again?"

Eddie said nothing, but stood and let Dwight push him down the hall to the holding cell. He cuffed him by one hand to the metal grating of the cell and locked the door behind him. About that time the smoke alarm started blaring. Dwight grabbed a fire extinguisher and ran to douse the trash can in the armory, then pulled out his phone and called for an ambulance as he jogged down the hall to Brenda.

He stopped in the doorway of his office. She had her head down on the desk, and she was so still he went ice cold. "Brenda?" he asked.

No reaction. Heart in his throat, he crossed the room and knelt beside her. When he laid his hand on her back, she stirred and raised her head. "What happened?" she asked.

"It's over," Dwight said. "Eddie's locked in a cell." He didn't tell her that he had shot him. She'd find that out soon enough. "Are you okay?"

She tried to smile, though succeeded only in lifting the corners of her mouth a scant half inch. "I've been better."

"Hang on," he said. "The ambulance is on its way."

"I'm not going anywhere." She rested her cheek against his hand and closed her eyes. "Not when I've finally found you."

He wanted to ask her what she meant by that, but had no time, as someone was pounding on the door, demanding to be let in. He stood and went to answer it, light-headed and a little unsteady on his feet, but how much of that was the adrenaline that had flooded him earlier draining away and how much was sheer love for this woman who had endured so much, he couldn't say.

Chapter Seventeen

Dwight sipped the tepid hospital coffee and tried to will away the fog of sleeplessness that dulled his senses. The early-morning hours had passed in a blur of dealing with the ambulance and the sheriff, who arrived as the paramedics were wheeling Brenda out of the sheriff's department. A second ambulance arrived a few minutes later to transport Eddie to the hospital. Travis agreed to go with Eddie, while Dwight followed Brenda.

They had agreed to team up this morning to question Eddie, as soon as doctors gave the go-ahead for them to do so. Dwight stared into the dregs of the coffee and decided he had had enough. He tossed it in the trash can and turned toward the door of the surgery floor waiting room just as Travis walked in. Despite having been awake as many hours as Dwight, Travis managed to look as sharp as ever. Dwight narrowed his eyes at his boss. "How is it you look ready to lead a parade and I feel like death warmed over?" he asked.

"I went home and showered and shaved," Travis said. "Gage is keeping an eye on Eddie, though I don't think he's in any shape to go anywhere."

"The bullet shattered his collarbone." Dwight grimaced. "If he hadn't jerked away, it would have been a heart shot."

Travis put a hand on Dwight's shoulder. "If you hadn't shot him, he would have killed you. Say what you will about the job Eddie did as a reserve officer, but he was always one of the top qualifiers at the range."

"I'd forgotten about that." Not that it would have made any difference in how he had reacted last night— his life had been in danger and his training had kicked in to protect him.

"His doctor says we can have a few minutes with him," Travis said. "He's on pain medication, but lucid."

"Let's hope the meds loosen his tongue enough for him to tell us what's going on," Dwight said. Though even then, a good lawyer might argue that Eddie had revealed information under the influence of narcotics. They had enough other evidence against Eddie that it was a chance Travis felt they could take.

"How is Brenda?" Travis asked.

"She's going to be fine." Saying the words out loud made him feel a little lighter. "The surgeon was able to remove the bullet, and he said there's no permanent damage. I looked in on her a little while ago, but she was still sleeping."

"I'm glad to hear it," Travis said. "Are you ready to talk to Eddie?"

"I am." He had a lot of things he would like to say to the man who had harassed and almost killed Brenda, but most of them he would have to keep to himself. Knowing Eddie was going to prison for a very long time to pay for what he had done would have to be enough.

Eddie's room was at the opposite end of the corridor from Brenda's. Since he was technically in the custody of the Rayford County Sheriff's Department, he rated a private room, and a guard on duty outside his door 24-7. Gage rose from a chair he'd placed against the wall opposite that door as Travis and Dwight approached.

"He's awake," Gage said after the three men exchanged greetings. "I looked in on him a few minutes ago and he wanted to tell me about how none of this was his fault, but I told him to save it for you two."

"Not his fault?" Dwight shook his head. "This should be interesting."

Gage checked his phone. "I need to get going if I'm going to make the auction."

"The auction?" Dwight asked. With everything that had happened in the last few hours, he had forgotten all about the museum's auction.

"Lacy and Paige decided that they needed to go ahead with it, since some of the bidders are here from out of town," Travis said. "They wanted to do it for Brenda."

"I'm sure she'll appreciate it," Dwight said. "Of course, the most valuable item is gone. All that's left of *The Secret History of Rayford Country, Colorado* is a bucket of wet ashes."

"They still want to get what they can," Gage said. "I'm going to run security, along with one of the reserve officers."

"You'd better go, then," Travis said. "We can handle things on this end." He pushed open the door to Eddie's room.

A muted television, and a bank of monitors provided the only illumination in the room. Eddie lay on his back in the bed, the head elevated forty-five degrees, a mass of white bandages around his left shoulder. His right hand was cuffed to the railing of the bed, an IV tube trailing from it. He turned his head toward them, his skin pale against a day's growth of dark beard and the cuts and bruises from his struggles with Dwight. "Hello, Sheriff," he said, his voice surprisingly clear.

"Hello, Eddie." Travis stopped beside the bed. "We need to ask you some questions about what happened yesterday."

"I know. And I can explain everything. I—"

Travis held up one hand. "Before you say anything, I need to tell you that you have the right to remain silent. Anything you say could be held against you in a court of law. You have the right to have an attorney present. If you cannot afford an attorney, one will be appointed by the courts."

"I know my rights," Eddie said. "I read them off to other people enough. I don't need a lawyer for what I have to say to you."

Dwight moved in on the other side of the bed. Eddie turned his head to look at him. "How is Brenda doing?" he asked.

"Why are you even asking?" Dwight said, unable to hold in his anger.

"If she'd just cooperated like I asked her to, none of this would have happened," he said, his voice a plaintive whine.

"Were you the one who sent those threatening notes to Brenda?" Travis asked.

"I didn't do it for myself," Eddie said. "It was a matter of national security. All she had to do was get rid of that book."

Travis's and Dwight's eyes met across the bed. *Na-*

tional security? "Why was that book so important?" Travis asked.

"The man who hired me told me I had to make sure it was destroyed so that it didn't fall into the wrong hands."

"Who was this man?" Travis asked.

"I don't know his real name," Dwight said. "He told me to call him B."

"Bee?" Dwight asked.

"The letter B. He called me E. They were, like, code names. He worked for a top-secret government agency."

"Did he show you credentials?" Travis asked.

"Of course he did." Eddie looked indignant. "I'm not stupid."

"And his credentials said his name was B?" Dwight asked.

"Yes." Eddie glared at them.

"What branch of the government was he from?" Travis asked.

Eddie frowned. "Something top secret. I mean, his credentials said Department of Homeland Security, but the more we talked, the more I got the impression that he was really CIA or something like that."

"What did he promise you in exchange for your help?" Travis asked.

"He told me he could get me a job with the Secret Service."

"Is that all?" Travis asked.

"He paid me a lot of money. Ten thousand dollars. Don't look at me that way! Since you fired me from the sheriff's department, my bills have been piling up. I needed that money."

Travis leaned over the bed railing. "Eddie, why would the Feds ask you to threaten Brenda Stenson?"

"I wasn't threatening her. I was just, you know, intimidating her so that she'd get rid of that book. B said it was a security risk and we couldn't let it fall into the wrong hands."

"Did he say why?" Travis asked.

"No."

"Did you ask?" Dwight asked.

Eddie looked even more sullen. "No."

"Did you burn down Brenda's house?" Dwight asked.

Eddie shifted in the bed. "I think I need to speak to my lawyer."

"You're in this so deep no lawyer is going to be able to get you out," Dwight said. "Your only chance is to help us get to the truth."

"B was putting a lot of pressure on me. He said I was failing my country. I figured if I destroyed her house, I'd destroy the book and the problem would be solved. I figured she had insurance, and I knew she wasn't home. I mean, I'd never hurt her, even if she does treat me like something she scraped off the bottom of her shoe."

"Where did you get that crime scene photo of Andy Stenson?" Dwight asked.

Eddie flushed and looked away. "I don't see why that matters."

"Did you take it from the case file when you were with the department?" Travis asked.

"You'll never prove it," Eddie said.

"What do you know about Henry Hake's death?" Travis asked.

"Nothing! I didn't have anything to do with that. All

I did was try to get Brenda to get rid of that book, like B asked. You find him and he'll tell you."

"How do we get in touch with him?" Travis asked.

"I don't know. He always got in touch with me. But he must be staying nearby. Maybe you could just call the Department of Homeland Security and ask."

"We will," Travis said. Though Dwight had his doubts they would find out anything.

"What was in the book that was so important?" Travis asked. "Did he give you any indication?"

"I already told you, I don't know. He said I didn't need to know."

No one would know now, Dwight thought, since the book had been destroyed.

"I know you think what I did was wrong," Eddie said. "But I didn't have a choice. B threatened to kill me if I didn't get the job done—the sleeping-pill-laced pizza was supposed to prove how easily he could get to me."

"Was B the man you were meeting with at the restaurant that night Brenda and Lacy and the others saw you?" Dwight asked. "Did he slash the tires on Parker's car?"

"I don't know anything about that. And I'm not going to say anything else." He sagged back against the pillow, his face pale. "I'm exhausted and in pain. You can't badger me this way."

Travis looked at Dwight and jerked his head toward the door. Dwight followed him out. "Do you buy his story, about all this being his patriotic duty?" Dwight asked.

"I think the money and the promise of the Secret Service job and the idea of being a hero would appeal to him," Travis said. "I'll talk to Lacy and get her description of the man who was with Eddie that night at the restaurant."

"I remember Brenda saying they didn't get a good look at the man—his face was in shadow."

"We'll get what we can."

"I'm wondering if B was Robert Brownley," Dwight said. "If he's the one who gave Eddie the doctored pizza, we know he was at the museum that evening."

"Good thinking," Travis said. "Get Brownley's description from Brenda and we'll compare notes."

"I'm going down to check on her now," Dwight said. "If she's awake, I'll ask her."

BRENDA HAD BEEN awake for some time that morning. There was nothing like a near-death experience to make a person take stock of her life. She had made some bad decisions, and had had more than her share of bad breaks, but instead of focusing on the past, she needed to come up with a plan for the future.

A light tapping attracted her attention to the door. Dwight leaned in. "Feel like some company?" he asked.

"Definitely." She found the controls for the bed and elevated the head so that she could get a better look at him.

"Why are you frowning at me?" he asked, coming to stand beside her.

"You look worn out," she said. Two black eyes from his broken nose and the dark shadow of beard along his jaw made him look dangerous—and utterly weary. "Have you been home at all since last night?"

"I'll go in a little bit. I wanted to make sure you were all right."

She reached up and took his hand. He squeezed it,

and the tenderness in his touch made her feel a little choked up. She cleared her throat. If she started crying, he would think something was wrong. "I'm going to be fine," she said. "The surgeon said so. I can probably go home this afternoon."

"You'll come back to my place," he said.

She might have argued, but why bother? With him was where she wanted to be. "That sounds good. But it's going to be a while, so you should try to get a few hours' sleep. I can get Lacy to take me to you if you aren't back when the doctor signs the discharge papers."

"Lacy is going to be busy for a while," he said.

"Oh? What? Did she and Travis decide to elope or something?"

He smiled, a little more life coming into his eyes. "Nothing like that. But she and Paige are handling the auction at the museum."

"The auction?" She tried to sit up, and regretted it as pain shot through her bandaged shoulder. With a groan, she settled back against the pillows. "I've been lying here, trying to convince myself that it didn't matter that we had to cancel the auction. But they're going through with it?"

"With some of the bidders here from out of town, they figured they had better."

"That's so sweet of them. Though the most valuable item we had is gone now."

"You still had a lot of items left. You'll bring in a good chunk of change."

Not enough, she thought. But no sense dwelling on that. "How is Eddie?" she asked. "I know they rushed him into surgery before me."

"His recovery is going to take a little longer, but

he'll live." Dwight certainly wasn't smiling now. "He admitted he sent you those threatening letters—and he burned down your house."

"But why?" She had scarcely said a dozen words to Eddie Carstairs in all the years they had both lived in Eagle Mountain.

"Apparently, someone posing as a federal agent offered him a lot of money to make sure the book was destroyed."

"What was so important about that book?" she asked. "I read through it more than once and I couldn't see anything significant there."

"I don't know. And Eddie says he doesn't know, either."

"Then why would he agree to do it—to harass me and commit arson—even threaten to kill the two of us? Surely he isn't that hard up and greedy."

"You know Eddie always wanted to be a hero. This man—who I don't for a minute believe was really with the government—convinced Eddie that he had to destroy the book to keep it out of enemy hands—that it was a matter of national security. When Eddie failed the first couple of tries, this mysterious agent delivered that doctored pizza—supposedly to prove how easily he could kill Eddie if he wanted to. That made him desperate to fulfill his 'mission.'"

Brenda tried to take this all in. "That's incredible. Do you think this mysterious secret agent is the one who ran me off the road and shot me?"

"Maybe."

"Did Eddie tell you how to find this supposed agent?" she asked.

"He says he doesn't know. The only name he has

is B. But I'm wondering if it was Robert Brownley—or rather, the man who came to you posing as Robert Brownley. I don't think that's his real name."

"He was very insistent on getting his hands on the book that night. And I'll admit he seemed rather menacing." She shivered, remembering being alone with the man.

"Do you think the man who attacked you and the man who posed as Robert Brownley were the same person?" Dwight asked.

"I don't know. It was dark and he wore that mask." She shook her head. "Maybe."

"I need you to give me your description of him again," Dwight said. "We're going to use every resource we can to find him."

She closed her eyes, trying to remember. "So much has happened since then," she said. "I don't know if I can give you enough information."

"Take your time. Describe him to me—what he looked like, as well as your impressions."

"He was in his forties, I think. Average height and build. Dark hair. His eyes were light—gray, I think, and really intense. I guess my biggest impression of him was that he was the kind of man who was used to getting what he wanted. Powerful—but personality-wise, not so much physically. He was well-dressed. His suit looked expensive, not off-the-rack. And he drove that black Land Rover—not a cheap car." Her eyes met Dwight's. "He looked like what he said he was—a rich businessman."

"I may ask you to look at some photographs later and see if you recognize him."

"I'll do whatever I can to help."

"We may be too late," Dwight said. "My guess is that now that he got what he wanted and the book is gone, he'll leave the county, maybe even the country."

"Give Travis my description and then promise me you'll go home and get some sleep," she said. "You're not going to be good to anyone if you fall asleep at the wheel of your cruiser."

"I could get used to you nagging me that way." He leaned over and kissed her on the lips. When he started to pull away, she grabbed his collar and prolonged the embrace. When at last she released him, he looked decidedly less weary. Later, they would talk, and she would tell him some things she had decided.

In the meantime, she liked giving him something to think about.

Chapter Eighteen

Dwight gave Travis Brenda's description of Brownley, then did as he had promised and went home, where he slept for four hours before a phone call awakened him. Groggily, he groped for the cell phone and answered it.

"You need to get back to the hospital," Travis said. "The judge is on her way over to conduct the arraignment for Eddie."

Dwight checked the clock at his bedside—it was almost one in the afternoon. "That was quick."

"Frank Rizzo is Eddie's attorney. He pulled some strings to rush the arraignment."

"Frank Rizzo? How did Eddie afford him?" Rizzo had represented a number of high-profile, very wealthy defendants.

"Eddie was as surprised to see Rizzo as I was," Travis said. "He said obviously the government had come through to support him. He's practically giddy, and I don't think it's all from the painkillers his doctor prescribed. He's convinced he's going to be exonerated as a national hero."

"I'm going to shower and change, and I'll be right over," Dwight said.

By the time Dwight arrived at the hospital, the lot

was crowded with news vans and broadcast trucks from every major television and radio network. Dwight's uniform attracted their attention, and he found himself pushing through a crowd of reporters with microphones who demanded to know what his role was in the case. He ignored them and made his way inside.

Fortunately, the hospital's corridors were closed to reporters. Travis met Dwight outside Eddie's room. "Did Rizzo alert the media?" Dwight asked.

"Probably," Travis said. "That's his style."

The man himself stepped out of Eddie's room and closed the door behind him. Clean-shaven and bald, dressed in a gray wool suit and wearing old-school horn-rimmed glasses, Frank Rizzo was well-known to television viewers and readers of the most popular gossip mags. From professional athletes to B-list celebrities to corporate moguls, his client list was a who's who of misbehaving millionaires. His eyes narrowed when he saw Dwight. "Deputy Prentice?" he asked.

Dwight nodded.

"You're the man who shot my client," Rizzo said.

"Your client was shooting at me at the time."

"So you say. My client has a different story."

Dwight kept quiet. Rizzo liked to goad his opponents into saying things he could use against them in court. Dwight wouldn't play his game.

"The judge is here," Travis said. The three men turned to see an older woman with silver-blond hair, dressed in a red business suit, striding down the hallway, followed by a young man who was carrying a court stenographer's machine and a second man who was probably the clerk of the court. Several feet behind them came a very tall man in a blue suit—District Attorney Scott Percy.

The woman stopped in front of them. "Judge Miranda Geisel." She shook hands with each of them in turn. "Let's get this proceeding started."

Travis entered the room first, followed by the judge and her attendants, the DA and Frank Rizzo, with Dwight bringing up the rear. He stationed himself by the door, while the others crowded around the bed, jostling for position in the small space.

The man who had harassed Brenda, destroyed her home and her car, and threatened to kill her, managed to look frail and vulnerable in the hospital bed, his shoulder bandaged and his unshaven face white with pain.

Judge Geisel looked around and, apparently satisfied that all was as it should be, nodded. "Let's begin, gentlemen."

The clerk read off the date, time and nature of the proceedings for the record, then listed the charges against Eddie. Though Dwight was aware of all of them, read together they formed an impressive list—everything from harassment to arson to theft to attempted murder. It would be a very long time before Eddie was a free man again.

"How does your client plead?" Judge Geisel asked.

"Not guilty, Your Honor," said Rizzo.

No surprise there, despite the fact that Eddie had been caught red-handed in the commission of the most serious charge, and had admitted to most of the others. Rizzo would no doubt be contesting those previous confessions. Dwight was almost looking forward to hearing the defense's case, especially if Rizzo could produce the mysterious B.

"I request that my client be released on his own recognizance," Rizzo said.

"The nature of these crimes are such that we request Mr. Carstairs be held without bail," Percy countered.

Eddie watched this exchange, wide-eyed, his gaze shifting from one side of the bed to the other.

"These are very serious charges," the judge said.

"Your Honor, my client has absolutely no record of previous violence," Rizzo said. "He isn't a flight risk. The man is seriously injured and will be recovering for some time."

"My understanding is that Mr. Carstairs could be released from the hospital as early as this afternoon," the judge said.

"If you will authorize his release, I will be personally transporting him to a rehab facility," Rizzo said. "You don't have to worry about him getting into trouble there."

"Your Honor, Mr. Carstairs tried to kill a woman and a police officer," Percy said. "He has been relentless in his pursuit of Mrs. Stenson and remains a threat to her still."

"As Mr. Rizzo has pointed out, Mr. Carstairs's injuries are such that he can't drive a car or go much of anywhere," the judge said. "I think that mitigates the threat. And I am cognizant of the burden on the county if he must remain in protective custody while undergoing rehabilitation and continued medical treatment." She turned to Rizzo. "I'm setting bail at $500,000."

"Your Honor, Mr. Carstairs is unemployed," Rizzo said. "He can't possibly afford such a sum."

"Yet he can somehow afford your fees," the judge

said. "Or are you doing pro bono work these days, Mr. Rizzo?"

Rizzo compressed his lips into a thin line and said nothing.

"Bail is set at $500,000," she repeated. "This arraignment is adjourned."

No one said anything while the court reporter packed up his recording equipment. Travis and Dwight left Rizzo to confer with his client and followed the court personnel and the DA into the hall. Percy waited until the judge and her staff had left before he spoke. "No surprise on the bail," he said. "And she's right—in his condition, I don't think he's a flight risk."

"I'm not so sure about that," Dwight said. "He's got someone behind the scenes pulling strings."

"I figured someone else was paying Rizzo's fees," Percy said. "Any idea who?"

"We're still digging," Travis said.

"All that stuff in the report you sent me about secret government agents—do you believe any of that?" Percy asked.

"No," Travis said.

The door opened and Rizzo stepped out. "I'm going to make arrangements for Eddie's release," he said. "I'll see you gentlemen in court."

They watched him walk down the hall and enter the elevator. "Want to bet he stops off downstairs to talk to the media?" Percy asked.

"No bets," Travis said.

"This is going to be an interesting one," Percy said.

They said goodbye and he left them. "I'll take over guarding Eddie," Dwight said. "I know you have things to do."

"I think it's best if you limit your contact with him," Travis said. "Just in case Rizzo follows through with any countersuit. Besides, I know you want to be with Brenda."

"She's supposed to be discharged this afternoon," Dwight said. "I'd like to take her home."

"Go." Travis clamped him on the back. "I'll take care of things here."

Dwight found Brenda in a wheelchair beside her bed, wearing a pink hospital gown and fuzzy pink socks. She could have been wrapped up in old sacking for all Dwight cared. The fact that she was upright and smiling made her the most beautiful person he would ever see.

"You look much better," she said, tilting her cheek up for him to kiss. "Did you get some sleep?"

"A little." He rubbed his smooth chin. "A shower and a shave helped, too."

"I just talked to Lacy. She said the auction made over $20,000. A lot more than I expected, since we no longer had the book."

"That will keep you going another few months at least," Dwight said. "It will give you more time to find a new benefactor."

"Professor Gibson may have come through for us there. He said he was so impressed with the museum, he's recommended us to the Falmont Foundation."

Dwight sat on the end of the bed, so that they were more or less at eye level. "What is the Falmont Foundation?" he asked.

"You know the Falmont family—Falmont semiconductors?"

He shook his head. "Never heard of them."

"It doesn't matter. They have a charitable trust that

gives money to worthy causes. Apparently, Julius Falmont was a great history buff. And Professor Gibson used to be on the board of the trust. He's recommended us for underwriting. This could be exactly what we've been hoping for." Her eyes shone, and Dwight couldn't remember when she had looked so happy.

"That's great," he said. "It's good to know all the hard work you've put into the museum is getting the recognition it deserves."

"I don't know about that—I'm just glad we don't have to close the doors and I don't have to start looking for another job."

He stood. "Are you ready to go home?"

"I'm ready, but we're still waiting on the doctor to sign the paperwork. A nurse is trying to locate him now."

Dwight sat back down. "We just had Eddie's arraignment," he said.

"Already?" she asked.

"The judge came here. It's not unusual when someone being charged with a crime is hospitalized. He's being released on bail. Somehow, he has Frank Rizzo as his attorney."

"He's being released?" Much of the elation went out of her face.

"To a rehab center." He took her hand. "He's not in any shape to harm you anymore—and I'll be keeping an eye out for you."

She nodded. "I guess I'm just surprised he would be released."

"He doesn't have a criminal history, and he's not considered a threat at the moment," Dwight said. "Plus, I'm sure having Rizzo as an attorney helped. He has a reputation for making life miserable for judges who don't do what he wants. He has lots of friends in the media."

"How did Eddie afford someone like Frank Rizzo?" she asked.

"I don't know, but that's one thing we'll try to find out." He squeezed her hand. "I don't want you to worry. I'm going to keep you safe—even though I know you don't like relying on others."

Her eyes met his, a new softness in her face. "I've been doing a lot of thinking, and I've come to some decisions," she said.

He tensed. Was this when she told him "thanks, but no thanks" to any prospect of a relationship? "I don't know that now is the best time to be making decisions," he said.

"Hush, and let me talk." She tempered the words with a smile. "I realized as I was lying in that bed, reviewing everything that has happened to me over the last couple of years, that I've been going about things the wrong way. I've been reacting to whatever happened by becoming defensive. Andy was killed and I kept to myself, upset and ashamed and really, not coping very well. Then I found out he was blackmailing people in town and using the money to renovate our house and I reacted again, this time by deciding not to trust other people—not to trust other men. Not to trust you."

He waited, afraid of saying the wrong thing if he interrupted her.

"But just reacting to what other people did was the wrong approach, I think. Instead, I needed to step back and focus on what *I* want to happen. Where *I* want to go in life." She took a deep breath and let it out slowly.

"It's time to follow my feelings instead of my fears. I love you, Dwight, and I think you love me."

"I do love you," he said. "I have for years."

She smiled again, and he felt like shouting for joy. But all he did was remain very still, holding her hand and waiting to hear what she had to say next. "Life is too short for us to be apart anymore," she said.

"Yes." Then he did what he had wanted to do for weeks now—maybe even years. He dropped to his knees in front of the wheelchair. "Brenda Stenson, will you marry me?" he asked.

"Yes," she whispered, tears glinting in her eyes.

He leaned forward and kissed her, a long, passionate kiss to seal their pledge. And that was how the doctor found them when he and a nurse walked in.

"Well, it looks like you're feeling much better," he said as Brenda and Dwight moved apart and Dwight stood. The doctor scribbled his signature on the papers on a clipboard the nurse handed him. "Follow the instructions the nurse will give you and I'll see you in my office next week."

The doctor left and the nurse took charge of the wheelchair. Dwight gathered up Brenda's things and followed her into the hallway. They stopped short at the turn to the elevator when they saw Eddie, also in a wheelchair, with Frank Rizzo at his side. "Stop," Brenda ordered.

They stopped and waited for Eddie and his attorney to pass. Neither man looked their way. When the elevator doors closed behind them, Brenda sagged against the chair. "Eddie looked bad," she said. "I'm still not happy about him getting bail, but he really doesn't look like a threat." She looked up at the nurse. "Okay, we can go now."

They arrived downstairs to a scene of chaos. People filled the front lobby, many of them members of the press with cameras and microphones. "I should have thought of this," Dwight said. "We need to go out the back entrance."

But they had already been spotted. A trio of reporters and cameramen surged toward them, shouting questions. Brenda covered her face. "No comment," Dwight shouted. He took control of the wheelchair and pushed toward the doors.

But their progress was blocked again by Frank Rizzo, who stood in the portico, holding forth to an audience of media and bystanders. More cameras flashed as he proclaimed his client's innocence. Eddie slumped in his wheelchair beside Rizzo, the picture of the aggrieved victim of injustice.

Dwight was searching for the best escape route when Rizzo concluded his comments, just as a black sedan pulled into the portico. Rizzo wheeled his client toward the waiting car, then someone screamed. At almost the same moment, the *pock!* of a silenced weapon sounded, and Eddie sagged further down in his chair.

"Get her inside!" Dwight shoved the wheelchair toward a man in scrubs, then sprinted toward Eddie. A bloom of red spread across Eddie's chest. Around them, people screamed, some dropping to the ground, others fleeing either back into the building or across the parking lot.

Another man, also wearing scrubs, reached Eddie at the same time as Dwight and felt for a pulse. He shook his head. "He's gone," he said.

Dwight looked around. Frank Rizzo and the black sedan were both gone also, though Dwight was sure the shots had come from farther away—possibly the parking garage across from the main hospital building.

Two uniformed police officers ran up to him. "Did anyone see the shooter?" the older of the two, a muscular black man, asked.

"No. But I think he might have been firing from the parking garage," Dwight said.

The officer studied the parking structure. "Long shot," he said.

"Not too long for a professional," Dwight said. He had no doubt Eddie's murder had been carefully orchestrated. Someone—B?—didn't want him to tell whatever he knew.

Dwight spent the rest of the day running down leads that went nowhere. He and local police searched the parking garage and the area around the hospital and came up with nothing—no video, no eyewitnesses, no bullet casings, no foot impressions—nothing. One more indication that whoever had killed Eddie was a professional.

Lacy showed up with Travis and offered to drive Brenda to Dwight's cabin—an offer she gratefully accepted. "If you need anything, call Mom," he told her as he helped her into Lacy's car. "I'll be there as soon as I can."

"Don't worry about me. Go do your job. I plan to take a nap and be there when you do get in."

"If you're tired, go ahead and go to bed," he said. "I'll just have a bunch of paperwork to deal with." This case had generated more than its fair share of forms and reports.

"Then I'll pour coffee and offer moral support," she said, before waving goodbye and settling back against the seat.

She had the right attitude to be a law enforcement officer's wife, he decided, then went to confer with Travis, who was on the phone with Frank Rizzo. He motioned Dwight to lean in, and together they listened to Rizzo's defense of his sudden departure from the hospital. "Clearly there was nothing I could do for Eddie and there was no sense staying around when there was a shooter on the loose."

"Who hired you to represent Eddie?" Travis asked.

"That information is confidential," Rizzo said.

"I can get a subpoena for not just that information, but anything having to do with Eddie Carstairs," Travis said. "If I have to do that, I promise to take up as much of your and your staff's time as possible. Or you could just answer my question now."

Rizzo's sigh was audible on the phone. "He said he was a friend of the family who wished to remain anonymous. He contacted me by phone—I never saw him, and the number was blocked."

"How did he pay you?"

"With a bank draft made out to my firm, delivered by a private courier within the hour."

"That didn't strike you as odd?" Travis asked.

"No. I deal with any number of very rich and sometimes very eccentric people. I don't question their methods as long as the payment is prompt and in full."

"Has he contacted you about a refund, since your

client is dead and won't be needing your services?" Travis asked.

"My fees are nonrefundable."

"Has this man or anyone else contacted you about this?"

"No."

"Let us know if they do," Travis said.

"I don't see how this relates to Mr. Carstairs's death," Rizzo said.

"You don't? You demanded and got bail for Eddie, which put him in a position where the killer could get to him."

Rizzo was silent for a long moment. "I hope you're wrong," he said. "And I have to go now."

The call ended. Travis put away his phone. "Want to bet we'll never hear from him again?" Dwight asked.

"I doubt B or whoever set this up will contact him," Travis said. "They knew when they paid him this case wasn't going to go to trial. They only needed Rizzo to get Eddie released on bail so that they could get a shot at him."

"It had to be a professional hit," Dwight said. "A military sniper couldn't have made a better shot, and the killer didn't leave a shred of evidence."

"Maybe it was a military sniper," Travis said.

"What do you mean?"

Travis shook his head. "I don't know. I'm not ruling anything out right now."

"What's next?" Dwight asked.

"Let's go through Eddie's apartment and try to figure out what he was involved in. So far, B has been very careful. I don't think we're going to find much."

The first item of interest in Eddie's apartment was

a box of yellow stationery, a row of cartoon flowers dancing across the bottom of each sheet. "We already knew he sent those threats to Brenda, but it's good to have confirmation," Dwight said.

Dwight flipped through the rest of the contents of the desk in Eddie's bedroom. He pulled a folder from the bottom drawer and looked inside. "Check this out," he said, and handed the folder to Travis.

The sheriff scanned the half dozen photocopies in the folder—all crime scene photos from sheriff's department case files. "Now we know where the photo on that note Eddie sent to Brenda came from," he said.

"That's sick," Dwight said. "It's a good thing you fired him when you did."

The rest of the apartment was full of used furniture, take-out cartons and dirty clothes. Dwight was grateful to leave it and head to his own comfortable home—and the woman waiting for him there.

Brenda smiled up at him when he entered. She was settled on the sofa, her injured arm propped on a pile of pillows. She had dressed and combed her hair and though she was still pale, the tension had faded from her face. Dwight sat beside her. "How are you feeling?" he asked.

"Better," she said. "Much better now." She turned his face toward hers and kissed him, long and hard. Not breaking contact, he slid one arm under her thighs and scooped her onto his lap, being careful not to jostle her injured shoulder.

When they did finally come up for breath, her eyes sparkled. "Tomorrow is my birthday," she said.

"I hadn't forgotten." He tucked a lock of hair behind her ear. "Not a very fun way to spend it."

"I don't know about that. I'm alive. I'm with you. It's funny—before all this happened, I was a little depressed about turning thirty. I felt as if I had reached a milestone in my life and I had nothing to show for it. I don't feel that way anymore."

"Do you think it's because you faced down death and lived?"

"Partly. But I also think it's because I had reached a point where I had lost everything—I was a widow, my job was in jeopardy, my house had burned down, and then my car was wrecked. I had nothing, but instead of all that making me feel defeated, it was incredibly freeing. I had nothing left to lose. I could do anything. I could be with whoever I wanted to be with." She stroked his cheek. "I don't have anywhere to go from here but up."

"As long as you go there with me."

"I've been thinking about my house," she said.

"What about it?"

"I want to rebuild it."

"Sure. We can live wherever you want to live." He would miss the ranch, but there were probably advantages to living in town. And he wanted her to be happy—she deserved that so much.

"I want to stay on the ranch, here with you," she said. "It's beautiful and peaceful here. I love it."

He hoped the relief he felt didn't show on his face. "Then what will you do with the house—rent it out?"

"Something like that. I don't want to build just one house. I want to build a triplex or a fourplex, and make it affordable housing—something Eagle Mountain really needs."

"That sounds like a great idea."

"I'm full of great ideas. I have all kinds of things I want to do at the museum with the money from the Falmont Foundation, and of course, we have a wedding to plan."

"I like the sound of that one. What other ideas do you have?"

"This one." She kissed him again. "And this one." She began unbuttoning his shirt.

"Hey." He wrapped his hand around hers. "You're supposed to be taking it easy. You're recovering from surgery."

"Oh, we can take it easy." She leaned forward and nipped at his jaw. "Slow and easy. Doesn't that sound good?" She leaned back, grinning at him. "Or if you'd rather, you can get a head start on all that paperwork."

"What paperwork?" He hugged her more firmly against him, then leaned over and switched off the lamp, so that the room was lit only by the glow of moonlight through the front windows. Then he pulled her close in a kiss once more. Paperwork could wait—but he didn't have to wait for Brenda anymore.

* * * * *

SPECIAL EXCERPT FROM

ⒽHARLEQUIN
INTRIGUE

After forensic investigator Lena Love is attacked and left with a partial heart-shaped symbol carved into her chest, her hunt to find a serial killer becomes personal.

Read on for a sneak preview of
The Heart-Shaped Murders,
the debut book in A West Coast Crime Story series, from Denise N. Wheatley.

Lena Love kicked a rock out from underneath her foot, then bent down and tightened the twill shoelaces on her brown leather hiking boots.

The crime scene investigator, who doubled as a forensic science technician, stood back up and eyed Los Angeles's Cucamonga Wilderness trail. Sharp-edged stones and ragged shards of bark covered the rugged, winding terrain.

"Watch your step," she uttered to herself before continuing along the path of her latest crime scene.

Lena squinted as she focused on the trail. Heavy foliage loomed overhead, blocking out the sun's brilliant rays. She pulled out her flashlight, hoping its bright beam would help uncover potential evidence.

An ominous wave of vulnerability swept through her chest at the sight of the vast San Gabriel Mountains. She spun around slowly, feeling small while eyeing the infinite views of the forest, desert and snowy mountainous peaks.

The wild surroundings left her with a lingering sense of defenselessness. Lena tightened the belt on her tan suede blazer. She hoped it would give her some semblance of security.

It didn't.

Lena wondered if the latest victim had felt that same vulnerability on the night she'd been brutally murdered.

"Come on, Grace Mitchell," Lena said aloud, as if the dead woman could hear her. "Talk to me. Tell me what happened to you. *Show* me what happened to you."

A gust of wind whipped Lena's bone-straight bob across her slender face. She tucked her hair behind her ears and stooped down, aiming the flashlight toward the majestic oak tree where Grace's body had been found.

Lena envisioned spotting droplets of blood, a cigarette butt, the tip of a latex glove…*anything* that would help identify the killer.

This was her second visit to the crime scene. The thought of showing up to the station without any viable evidence yet again caused an agonizing pang of dread to shoot up her spine.

Grace was the fifth victim of a criminal whom Lena had labeled an organized serial killer. He appeared to have a type. Young, slender brunette women. Their bodies had all been found in heavily wooded areas. Each victim's hands were meticulously tied behind their backs with a three-strand twisted rope. They'd been strangled to death. And the amount of evidence left at each scene was practically nonexistent.

But the killer's signature mark was always there. And it was a sinister one.

Look for
The Heart-Shaped Murders *by Denise N. Wheatley,*
available June 2022 wherever
Harlequin Intrigue books and ebooks are sold.

Harlequin.com

Love Harlequin romance?

DISCOVER.

Be the first to find out about promotions,
news and exclusive content!

Facebook.com/HarlequinBooks

Twitter.com/HarlequinBooks

Instagram.com/HarlequinBooks

Pinterest.com/HarlequinBooks

YouTube.com/HarlequinBooks

ReaderService.com

EXPLORE.

Sign up for the Harlequin e-newsletter and
download a free book from any series at
TryHarlequin.com

CONNECT.

Join our Harlequin community to
share your thoughts and connect
with other romance readers!
Facebook.com/groups/HarlequinConnection

HARLEQUIN

Heartfelt or thrilling, passionate or uplifting—Harlequin is more than just happily-ever-after.

With twelve different series to choose from and new books available every month, you are sure to find stories that will move you, uplift you, inspire and delight you.